ABOUT THIS BOOK

Three novellas (books 23-25) in the young adult paranormal fantasy series Havenwood Falls High, Home of the Dragons – and vampires, wolves, fae, and much more.

Finding Infiniti by **Rose Garcia**
    Sequel to *Saving Infiniti*
    Joe Greg reunited with his soul mate Infiniti Clausman only to lose her in a cruel twist of fate. Separated by time and space—and a memory ward that has wiped him from her mind—he vows to do whatever he can to find her, but so far nothing has worked. Infiniti Clausman feels like something isn't quite right. Like she's stuck, as if she can't move on, as if she's missing something or someone. She tries to dismiss the sensation, but then her psychic neighbor tells her about a quantum event that's been happening since last December, and her world turns upside down.

Unicorn's Lament by **Megan Linski**
    Thea has no idea what her future holds. When she's whisked off to a mysterious town in the mountains, she finds out magic is real—and so are unicorns. If that wasn't shocking enough, she also learns that her mom's an evil sorceress who desires to destroy the unicorns, and all of Havenwood Falls is in danger. Thea has until her eighteenth birthday to learn how to control her magic, lead the herd . . . and maybe kiss the cute girl at Havenwood Stables.

Paper Bird by **Amy Richie**
    Ava Tate has never had what anyone would call a fairy tale life. A dead mother, an absent father, and an uncle who doesn't want her. One more year of high school and she'll be able to live on her

own. But after another run-in with the cops, her uncle sends her away to live with a father she's never even met before in a town she's never heard of. Ava isn't counting on meeting Toby, though. Suddenly, all the rules seem to be changing, and if she doesn't keep up, her very existence will be wiped away.

HAVENWOOD FALLS HIGH BOOKS

Written in the Stars by Kallie Ross

Reawakened by Morgan Wylie

The Fall by Kristen Yard

Somewhere Within by Amy Hale

Awaken the Soul by Michele G. Miller

Bound by Shadows by Cameo Renae

Fata Morgana by E.J. Fechenda

Forever Emeline by Katie M. John

Reclamation by AnnaLisa Grant

Avenoir by Daniele Lanzarotta

Avenge the Heart by Michele G. Miller

Curse the Night by R.K. Ryals

Blood & Iron by Amy Hale

Shadows & Spells by Cameo Renae

Falling Deep by J.L. Weil

Saving Infiniti by Rose Garcia

Willful by Liz Ferry

Cast in Moonlight by Ali Winters

Promise the Moon by Kallie Ross

Blurred Lines by Daniele Lanzarotta

Ascending Darkness by J.L. Weil

Finding Infiniti by Rose Garcia

Unicorn's Lament by Megan Linski

Paper Bird by Amy Richie

Predestined by Valia Lind

Rediscovered by Morgan Wylie

Ashes of Fate by Apryl Baker

Stay up to date at www.HavenwoodFalls.com

HAVENWOOD FALLS HIGH VOLUME EIGHT

A HAVENWOOD FALLS HIGH COLLECTION

ROSE GARCIA   MEGAN LINSKI   AMY RICHIE

FINDING INFINITI

ROSE GARCIA

HAVENWOOD FALLS HIGH

Finding Infiniti

ROSE GARCIA

~ A Havenwood Falls Young Adult Novella ~

ALSO BY ROSE GARCIA

FINAL LIFE

To everyone who believes in second chances.

CHAPTER 1

*J*oe Greg studied every detail of Infiniti Clausman, desperate to sear her image in his brain because he didn't know if he'd be able to find her once she left Havenwood Falls. Long dark hair, ivory skin, the most gorgeous face he'd ever seen. She had time traveled with a Transhuman guy named Fleet from Houston to Havenwood Falls so she could find a protection spell. With their mission complete, they were about to return to their proper place and time, and Joe could hardly bear it. Her magnetic beauty had sparked a connection deep within him, so deep that he was called to her and would be bound to her forever—a wolf shifter and a human. Together against all odds, yet about to be separated in a cruel twist of fate. He knew he'd never be the same without her.

Her lips parted, as if she wanted to say something, just before she vanished from view.

"Infiniti!"

Joe dashed to the spot where she had been standing. Dust particles from Fleet's supernatural energy stream floated in the air. A warm electrical charge filled the cool space. Joe glanced around, as if they'd reappear, but they didn't.

They were gone. She was gone.

Heartbreaking silence filled the room.

"I'm very sorry, Joe," Ms. Howe said in a low voice, still clutching the book she had used to cast her protection spell on Infiniti.

Joe nodded, his heart crumbling. A lump the size of a football lodged in his throat. He felt as if a piece of him had been ripped away. And he didn't know if he'd ever get it back.

"I'll let you have a minute," Ms. Howe added, leaving the room.

Joe couldn't remember the last time he had cried, but watching Infiniti disappear brought hot tears to his eyes. He rubbed them away with the back of his hands, forcing himself not to lose it.

Not here anyway.

He tucked his crutch under his arm, his body throbbing with pain from the wild wolf attack at the Mills Mansion during the Cold Moon Ball earlier. He drew in a deep breath, then hobbled out of Ms. Howe's office and to the front of the herbal shop. He needed to get out of there. He kept his gaze down, avoiding eye contact.

"Thanks for everything, Ms. Howe."

"Sure thing, Joe."

He fumbled with the keys in his pocket as he painstakingly made it out of the shop and into his car. He sat there for a minute, letting the frigid air wrap around his body as the smell of the shop's herbs left his lungs, replaced by the scent of his newly washed car.

Twinkling white, red, and green holiday lights were strung up and down the street. Yet their cheerful and festive message fell flat on Joe. Despair had taken him over. Hours earlier, Infiniti was sitting next to him, dressed like a princess for the ball, and now she was gone. He leaned his head back against the headrest, thinking of their amazing kiss and the promise he had made to find her.

Could he really do it?

He started his car and headed home. Driving through the quiet streets of the town, a slew of memories exploded in his brain. A few months after Infiniti had vanished back in December 2012, he had a series of dreams of horrible things happening to her, incidents that all resulted in her death. Another car accident, being swept away by a tornado, drowning in the ocean, even catching on fire. He shuddered as dread worked its way through him.

He thought of that damn reaper, Shade StormIron, and his words: "The doll's soul still wants me. I can feel it. I'll be back in due time."

A blast of icy fear invaded his senses. Had they sent Infiniti back to 2012 only to die?

He slammed on his brakes and screeched to a halt. He made a U-turn in the middle of the road and sped back to the herbal shop. He parked the car, hopped out, and rushed over to Ms. Howe as she emerged from the door.

"It didn't work!"

She huddled into her long dark coat and wrapped her arms around herself. "What do you mean, it didn't work?"

"We sent Infiniti back to 2012, and she's going to die there! I know it!"

Ms. Howe looked away for a second, as if contemplating the possibility.

"Listen, Joe. I don't know if you're right or if you're wrong, but I do know a thing or two about destiny, and I can tell you that destiny cannot be changed. Not ever." She stared up at the night sky. "It's like telling the moon not to be bright. It simply can't be done." She flashed him a look of concerned sympathy. "So whatever will be, will be."

He looked down at the sidewalk, wracking his brain for a response, when an idea came to him.

"Okay, fine, I get that about destiny, I really do. But what if her coming here was another type of destiny? A way for the right destiny to counter the wrong destiny?" He stopped, thinking his words weren't making any sense, but went on anyway. "I mean, we didn't bring her here, yet she showed up needing our help. Maybe she needs our help again."

He hobbled forward, waiting for the red-haired witch to give him some sign of hope that she understood what he was saying and would help him.

She nodded but held a pensive look on her face. "Maybe she does, Joe. Maybe she does. But let's get through the holidays first, okay? We can take up this conversation later."

"Okay," Joe said, trying to calm his excitement. "That sounds great. I'll come by after the new year. Thank you, Ms. Howe."

Joe felt better, but there was no way he could wait until after the holiday break to do something about finding Infiniti. He got back in his car and drove home, his mind searching for his next move. Once home and in his room, he texted Kase, knowing he'd still be up.

Me: Dude

Kase: Sup

Me: Need your help

Kase: About the girl? Did it work? My dad told me

Joe wasn't surprised that Sheriff Ric had said something to Kase about what had happened to Infiniti, and he didn't mind. Kase was his best friend. He would've told him everything anyway.

Me: Yeah, I think. And now she's gone

Kase: Sorry

Me: It's ok. But I have an idea. Come over tmr. I'll fill you in

Kase: Ok

Joe set his phone down and lay on his bed, exhausted and feeling like crap. But more than anything, he was determined to find Infiniti Clausman. And no one could stop him.

He turned off his bedside lamp and eyed the streaks of moonlight that poured through the blinds of his window. His mind swirled with different ideas of how he could find her when a soft knock sounded on his door.

"Joe, it's Mom. Can I come in?"

"Yeah, sure."

He sat up and switched his lamp back on. The soft light illuminated his blue-and-gray-hued room. His mom sat on the edge of his bed. Her long blond hair was wet from a recent shower.

"I heard you come in and wanted to check on you." She patted his leg and gave him a reassuring smile. "You okay?"

His fight with the wild wolf pack back at the Mills Mansion had left his body cut and bruised, but nothing could compare to the pain crushing his heart. He rubbed his head, masking his emotions, and focused instead on his physical pain.

"I'm fine. Just a little sore."

She gave him the all-knowing mom look. "I wasn't talking about your wounds, son."

"Oh," he murmured, not wanting to go there with his mom. "You mean Infiniti?"

"Yes, I mean Infiniti."

He thought of telling her his fears about Infiniti returning home only to die, but decided against it. She'd never let him try to find her. Neither would his dad. And really, he couldn't blame them. Try to find a time-traveling human girl he was called to? It was a crazy idea. Besides, they didn't even know he'd been called to her.

Joe shrugged. "She came here to do what she needed to do, and she's gone now."

His mom gave a slight nod. She patted his leg one more time and stood up to leave. "I'm very sorry, Joseph."

"Me too."

Alone again, Joe eased himself back into bed. He stared at the ceiling until the night crawled by and transformed to day. And when Kase finally showed up at his house later that morning, he hadn't slept a wink. He also hadn't formulated a plan for how he was going to find Infiniti.

"Dude," Kase said, looking his friend over. "You look like hell."

"You don't even know the half of it."

Joe limped his way down the hall, leading Kase to his room. He locked the door so they wouldn't be disturbed by his little brother, Boris.

Kase kept staring at Joe's bruised face. "My dad told me you were in a fight, but he didn't mention you got your butt kicked."

"I was swarmed. If that Transhuman guy Fleet hadn't shown up when he did, I don't know what would've happened."

Kase shook his head. "I wish I could've been there for you on that back patio instead of inside the Mills Mansion with Elle. I guess I was so wrapped up with her, I didn't even catch on that you needed help."

"Well, you can still help. That's why I texted you to come over."

Kase sat on the chair at Joe's desk. His leg bounced. He rubbed his hands together, ready for action. "Sure. Whatever you need."

Joe waited a few seconds before he continued.

"I need you to help me get to 2012."

Kase's eyes widened. He eyed Joe for a minute before laughing. "Uh, what?"

"Infiniti is in trouble. I felt it back in 2012 when she disappeared from the medical clinic, and I feel it again now. So I need to go to her. Right away. Before it's too late and something happens to her."

Joe kept a steady gaze on Kase, letting him know he wasn't kidding. The message finally sank in.

"You're serious?"

"Yeah, I am."

Joe moved across the room. He peered out the window and eyed the wintry landscape, wondering if Infiniti was still alive, when an idea came to him.

"I'm so stupid!" he called out. He snatched his laptop from his backpack and opened it on his bed. He ran a search for Infiniti Clausman Houston.

"Good idea!" Kase said, looking over his shoulder. "We can find her and help her from here. Time travel not required."

Joe's search turned up zero results. "Crap," he mumbled. "Nothing."

"Gimme that." Kase turned the laptop toward him. He typed Infiniti Clausman Texas. He clicked the search button. Still no results.

"Boys!" Joe's mom called from the other side of the door. "I've got some snacks if you're interested."

Joe's fingers hovered over the keys as his mind raced. There had to be a way to find Infiniti online. There just had to be. Or maybe there was no information on her because he was too late and she was dead.

His gut clenched tight. A knot formed in his throat.

"Be right there, Mrs. Greg!" Kase answered. He rested his hand on the laptop screen before closing it shut. He eyed his friend. "Joe, dude. She's back where she belongs, six years in the past. You need to let her go."

Joe knew right then and there that he couldn't involve Kase any further in his search. It'd be too dangerous, too risky. Plus, Kase didn't understand what it was like to be called to someone and have them ripped away. He'd have to go it alone. He forced a smile and put his hand on Kase's shoulder.

"You're right," he blew out, faking defeat. "I need to let her go."

"Exactly," Kase said with an encouraging smile. "Now, let's go eat."

Kase and Joe's little brother Boris dove into a mound of fritule pastries as if they hadn't eaten in days. Joe's mom made the donut-like fried Croatian delicacies every holiday. It was her most prized recipe that had been handed down from generation to generation. Joe usually had no problem matching their enthusiasm for food, especially for fritule, but this time he could barely finish a few bites. His stomach had twisted into a permanent knot, and he couldn't get his mind off Infiniti. Plus, exhaustion was beginning to set in after a night of life-altering events and no sleep.

Joe's mom caught on right away. She started clearing the kitchen table.

"Maybe you should rest, Joe. Take a nap or something. You did have quite the eventful evening."

"Yeah," Joe said, his eyelids so heavy he struggled to keep them open. "I could use a nap."

Kase got up and stretched. "Yep, I could use a nap, too. Thank you, Mrs. Greg." He patted Joe on the back. "See you later, dude."

Joe rubbed his throbbing shoulder, wincing a little from the sting of Kase's pat. He wondered when his wolf-shifter healing abilities would kick in as he retreated to his room. He eased himself onto his bed, his bones so sore he could hardly move. But as tired as he was, his mind was too busy to sleep just yet. Instead, he started formulating his plan. Go to Ms. Howe after the holiday and see if she'd help him. If she couldn't or wouldn't, then he'd have to find someone else to help him time travel to Infiniti. Question was, who could do it? And would they? He wasn't sure, but he was determined to find someone.

With a long yawn, he draped a blanket over himself. His body melded into the soft cotton while exhaustion took over and his brain finally shut off.

Early the next morning, Joe was back at it. He scoured the internet for any mention of a death of a Houston teen girl in 2012 but found nothing that matched Infiniti's description. He took that as a good sign and decided to go with the theory that she was still alive.

With his online search pretty much exhausted, he started looking into time travel. He spent days at the Sun and Moon

Academy library reading every book on magic and time travel he could find, but couldn't make any of the spells work for him. He thought of talking to Gallad Augustine or even Addie Beaumont to see if they'd help him, but their connections to the Court of the Sun and the Moon would be too risky. The last thing he needed was to cross the leaders of the town. His dad would be furious.

With the holiday break finally over, Joe went to see Ms. Howe at her herbal shop. She ended up giving him a long explanation for why he shouldn't meddle with fate and destiny. When school started, he subtly brought up the topic of time travel with some of his teachers, but nothing they mentioned helped him.

Days turned into weeks. Weeks morphed into months. Joe was beginning to think he'd never find Infiniti. Desperate and fresh out of ideas, he decided to change his tactic. Instead of searching for Infiniti in the past, he'd search for her in the present. He'd go up and down every single street in Houston if he had to. He didn't care if there was a six-year difference between them. Couples had age differences all the time. And in the larger scheme of things, six years was nothing. But what if he found her and she thought he was crazy? Or what if she was married? Or maybe she really was dead. He forced himself not to think of worst case scenarios. He had to keep trying until he found her.

But still, deep down, he couldn't shake the overriding feeling that he wouldn't be able to find her in the present because something horrible had happened to her in the past.

"Hang on, babe," he said as he started a fresh search on his laptop. "I'm coming."

This time he searched for flights to Houston for after graduation. He scribbled the prices on a piece of paper. Factoring in food and thinking he could sleep on park benches, he'd need at least eight hundred dollars. With the graduation money he thought he'd be getting, plus the money he'd be making over the summer, he'd have more than enough. As for his parents, he knew they'd be pissed, but he didn't care. He had to go.

The seasons changed from freezing to mild to sunny, and

before Joe knew it, the end of the school year had arrived. Graduation had come and gone. His friends were either making plans to go away for college or stay nearby and attend the new Sun and Moon Academy College of Supernatural Guardians. He had been invited to be a member of the inaugural class of the college, but had turned it down. He needed to focus on finding Infiniti. Nothing else mattered, and his flight to Houston couldn't come fast enough.

CHAPTER 2

*I*nfiniti blasted her music, eyeing the jam-packed closet her mother had been begging her for weeks to clean and organize. Kicking her shoes around, she started making a pile of stuff she didn't want anymore. She laughed at the absurdity of some of her older fashion choices.

"Well, look at that," she said, spying a worn-out shirt with a giant purple smiley face she had worn all the time when she was in middle school. "Cute and cringeworthy all at the same time."

She yanked the shirt from the hanger and tossed it in the give-away pile. The fabric bunched together into a pathetic looking bundle. Looking at the crumpled expression that now resembled a sad face instead of a smiley face, she couldn't help but feel sad, too. She scooped it up and held it close, feeling guilty at having dismissed it so harshly. Her mind replayed all the good memories from her youth—sleepovers, movie nights, roller skating parties. Now she had to go to college and get a job.

"Growing up sucks," she grumbled.

She folded the shirt neatly and placed it in her dresser with her other collectible tops. Fishing through the remainder of her wardrobe, she came across her senior year class shirt. It had a large rocket ship blasting into space on the front. On the back it said

Senior Odyssey 2013. The last time she had worn that shirt was the last day of school. She smiled, thinking of her fun times at Harmony High, then placed it with her smiley face shirt.

Senior year was over, summer had arrived, and college was around the corner. Infiniti wasn't ready at all. Something inside of her felt off. Weird. Like she was missing something. And it had all started around the Christmas break, right after her trip to Breckenridge, Colorado. Ever since that trip she'd been plagued with dreams of dying. She had searched for dream meanings and found an article that said dreaming of death signified transformation. The theory made perfect sense to her. She chalked up her nightmares to the whole college transition thing and dismissed her feelings as "graduation blues," yet the dread in the pit of her stomach seemed way more than that. She thought the strangeness would fade, but the sensation had only started to magnify.

"Stop being so emo," she ordered herself with a sigh, plopping down on her window seat.

She folded her legs, wrapped her arms around them, and gazed out at the sunny August day from her second-floor window. Branches and leaves from the tall oak outside crisscrossed her line of sight, providing the perfect view for her melancholy thoughts.

All of her friends had left for college already, and she had decided to go to the local community college at the last minute. She had told everyone, including her mom, that she had changed her mind because she wanted to get her basics out of the way, but deep down she felt as if she needed to stay in Houston for something. But what? Alone in her house, she was kind of regretting her decision.

Her stomach rumbled. "Food," she announced, perking up. "Yep, I need some food. Food makes everything better."

She started to get up when movement on the sidewalk caught her eye. It was a little girl she hadn't seen before. With her babysitting experience in the neighborhood, she thought she knew just about every kid in Rolling Lakes.

The girl was around five or so. She wore a white dress, and her long fair hair practically blended in with the material. The girl stopped, as if sensing Infiniti's stare. She shaded her eyes with one hand, looked up to where Infiniti was, then waved with her other hand.

Infiniti raised her hand in acknowledgment, watching as the girl dropped her hand and strolled up to her across-the-street-neighbor Jan's house. Her small frame slipped from view the closer she got to the door.

Infiniti searched her mind for any memory of Jan mentioning a granddaughter, but couldn't recall anything. She leaned down, so she could see better, but the overhang by Jan's front door obstructed her view.

"Huh," Infiniti muttered to herself, wondering who that was.

Her stomach issued a fresh reminder of its hunger. This time she obeyed the call. Traipsing down the stairs, she rounded the foyer when she glanced out her beveled-glass front door and saw the little girl again. She was standing by Jan's front door, facing Infiniti's house. She seemed to be looking straight at her.

Infiniti froze.

The little girl beckoned her to come over with a series of rapid hand gestures.

"Me?" Infiniti muttered out loud, although the little girl couldn't hear her. She moved closer to the door. She looked to the right and then to the left to see if anyone else was outside, but she didn't see anybody. When she brought her attention back to the girl, she was gone.

Infiniti gasped. A shiver raced down her spine. Was the girl a ghost? Even though she loved all things supernatural, deep down she was the biggest scaredy-cat she knew. She rested her hand on the brass doorknob. Should she go over there to investigate? And then she thought of Jan. Was there something wrong with her? She had known Jan her whole life. She had become like family to Infiniti and her mom over the years, especially since Infiniti's mom traveled a lot for work. If something was happening at Jan's, she had to help.

"Come on," she said out loud, mustering up her courage, telling herself that if it was a ghost, it was only a little girl. Plus, it was daylight. Nothing bad happened during the day, right?

She approached Jan's with caution. She rang the doorbell. She kept an eye on her surroundings when the door swung open.

"Infiniti, dear. How nice to see you," Jan said with a deep voice and a wide smile. Jan was a tall woman with deeply etched lines riddling her face and puffy gray hair that rested on her shoulders. Even though it was summer, she wore her usual long-sleeved shirt, long skirt, and socks with loafers.

"Hey, Jan." Infiniti scanned the crisp white walls and dark wood floors, wondering if the little girl she had seen would appear. "Is anyone . . . here with you?"

"No, it's just me. And Tinker, of course." Hearing her name, Jan's fluffy cat strolled into the room. "How about some tea? It's been a while since we've chatted, so I'd say we're due for a nice visit."

Tea and cookies was Jan's customary way of greeting visitors. Infiniti and her empty stomach had no complaints. "Sure. That'd be great."

"Is your mom away for business, dear?"

"Yeah. She'll be back tonight."

Infiniti followed Jan into the kitchen and took a seat at her small square-shaped wooden table. Jan chatted about the weather while she set a teapot on the stove and then disappeared into her walk-in pantry. She emerged with a plate of cookies and placed them in front of Infiniti.

"Well, my dear, it's been what, since the Cold Moon that we've had a proper visit?"

"That's right, the Cold Moon," Infiniti echoed, remembering how Jan had told her the full moon last December was called the Cold Moon. She also thought about the strangeness inside of her she'd been feeling ever since then. "It wasn't so long ago, yet it seems like a lifetime away."

"Interesting choice of words," Jan said.

Infiniti was about to take a bite of her cookie, but stopped. "What do you mean?"

The teapot whistled before Jan could respond. "Let me get that. Hold on to that thought, dear."

Jan removed the pot from the stove. She poured the boiling water into two dainty teacups. She put the cups on the table and offered Infiniti some tea bags. They started dunking their bags in the hot water, and soon the aroma of mint and herbs filled the air.

"Now, I didn't want to bother you, what with all your end-of-the-year school activities and graduation, but I've noticed a significant energy shift since the Cold Moon."

Infiniti's eyes grew wide. She leaned in. "You have?"

"Yes, I have." Jan sipped her tea. "You're pretty in tune with nature. Have you noticed anything odd?"

"Oh my god, yes!" Infiniti scooted her chair in closer, relieved that the bizarreness she'd been feeling wasn't just her. "I thought I was feeling all weird because I was graduating, but it wasn't making any sense. I spent my entire high school career looking forward to getting out of Houston, but now I feel like I can't leave. And I don't want to. Like I need to stay here for something, or even someone. It all started right after the holiday break, and it's only getting worse." She lowered her voice. "And by the way, I thought I saw a ghost girl or something outside your house just now." Infiniti let out a nervous laugh. "It's crazy, isn't it? I'm going crazy. Happy graduation, now you're nuts."

Jan put her thick wrinkly hand on Infiniti's small one and squeezed. "Nothing is crazy, especially not you."

Infiniti blew out a sigh of relief. "Okay, then what the heck is going on?"

Infiniti hoped Jan would have an answer. Jan was wise in a mystical way. She called herself a homegrown psychic and was into all things otherworldly. Together they'd used the Ouija board, dabbled in tarot cards, and even had fun with Jan's theory of everyone having nine soul lives on Earth. Jan had a way of explaining the unexplained, and Infiniti was ready for a rational explanation for everything.

Jan cleared her throat. "What color is Tinker's coat?"

Infiniti stitched her brows together, thinking for sure Jan would've asked about the girl she'd seen outside. But instead, she wanted to talk about the color of her cat?

"Huh?"

"Follow along with me on this, okay?" Jan paused for effect before repeating, "What color is my cat Tinker?"

Infiniti knew Tinker as well as if she'd been her own. She'd been playing with Tinker for years. She even took care of Tinker every time Jan went out of town. She loved that cat.

"Um, white, of course," Infiniti answered. "From her head to her toes. Pure white."

Jan lifted an eyebrow. She snapped her fingers a few times. "Tinker! Come, girl!"

Tinker trotted into the room. Infiniti scanned the feline— white body, a long fluffy white tail, and black paws. She did a double take. Black paws?

Infiniti's mouth dropped.

"W-w-w-hat?!" Infiniti stared at the cat, wondering if she was seeing things. "She's white . . . and black?"

"Yes," Jan acknowledged. "One day, I noticed she was different. Like something wasn't quite right with her. I couldn't put my finger on it, but then, as I studied her, I had a memory of her being all white."

Infiniti stared at Tinker and then back at Jan. She forced herself to follow Jan's explanation. "So . . . your memory didn't match reality?"

"Exactly, my dear." Jan's eyes took on a faraway look. "I've noticed differences with other things, too. I could've sworn the color of my favorite book was red, when in fact it is blue. Even the name of my favorite restaurant is spelled differently than I thought." She narrowed her attention on Infiniti. "It's subtle, small things someone might not recognize at first, but when added up with everything else, is actually quite significant."

Infiniti pushed the plate of snacks away, suddenly losing her appetite. "I-I-I don't know what to say. I mean, when I walked in, I saw Tinker, and I didn't notice anything out of the ordinary. But there she is," Infiniti gestured to Tinker, "with black paws."

"You didn't notice because your mind and your eyes were not in sync. And now that I've pointed it out to you, the truth has been unveiled."

"How is this even possible?" Infiniti continued staring at Tinker, as if she had come from another planet.

"I've been looking into it, and I believe there's been a quantum event." Jan paused for a long while before she went on. "I think we have slid into an alternate reality. A different timeline, if you will."

"Holy shit," Infiniti whispered. She bit her lip because she had never cussed in front of Jan. "Sorry."

"It's okay." Jan chuckled. "If there's any time to issue an expletive, this would be the time."

Infiniti sipped the tea, thinking it'd calm her, but it didn't. Her heart raced out of control while her mind started picking away at her life. She couldn't pinpoint any solid differences in anything else, other than Tink's differently colored paws staring her in the face, but the unease that had settled deep within her told her that Jan was right. The world was *off*.

"And the ghost girl," Jan said in a lowered voice. "I've seen her, too."

Infiniti sucked in a breath. She held it for a while before squeaking out, "You have?"

"I have indeed." Jan reached out for Infiniti's hand. She held it in a death grip. "Her name is Abigail, and she says you need to go back."

Infiniti's mind reeled. Her heart catapulted against her chest. She stared at her fingers that were turning purple from Jan's hold. "Go back where?"

Jan released her. "I don't know, my dear. She disappeared before she could explain." Jan looked up and away, as if lost in thought. "That was a few weeks ago. Despite my best efforts, I haven't seen her since."

The old-fashioned cuckoo clock in the kitchen started chiming.

"Oh my, the time!" Jan got up. She placed the teacups in the sink. "I'm so very sorry to cut our conversation short, but I have an appointment to get to. How about we chat again tomorrow?"

Infiniti rose to her feet while Jan bustled about. The earth was experiencing some weird timeline shift, a ghost girl named Abigail wanted her to go back to wherever, and now Jan had to leave for an appointment? Talk about terrible timing.

"I guess I'll come back tomorrow, then."

"Yes, tomorrow," Jan agreed. She ushered Infiniti to the front door. Stopping at the threshold, she put her hands on Infiniti's shoulders. "We'll figure this out. Easy peasy."

Infiniti gulped. Jan only said "easy peasy" when something was *not* easy peasy. As in the opposite of easy peasy. She wished Jan hadn't said that, because now she was freaked.

"Okay," Infiniti said. "See you then."

Once outside, Infiniti breathed in the warmth from the summer air, trying to erase the fear building inside of her.

"I'm cool," she said out loud. "Everything is totally cool. Easy peasy can sometimes actually mean easy peasy."

She looked down the street to the right and then to the left. Not seeing anyone, ghost or otherwise, she booked it back home, slammed the door behind her, and locked it.

She took out her phone and texted her mom.

Infiniti: What time ya coming home

She went to the kitchen and ripped open a bag of Flamin' Hot Cheetos. She shoved the fire-hot crispy goodness in her mouth and started crunching while keeping her eye on her phone.

Mom: Should be there around 9

Infiniti: K, see you then

Mom: Love you
Infiniti: Love you

She tucked her phone into her back pocket, then finished off her snack. She thought her favorite junk food would make her feel better, but it didn't. Fear of ghosts and quantum events swirled in her head.

"Okay, I'm not doing this," she commanded herself, pushing every eerie thought out of her brain. "Back to the closet."

She went up to her room, closed her door and her blinds, lit some incense, and started sorting through her clothes, telling herself everything was going to be okay.

Easy peasy.

CHAPTER 3

Fleet bolted upright in bed, panting from the nightmare he'd been having. He kicked off his covers, swung his legs over the edge of his bed, and planted his feet on the ground. He ran his fingers through his thick dark hair while his breathing settled. Eyeing his clock, he saw it was five in the morning.

"Son of a bitch."

Fleet knew there was no way he could go back to sleep, so he got up. He slipped on a white T-shirt and dark sweatpants and headed for the kitchen.

"Another dream?" Fleet's brother, Farrell, was standing by the coffee machine as it spewed hot brown liquid.

"Yeah, you too?"

"Yeah."

They were practically mirror images of each other, except Fleet had dark hair while Farrell had blond. They crossed their arms at almost the exact same time and waited for their brew to finish. When the machine sputtered out its last drops, they poured themselves two oversized mugs of coffee and sat on the sofa in the living room. Windows lined the back wall of their log cabin in the Michigan woods—the cabin they had called home for lifetimes.

"What did you dream about this time?" Farrell asked.

Fleet blew out a long breath. "Infiniti. She keeps popping up in my head. Always dying, always pleading for me to help her. Like a damn movie stuck on repeat." He peered out the windows, searching for any sign of daylight, but didn't see any. "What about you?"

Farrell kept his eyes down. "For me it's Dominique. Over and over."

Farrell never elaborated about his dreams of Dominique, and Fleet never asked. Too much had happened between the three of them, and he didn't need to know his brother's hidden thoughts.

Fleet rubbed his stubbled face, reminding himself that he and Farrell had agreed to stay away from Dominique, Trent, and Infiniti. But something about Tiny's pleas wouldn't let him go.

"What if I need to help her?" Fleet asked. "What if her story isn't finished?"

Farrell shifted and faced his brother. "What do you mean?"

"I don't know, and I can't explain it. But something inside me is telling me this is different. That she really does need my help."

Farrell let the idea sit with him for a few seconds. "But we agreed to stay away from them. Remember?"

"Yeah, yeah. I remember."

Fleet got up and faced the windows. After everything they'd been through with Dominique's final life, he didn't know why Infiniti of all people would somehow need his help. Infiniti had played a major role in Dominique's story, but everything was over now. And as far as he knew, she was safe and sound in Houston, probably getting ready for college.

"You helped Infiniti in Havenwood Falls."

Fleet spun around and saw Abigail. He recognized the ghost girl right away. He hadn't seen her in a while and had no idea what she was talking about.

"I helped Infiniti in Havenwood Falls?"

Transhumans knew about the supernatural town of Havenwood Falls without having any specific knowledge about it, other than it was located somewhere in Colorado. It was an agreement made between Transhumans and the founding members of the town in case the town ever needed their help. But Fleet had never stepped foot in the place. In fact, he didn't know of any Transhuman who had. Surely the girl was mistaken.

He threw Farrell a curious look. He could tell by the puzzled expression on his brother's face he didn't know what Abigail was talking about either.

"You must be confusing me with somebody else. I've never been to Havenwood Falls," Fleet said, approaching the girl with caution.

"Neither have I," Farrell added, on his feet now too and standing by Fleet's side.

Abigail pointed at Fleet. "You've been there, with Infiniti, though you don't remember it. She doesn't remember either. The town spelled you both to forget when you left," she said in her young ethereal voice. She looked away, as if dismissing that part of the conversation. "But that's not important right now. The important part is you need to go to her. To her house in Houston. She's in danger."

"She's in danger?" Fleet asked. "Explain."

Abigail's form started fading. "That's all I can say. The rest is up to you," she said as she shimmered out of view.

"Wait!" Fleet called out.

The small girl disappeared, leaving Fleet with a thousand questions and no answers. He eyed his brother. "That's just great. A cryptic message about a supernatural haven I've apparently been to but don't remember. And I have to help someone you and I agreed we'd stay away from."

Fleet studied his brother, waiting for him to say something.

"You need to go to her," Farrell said after a while. "Your dreams and now Abigail appearing and saying Infiniti needs you? It can't be a coincidence."

Fleet knew Farrell was right. There was no such thing as

coincidence. "What about Havenwood Falls? What do you make of that?"

Farrell shrugged his shoulders. "I guess you'll figure it out as you go along."

Fleet lowered his coffee mug. "Wait a minute. You're not coming with me?"

Farrell looked away, and Fleet knew why. It was Dominique, but Fleet knew his brother didn't want to say.

"I should stay here," Farrell explained. "If Infiniti needs you, then maybe," he paused, "someone else will need me."

Fleet placed his hand on Farrell's shoulder, letting his brother off the hook. "Understood. I'll go it alone. I'll call for you if I need backup."

Fleet stood with his brother in silence while streaks of morning sunlight began to filter into the woodsy cabin. Fleet studied the budding summer day as his mind cluttered with everything he'd been through—love, death, betrayal. So much pain and hurt over so many lifetimes. He thought it was all over, but now Tiny needed him. He couldn't even imagine what for, but he needed to see it through.

"Should I zap over there? Or drive?" he asked Farrell. They had decided to use their abilities only when necessary so they could keep off the grid. He wondered if the call to aid Tiny qualified as necessary.

"I think you should err on the side of caution and drive. Besides, you may need a car while you're there."

"You're right. I can make it there by nightfall if I drive straight through." He rubbed the back of his neck. "Guess I should go pack."

Back in his room, Fleet got dressed in a hurry, anxious to get on the road. He threw some stuff in a duffel bag, then did a last minute scan of his room to make sure he wasn't forgetting anything. Ready for the drive to Houston, he said a quick goodbye to his brother and left.

Fleet drove into the day, his mind picking apart his lifetimes.

He searched for any clue about why Tiny would need his help now and why Abigail said he'd been to Havenwood Falls when he had no recollection of it. None of it made any sense. He only hoped that whatever was going on wouldn't be that bad.

But he knew better.

Shit always happened to him.

CHAPTER 4

*G*azing out his bedroom window at the bright August sky, Joe couldn't believe so much time had passed since Infiniti left Havenwood Falls. He remembered the Cold Moon Ball as if it were yesterday. He closed his eyes, picturing blankets of snow covering the town, holiday decorations that sprinkled homes and businesses, Infiniti looking beautiful in her purple dress, and the amazing kiss they had shared.

He opened his eyes, returning to reality and the backpack on the floor he'd been packing for his trip to Houston in the morning. He'd spent the summer saving money and preparing, and the time to go was finally arriving. Maps of the massive Texas city were strewn about his bed. Most were of neighborhoods and streets; others were of major roads and highways. He had planned his search in grids, focusing on the innermost parts of the city first and then branching out. He hoped it wouldn't take too long to catch her scent, but he needed to be prepared for a long stay just in case.

He folded the maps carefully and stuffed them in the inside pocket of his backpack. He followed that with clothes and toiletries. With his pack loaded, he took the plane ticket he had purchased from a travel agent a few towns over and placed it in the oversized envelope that held enough cash to last him a few weeks.

A light rap sounded at his door. Joe froze. He eyed his things and started scooping everything up.

"Joe? It's Mom. Can I come in?"

"One sec," he said, shoving his pack in the back of his closet. He threw a blanket over it for good measure.

Trying to look as casual as possible, as if he hadn't just been planning his big getaway, he opened the door.

"Hey, Mom. What's up?"

She was wearing jeans and a floral printed blouse. Her long blond hair was pulled up in a ponytail. "I just got a call from Dr. Underwood. He wants you to come in today for a checkup. Says he cleared some room in his schedule for you."

"A checkup? What for?"

Even though he had asked, Joe knew the reason. He'd been wasting away for months. His clothes hung loose. He hadn't had a haircut or a shave since graduation, though he was meaning to clean up before his flight to Houston.

"Well," his mom said, fidgeting with her hands, "I saw Dr. Underwood earlier today at Coffee Haven. He asked me how you were doing. I told him you still had your limp from the scuffle at the Cold Moon Ball."

"Mom, why did you say anything? It's just a limp. It's no big deal."

"It should've gone away by now, son." She eyed him with determination. "You know I'm right."

Joe's hand went to his leg. Deep down he'd been worrying about why he hadn't fully healed, and it seemed his mom had the same concerns. Probably his dad, too. Guilt struck him at the pain he knew she and his dad would go through when he left. The least he could do was go with her to the doc. Besides, maybe the doc could help him. Having a limp was sure to slow down his search.

"Fine," he said. "I'll go. Do I have time to shower?"

"Sure. I'll be waiting in the kitchen. But please don't take too long, okay?"

"Yeah, okay."

Standing in the hot stream of water, Joe's mind rehearsed everything he needed to do to leave town. Fake needing to leave early for a hike, head to the bus station for a ride to Montrose, Colorado, then catch his flight from there. He'd text his parents and let them know what he'd done once he made it to Houston.

When he finished his shower, he dried off and stood in front of the mirror.

"Damn," he whispered, taking a good look at his reflection for the first time in a while. He hardly recognized himself. His usually short-cropped blond hair had grown so much it covered his ears and hung in his eyes. He leaned forward, rubbing the scruff on his face. It wasn't a full beard, but pretty close. Assuming Infiniti would have any chance of remembering him, it wouldn't be like this.

Lathering up his face with shaving cream, he started taking off the facial hair. And when he finished, he thought he looked more like himself. The next thing he needed was a haircut. Maybe he could get one after seeing the doc.

Dressed and ready, Joe got in the car with his mom. She tried to strike up a conversation with Joe about his friends and what they had been up to, but there wasn't much to say, since he hadn't really seen them in a while. Eventually, he and his mom resorted to silence as their small-talk faded.

After a few minutes, the Medical Center came into view. Only a few cars lined the parking lot of the converted white house with blue trim. Joe hoped that meant his appointment would be quick. Down the way, he spotted the shopping center and Burger Bar. He thought of how Infiniti had ended up at the clinic in December and then wandered down to Burger Bar because she was hungry and needed a phone. That was before she found out she had time traveled.

"You hungry?" Joe's mom must've followed his line of sight. Optimistic yet subtle enthusiasm laced her voice. "Want to get a burger when we're finished?"

Joe had no appetite, but didn't want to disappoint her. "Yeah, maybe." He ruffled his hair. "What I could really use, though, is a haircut."

His mom parked the car with a smile on her face. "A possible burger and a haircut. Sounds like a plan."

They were escorted to an exam room in the back of the clinic. Joe's mom took a seat on the chair in the corner of the room.

"Mom, really? I'm not a kid anymore. I got this."

"Oh." She got up, looking a little surprised. "Sure, of course. I'll be out in the lobby."

Joe paced about the room for only a few seconds when a knock sounded on the door and in walked Dr. Jasper Underwood. He had salt-and-pepper hair and wore khaki pants with a button-down shirt and a white lab coat. He held a chart in one hand and extended his other hand for a shake.

"Joseph," he said with a warm smile and strong grip. "Thank you for coming to see me today. And congratulations on graduating!"

"Thanks, Doc."

"What are your plans after summer?"

"I'll be taking online college classes and working full time with Sheriff Kasun."

"You won't be going to the new college? The Sun and Moon Academy College of…" The doc's voice trailed off. He tapped his forehead, searching for the full name of the new school.

"…Of Supernatural Guardians. No, I'm not. There's too much work to be done here," Joe explained, issuing the canned response he used any time someone asked him about his college plans.

"Ah, a young man of duty. I admire that, Joseph."

Dr. Underwood patted the paper-lined exam table, and Joseph hopped on. The doc rolled a stool over from the corner of the room and took a seat. He opened the chart and started reading to himself.

"I saw you back in December after that event with the wild wolf pack, then three months later to check on your healing. And then this morning, I ran into your mother at the coffee shop. She says you're still limping. Does that sum it up?"

"Yeah," Joe said. "Pretty much."

"Hmm," the doc said, rubbing his chin. "Let's do all the regular stuff before we look at that leg, shall we?"

Joe rubbed his hand on his jeans. "Okay."

The doc set his chart down. "I'm going to give it to you straight, Joseph. You're not looking so hot. Though I do appreciate the fresh shave." He winked. "Other than the limp, how are you feeling?"

Joe knew he wasn't looking his best, but hearing the doc say something out loud made him think he looked way worse than he thought.

"I'm feeling all right."

Dr. Underwood took the blood pressure cuff from the hook on the wall. He wrapped the arm band around Joe's bicep and started pumping.

"You've been struggling since your scuffle at the Cold Moon Ball. Is that right?"

"Um, yeah. That's right."

"And you don't seem to be getting better?"

Joe thought of hiding the truth, but then decided to be honest. "No. Not really."

Joe's arm was squeezed tight until the arm band started releasing in intervals. Dr. Underwood watched the numbers. He removed the cuff and hung it back on the wall where it belonged.

"Numbers are low, Joseph."

A twinge of panic struck Joe. "Is that bad?"

"Well, for your age not necessarily. You may just be a little dehydrated, but let's finish the exam." Dr. Underwood motioned toward the scale. "Let's get your weight."

Joe walked across the room. He stared at the scale for a few seconds before stepping onto it slowly. The numbers blinked until they stopped on a weight that was almost fifteen pounds below his normal.

Dr. Underwood made a notation in the file. "Are you trying to lose weight?"

"No. I'm just not as hungry as I used to be, I guess."

"I see," Dr. Underwood mumbled, scribbling on the chart. "Hop back up on the table."

Dr. Underwood held Joe's wrist and started taking his pulse. "Would you say your limp is the same, better, or worse since the Cold Moon Ball?"

"Ummm," Joe had been trying to hide his limp for months, but hadn't really thought of it in terms of comparing it to the initial injury. He shrugged. "I guess it's a little better?"

The doc released his hold. He scribbled more notes, then took a penlight from his medical coat pocket and shined it in Joe's eyes. When he finished, he dropped the light back where it belonged.

"Pulse is a little elevated, but your eyes are dilating fine."

Joe breathed a sigh of relief. "That's good at least."

Dr. Underwood set his stuff aside. He crossed his arms. His usual positive facade gave way to a serious look.

"Good is a relative term. If you were an ordinary young man, I'd say you were simply lovesick. But you're not an ordinary young man. You're a wolf shifter. Your wounds from that attack should've healed months ago, and they haven't."

Joe wondered if there was something *really* wrong with him. He'd heard of other shifters going insane when separated from their mates, but he'd never heard of it happening to anyone in his pack. Maybe something else happened to his pack, like some sort of slow and painful deterioration. He let out a nervous laugh, hoping he was wrong.

"Do I need to be worried?"

"The girl, the time traveler, you were called to her—am I correct?"

36

Joe's face grew hot. The image of Infiniti's bloodied body at the car wreck flashed before his eyes. Other than Fleet, he hadn't told anyone about his connection to Infiniti.

"Yeah, I was twelve when it happened."

Dr. Underwood rubbed his chin. "Lovesickness is a real thing, Joseph. It can cause all kinds of ailments, similar to the ones you're experiencing—weight loss, withdrawal, and even improper healing when the body is compromised."

"Wait a minute," Joe cut in. His mind raced, thinking of how he had felt when Infiniti disappeared in 2012. She had most definitely plagued his thoughts and dreams, but he had never gotten sick. "Why am I feeling all this now and not then?"

Dr. Underwood stitched his brows together. "Good question, Joseph. I surmise it's because you were so young the first time she was here. Plus, she disappeared quickly. But this go around you're much older, and you spent significant quality time with her. And I'm assuming she bonded with you in turn. Am I right?"

Joe thought of their kiss and how Infiniti had begged him to find her. "Yeah, you're right." His heart hurt, as in actual physical pain. The type of pain he knew would never go away. "So I'm lovesick."

"You are indeed. But the difficulty with someone like you being lovesick is that you are not a normal young man. You are a wolf shifter, and you've lost your mate. Some wolf shifters adjust to a loss like that and move on. Others . . ."

Dr. Underwood's voice trailed off as he appeared to be searching for the right word.

Joe sat forward. "Others what?" he prompted, needing to hear the truth.

"Others don't recover."

Joe gulped as ripples of goose bumps raced across his skin. He feared not being able to make it to Houston to look for Infiniti. And then he envisioned a tombstone with his name on it.

"Doc, what do you mean? Don't recover? As in—"

The door swung open, and Joe's dad entered the room. He

was almost an exact replica of Joe, tall with blond hair. His build was thick and muscular. Joe used to be pretty muscular, too. Now he felt like skin and bones. He was wearing his usual patrol jeans, tucked-in Henley shirt, and leather jacket. He even had his gun still strapped at his waist. Joe's mom came in right behind him. They both wore worried expressions, but Joe's dad quickly erased his. He patted Joe's shoulder, then shook Dr. Underwood's hand.

"Sorry I'm late. Had to finish up a report before I could leave the station."

"That's okay, Ivan. I was just about to ask Katarina to come back in. You both need to be in the exam room for this next part."

"Dad?" Joe looked from his mom to his dad. "I didn't know you were coming."

"We're all in this together, son."

All in this together? Joe's stomach tightened even more. He thought for sure he was dying, and they all knew it.

Dr. Underwood motioned for his parents to shut the door behind them. "I was about to explain to Joseph how some wolf shifters don't recover when they lose their mates."

"I knew it," Joe's mom uttered.

"Wait a minute," Joe said. "Knew what? That I was called to Infiniti or that I'm dying?"

"No, no, no," Dr. Underwood cut in with an apologetic tone. "Joseph, you are frail and weak and could possibly never regain your robust nature, but to say you're dying would be quite the worst case scenario."

"But a possible scenario nonetheless?" Joe asked.

"Joseph," the doc said, meeting him eye to eye. "Right now, you are not dying."

The doc's words fell far short of making him feel better, because saying *right now you are not dying* was not the same as saying *you are not dying.* But Joe figured he'd take what he could get. Glossing over his parents suspecting he was called to Infiniti, thinking that detail was not that important under the circumstances, he wondered what it meant to never regain his robust nature.

"Fine. I'm not dying right now, but I'm gonna be skinny with a limp and feel lost and hopeless the rest of my life? And maybe die somewhere down the road? I don't think so."

He didn't want to die, not at all. But he also didn't want to continue living like he had for the last few months. That's why he had to go to Houston.

"We are all in agreement that something needs to be done, Joseph," his mom said.

"Dr. Underwood is going to try to heal you," his dad tacked on with a hopeful tone.

Joe perked up. He studied the doc's navy-colored eyes. He hadn't even thought about the doc being a fae but now was thinking of nothing else.

"That's right. Doc, you can heal me!"

Excitement at being strong and healthy again exploded inside of him. Determination spread through his veins. If he got well, he'd have a better chance at finding Infiniti.

Joe clapped his hands together. "Let's do it."

"All right," Dr. Underwood said with a smile. "Let's give it a go. All you need to do is be still, okay?"

Joe nodded. "Be still. Got it."

Dr. Underwood raised his hands. He brought them to either side of Joe's head, right at the temples. He closed his eyes. The touch warmed Joe's skin ever so slightly.

"I'm reading your body," Dr. Underwood explained. "Like a scan."

"Okay," Joe whispered.

After a few long seconds in that position, the doc moved his hands down. He rested them on Joe's chest, right over his heart. Joe looked down and saw light glowing all around the doc's hands. A slight warmth penetrated through his shirt, as if someone had lit a fire before him. He watched as the glow waned, then flickered, then waned again, as if struggling to hold steady.

Joe didn't think that was supposed to be happening.

He brought his gaze back up to the doc and saw his face straining from effort. His lips quivered. The heat on Joe's skin magnified until it almost burned. Joe held his breath, wondering if he should break contact, when the doc dropped his hands with a grunt.

"Doc, are you okay?"

"Yes, I'm fine." Dr. Underwood took a handkerchief out of his pocket and wiped his brow. "But I'm sorry to say I was unsuccessful. I'm very sorry, Joseph. Seems your heartbreak is a lot deeper than I thought."

A heavy silence filled the room as Joe considered the implication of Dr. Underwood being unable to heal him. Did that mean the worst case scenario was an actual possibility now? Had his death sentence kicked in? He thought so, but didn't want to say it out loud. Saying it made it real.

Joe patted his chest, just to make sure he was okay. "Well, now what?"

"Plan B," Dr. Underwood announced.

Joe raised his brows. He eyed his parents, catching on that they and the doc had been plotting this whole visit for a while. A plan A and a plan B didn't just happen.

"What's plan B?'

The doc crossed his arms. "In the event the healing didn't work, your parents and I discussed petitioning the Court to help you find Infiniti."

Joe hopped off the table. He smiled with excitement and disbelief. If they could convince the Court of the Sun and the Moon to help him, the governing body of the town and the supernaturals, his search would be a whole lot easier.

"Really?"

"Yes, really." His dad smiled back. "Your mom and I couldn't bear to see you like this any longer."

"Well, let's go. Now. To the Court. Let's do this!"

Dr. Underwood shushed Joe. "I know you're excited, Joseph, but don't forget we have other patients in the clinic."

"Oh, that's right. Sorry." Joe shrugged but couldn't keep the smile off his face.

"And we just can't waltz into the Court with something like this," Joe's dad said in a lowered tone. "We need a Court hearing and a witness."

Joe's shoulders dropped. So did his smile.

"But we had anticipated this as a possibility," Joe's mom went on. "We have our witness right here with Dr. Underwood. And our hearing is set for tomorrow morning. So your arrangements to fly to Houston will have to wait."

Joe's mouth dropped. He eyed his parents. "You knew about that?"

Joe's dad nodded. "Son, I'm a police officer. Everyone in this town and in the neighboring towns knows me. So if my son is going to buy a bus ticket and a plane ticket, you'd better believe someone is going to tip me off."

Joe felt so dumb. He should've known someone would spot him and tell his dad. Sometimes it really sucked having a cop for a dad. But in this particular instance, he had no complaints.

"Sorry, Mom and Dad. I didn't think you'd let me go."

"You're right about that. We wouldn't have because she's not there. At least, not right now," his dad explained.

"Huh?"

"When I got wind of what you were doing, I decided to do my own searching. There's no trace of Infiniti Clausman in Houston, or even Texas."

Joe tightened his fist. "I knew it."

"That's why the Court is our only answer," his mom said. "If you're going to find her, you need to go to the past."

Joe couldn't believe his ears. His parents were on his side and had arranged for a meeting with the Court. That was when it hit him. They were suffering just as much as he was, maybe even more. For them to be working behind the scenes to help him like that, not only with the doc but with the Court, made him feel beyond grateful. He didn't know how he could ever thank them.

"Thanks, Mom, Dad," he said bringing them in for a group hug.

For the first time in a really long time, hope soared inside of him. He was going to find Infiniti. He finally had real help and a real shot at truly finding her.

He hoped it wasn't too late.

CHAPTER 5

*P*ushing her fear of ghosts and quantum events out of her mind, Infiniti finished going through her closet and her drawers. She eyed her huge piles of clothes to donate, proud of her accomplishment. She shoved everything into garbage bags and hauled them downstairs. She plopped them by the kitchen table, then glanced at the clock. It was only six. Three more hours until her mom got home.

She hadn't eaten anything other than a few cookies at Jan's and a bag of Flamin' Hot Cheetos after that. She was ready for something more substantial. She opened the pantry, scanned her options, and settled on a bag of Ramen. Not the best or healthiest of meals, but it would do. Besides, she loved noodles.

With her dinner ready, she parked herself in front of the TV and put on a movie. Something light and funny. Finally, at nine o'clock, the back door swung open.

"Hey, Fin," her mom said.

"Hey!" Infiniti popped up from the couch, relieved to see her mom, but playing it cool. She knew her mom would roll her eyes if she mentioned her earlier conversation with Jan, so she had decided to keep it to herself.

"How was your trip?" Infiniti asked.

"The usual. Meetings, paperwork, blah, blah, blah. I'm just glad I made it home tonight. I almost missed my flight."

"Wow. I'm glad, too." Infiniti watched her mom put her stuff on the kitchen table, shuddering on the inside at the idea of almost having to sleep alone in the house with a ghost girl somewhere loose in the neighborhood. That would've sucked.

Her mom smiled, motioning at the bags of clothes. "I see you had a productive day in your closet."

"Yep, I sure did. Now I need a new wardrobe. I'll be ready to go shopping tomorrow."

Her mom laughed as she trudged her way to her room. "We'll see about that." Then she added, "I'm gonna shower and hit the hay, if that's okay. I'm beat."

"Yeah, that's fine. Goodnight."

"Goodnight, honey."

Infiniti popped some popcorn and put on another movie. She chose another light and airy comedy, still trying to erase the fear within her. By the time it ended, she could barely keep her eyes open. She turned off the lights and headed upstairs.

After a nice hot shower, she snuggled into her bed. She started drifting to sleep when she felt a presence in her room, as if someone was watching her. She cracked one eye open, not wanting to alert her intruder that she was awake, as if that would help anything. And then she thought of the creepy ghost girl she'd seen. The girl Jan had called Abigail.

Please don't let there be a ghost in my room, she thought to herself.

Ripples of panic crawled down her spine. Her heart slammed against her chest. She covered her head with her comforter, then pulled it down slowly right below her eyes. She peered about, afraid she'd see the girl, but instead spotted a tall, dark shadow of a man in the corner of her room. She opened her mouth to yell, but nothing came out.

"Listen, doll, you can't scream. You can't even run. It's just you and me, together in your dreaded nightmare."

He stepped forward. The dim light from Infiniti's alarm clock revealed a guy with short hair and a trimmed beard dressed in dark jeans and a T-shirt. Infiniti propped herself up on her elbows, thinking she could smell something burning. She studied her room, then looked back at her visitor.

"I-I-I'm dreaming?"

"That's right, doll. For now you are, and I'm here enjoying the view, waiting to claim what's mine."

She sat up even more, still smelling smoke. "Who are you?"

The guy bowed in acknowledgment. "Shade StormIron at your service, and you are Infiniti Clausman." He wagged his finger at her. "Tsk, tsk, tsk. You are quite the time traveler. You are here, you are there. It's really something keeping up with you. But my boss says I need to bring you in." He grimaced. "And I always do what my boss says."

A glow shone from under Infiniti's door. She narrowed her eyes and studied it, wondering what it was, the burning smell in her room growing stronger.

"Bring me in? Boss? What does that mean?"

Shade swooped in closer to her. He brought his face up to hers.

"It means you're dying, doll."

Infiniti's eyes snapped open.

She shot upright in bed.

Smoke filled her room. The smell of soot and ash clogged her nose and throat.

"Oh my god, oh my god," she whispered, realizing her house was on fire. Her brain somehow remembered she needed to drop to the floor, and she did. "Mom!"

She crawled to the door. She reached up and grabbed for the knob, but her hand slipped.

"Mom!"

She lunged for the knob again, catching it in a desperate hold. She turned it fast. The door swung open, and a gust of smoke rushed her room, spraying her face with heat and soot. She lay flat on the floor, pressing her cheek against the shag carpet while hacking out a series of coughs. Hot air smothered her. Tears stung her eyes. She started crawling again, military style, desperate to get downstairs to her mom's first floor room.

"Mom!"

She bumped into something in her way. She looked up and saw the tall guy from her dream. The guy that had emerged from the shadows. He was real. Smoke billowed all around him, as if he had ascended from the fiery gates of hell. Her heart slammed against her chest.

"What are you?" she choked out.

"I am a reaper." He crouched down and smiled. "You almost ready to come with me?"

Disbelief crowded her senses, followed by anger. She needed to get to her mom, and he was in the way.

"No," she squeaked out. She clenched her first, pounded at his boot, and said again, "No."

Smoke and heat filled her lungs, strangling her, forcing out a fresh spasm of coughs. She looked up at the reaper, thinking there was something oddly familiar about him, when she heard someone yelling her name.

She tried to holler back to whoever it was so they would know she was upstairs, but she couldn't speak. Her throat had shut tight.

She was dying.

She mustered all her strength to raise her arm. She swatted at the reaper, thinking to herself, *Hell no you're not taking me*, but knowing he probably would.

Everything dimmed.

Her vision tunneled.

And she plunged into darkness.

CHAPTER 6

*J*oe had prepped all night with his parents and Dr. Underwood. By morning he was as ready as he'd ever be. Facing a new day with rattled nerves and high anxiety, he studied himself in the mirror. Fresh haircut, still clean shaven from the day before. He almost looked like his old self. And with Infiniti, he'd be complete again.

His mom appeared at his door. He eyed her in the mirror.

"You sure I shouldn't wear my suit?"

He was wearing some of his old clothes since everything he had was loose. Dark jeans and black T-shirt.

She nodded. "Yes, I'm sure. If the Court approves your request, they might send you on the spot. So you need to be ready for travel."

"They'd really do that?" he asked, excited at the idea of going right away to find Infiniti, but not really believing it would happen.

"Anything is possible with the Court," she answered. "Now grab that backpack, and let's go."

"I guess it's a good thing I was planning on leaving, because now I have this backpack all ready," he joked.

She shot him a look. "Don't push it."

In the car, Joe went over everything he and his parents and the doc had discussed the night before. And when he pulled up to the parking lot of City Hall, something occurred to him. What if the Court said no? He forced that thought out of his mind, telling himself there was no way they'd say no. Especially with the doc on his side.

They entered through the secret door at the back of City Hall and descended a flight of stairs to the basement. Once at the bottom floor, they made their way down a long hallway until they came upon a reception area with a couple of chairs. Addie Beaumont was sitting in the seat closest to the hallway. She was wearing black denim pants, a plain black T-shirt, and a long dark jacket. She was the manager of the Court and pretty much knew everything going on in the town.

She peered at them from over her dark-rimmed glasses. "We just need Dr. Underwood and then—"

"I'm right here!" the doc called out, hurrying toward them.

"All right, then," Addie said to the group. She tucked her long brown hair behind her ears. "Follow me, please."

Addie went to a door on the far side of the room. She held it open. When Joe walked by her, she whispered, "Go get 'em, Joe."

Joe smiled, feeling a surge of confidence knowing he had her support, but then lost all his courage when he entered the windowless candlelit room. The place reminded him of a dungeon. A deadly dungeon. The kind of dungeon people didn't emerge from.

He followed his mom, dad, and Dr. Underwood to a long table in the middle of the room. Before him was a raised dais. The scene reminded him of the setups he'd seen on TV involving government hearings and things. Joe took a seat at the middle of the table and placed his backpack by his feet. His parents sat to his right, and Dr. Underwood filed in to the left. Joe studied the faces of the members that looked down on him. Although he knew them all, he didn't really *know them* know them, except for Sheriff Ric. He was relieved to see his pack leader up there.

Saundra Beaumont, one of the oldest witches in town, sat in the middle of the group, her silvery-white hair pulled up in a twist. She cleared her throat, silencing the murmuring in the room. She lifted a piece of paper and started to read.

"The Court of the Sun and the Moon is now in session. We are here today in the matter of a request by Joseph Greg. To wit, Joseph Greg, the petitioner, by way of his parents Katarina and Ivan Greg, with the supporting testimony of his doctor, Jasper Underwood, requests permission to time travel outside of Havenwood Falls for the purposes of locating his mate, Infiniti Clausman, a human. Said request is being sought due to the petitioner's severe and declining health. As part of the security detail of Havenwood Falls, this decline poses a serious detriment to his pack and the overall safety and security of the town. "

Joe gulped as the stately witch laid the paper down and narrowed her gaze on him.

"Does that sum it up correctly, Petitioner?"

Joe got to his feet, like his parents had instructed. "Yes." His voice cracked a little, and he felt his face flush. He swallowed and said again, "Yes. That's correct."

Saundra Beaumont studied Joe with laser focus. "Before we proceed with the hearing, I want to caution the petitioner on the seriousness of his request."

Joe felt as if every member of the Court leaned in a little. He clasped his sweaty palms behind his back, not knowing how to respond, so settled on a nod.

"Matters of time travel are fraught with danger. If you are successful here today and time travel in search of your mate, there's a possibility you will *never* return. In the event you do return, there's a possibility nothing will be the same when you get back. You might alter your life in such a way that you may never see your parents again, or this town. At least, not like you know it. Your connection to the wards may falter, and if it does, every memory of your time here will be erased. Permanently. With no chance for reversal."

The pitch of her voice grew louder with each word, and each sentence sounded almost like an argumentative plea for Joe to change his mind. As if checking herself, she paused, then added in a more controlled tone. "The risks are endless, which is why the Court would normally never entertain such a request." She folded her hands together before her. "Knowing this, are you sure you wish to proceed?"

Joe knew what he was asking. He'd gone over the severity of his request with his parents and the doc, but hearing the witch detail the perils made every hair on his body stand on edge. His gut twisted so tight it hurt. But his mind was set. Infiniti needed him, and he was going.

"Yes," he nodded. "I wish to proceed."

"And if I may add," Joe's mom said, getting to her feet. "None of us take this matter lightly. We know the dangers associated with time travel, but my husband and I cannot stand idly by while our son wastes away. The stars are aligned for good fortune and good travel. All three members of the Luna Coven's High Council are present here today. The energy in the universe supports us. I can feel it. So can my husband and our doctor. We are ready for the outcome, whatever it might be, but hold on to guarded optimism. And we do appreciate the Court's warning."

"Very well," Saundra said, looking at the Court members to her right and then to her left. "Let's get on with it, then."

Joe's mom gave him a quick squeeze before sitting back down.

Saundra shuffled her papers. "Petitioner, please explain why you seek to time travel. Why not just get on a plane and go to your mate right now?"

"Well, I was actually going to do that, except there's no trace of her today. My father can confirm that."

Joe's dad stood. "I've searched every database at my disposal. There's no record of an Infiniti Clausman anywhere in Houston or even Texas."

"Is that so?" Saundra asked.

"Yes," his dad continued. "Joe will need to find this young lady in the timeline she was returned to."

"And she's in danger," Joe blurted. "That's why I need to go to her right away."

"Hmm," Saundra said. "And what makes you think this?"

"Well," Joe explained, "when she originally left back in 2012, I had several dreams of her dying. The feelings have come back with a vengeance following her second departure this past December. Plus, the fact that she can't be located today kind of supports my theory."

"I want to hear from Dr. Underwood," Elsmed Fairchild cut in. The fae's glamour had been lowered, revealing the tips of his arrow-shaped ears. His flat nose almost touched his chin.

Joe and his dad sat while Dr. Underwood stood.

"For the record, and so it's perfectly clear, Joseph Greg has been called to Infiniti Clausman." The doc paused for a second so that the Court would understand the gravity of Joe's connection to Infiniti. "Now, I've been witnessing the decline in my patient since the departure of his mate on the eve of the Cold Moon Ball. As you all may know, he was attacked by a wild wolf pack on that evening, and I've been tending to him since then. His cracked femur has failed to heal properly, he's lost weight, and he's suffering from dehydration and tachycardia. I fear he will maintain a steady decline if not reunited with the human."

"To what end?" Elsmed asked. "Is this condition fatal?"

Dr. Underwood hesitated a moment. "It's quite possible."

Joe's stomach dropped. Hearing the doc confirm that he could be dying cemented his worst fears. Everything depended on this hearing now.

"And what if he can't find her? Or if she doesn't want to be reunited?" the fae asked in a serious and stern tone. "What of his health then, Doctor?"

"Then he'll know the truth," Dr. Underwood explained. "And can move on without her, and his health will rebound."

"Will it?" the fae pressed.

"Yes, it's my belief that it will."

A sliver of relief entered Joe, hearing that his health could rebound, but it didn't last long. He still needed the Court to rule in his favor.

"Closure," Lilith Blackstone offered. "Is that what you seek, Petitioner?"

The doc sat down while Joe got back up. He faced the petite blond-haired witch hunter he'd met once when he visited her vineyard. Her daughter, Macy, graduated a year ahead of him.

"Well, yes. If I find her, I believe she'll come back with me because she feels for me the same way that I feel for her. But if I'm wrong and she doesn't want to come with me, then I'll know and I can move on." He paused for a few seconds while the feeling of her being in danger surged inside of him. "My biggest concern, though, is getting to her before it's too late."

"Let's address this business of being too late," cut in frost dragon shifter Lawrence Mills, his white hair looking as wild as ever. Joe knew his granddaughter Zoey from school. "What does that mean exactly?"

"Well, I believe Infiniti's life is at risk, sir. It's my hope that she can come back here with me to Havenwood Falls and, um, live here in safety."

"One minute," the mage Roman Bishop said, raising his hand in a subtle yet commanding gesture, announcing to the other members he was about to speak and for them to be quiet. He was as imposing as ever with his slick black hair, tanned skin, and penetrating deep blue eyes. Joe had been told to be careful with him. "Meddling with humans bores me. Even if she is in danger, and even if one of our own is ill. I say we mind our own business."

"I agree with Roman," Old Man Mills added in his usual crotchety voice. "We should not stick our noses where they do not belong."

"Joseph Greg *is* our business, Lawrence," Saundra shot back with vigor. "I mean, look at him. His health is at risk. Can't you see that? And his true love may be in danger."

"So she comes here and then what?" Roman said between thin lips. "Where will she live? What will she do? Who will speak for her?"

Sheriff Ric rose to his feet. "I may have no vote here, but I have a voice, and my pack will speak for her. We'll speak for Joe and the entire Greg family, too, for that matter."

Joe admired Sheriff Ric already, but even more so now. He nodded at his pack leader and mouthed a quick thank you. Sheriff Ric nodded back.

"Well said, Ric," Lilith Blackstone added. "I will speak for the human, too. I am a believer in second chances. There is room at NamaStays Inn on my vineyard. She can stay there until she finds a more permanent situation."

"She can also stay with me," Saundra added, tossing Roman Bishop and Old Man Mills a look. "And I'm sure my daughter Lyra would offer the same, especially since the young lady has stayed with Lyra previously." She smiled at Joe. "I too am a believer in second chances."

"Me too," offered fae Teeny Weeny Tahini, a glittery glow shimmering about her. "I am a believer in second chances."

Joe struggled to remain calm on the outside while on the inside he was celebrating. Things were going his way!

"Fools," Roman Bishop muttered. "Meddling fools."

Old Man Mills leaned over. He eyed Roman. "Indeed," he huffed.

Joe studied the other members, wondering if they'd chime in, when Mathilde Augustine spoke.

"What of the wards? No one has mentioned them and their effect on the human."

Joe studied the powerful witch who looked like an ordinary grandmother, gathering his thoughts before he replied. He and his parents had talked about Infiniti not remembering anything and how it might be impossible to establish a connection with her again, but he had pushed that possibility aside. Failure to reach her wasn't even an option, but what if it became a reality?

He had to consider that might happen even though he didn't want to.

"I haven't forgotten about the wards. I know Infiniti won't remember me or her time here, but I still need to go. I still need to find her. And I believe—no, I *know*—I can get through to her." He clenched his jaw, his determination taking over any doubt in his mind. "I know it."

No one else said anything, and it seemed as if everyone in the room held a collective sigh of pity for Joe, but he didn't care. He was called to Infiniti, and she was connected to him, too. If he could find her, he could get through to her.

Saundra Beaumont eyed the other members of the Court, waiting to see if anyone else had any questions, when Mayor Barbie Stuart, a human, chimed in.

"Well," she said, breaking the tension in the room, "I want to make sure I'm understanding the mission of this brave young man." She had puffy blond hair and wore a low-cut top. "So the mission is to find Infiniti. Bring her back to Havenwood Falls present day if she wants to come, but leave her in her time if she wants to stay. And either outcome will restore the health of this young man, and he could possibly even be saving her life."

"Correct," Dr. Underwood said. "Thank you, Mayor, for putting it so succinctly."

With no one else speaking up, Saundra said, "Very well. Let us take it to a vote. All in favor of the Petitioner's request, raise your hand."

Everyone raised their hands except for Roman Bishop, Elsmed Fairchild, and Old Man Mills.

Saundra Beaumont banged her gavel. "With a majority, the petition passes. And in light of the decline in the petitioner's health, I recommend the petitioner be sent on his way posthaste."

Joe had been ready to celebrate when the words "posthaste" stopped him short. He shot his parents a questioning look.

"What does that mean?" he asked in a whisper.

"Now, Joseph. Posthaste means now," Saundra Beaumont

responded. She opened a box Joe hadn't noticed before and took out what looked like a small purse. "Miss Clausman's wallet was found after the thaw. We know exactly where she may be, and we are going to send you there now."

Joe couldn't believe it. He'd been searching for that wallet for months, and there it was, with the Court. And now he was being sent by the Court to find her!

His celebratory reaction was cut short when everyone started moving about with purpose. Saundra, Mathilde, Roman, and Addie gathered in the open space before Joe while the other Court members hung back. Addie waved him over. Before he went to her, Joe's mom and dad brought him in for a quick hug.

"Love you, my son," Joe's mom said in a choked voice.

"So much," his dad added.

"Love you both, too," Joe said, trying not to think of their exchange as a goodbye. "And I'll be back soon. I promise."

With a pat on his back from Dr. Underwood, Joe went to Addie and the others.

"Ground rules," Addie said. "Your tattoo prevents you from talking about the town outside the wards, as you know, but I'm gonna spell it so you can talk about it in general terms. Okay? Nothing specific."

Joe's mind scrambled with how he'd be able to talk about Havenwood Falls without really talking about it. "Okay."

"Where's your tat?" she asked.

Joe put his hand over his right bicep. "Should I take my shirt off?"

"Not necessary, I can do it through the fabric." She took a hold of his bicep and squeezed. She looked at the ground and mumbled something he couldn't make out. "There, it's done," she said, releasing him.

Saundra Beaumont approached next. "Think of the time when you want to go." She slipped a necklace around Joe's neck. "When you're ready to come back, step on the stone on this chain, and you should return to this time and this place, along with Infiniti, should she choose to come with you." She backed away and took her place in the circle. "You have seventy-two hours to accomplish your task. Before then, the stone should work. Beyond that time, it definitely will not."

"Only three days?" Joe asked.

"Longer than that would be too disruptive to the timeline," Saundra answered.

Joe's body tingled with fear and anticipation as Saundra, Mathilde, Roman, and Addie circled him. A flood of excitement mixed with trepidation soared inside of him as he watched the most powerful people in the room join hands. They started chanting, taking on expressions of concentration. The floor beneath his feet started to swirl. Slow at first, it picked up speed until it resembled a churning tornado. Joe slammed his eyes shut. He pictured Infiniti clearly in his mind. He silently repeated over and over *2013, Houston, Texas*, willing himself to go to her exactly six years in the past.

Weightlessness overcame him. His stomach turned. His body dropped into a free fall. He braced himself when his feet landed on solid ground. He opened his eyes and found himself in front of a burning house. Sparks illuminated against the dark night. Streams of black smoke wafted into the air.

"No, no, no."

Fear strangled his heart. Infiniti was inside! He knew it! And she was dying!

He started to bolt for the door when a hand jerked his arm back. Joe spun around and saw Fleet, the Transhuman who had helped Infiniti get to Havenwood Falls.

"Fleet!"

Fleet narrowed his eyes. "You know me?"

"Yes!" Joe yelled, but he knew Fleet had no memory of him. Joe shook his head. "It doesn't matter. Infiniti is in there, and she needs our help!"

Fleet studied the house for a quick second before he let go of

Joe's arm. "The fire is stronger in the rear of the home. I'll take the first floor. You go upstairs. Let's go."

Fleet ran for the door. He blasted it away with a stream of energy and disappeared inside a cloud of black smoke. Joe darted in after him. Heat stung his face and eyes. His throat and lungs clogged with deadly vapor. He dashed up the stairs, calling out for Infiniti. He didn't have to go very far when he found her sprawled out on the floor in the hallway. He scooped up her limp body and hauled her out of the house.

"Over here!" someone hollered at him.

Bystanders swarmed the area. Red lights from an ambulance and a fire truck filled the night. A paramedic ushered Joe over to a stretcher.

"Here, put her here," the man urged.

Joe laid her down gently and stepped back. He watched as the team from the ambulance descended on Infiniti's motionless form.

Fleet rushed over with a woman in his arms. Joe thought it must've been Infiniti's mom. Blackened splotches covered her face, blending in with her clothing so that Joe didn't know where skin ended and clothing began. A putrid smell filled the air. He covered his mouth and nose and turned away. Half of the team working on Infiniti broke away and started working on her mom.

Joe's head reeled. His heart shattered in a million pieces. He walked away, unable to watch Infiniti or her mom die. His vision blurred as tears filled his eyes.

"It's okay, man." Fleet said, placing his hand on Joe's back. "It's gonna be okay."

Joe's world was crashing down on him. Guilt over not acting sooner descended on him. Infiniti and her mom were dying, and it was his fault.

"I was too late," he muttered. "I got here too late."

CHAPTER 7

Fleet gave the guy some space, wondering how he knew who he was. He'd never seen the guy before. But obviously he knew Infiniti and had a deep connection with her, because he was crumbling. Fleet couldn't blame him. He knew all too well the pain of being in love with someone and having them ripped away.

The house crackled while it blazed with flames. Fire trucks blasted the inferno with streams of water. Neighbors gathered all around, either dumbstruck or crying or both. And Fleet couldn't do a damn thing. Transhumans, at least the good ones known as the Pure, didn't interfere with fate and destiny. Only the Tainted meddled in human affairs.

He moved closer to the area where the paramedics were working on Infiniti and her mom. They were being strapped into place for transport. Oxygen masks covered their faces. Fleet eyed their chests, looking for movement, hoping they were alive, but the bustling about of the paramedics obstructed his view.

"Looks like you and the Havenwoodie were just a little too late, cupcake."

Fleet spun around and saw Shade StormIron. His arms were crossed as he leaned against the ambulance. Of all the reapers he'd encountered over the years, Shade irritated him the most. Fleet clenched his fists at his side.

"You son of a bitch."

"Yep, I'm that, and other things. And as much as I'd love to sit here and chat with your moody self, I need to catch my ride."

The reaper dissolved into a stream of black and filtered into the ambulance as it drove off.

"Dammit," Fleet muttered, wondering whose life the reaper was going to claim, thinking the mom for sure but uncertain about Infiniti.

He stood in the middle of the street, angry as hell, determined to do whatever he could to help Tiny and her mom. He stomped over to the guy the reaper had referred to as a Havenwoodie, wondering why someone from Havenwood Falls would be in Houston with Infiniti, but starting to piece things together. Everything had to do with Abigail's cryptic message.

"Hey, man, what's your name?"

The guy wiped his face with his shirt sleeve while he pulled himself together. "Joe. My name is Joe."

"Okay, Joe. Come on. We're following that ambulance."

They got into Fleet's car down the street and sped up to the ambulance. The lights were blinking; the siren was blaring. Fleet knew the display wasn't a good sign. After about ten minutes of driving, they arrived at a hospital. Fleet parked in the nearest spot, and he and Joe hurried over to the emergency entrance.

A team of doctors and nurses dashed out of the building. They stood behind the ambulance while the doors opened. A stretcher with a body covered in a sheet came out first.

Fleet halted. So did Joe. Time stood still for a few seconds until Infiniti came out in the second stretcher.

"Damn," Fleet mumbled. Even though a part of him was happy to see that Infiniti had made it, he didn't want anyone to die. He knew Infiniti would be devastated. She and her mom were close, and she was the only family Infiniti had.

The stretchers disappeared inside the hospital. Fleet and Joe were about to follow them in when one of the paramedics spotted them.

"Hey, the guys from the fire. Y'all okay?"

Not knowing anything about Joe, Fleet thought being seen by a doc might do him good. Even though he wasn't in the house long, Fleet suspected he'd taken in a lot of smoke. Plus, they'd be closer to Tiny.

"We're no worse for wear, but could use a once over. And hey, I'm sorry the mom didn't make it."

"Us too," the guy said, shaking his head. "We did everything we could. Losing someone never gets easier."

"And Infiniti? The girl?" Joe asked. "She's gonna be okay?"

"I'm pretty sure she is." The paramedic led them to the hospital entrance and called one of the nurses over. "It's a good thing you two were around. A few more minutes and she would've ended up like her mom."

A nurse with a clipboard put Fleet and Joe in a room. She started Joe on oxygen right away. She handed a mask to Fleet, but he held up his hand.

"I'm fine."

The nurse eyed him. "Suit yourself."

"So, Infiniti is okay?" Joe asked her. "The paramedic said she was, but is she really?"

"The young lady? Yes, I believe so," the nurse said.

"Can I see her?"

Fleet thought Joe would come unglued if he couldn't see her soon.

"Are you family?" the nurse asked.

"No, but she's very special to me."

"I'll see what I can do, but let me get your information first." She took out a pen from her pocket and handed it over with clipboard.

"I can fill those out," Fleet said.

"You two related?"

"Yes," Fleet said. "We are." He was a pro at filling out forms with the go-to fake information he and his brother had used for years.

"Okay, then," the nurse said. "You fill those out, and I'll be back with a doctor as soon as one is available. It's a busy night, so it may be a while." She nodded at Joe. "I'll see what I can do about that visit."

Alone now, Fleet moved his chair in front of Joe's. He leaned over, resting his elbows on his knees.

"Okay, let's hear it. How do you know me, and what's the situation with you and Tiny?"

Joe took off his mask. "That's right, you call Infiniti Tiny."

"Yeah, I do. Now spill."

"Well, I'm Joe, like I said, and I know you and Infiniti from the future, where I'm from." Joe paused, as if waiting for Fleet to react, but he held a steady expression. He'd done enough time traveling and had lived enough lives to know anything was possible.

"I'm from H—" He stopped, looking dumbfounded, as if he'd forgotten what he was going to say. "I'm from H-H-H, argh, I can't say it."

Fleet raised a brow. He knew exactly where the guy was from. Shade had called him a Havenwoodie, and Abigail had mentioned Havenwood Falls. Fleet figured the guy was from there but couldn't talk about it because of the town enchantment Abigail had mentioned.

"You're from Havenwood Falls," Fleet said.

"Yes!" Joe said, blowing out with relief. "You and Infiniti came to town in December 2018. Actually, she first arrived December 2012."

Fleet sat back and crossed his arms, absorbing the information. "That makes no sense."

Joe ran his fingers through his hair. "Infiniti was in a car crash that happened outside of town in December 2012. She was brought to the medical center. She disappeared, but then reappeared in December 2018. And when she reappeared, you were with her."

Joe paused to see if Fleet had any questions, but he didn't. Not yet anyway.

"We figured out she needed something from my time—a spell to make her a void so harmful magic couldn't hurt her. The spell was performed, and then the two of you left and came back here to your proper time to help someone named Dominique. You guys don't remember any of it because of the protective wards around the town that wipes everyone's memories of their visit when they leave."

Fleet rubbed the back of his neck. "Then how do you remember all this? We're not in Havenwood Falls."

Joe shifted in his seat. He stitched his brows together. "The memories fade over time, but I just got here. That's how I still remember. But I've also been released from some of the magic of the wards so that I can say a few things about where I'm from. And I only have seventy-two hours."

"Seventy-two hours for what?"

"To get back home with Infiniti."

Fleet got up and started pacing the room, analyzing Joe's words. So Abigail was right. He had been to Havenwood Falls with Infiniti to help her find a spell. And now he had helped save her from a fire. But to what end?

"Hey, did everything work out with that Dominique person?" Joe asked.

Fleet stopped in his tracks. The story of Dominique's final life and everything he, Farrell, Dominique, Trent, and Infiniti had been through was long and complicated. He didn't think Joe needed all the gory and gut-wrenching details.

"For some it has."

Fleet continued pacing. He still didn't know why Joe was here.

"So why come back? Why risk traveling from your time to this time? Why are you—?" Fleet stopped mid-sentence because he knew the answer. It was love. Love made people do dumb-ass things.

"You're in love with Infiniti."

Joe rubbed his hands on his jeans. "Yes, but it's way more than that. I'm a wolf shifter, and I'm called to her. She's my mate. For life. During our time together, she developed strong feelings for me, too. When she left, she made me promise to find her." He looked away for a few long seconds. "I've been trying to make good on that promise since December, hoping I could find her and bring her back with me. Not only because of my connection to her and my failing health since she's been gone, but also because I kept feeling like she was in danger here." He lowered his head. "And she was."

When Joe finished his story, Fleet saw him in a different light. Gaunt face, tired eyes. Through the soot and ash on his face and body, Fleet could see the guy was wasting away from heartache. Plus, he was right. He had saved Infiniti. In light of Abigail's message, Fleet thought her life was still at risk, but didn't want to say so unless he knew for certain.

"What if Infiniti doesn't believe your story? What if you can't get through to her? Or what if she doesn't want to go with you?"

"I have three days to try my best. Assuming the worst case scenario and things don't go my way, I return home. My doc thinks my health will rebound because at least I would have tried."

The theory made sense to Fleet. Getting over a heartache was much easier when the affection was one-sided. "Okay, fine. So why do you need me then?"

"I don't know," Joe said. "I guess we still need to figure that part out."

Fleet and Joe fell into a lull of silence. After about an hour, they decided it was best to not see the doctor after all and told the nurse they'd be in the waiting room, hoping to see Infiniti.

They stayed in the overcrowded room all night. Sitting in the corner as far away as possible from the coughing and sneezing people in the cramped space, they spent their time analyzing their situation. And while the minutes ticked by, Fleet kept wondering how Infiniti would react when she finally saw him and Joe. Would she remember all the crap they'd been through during their ordeal with Dominique? Would she see Joe and remember her feelings for him? And was she still in danger?

He had no idea, but sooner or later they were going to come face to face with her and find out.

CHAPTER 8

Something felt stuck in Infiniti's throat. Like a piece of food—a noodle or something. She'd eaten ramen for dinner, so thought maybe that was it. With her eyes closed, she reached over to her bedside table for the water bottle she kept there. That's when a flood of awareness washed over her.

She remembered smoke and fire. She could practically feel the heat from the flames, could taste the soot in her nose and throat. She jolted upright in bed. Tingles of fear raced over her body. Her breathing came out in panic-filled bursts.

Fire! Her house was on fire!

"Mom!" she shouted in a hoarse voice, her airway throbbing with pain.

"Shh, Infiniti. It's okay."

It took Infiniti a few seconds to see Jan standing next to her, holding her hand. Tears filled her neighbor's eyes.

"I'm right here, dear. I'm right here."

Infiniti struggled to speak, not even knowing what to ask. She eyed her surroundings and found herself in a hospital room. An IV was attached to her arm. Her hands patted their way up her chest and to her nose, where plastic prongs nestled in her nostrils.

Her breathing steadied, but not by much. "W-w-what happened? W-w-where's my mom?"

Jan looked down while Infiniti's heart pounded out of control. Shivers rippled up and down her body as she waited for her neighbor to speak.

"My dear, your house caught on fire. You and your mother were pulled out and brought to the hospital by ambulance. You've suffered moderate smoke inhalation, but," Jan's voice choked up, "your mother's smoke inhalation was severe." Jan struggled to silence her sobs. "And . . . she didn't make it."

Infiniti stared at Jan, wide-eyed, struggling to make sense of her words as they swirled in her head like a foggy storm. Tears welled up in her eyes.

"What? She didn't make . . . what?"

Deep down, Infiniti knew what Jan meant, but needed to hear the words. It wasn't real without the words.

"She didn't survive. She passed away in the ambulance."

Infiniti's heart shattered into a billion pieces. Her body shook uncontrollably. A flood of tears gushed out of her. She clutched Jan and held her tight, letting every tear spill out of her as she tried to make sense of what had happened.

She had lost her mom, the only person in the world she had. Infiniti didn't want to stop crying, didn't want to let go of Jan, but someone opened the door of her room.

"Ladies, my apologies, but I have some questions for Miss Clausman."

Infiniti looked up and saw a portly white-haired police officer with a full beard.

Jan huffed. "Officer, please! Can't this wait? The fire just happened tonight! Give us some time!"

He came in all the way and shut the door behind him. "It can't. My apologies again. I have a few questions while everything is fresh in mind. It's procedure."

Infiniti pulled her hospital sheet up to her face and wiped her cheeks. "It's okay," she said to Jan. "I-I-I think I can do it."

"Okay," Jan said, moving to the other side of the bed, giving the officer room for his questioning. "I'll be right here, and if you want to stop, you let me know," she said to Infiniti. She directed a scowl at the officer. "You have two minutes, Officer."

The officer cleared his throat. "I'm very sorry about your loss, young lady. I promise to make this as short and painless as possible." He took a small pad and pencil out of his shirt pocket. "Tell me everything you can about the fire. Anything you remember."

Infiniti thought back to her evening. "Well, my mom came home from a business trip. She put her stuff on the kitchen table and then went straight to bed. I stayed up and popped some popcorn and watched a movie. When it was over, I showered and went to bed too. And then I woke up because I smelled smoke."

"So everything was normal? Nothing out of the ordinary?"

Icy fear coursed through Infiniti's veins when suddenly she remembered a dream she was having right before she woke up.

"I was having a nightmare," she half whispered.

The officer gave Infiniti a curious look. He moved in closer. "A nightmare?"

Infiniti's head pounded with pain, but she forced herself to recall the dream. "I dreamed there was a guy in my room. He told me I was dying. And then, when I woke up, I saw him."

The officer stopped his note taking. "There was an intruder in your house?"

"No, I mean, yes, I mean . . . he was a reaper."

The officer looked from Infiniti to Jan back to Infiniti. "Miss Clausman, was there a person in your house? I'm not talking about dreams or make-believe creatures. Was there a real live person in your residence?"

"If she said it, then she saw it!" Jan declared, coming to Infiniti's defense.

Infiniti's lip started quivering. She knew what she had seen. But she also knew how it sounded. A reaper from her dreams actually appearing before her? Who would believe that? She glanced at Jan, grateful for her neighbor's support, but second-guessed herself. Maybe the smoke had caused her to hallucinate. Maybe she hadn't really seen what she thought she had. Maybe losing her mother was making her crazy.

She rubbed her forehead. "I don't know. There was a reaper in my dream. And then I thought I saw him. But I must've been imagining it, because reapers don't exist, right?" She eyed Jan. "Right? They don't exist?"

Jan placed a reassuring hand on Infiniti's shoulder. "They do not, dear."

Infiniti stared up and away, picturing the reaper clearly in her mind. And then she remembered the smoke. "There was smoke everywhere."

"There was smoke everywhere and then what?" the officer asked, glazing over the reaper part, dismissing it entirely.

"I fell to the ground like you're supposed to do in a fire, and crawled out of my room trying to get to my mom. I made it into the hallway and . . ." She could still see the reaper's boots before her, could see his face and hear his words, but she didn't say so. "And I couldn't breathe and I guess I passed out."

"And it was only you and your mom in the house, correct?"

"Yes." Fresh tears spilled out of her. "It was just the two of us. It was always just the two of us."

Jan cut in with a curt tone. "Elizabeth Clausman was a single mother. She had no husband and no other family. Is that enough for now?"

The officer turned his attention to Jan. "Yes, ma'am. Thank you. And you are?"

"My name is Jan Kelly. I live across the street from Infiniti. I've known Infiniti her entire life. She and her mother are family to me."

He handed Jan the notebook. "Please put down your name, address, and contact numbers in case I need to reach you."

Jan jotted down the information and handed the notebook back to the officer. He closed it up and put it back in his pocket.

"That's all I need right now. Thank you both very much. I'll be in touch should I need anything further. And my sincerest condolences."

When he left the room, Infiniti pulled Jan's arm, desperate to talk about what she had seen.

"There really was a reaper. He said his name was Shade StormIron. He said his boss wanted me."

Jan placed her hands on Infiniti's shoulders. She helped her ease back into the bed. "Dear, I believe you. I really do. But it's three in the morning, and you need some sleep. We can talk more after you've rested."

Infiniti let herself fall back onto her pillow, but couldn't relax. Her neck and shoulders were stiff and tight. A sick feeling had sunk so far down in her stomach she could barely breathe.

"Where's . . . my mom?" she asked in a hushed tone.

"She's here, in the hospital. Being prepared for the next step in her journey."

Infiniti had talked with her mom about death and dying and knew she wanted to be cremated. But the idea of handling all that was too much for her.

"Jan, I can't be the one to make any decisions about—"

"I'll see to it, dear. I know what your mother wanted. I'll make all the arrangements."

Infiniti nodded.

"I'll let you rest now."

Another nod.

Before Jan could say anything else, Infiniti popped up. "How did I get out of my house?"

"A young man ran in and carried you out. Another young man carried your mom. Now sleep. It's late, and a new day will be here soon."

Fear clenched Infiniti's insides as Jan turned off the light and rested her hand on the door.

"You're leaving?"

"Only to secure my house, look in on Tinker, and gather some things we'll be needing. And then I'll be right back. I promise." She pointed at a chair in the corner. "I'll be snoozing right there with you before you know it."

Infiniti didn't want Jan to leave. She was terrified of being alone, but understood why Jan needed to go.

"Okay. Just hurry, please."

"I will."

Infiniti rested her head back down, watching as the door slowly swung shut. A steady stream of tears rolled down her face and onto her pillow. She decided to forget about the reaper, telling herself he wasn't real as she cried herself to sleep.

Infiniti's eyes flitted open when she heard someone rustling about in her room. After a quick moment of fear, she saw her nurse standing beside her.

"I'm checking your vitals," she said with a smile. "I didn't mean to startle you."

Disoriented, Infiniti let the nurse do what she needed to do as she scanned her room. She studied the hazy glow of early morning sunlight peeking through her blinds.

"What time is it?" Infiniti muttered.

"It's five thirty in the morning," the nurse answered, then left the room.

Infiniti's gaze went to the chair, and sure enough, there was Jan, head pressed against a pillow that had been propped against the wall. Her shoulders eased when she saw her neighbor, and she lay back down. She thought of everything that had happened, playing the evening over and over in her mind on repeat until Jan stirred, her bones creaking and popping as she shifted.

"Jan?" Infiniti asked. "Are you awake?"

"Yes, I am," Jan answered, rubbing her leg. She sat up all the way, moving her pillow to the floor. "Did you sleep okay?"

"No. Did you?"

"Not really." Jan smiled.

The stink of smoke and soot still permeated Infiniti, and she needed to get rid of it. "I could use a shower," she said to Jan.

"Good," Jan said. "Let me get a nurse to unhook you from your contraptions."

Infiniti sat in a daze while the nurse came back in and started working on her. Once she was free of the oxygen and the saline bag, both of which the nurse said she didn't need anymore, she took a long hot shower. She washed away the residue from her ordeal, but couldn't do anything about the pain in her heart.

What was her life going to be like now? Where would she live? What would she do?

After her shower, she dressed in new clothes Jan had purchased for her and started nibbling on the hospital breakfast. A knock sounded on the door, and a woman dressed in a business suit came in.

"Miss Clausman, my name is Jessica Ramirez. I'm the hospital administrator. I have a few things to go over with you about your mother—things Ms. Kelly and I went over last night while you were asleep."

Infiniti pushed her food away while her gut clenched and a new supply of tears welled up in her eyes.

The woman had light brown hair and a kind smile. She handed Infiniti a box of tissues, pulled up a chair, and sat down. "I know this is difficult, and I'm glad you have your neighbor here to help you. These conversations are not easy, but we need to discuss arrangements for your mother. I'd like for you to confirm what Ms. Kelly has authorized."

The woman opened her notebook. "Ms. Kelly has arranged for a funeral home to retrieve the body and make preparations for cremation. As the only surviving relative, can you confirm that's what your mother wanted?"

"Yes," Infiniti said in a hoarse whisper. "That's what she wanted."

"Once the body leaves the possession of the hospital, we will require no further documentation besides financial settlement for our services." The woman handed Infiniti a piece of paper. "This details what I've just explained. If you can please sign at the bottom." Infiniti took a pen from the woman and signed her name. "And this is for your records," the woman concluded. She handed Infiniti a set of the papers she had just signed. "The official death certificate should be ready in about two weeks."

Infiniti blinked as those words sunk in.

"Anything else?" Jan asked.

"The doctor has cleared Miss Clausman for release. However, you can stay here another night if you feel observation is necessary. It's up to you."

"I want to leave today and go . . ." Infiniti's voice trailed off because she had no idea where she would go.

"My house," Jan offered. "Infiniti will come to my house."

"Very well," the woman said. She got up to leave. "Once again, on behalf of the hospital, we offer our sincere condolences."

Infiniti eyed the paperwork, feeling sick to her stomach. "People get certificates for dying? Like, good job, here's your certificate?"

Jan took the papers and stuffed them in her oversized bag. "I never thought of it that way, but you're right. It's a ridiculous thing to call it."

The door opened again. A nurse Infiniti hadn't seen yet entered the room.

"Pardon my interruption, but the two young men from the fire last night are still in the waiting room. They would like to see you."

Infiniti wiped her eyes with a tissue. She sat up. "The ones who carried me and my mom out of my house?"

"Yes. They didn't want to leave without seeing you."

Infiniti wondered who had run into her burning house. Who would risk their lives like that?

"Well, I guess I should thank them." She turned to Jan. "Right? I should see them and thank them?"

"It's up to you, but it would be a nice gesture."

It had to have taken a lot of courage and bravery to run into a flaming house for a stranger. The least she could do was see her rescuers.

"They risked their lives for me and my mom. So yes, I'd like to thank them," she said to the nurse.

"I'll bring them up, then."

The nurse left as another person came in with even more check-out paperwork. Infiniti was glad for all the interruptions. It kept her mind off the horror of her situation. Jan went outside with the woman, leaving Infiniti alone. Not a minute later, the phone by her bed rang, startling her. She answered the call.

"Hello?"

"Fin! It's Trent!"

A fresh flood of tears rushed to her eyes, clogging her throat and strangling her words. Trent was her best friend in the whole world. He'd left for college a few weeks earlier.

"Fin, are you there?"

"Yes," she squeaked out, but couldn't fight the tears anymore. "Trent," she said between blubbering sobs. "My house caught on fire, and my mom—"

Pain and heartache wrestled her so tight she couldn't get the words out.

"I know, Fin," he said in a low voice. "I know. I'm so sorry. I saw the news. I've been trying to reach you for hours."

The last time she had used her phone was in her bedroom before she went to bed. For all she knew, it had burned to a crisp. "I don't have a phone anymore," she sobbed. "I don't have anything anymore."

"I can't get to you for few days, but I'm coming. Okay? I'll be there."

She wiped her tears away. "Okay."

"Where will you be?"

"Jan's."

"Okay, I'll be there, Fin. Everything will be okay. You just hold on."

"Okay."

She hung up and dragged herself over to the bathroom. She splashed cold water on her face, thinking she'd never get over losing her mother. She was back on her bed, feeling completely drained, when her door cracked open.

"Miss Clausman, I have your visitors, if you're ready."

She wasn't ready at all, but wanted to thank the guys who had rushed into her house. It was the least she could do.

"All right," she said, smoothing out her crisp new shirt. "I'm ready."

The nurse opened the door all the way and in walked two guys —a tall slender one with short blond hair and hazel green eyes and another guy who was even taller with short dark hair and a trimmed beard. Ash residue stained their shirts and jeans. Taking them in, she thought she'd seen them before, especially the blond guy. Something about him reminded her of someone she knew, though she couldn't figure out who.

"Here are the young men, Miss Clausman," the nurse said with a nod before leaving the three of them alone.

Infiniti tucked her hair behind her ears. It was still damp from her shower. "So, you're the ones who ran into my house?"

The guy with dark hair dropped to the back while the slender guy with blond hair moved forward. "Yes, we did. I'm Joe, and this is Fleet. We wanted to check on you and make sure you were okay. We're very sorry about your mom."

A surge of recognition tugged at her, as if she recognized his voice.

"Thank you," she said after a long pause. Her eyes watered over again, but this time she managed to stop the flow. She looked away from her visitors, embarrassed for them to see her like this.

"I'm so sorry," she said, dabbing at her eyes with a tissue. "I can't seem to stop crying."

"It's okay, Infiniti," Joe said, getting closer. "You don't have to apologize."

Staring into his beautiful face, she thought he was looking at her as if he'd known her forever. As if he really and truly cared about her.

"Do I know you?' she asked. "Have we met?"

"I'll leave you two alone," the dark-haired guy said. "I'll be right outside, Joe."

Infiniti didn't pay him any attention as he left. She couldn't keep her eyes off Joe.

He stuffed his hands in his jeans pocket. "I've seen you around, but we haven't exactly met."

"Oh," she said. "I guess that must be it then, because you seem so familiar to me."

"Yeah." He smiled. "That must be it."

A long silence grew between them while Infiniti thought of her usual hangouts where she might've run into Joe but couldn't pinpoint him at any particular place.

"So," she said. "I guess you were by my house when it caught on fire?"

"Um, yeah, I was. Fleet came up, and we ran in together."

She pointed her finger at the door. "Fleet came up to you? So he wasn't with you?"

"No, we kind of saw each other on the sidewalk and then teamed up together."

"So you don't know him?"

Joe hesitated for a few seconds. "I know him, but not that well."

"Oh," Infiniti said, trying to make sense of it all.

Jan waltzed back in, nearly bumping into Joe.

"My apologies," she said. "I didn't know you had company, dear."

"This is Joe. He's one of the guys that came into the house for me and mom."

Joe held out his hand for a shake. "I'm Joseph Greg. Nice to meet you, ma'am."

"I'm Jan Kelly. Thank you so much for your bravery and heroism. The world needs more young men like you."

The name Joseph Greg sparked a recognition deep within Infiniti. She knew, without a doubt, she'd heard his name before. But from where?

She tilted her head. "Your name is Joseph Greg?"

"Yes," he said, his eyes lighting up. "Do you recognize my name?"

"I think so, but I'm not sure. Maybe you just have one of those names."

"Maybe I do," he said, looking a little defeated, but still holding a hopeful look on his face.

"Infiniti," Jan said, interrupting them. "We can leave now. I've taken care of all the paperwork."

Infiniti swung her legs to get out of bed. Joe extended his hand to help her up, and when she put her hand in his, a weakness struck her knees. A flurry of butterflies exploded in her stomach. She looked up at him, wondering if he felt what she had, but didn't want to ask. She had lost her mom and had almost lost her own life, and here she was having feelings for her rescuer? It was the worst timing ever, but she couldn't help herself.

A nurse entered the room with a wheelchair.

"I have to go now," she said, suddenly not wanting to leave him. "I'll be going to Jan's house. She lives across the street from me." She paused, feeling crazy for asking him to come over but overcome with the need to see him again. "In case you maybe, I don't know, want to check on me or something."

"Yeah," he said. "Sure. I'd like that, if that's okay."

"Yeah, that would be okay. Thank you again, Joe. And tell your friend Fleet I said thank you."

"Of course," he said. "I will." And then he added before she left, "I'm really glad you're okay, Infiniti. Really, really glad."

She tilted her head a little at him, thinking there was

something about him that was comforting and lovable. She mustered a weak smile. "Me too."

Infiniti eased herself onto the wheelchair. The nurse rolled her out of the room, and Jan walked by her side. Her thoughts flooded with competing feelings—grief over losing her mother and a deep connection to Joe. She pushed it aside, not able to deal with the warring emotions, when the wheelchair stopped at the elevator bank. Infiniti's gaze landed on a nearby bulletin board. She spotted a piece of paper with thick black lettering. She peered closer.

Infiniti,

I'm coming for you.

Death

Infiniti gasped. She grasped Jan's arm.

"What is it?" Jan asked. "Are you okay?"

Infiniti glanced at Jan, then pointed at the note, but the message was gone. Instead, the note contained an ad about a nearby sandwich shop. She shook her head.

"I thought I saw—" The elevator door opened with a ding, and Infiniti scooted the wheelchair forward with her legs.

"Miss, are you okay?" the young nurse asked, helping Infiniti get into the elevator with a gentle push on the wheelchair.

"Yes," she said, slapping the button for the first floor. "I just want to get out of here."

"Infiniti?" Jan asked. "What in the world?"

"Please, Jan. Let's just go," she whispered, pinching the bridge of her nose and telling herself her eyes must've been playing tricks on her. Just like they did back in her room with that reaper.

Once in the car, she and Jan drove in silence. As they got closer to their neighborhood, Jan started warning Infiniti about the condition of her house. But when they rolled down the street, nothing could've prepared her for the horrific sight of her childhood home.

She covered her mouth with her hand.

"Oh my god," she uttered between her fingers.

The scene reminded Infiniti of something she might see in a

war movie. Windows were busted out. The front door and entry looked as if it had been blasted by a bomb. Streaks of char covered the left side of the house, spreading across the first floor and reaching up into the second. Yellow caution tape circled the premises. She didn't feel the tears streaming down her face until Jan handed her a fresh tissue.

All of her things were ruined. The memories of her childhood altered forever in the most horrendous way. She knew she'd never be the same after this.

CHAPTER 9

*J*oe wanted nothing more than to hug Infiniti, cradle her in his arms, kiss her, and tell her everything was going to be okay, but he couldn't. She didn't know him. To her, he was a stranger who'd run into her home and carried her out. Yet despite that, he could tell something about him seemed familiar to her. He replayed their conversation in his mind, wondering if he should've said more, but he knew it would've been too much for her. She was crushed from the loss of her mother.

"What happened?" Fleet asked, coming into the room.

"She remembered something when I touched her hand. There was a spark in her eyes. She even thought my name sounded familiar."

Fleet crossed his arms. "That's a good sign. Now what?"

"She told me where she was staying. Even said I could go check on her."

Fleet patted his back. "Okay. So all you need to do is go over there and get through to her."

Joe glanced at the clock on the wall. His time was ticking, and even though he didn't want to be too pushy, he realized Fleet was right. He needed to go to her and right away. Especially since he still felt as if she could be in danger.

"What is it?" Fleet asked. "You've got a look."

Joe rubbed the back of his neck. "I can't shake the feeling that something horrible is going to happen to her."

"Still? More than the fire?"

"Yes."

"All right then," Fleet said. "Let's regroup, but not here. I saw a shopping center down the way and a motel. We could both use a shower and a fresh change of clothes. Come on."

"Good idea," Joe said. And then he remembered the backpack he'd left back in the Court chambers.

"Uh," he said. "I have no money."

"I've got it. Don't worry."

After making a quick stop for new clothes, they grabbed some burgers and drinks and got a motel room not far from Infiniti's house. The beige-on-beige room with two double beds promised a hot shower and a place for them to strategize.

"I'll go first," Fleet said, disappearing into the bathroom.

Joe eyed the pillow. He hadn't slept hardly at all in the hospital waiting room and could use a quick rest. He eased himself onto the bed. His fatigued body ached all over. Even his limp felt worse, as if his bones were revolting against him. He stared at the popcorn-textured ceiling and thought of Infiniti. He had to get through to her before something else happened and before his time was up, and then he could smash the stone on the necklace Sandra Beaumont had given him and he and Infiniti could go back home. She'd be safe back there.

"It's gonna work out," he whispered to himself. "It has to."

He thought about the necklace. Everything had been happening so fast, he hadn't had time to even look at it. He reached for it, but didn't feel it around his neck. He jolted upright. He patted his shirt up at the front near the collar, then all the way to the back. He dropped to the floor, looking all around the carpet. He took Fleet's keys and hurried to the car parked outside their room. He searched every nook and cranny, but it wasn't there either.

He trudged himself back to the room. He pressed his palms against the wall. How were he and Infiniti going to get back to Havenwood Falls and 2019 now? Frustration starting building inside of him. How could he have lost the one thing he really needed? Seething with anger at himself and his messed up situation, he slammed his fist into the wall.

Fleet came out of the restroom. "Whoa. What's up with you?"

Joe pulled his hand out of the sheetrock. He rubbed his knuckles. "I lost it."

"I can see that." Dressed in new jeans and a T-shirt, Fleet toweled off his wet hair. "Or did you actually lose something?"

Joe blew out. "I punched the wall because I lost mine and Infiniti's ticket back home to H-H-H." Joe growled, wanting to punch his other hand through the wall, pissed that he couldn't talk about his home.

"Havenwood Falls," Fleet said, completing the sentence.

"Right. I lost our way to get back there."

Fleet raised an eyebrow. "What do you mean?"

"I was given a necklace with a stone that I was supposed to use to take me and Infiniti back to where I'm from." He kicked at the wall. "And I lost it."

Fleet sat on a wooden chair by the window of the room. "Well, maybe that's why I'm here. Maybe I'm your way back."

Hope filtered into Joe. "That's right. I've seen you in action. You can do your thing and get us home."

"You've seen me in action?" Fleet asked, looking doubtful.

"Yeah, back in H-H-H—my home. I saw the stream of energy pouring out of your hands. It swirled around the room until you and Infiniti vanished into it."

Fleet tossed his towel on the bed. "Sounds about right."

Joe faced Fleet, thinking of his Transhuman skills. "It'll work, right? You can do it again?"

"Of course it'll work. Now go shower. We've got shit to do."

Joe hobbled his way to the bathroom. He turned the water as hot as he could and let it pummel his worn-out body. He watched as dark residue pooled around his feet from the ash and soot he'd been carrying for hours. He thought of all the things Infiniti had lost in the fire, including her mother. It seemed like the odds were stacked against them. He wondered if the tides would ever turn their way.

Standing in the hot stream, Joe resigned to trust Fleet's ability to send them home. All he needed to do was get through to Infiniti. He lathered up the soap while racking his brain with ways to see Infiniti again when flowers popped into his mind. He could take her some flowers and maybe she'd invite him inside and they could chat. But then what? How could he even begin to tell her that he was from the future and that they had fallen in love when she had transported there? And that he thought she was in danger and should go back with him? Not to mention the whole wolf shifter thing. He leaned his forehead against the shower tile and groaned.

Why couldn't anything be easy?

He finished up in a hurry, got dressed, and joined Fleet in the main room. Fleet pointed at his leg.

"What happened to you?"

Joe rubbed his thigh. "Funny you should ask, because you were there when this happened. I was attacked by a pack of wild wolves. I would've been much worse off if you hadn't shown up when you did."

"Why didn't you heal up? You are a wolf shifter, right? Aren't you supposed to heal fast?"

"I am, and the break should've healed long ago, but this whole thing with Infiniti has me messed up."

Fleet rubbed his chin. He eyed Joe's leg. "Want me to take a crack at it?"

There was a lot Joe didn't know about Transhumans, but if Fleet could fix his leg, then he was all in.

"Sure. I'd love to be able to walk without an old-man limp."

Fleet motioned for Joe to sit on the edge of the bed. He scooted the chair over and sat in front of him. He narrowed his eyes while he hovered his hands over Joe's leg. He moved them up and down, then stopped midway between the hip and knee.

"There it is," Fleet said. "Hold on."

Fleet closed his eyes. He placed his fingers on the spot. His hands started to glow, reminding Joe of how Dr. Underwood had tried to heal him. The light from Fleet's hands intensified until a gray mist started trickling out of his palms. Fleet grimaced, and a crackle of electricity shot out of his hands. Joe's leg spasmed.

"This is deep," Fleet said between gritted teeth. He held his touch a few more seconds before he dropped his hands.

Joe rubbed his leg. "Did it work?"

"Not completely, but you should be able to walk better."

Joe got up and walked around the room. His limp wasn't completely gone, but it was much better. "This is good. Thanks, Fleet."

Joe continued moving about the room. "So I've got an idea about Infiniti. She told me she was staying with her neighbor across the street. The lady from the hospital. What do you think if I went to see her with some flowers? Maybe she'd invite me in, and I could, you know, try to get through to her."

"That's not a bad idea. While you're visiting, I can sift through the rubble of her house and look for your necklace."

A twinge of worry struck Joe. "I thought you said we didn't need it."

"Just in case."

Those three words stayed with Joe while he and Fleet went to a nearby florist and then to Infiniti's. The idea of needing a "just in case" option set his nerves on edge and soared within him as they drove to Infiniti's house. And when they parked in front of the burnt remains of her home, Joe couldn't believe his eyes.

"Damn." Fleet whistled.

"We ran into that," Joe gulped.

Seeing the destruction made him realize how lucky he was that he found Infiniti so quickly and got her out before it was too late. And even though he could've died, he'd do it all over again. His gaze went to the house across the street where Infiniti was staying. He hoped she was okay.

"Come on," Joe prompted, eager and nervous all at the same time. "Let's see if she's there."

He approached Jan's house first while Fleet hung back a little. He rang the doorbell. After a few long seconds, Infiniti opened the door.

"Hi," Joe said awkwardly, trying not to be too excited. With everything she'd been through, he needed to play it cool.

"Hi," she said with a fragile smile.

Her eyes were puffy from crying, and the tip of her petite nose was red, but she was still the most beautiful girl he'd ever seen.

She motioned at the flowers. "Are those for me?"

"Oh, yeah, here." He handed her the flowers he'd almost forgotten he was holding.

"Thank you, Joe. They're beautiful."

Joe had no idea what to say next, but luckily Fleet saved him. "Joe wanted to make sure you were okay." Fleet pointed his thumb over his shoulder at Infiniti's house behind him. "And if you don't mind, could I check your yard for a necklace Joe lost?"

She eyed her house with the saddest look Joe had ever seen.

"Sure," she said to Fleet. "Go ahead."

Fleet left them, and Joe searched for what to say next.

"So, you're doing okay?"

She shrugged her shoulders. "I guess I'm okay."

"Good," he said. "I'm glad."

A few more awkward moments of silence set in.

"Do you want to come in?"

"That would be great," he said, relieved.

He followed her to the kitchen and watched as she got a vase from under the sink. She put the flowers in it and started filling it with water.

"Are you by yourself?" he asked, looking around the room.

"Yeah, Jan left not too long ago for the store."

Joe studied the traditional kitchen with dark-grained cabinets and white laminate counters. He thought everything looked a little dated, especially now that most people had granite countertops. He still remembered when his own kitchen back home was updated. It was the first time he thought of being in a different time, and he instantly thought of his family. He hoped they weren't too worried about him.

"You're lucky to have someone like her."

"I really am. Thanks." She put the vase on the middle of the wooden kitchen table and sat down. Joe took a seat across from her. He held on to his knees under the table, forcing himself to relax.

"So," she said, as if searching for what to say. "Where do you live again?"

His mind scrambled as he tried to figure out what to say. He didn't have a whole lot of time, and this was his chance to make some progress with her.

"I'm from a small town in Colorado. H-H-H—" He stopped, feeling like an idiot. "Let me try that again," he said with a nervous laugh. This time, instead of saying Havenwood Falls, he went with a town nearby. "I'm from Montrose, Colorado. It's a small town near Telluride. I'm just here visiting."

"Oh," she said, looking confused. "But I thought you said we'd seen each other around."

Joe had forgotten he'd said that at the hospital. He had to think fast.

"Well, I've been here before, so that's what I meant," he said. He hated lying to her and quickly redirected the conversation. "Have you, um, been to Colorado?" he asked, hoping to spark a memory in her.

"Actually, yes. I was there this past Christmas."

"Oh yeah? Where did you go in Colorado? What did you do?" he probed.

"My mom and I went to Breckenridge for the holidays." Her

eyes took on a faraway look, as if she'd been sucked into a sad memory.

"We don't have to talk about it," Joe offered. He started to reach across the table for her hand but stopped himself.

"No, it's okay. Jan said I should never stop talking about my mom or remembering her. She said my stories will keep her alive. And I want to keep her alive. She was my mom and my best friend."

Her sorrow-filled big brown eyes tugged at his heart. And this time, he couldn't stop himself. He reached over, took her hand, and squeezed. She gave him a curious look, making him think the gesture might be too much. He started to let go, when she held on.

"Are you sure we don't know each other? I mean, it may sound crazy, but I swear I know you."

She knew him! She really and truly knew him! But what should he say? He didn't want to scare her or freak her out.

"No, it's not crazy at all." He leaned toward her. "In fact, I feel the same way."

She leaned closer to him, too. "You do?"

"Yes, I do. It's like . . ." He stopped so he could search for the right words.

"We've been together," they said at the same time.

Infiniti's lips parted in surprise. "We just said the same thing."

"We sure did," Joe said, wanting to get closer to her, but the table was in the way.

The front door opened, then slammed shut. Joe pulled his hand away from Infiniti's and sat back as Jan came in with two brown sacks of groceries. He got to his feet right away.

"Here, let me help you."

"Oh, the young man from the hospital. Thank you," Jan said. "Joe, is it?"

"Yes, my name is Joe. And you're welcome." He took the bags and set them on the table. "Are there any other bags?"

"No other bags. Thank you for asking."

Jan spotted the flowers right away. "How thoughtful of you to come by and bring flowers."

Infiniti got to her feet. "Yeah," she said. "Aren't they beautiful?"

"I should say so," Jan replied.

"It was the least I could do." Joe shoved his hands in his jean pockets, not really sure what he should do now that Jan was there.

Jan rubbed her forehead. "I'll leave you two, if that's okay. The hectic evening and the trip to the store has worn me out, and I could use a rest."

Before Joe could respond, Infiniti asked, "Is it okay if Joe stays for a while?"

"Of course. He is more than welcome to stay." Jan patted Joe on the shoulder, then shuffled away, leaving him and Infiniti alone again.

"So," Infiniti said, fiddling with her long, wavy brown hair. "Do you want to go to the other room where it's more comfortable?"

"Sure," Joe said, excited to get closer to her.

He followed Infiniti out of the kitchen and into the living room. They sat on a fluffy oversized white couch. They angled their bodies so they'd be facing each other.

Infiniti leaned her head against the couch cushion. "Tell me about yourself, Joseph Greg."

Something about the way she said Joseph Greg made him want to pounce her. He didn't know if it was her Texas accent, her natural beauty, or a combination of the two, but he forced himself to stay calm. And even though they'd had a similar conversation back home in December, he didn't mind doing it all over again. He could talk to her for hours.

"Well, it's just me, my little brother who's twelve, and my parents. My mom makes jewelry out of the house, and my dad is a police officer."

"A police officer? Wow, what's that like?"

"It actually sucks." He laughed. "My dad knows everything I'm doing before I even do it, so it's hard to get away with stuff."

She smiled. "That does sound sucky."

He shrugged, thinking about how his parents had stepped in to help him with the doc and the Court. "It does, but it's not all bad."

Infiniti interlocked her fingers with his as if it was the most natural thing to do, but then realized what she was doing and dropped his hand.

"I'm, uh, sorry."

"No, don't be sorry," he said, boldly taking her hand back.

This time she didn't let go. Playing with her fingers, he tried to think of a way to ask her about herself without eliciting a fresh wave of sorrow. Luckily for him, she started talking.

"Well, as for me, it's just me and my mom. She's a single mom, so it's always just the two of us." Her voice cracked. "I guess I should say was and not is, since she's not here anymore."

Her eyes watered over. She leaned into him and cried into his chest. He held her gently and rubbed her back. "Everything will be okay, Infiniti."

She pulled back and looked into his eyes. "Will it? Because I feel like it won't."

He wiped the tears from her cheeks, his heart exploding with so much love for her it hurt. He traced her face with his fingertips.

"Of course it will."

Their eyes locked. Their bodies moved closer together.

"Joe," she whispered. "I don't understand it, but I have really strong feelings for you."

"I know what you mean."

"You do?"

"Yes, I most certainly do."

She leaned closer, her eyes closed. Their lips were about to meet when Jan burst into the room. A terrified expression plastered her face. She was clutching her shirt at her chest, taking in frantic breaths.

"My dear!" she called out. "You are in grave danger!"

CHAPTER 10

Fleet left Joe and Infiniti and walked across the street. He stared at the damaged and charred structure. From his vantage point, and from what he remembered when he had charged into the flames, the brunt of the fire had blazed to the left of the home and at the rear. Luckily for Infiniti, her room was upstairs on the right. Her mom, on the other hand, had no chance with her room downstairs and in the thick of the flames. Fleet figured the fire must've started in her room.

Focusing on the spot where the ambulance had parked, he walked around, searching for Joe's necklace. Finding nothing, he canvassed the sidewalk and yard.

Still nothing.

He ducked under the yellow caution tape around the house and headed inside. He eyed the space all around the foyer. The stench of water-soaked soot assaulted him as he picked his way over clumps of ash. Keeping a laser focus for any hint of a chain or a stone, he went upstairs and made his way to the first bedroom on the right.

The space exuded Tiny with its purple-on-purple color scheme. The waterlogged room had purple walls, a purple rug, and a giant purple *I* painted on her door. The only break in the color scheme was a soggy white comforter. Dark splotches of carbon marred the walls and ceiling, and a thin layer of ash covered the drenched belongings.

He moved around slowly, eyeing every inch of the floor, but didn't see a necklace. He turned to head back out when a voice spoke to him from behind.

"Leaving so soon, Fleet the Transhuman?"

Fleet froze. His body tingled with icy dread. He recognized the gravelly, deep voice right away. He turned around with slow steps and saw Death in the middle of the room. Tall and wide, dressed in his perfectly tailored black suit, he narrowed his dark menacing eyes on Fleet.

Death kept away from Transhumans for the most part, satisfied to have Tavion taking on the role of the villain, even if Tavion acted independently. Some beings were pure evil without Death's influence.

"What the hell do you want?" Fleet asked.

Death lifted his chin. He huffed. "I could kill you on the spot for being a smart-ass, you know, but I'd prefer to keep you alive. You and your people have provided me much entertainment over the centuries." He clicked his tongue. "Much entertainment."

Fleet clenched his jaw. "Then what is it?"

He knew the monster wanted Tiny, but waited for confirmation.

Death studied Fleet for a long intimidating moment. "It's this human. Infiniti Clausman. She keeps eluding me. Here, in the future, in this reality, in an alternate, she keeps dodging my sentence. Frankly, I'm fucking tired of it. My faithful servant Shade is also weary of her. And so, lucky you, or I should say lucky her, I've decided to handle her demise myself. Once and for all. But not before a little gamesmanship."

Fleet's head reeled. He scrambled for something to say, anything to keep Tiny safe. He thought of offering a trade, but feared Death would want Dominique or even his brother, Farrell. Or maybe even

Joe. He imagined how shitty that would be, Joe trying to save his true love only to trade places with her. Death operated on the cruelest possible level. No way could Fleet risk that. Besides, trading a life for another life was never the solution. He knew that already.

Fleet eyed the window. The sky outside was starting to grow dark. Soon it would have been twenty-four hours for Joe, which meant he only had another forty-eight left. Maybe if he could get Joe and Infiniti safely to Havenwood Falls, the people there could find a way to protect them. He only needed to stall Death long enough for him to accomplish the task.

"How long does she have?" Fleet asked.

Death's lip curled with amused satisfaction. A wide, toothy, ultra-bright grin spread across his angular, clean-shaven face. "Maybe now. Maybe a day. Maybe a week." He shrugged his shoulders. "It's hard to know. But I wanted to alert you of my design. I like seeing you squirm."

Even though Fleet knew none of his attacks would work on the bloodless beast, he wanted nothing more than to charge him head on. But he held back.

Fleet clenched his fists at his side. "Give it your best shot."

He turned his back on Death and started walking out of the room. After a few steps, he heard a swish. He knew Death had left, but he refused to look back. No way in hell would he give that maniac any kind of satisfaction. He needed to play it cool, even if on the inside he was ready to explode.

He scanned the hallway once more for the necklace, then the stairs, and then the foyer before he walked with speed back to the house across the street. He rang the doorbell.

The old woman from the hospital cracked the door open. She peered out. She sighed with relief when she saw Fleet and swung the door open all the way.

"Thank goodness it's you. Come in, hurry."

She ushered him to the living room, where he was surprised to see Joe and Infiniti hand in hand. It seemed whatever he had said to her worked. But then he noticed something else in their expressions.

Fear.

"What happened?" he asked Joe.

"It's Infiniti. Death is after her."

Fleet's blood boiled with anger. The menacing beast was wasting no time with his mission. "How do you know?"

"He told me," Jan said with a worried frown. "I was taking a nap, and he spoke to me through my dreams." She glanced up and away as if going back to that moment. "I dreamed I was in the kitchen, cutting vegetables for soup. A gust of wind blew over me, and a swishing sound filled the room. When I turned to see what it was, I saw a thick man sitting at my kitchen table. He wore a black suit and had dark penetrating eyes. The kind of eyes that look endless. He spoke to me in a deep, throaty voice. He told me his name was Death, and that he was coming for Infiniti. He disappeared, and then I woke up."

Jan wrapped her arms around herself, as if the recollection of her conversation with Death chilled her to the bone.

Infiniti put her hand on Jan's arm. "He sent me a message too," she said to Fleet. "When I was leaving the hospital, I saw a note by the elevator from Death saying he was coming for me. I thought I was seeing things, so I ignored it. But now I know I wasn't imaging anything after all." Infiniti lowered her voice. "He's coming for me."

Fleet ran his fingers through his dark hair. "He came to me too, just now when I was across the street. He's probably the one that started the fire at your house."

Nobody spoke for a few minutes as everything sank in. Fleet eyed Infiniti and Jan, thinking they were taking everything in stride.

"You two seem oddly okay with all this."

"Okay with Death being a terrorizing entity after Infiniti? And responsible for killing her mother?" Jan asked. "Not in the least! He is a vile despicable being! But do I believe it's all real?" She sighed. "Sadly, I do. I also believe Infiniti saw a reaper. I'm a psychic, so I understand a thing or two about the unexplained."

Fleet shot Joe a look. "Joe, she understands the unexplained. Probably Infiniti too. I'd say now would be a good time to get everything out in the open."

Infiniti eyed Joe. "Get what out in the open?"

Fleet hung back and let Joe take over. The lovestruck guy rubbed the back of his neck. He faced Infiniti as if she were the only person in the room.

"Well," Joe said, pausing to formulate his next words. "What I'm about to say may sound crazy, but please hear me out. And please believe me. Okay?"

Infiniti nodded with wide eyes. "Okay."

Joe blew out a breath. He shoved his hands in his pockets. "The thing is, I'm from the future. Six years into the future, to be exact. We met when you went to Breckenridge this past Christmas, but you didn't exactly make it to Breckenridge. Your car crashed and you ended up in my town. You just don't remember any of it."

Infiniti sucked in her breath. She held it for a time before saying, "I always dream of car crashes. Mostly they happen in the snow, with me driving off a cliff. Are you saying that really happened? I mean, I would've remembered something like that. Right?"

"Yes, it really happened." Joe let that soak in before he continued. "After your crash in December 2012, you were taken by ambulance to my town. Once there, you and Fleet ended up time traveling to December 2018 because you needed a spell to protect you from evil magic. You don't remember any of your time there because your memories of the town were wiped when you left my time and came back to your own. Both yours and Fleet's. But while you were there in my time, we met, and we spent a lot of time together, and we . . ."

"Fell in love," she whispered.

"Yes," he said. "We did." He waited a few seconds before he

went on. "When you left, you told me to find you, and I said I would. And while I searched for a way to get to you, I started feeling like you were in danger."

"The fire," she whispered.

"Yes, the fire," Joe said.

Infiniti turned to face Fleet. "You don't remember any of this either?"

"Not a thing. But I've done enough and seen enough to believe it."

Even though Infiniti looked shell-shocked, Fleet thought it best for Joe to get everything out. "But there's more," Fleet prompted. "Right, Joe?"

Infiniti placed her hand up by her throat. "There's more?"

"Dear spirits," Jan whispered. "There's more than the reaper, the fire, the messages from Death, the car crash Infiniti doesn't remember, and the time travel?"

Joe cleared his throat. He wiped his hands on his jeans. "There's nothing worse than that, but I haven't explained why I'm here yet."

"Oh," Infiniti muttered. "That's right, you haven't."

Joe moved closer to Infiniti. "When you left, I became lovesick. As in, really, really sick, because my love for you is a forever thing."

Her brows stitched together. "A forever thing?"

"Yes, a forever thing. You see, I'm a"—he paused for a really long second—"a wolf shifter."

Infiniti's mouth fell open. She didn't say anything, so he went on.

"My feelings for you were so deep and so intense that I was called to you, and I will remain called to you forever."

Joe stopped again so Infiniti could take it all in. Fleet watched, waiting for her to say something.

"You're . . . a . . . wolf shifter," she repeated.

"Yes," Joe answered. "I am."

"Are you here to ask Infiniti to go back with you to your time?" Jan asked, connecting the dots.

"Yes," Joe said. "To my town and my time, 2019."

"Oh," Infiniti said, taking on an expression of understanding. "Six years into the future," she whispered. "To Montrose, Colorado."

Joe pointed at Fleet, signaling him to correct her. "To Havenwood Falls, Colorado," Fleet clarified. "Joe's spelled so that he can't say the name of the town or talk about it too much."

"Then why can you say it?" Infiniti asked.

"It's a long story," Fleet said, not feeling like getting into how he knew about the town. Besides, it was totally irrelevant where she was concerned.

"Oh," she said.

Joe moved in front of Infiniti, as if nobody else was in the room. "As soul mates, we're linked. And we belong together. That is, if you feel the same way and want to come with me."

Infiniti sank down to the couch while a look of bewilderment spread across her face. Joe knelt on the floor in front of her. He took her hands.

"It's a lot, I know."

Fleet crossed his arms. Death's smug expression replayed in his mind. He needed to impress upon Infiniti the gravity of the situation.

"Listen, Tiny. Joe's right. It is a lot. But we don't have the luxury of time to go over everything in more detail. Death is coming. Getting you to Havenwood Falls may be your only chance for survival."

*I*nfiniti couldn't believe what she was hearing, but at the same time, also could believe it. The feeling of missing something or someone had been growing in her since the Cold Moon. Add the dreams of car crashes and the visit from Abigail, and it all made sense.

She'd been missing Joe.

Gazing into his hazel eyes as he knelt before her, she could feel the intense connection with him. But to learn he was a wolf shifter from a town of supernaturals and that she needed to go with him to the future because Death wanted to kill her? It was a lot to take in.

Death had taken her mom and now he wanted her. She knew her mom would say to fight like hell and do whatever she could to be safe. But leave her home? And go to the future with Joe? She wasn't sure.

Infiniti looked to Jan, the closest person to her alive. She trusted Jan and knew Jan had her best interests at heart.

"What should I do?"

Jan pursed her lips, then gave a swift nod. "You live."

Live? She already had to live without her mom, but what about everything else? But then she remembered she didn't really have anything else. Her house was gone. She didn't have any other family. Her friends had all left for college. Trent had said he'd come see her, but he'd be a few days.

"And if living means leaving you and everything I've ever known? And going to a town six years in the future?" she asked Jan.

"Then you leave here and go to a town six years in the future. And I'll come visit you, in six years. With more wrinkles and more gray hair."

Infiniti eyed Joe. "Can she do that? Come visit me?"

"Of course," he said, releasing her hands and sitting next to her. "The supernatural power of the town doesn't prevent us from having visitors. And unless someone is a supe, no one even knows about the magic." He lifted his shoulders. "It's really just a normal and beautiful place. You can work, go to school, all of it. You can even come visit Jan, without the time travel part that is. You'll just have to follow the magical rules of the town. I can fill you in on all that when you get there. If you decide to come with me, that is."

Infiniti thought about seeing Jan in six years and how weird that would be. And then she wondered if Jan would even be alive in six years. She pushed those morbid thoughts away, telling herself Jan had way more than six years left in her.

"And you'll be well taken care of," Jan added. "Your mother had a two-million-dollar insurance policy with you as the beneficiary."

Infiniti gulped. "She did?" Tears sprang to her eyes. It was just like her mom to do that. She was always doing whatever she could for Infiniti. And that's when Infiniti knew she needed to do whatever she could for her mom.

And that included living.

She brought her attention to Joe, the wolf shifter she had met in the future and fallen in love with, who had come to the past to save her. Her heart and soul hadn't forgotten him, even though her mind had.

"I'd like to talk to Joe alone for a minute," she said to Jan and Fleet.

"Sure," Fleet nodded.

"We'll be in the other room," Jan added.

Infiniti folded and unfolded her hands in her lap while she processed everything. Joe placed his hands on top of hers, his touch instantly calming her. She stared at their intertwined hands.

"Yesterday I was cleaning my room, trying to make sense of my future. Today my whole world has changed."

"I know," Joe said. "And I'm so sorry. Your life may never be the same, but I promise it can still be amazing."

"If we can make it out of here," she tacked on.

"We'll make it," Joe urged, his eyes taking on a fiery look. "I know it."

Seeing the determination in him ignited the spirit of her old self that had been buried under her grief. Her mom didn't raise a quitter. She decided to hold on to who she was, no matter how hard. She wasn't going to let Death win. With Joe and Fleet on her side, and with Jan's support, she felt like everything would turn out okay.

"All right," she said, deciding to take a huge leap of faith. "I'll go with you."

A look of surprise mixed with relief washed over Joe. "You will?"

She smiled. "Yes, I will."

His gaze drifted to her lips, lingering there for a quick second before coming back up to her eyes. The vulnerability of the move made her heart flutter and her insides tremble. He was the perfect blend of sexy and adorable, and in that moment she wanted nothing more than to feel his lips on hers. He must've felt the same way, because he scooted closer.

"It's terrible timing, Infiniti, but I really need to kiss you."

"I need to kiss you, too," she said, giving in to her impulses.

They moved closer and closer to each other. Their mouths opened, their lips met, and finally they kissed. It was sweet and tender and familiar and provocative. Her head soared in the clouds while longing spread throughout her body.

She parted from him slowly, not wanting to break away, but feeling weird that Jan and Fleet were in the other room.

"Wow," Joe said.

"Very wow," she echoed.

Unable to stop themselves, they kissed again. This time they swooped in and wrapped their arms around each other. It was the kind of embrace that came from being scared of losing something new and wonderful. And if she could, she'd stay like that with him forever. But they didn't have forever. She figured they needed to tell the others about her decision. Especially since time wasn't on their side.

"I guess we should call Jan and Fleet back in," she said against his lips between panting breaths.

"Probably."

He kissed her once more before they separated completely. He got off the couch and helped her to feet.

"Jan, Fleet," she called out, smoothing her long brown hair away from her face. "Y'all can come back now."

Together again in the living room, Infiniti announced, "I've decided to go."

"That's my girl," Jan said.

Fleet rubbed his hands together. "With that settled, I suggest we get a move on."

"You mean leave now?" Terror struck Infiniti, along with the realization that all she had was the clothes on her back, clothes that Jan had purchased for her while she was in the hospital. Jeans, a plain white T-shirt, and white tennis shoes. "What I'm wearing is all I have. Everything else is ruined."

Jan placed her hands on Infiniti's shoulders. "I'm sure they have nice stores where you're going. And if they don't, you raise a fuss."

Infiniti hugged Jan tightly. "I will."

"Good," Jan said, ending their embrace with a reassuring rub on the back. She motioned to Fleet. "This young man will come back here after he's seen you and Joe safely to Havenwood Falls, and he'll help me get your money to you." She smiled. "And then I'll see you in six years. Easy peasy."

Infiniti nodded and smiled while her stomach clenched. There was that phrase, the one Jan always used for things that were anything but easy. She mustered up her courage and swallowed the lump in her throat.

"Easy peasy," she repeated back.

Tinker trotted into the room. She rubbed her furry body against Infiniti's legs, purring loudly. Infiniti crouched down to pet her, still marveling at how she wasn't all white anymore but now understanding why. When she stood back up, Trent popped into her mind. He said he'd be coming to see her. She wondered if she should call him, but quickly decided against it, because what would she say?

"Jan, Trent's supposed to be coming to see me."

"I'll handle it all, dear. Don't you worry."

Forcing herself to keep a stiff upper lip, she nodded. Hand in hand with Joe, she went outside with him and Fleet to their car. Before she got in, she stopped and studied her house across the street. Memories of good times flashed before her eyes—movie nights with friends, parties, conversations with her mom. She vowed to keep the memories and love alive inside her. She also vowed to somehow return to Houston again. And then she started imagining what Jan would say to explain her disappearance. She hoped it wasn't something completely off the rails, like joining the circus or a monastery. As if any of her friends would believe a monastery cover story. The circus, maybe.

Fleet drove while Infiniti sat in the back with Joe. Fleet suspected he'd have better luck transporting her and Joe six years into the future to Havenwood Falls if he could get as close to the town as possible. But since Fleet didn't know exactly where the town was, and Joe couldn't say because of the protective magic that bound him, they settled on getting to Montrose, the nearest city Joe could talk about.

Minutes turned into hours, day turned into night, and a sense of safety started to set in. Maybe Death would let them go. Maybe he was busy with other things. With her mind a little at ease, Infiniti turned her attention to Joe. She wanted to know all about him and their time together. How did they meet? Where did she stay? What did they do?

She scooted closer to Joe as he filled her in on everything she didn't remember. Staring into his dreamy hazel eyes and admiring his perfectly angular features, she listened to their love story. As he spoke, everything about him drew her in—his smile, his laugh, the way he traced her hand with his fingers but slowly pulled them away because he didn't know if it was too much, but then went back to touching her again because he couldn't help himself. She didn't want him to stop. She might have had her doubts when he first told her everything, but being with him made her heart swell and the entire world around them melt away. It was just her, Joe, and the amazing connection between them she had felt right away but didn't understand.

After a while, she realized how exhausted she was. But before she could sleep, she needed to go to the bathroom.

"Hey, Fleet, I really need to make a stop."

"Okay," he said. "I saw a sign for a rest stop a couple of miles ahead."

The hot August night sky was sprinkled with a host of shimmery stars, stars Infiniti really couldn't see from home because Houston was so bright and big. Finally she spotted a neon blinking sign that promised *Tasty Jerky* and *Clean Restrooms*.

Fleet parked in a spot farthest away from the entrance. He turned off the car. He thrummed his thumbs against the steering wheel. "We go in fast and get out fast. Everyone stay close. Got it?"

A wave of shivers raced across Infiniti's spine. The fear and panic that had disappeared sprang fresh inside of her. She eyed the busy parking lot and watched people either pumping gas in their cars or filtering in and out of the store.

"We'll be okay with all the activity, right?" She let out a nervous laugh. "You know, safety in numbers and all that?"

"Should be," Fleet said.

"I'll be right beside you," Joe reassured her.

"Me too, Tiny." Fleet eyed her through the rearview mirror. "Now let's do this."

Infiniti laced her fingers with Joe's and held him close to her as they followed Fleet into the busy store. They hurried to the back, where the restrooms were. Infiniti paused as she stared at the separate section for women.

She gulped, eyeing Joe. "I have to go alone," she said, not wanting to leave him, suddenly wishing she had squatted behind the car instead. But they were already inside. It was too late to go back now.

"I'll be right here," Joe promised. "It'll be fine."

Slowly releasing her hold from his, she went in. She made her way to the first empty stall and did her business fast. When she came out, she went to the sink and started lathering her hands. Glancing at herself in the mirror, she saw thick red letters sprawled across the glass.

YOUR TIME IS COMING

Infiniti shrieked, and Joe bolted into the restroom.

"What is it?" He glanced about. "What happened?"

She pointed at the glass. Her hand shook like uncontrollably. "There was a m-m-message, right there. But now it's g-g-gone."

Fleet ran in, followed by a stout female worker wearing jeans and a company logo shirt.

"Everything okay?" she asked with a Texas twang. "I heard screaming."

"Uh, she fell," Joe hurried out. "And she yelled. But she's fine now. Everything is okay now."

Infiniti stilled her hands by shoving them in her jeans pockets. "Yeah, I slipped. But I'm okay."

The woman nodded, while studying the floor as if looking for a slippery spot.

Fleet jerked his chin to the exit. "We'll get out of your way, ma'am."

They filed out of the restroom and left the store in a hurry. Infiniti's heart raced out of control. Her nerves were on edge and her eyes flickered about as she wondered if Death would deliver another message.

Fleet sped out of the parking lot, increasing their distance from the store. He slowed down enough to join the flow of traffic. Maintaining a steady speed, he said, "Let's hear it, Tiny. What did the message say?"

Infiniti had been working on her breathing to steady herself. "It said, 'Your time is coming.'"

"Not if I can help it," Joe said.

Infiniti stayed on the edge of her seat. She eyed their surroundings, as if Death would fall down on them from above, when she noticed the weather changing. The dim streetlights that dotted the sides of the roads illuminated with enough light for them to see thick puffs of clouds gathering overhead. The mass stretched out as far as the eye could see. Pellets of rain started hammering the car. The winds gusted so hard the car rocked from side to side.

"This is tornado weather," Infiniti warned, scooting closer to Joe. She searched the horizon, looking for a break in the clouds, but didn't see one. "Is Death doing this?"

"Probably," Fleet said. He kept both hands on the steering wheel, holding it in a firm grip. His jaw clenched. "But don't worry, I got this."

Infiniti and Joe sat back. They stayed close together. "You know what would really suck?" she asked him.

"You mean, what would suck more than this weather and Death being after us?" He smiled, trying to lighten a terrifying situation.

She wanted to laugh too, but suddenly couldn't. Her heart had been through too much. "What would suck is reuniting with you only for both of us to die. Then I'd be losing two loved ones."

He traced the side of her face with his fingers and tucked her hair behind her ear. "Yeah," he whispered. "That would really suck. Luckily for us, that's not gonna happen."

The storm clouds and the hard rain followed them as they made their way from Texas to New Mexico. On edge, making quick stops, trading off naps with Joe, it was the worst and most stressful road trip of her life. Yet each mile they advanced and each city they passed, hope that they'd make it grew inside of her.

Maybe Death had found someone else to torment.

They arrived in Colorado well into the next day. Driving into the plains with majestic mountains off in the distance, Infiniti noticed the sky clearing a little. The ominous dark clouds were giving way to slivers of blue sky.

"I think we've made it through the storm," Infiniti said with reserved optimism. She kept peering about, looking for the sun, but didn't see it. "At least, I think we have."

"I think you're right," Joe said, craning his neck and looking out the window too. "I think the worst is behind us now."

"Maybe," Fleet said. He glanced over his shoulder at Joe. "A few more hours and we'll be in Montrose. And then this will all be over."

Infiniti sat back in her seat. Something in Fleet's tone and choice of words told her he didn't share the same outlook as Joe. And whatever he was feeling filtered into her. Her stomach twisted into a brand new knot. Any sense of hope she'd been storing up started slipping away.

Joe placed his hand on her knee. "We're gonna make it," he whispered.

Infiniti thought of losing her mother. She never wanted to feel that level of pain ever again. And then she remembered asking Jan what she should do, and Jan telling her to live. She resolved to do exactly that. For herself, for her mother, for Jan, and even for Joe, who had crossed six years of time to find her. She was going to push every shred of fear and doubt out of her mind and fight for her survival.

After a quick snooze and a few more hours of driving, Fleet turned onto a small two-lane dirt road hidden between massive pine trees. He slowed down as the car worked its way over bumps and rocks. After a while, they came upon a clearing and parked on the far side of the open space. Everyone got out of the car quietly, as if Death hovered nearby, watching and listening.

Fleet rubbed his hands together. He intertwined his fingers and popped his knuckles. "This is it. You both ready?"

"Yeah," Infiniti and Joe said at the same time.

"Good," Fleet said. "Now let's stand in a circle and hold hands. Joe, you concentrate hard on where you want to go."

Fleet walked to the middle of the clearing. Infiniti and Joe followed. They started getting into position when a deep, menacing laughter filled the air.

"Look at the three of you, joining hands in a kumbaya moment. How pathetic."

An army of goosebumps raced across Infiniti's skin when she saw Death. Or, at least, she thought it was Death. She'd never seen him before. He was a towering figure, dressed in an all-black suit. He was leaning against the car with his arms folded.

"You're dead. I mean, Death," she muttered.

His thin lips curled into a menacing smile. "I am indeed. To both. And you're about to join me. I hope you're ready." He licked his lips. "I know I am."

CHAPTER 12

*J*oe eyed the dark, hulking figure standing by the car. He halfway expected a skeletal figure in a grim reaper outfit, but instead Death was dressed in all black, like the owner of a funeral home. And he may as well have been one. He took souls for a living.

Joe glanced at Infiniti. Dark circles encased her terror-filled eyes. Her skin had paled from her grief. He needed her to hold on a little longer despite Death's threats.

She's not going anywhere with you," he said, sidling in front of Infiniti.

"Of course she is," Death sneered. He eased himself from his resting position beside the car and brushed off his suit jacket. He approached with slow, calculated steps.

Fleet moved beside Joe. His hands crackled with energy.

"You and Infiniti run when I say," he urged in a low whisper.

Letting them know he could hear them, Death taunted, "Run? Please do. I welcome a good ol' fashioned game of chase. We can even play tag. I'll be it, of course."

Death moved closer. His sparkling toothy grin covered half his face. He lifted his hand and swiped the air with his fingers. A snapping sound filled the space all around them, followed by a crackling of splintering wood as a massive tree came crashing down. Fleet flung out a stream of energy, blasting the timbering pine into smithereens. Leaves and branches showered all around them.

"I am having so much fun with the three of you," Death chided, still smiling, still advancing. "It'll be a shame when all this is over. But when your time is up, it's up."

Joe scanned the area, looking for a place to run and hide with Infiniti. He started backing up with her when Fleet powered up his energy. He hurled a series of blasts at Death that were easily deflected by the towering monster, as if he were batting away at bubbles.

"Shit," Fleet muttered.

"One of yours for one of mine," Death countered.

Death frowned. He narrowed his eyes. He raised his hands and clawed at the air with angry force. Explosive blasts erupted all around. Trees and shrubs careened through the air. Fleet flung his energy streams, deflecting the onslaught while Joe knocked Infiniti to the ground and covered her with his body. She buried her face in the crook of his neck and held onto him for dear life as the ground beneath them shook like an earthquake.

And then, all at once, the melee stopped.

Infiniti hugged Joe while her body trembled. "Is it over?"

Joe lifted his head. He peered about. The place looked like a tornado had barreled through the clearing. Clumps of trees and debris covered the ground as far as the eye could see. Joe caught a glimpse of Fleet leaning over in the middle of the disaster, hands on his knees, but otherwise looking okay. He didn't see Death anywhere.

"I don't think so," Joe answered. As a wolf shifter, he knew hunters never released their prey. And Death was the ultimate hunter. He got up and helped Infiniti to her feet. He spun around, searching the area for the madman as he approached Fleet, but he didn't see him. He placed his hand on Fleet's shoulder.

"Fleet, you okay?"

Fleet rose to a standing position. "That son of bitch is playing with us," he said, gulping for air. "Do you see him?"

Joe pulled Infiniti close. He kept scanning the field, his wolf shifter eyes and ears kicking into high gear.

"No, I don't."

"Should we hurry and do the transport now? Before he comes back?" Infiniti asked in a panic-filled tone.

A cackling laugh whispered through the winds. A flock of crows started gathering overhead, cawing as they began flying in a circle formation.

"Son of a bitch," Fleet said under his breath.

"What now?" Joe asked.

"Now I call for backup," Fleet answered. "Hold on."

Joe watched Fleet close his eyes. His lips moved as he mumbled under his breath. When he opened his eyes, a flash of lightning crashed all around him. When the light faded, a guy who looked just like Fleet but with blond hair appeared. He marched over to Fleet's side. Joe thought for sure they were brothers.

"What's happening?" the guy asked Fleet, acknowledging Joe and Infiniti with a quick nod.

"These two need to get to Havenwood Falls, but Death is being an asshole."

"Okay, and the plan?"

"Put a protective shield around us while I get them home."

"Okay," the guy said. "Let's go."

Fleet eyed Joe and Infiniti. "Get together," he commanded, moving toward them. "And hold hands."

Joe moved even closer to Infiniti. He grabbed her hands as the crows cried louder, their swarm flying closer. The newcomer knelt down in front of Joe and Infiniti. He placed his hands on the ground. Streams of white mist poured out of his arms and hands, oozing underneath their feet and then stretching upward, forming into a vaporized bubble that grew until it encased their group like a shimmering dome.

"Whoa," Infiniti whispered.

"Okay, Fleet," the guy said between clenched lips. "Do it."

Fleet placed one hand on Infiniti's wrist and the other on Joe's. "Think of your time and your place," Fleet ordered Joe.

Joe nodded, keeping his eyes on the skies as the black birds started dive bombing them, sizzling away as they made contact with the supernatural shield. He forced himself to keep calm as the birds gathered in so tightly, their chaotic movement blocked out everything else.

"Oh my god," Infiniti muttered, flinching at each black-winged strike against the energy surrounding them.

"It's gonna be okay," Joe urged. "Just focus on me."

"Joe! Think of where you want to go!" Fleet hollered.

Focusing on his directive, he embraced Infiniti in a bear hug. He lowered his eyes. He thought of Havenwood Falls and his family, but his concentration kept breaking with the clamoring and commotion all around him.

"My home," he said out loud, thinking the verbal command would help him stay focused. Repeating his destination, he caught sight of Fleet's gray power. It seeped out all over the place until the ground started churning with power.

"My home," Joe repeated, struggling to block out everything else when he noticed a group of birds landing on the barrier. Joe watched in horror as they hammered at the sphere with their beaks like possessed demons, despite the zapping that shocked them with each peck. One made it through the enclosure, and then another. They bounced all around like crazed pinballs inside Fleet's contained energy storm.

"Hurry," the guy urged Fleet. "I can't hold it much longer."

"Just a little more," Fleet grunted out.

Joe squeezed Infiniti even tighter to him, thinking of his home, trying desperately to keep the image in his mind, when a feeling of weightlessness swept over him. A supersonic boom shook him to his core as he felt Fleet release his hold, and he and Infiniti plunged into a free fall.

CHAPTER 13

*J*oe held on to Infiniti as they toppled to the ground amidst an explosion of dirt and electric particles. He cradled Infiniti's head, waiting for everything to stop, then cautiously scanned the area. The birds were gone. The leveled field was gone, too, replaced with tall grass and mid-sized trees.

"Did we make it?" Infiniti asked, uncovering her face.

From the look of the growth all around them, they had definitely time traveled. He had to assume he was in the same spot but in his proper time.

"I think so," Joe answered, getting up and helping her to her feet.

Infiniti smiled. "I think so, too."

There was no shield. The blond-haired guy that Joe assumed was Fleet's brother, because they looked so much alike, was gone too. Only Fleet remained, standing nearby. Death had to have been left behind.

"Hey, Fleet, did we make it?"

Fleet dusted off his pants. He turned and smiled, and Joe staggered back. Fleet's eyes had turned from green to pure black. Infiniti clutched Joe's arm in a death grip.

"Oh no," she uttered.

Joe pushed Infiniti behind him and stepped back, increasing the distance between them and Fleet.

"What have you done with Fleet?" Joe demanded.

Death formed a ball of electricity in Fleet's hands. He tossed it in the air and caught it with his other hand.

"Nothing," he said in Fleet's voice. "I'm merely trying him on for size. I have always been a huge fan of Transhumans. Really, any humans."

Death smiled, then morphed from Fleet's form into Infiniti's mom. Like Infiniti, she was petite with long wavy hair, but instead of rich brown locks, her hair was strewn with white streaks.

"Infiniti," Death said in a hoarse voice. Her face started crisping with burn marks. "Why did you leave my cold, dead body in Houston? What kind of daughter are you? Don't you love me? Or was that all a lie?"

Infiniti gasped, digging her nails into Joe's skin. "You monster," she choked out between anger-filled tears.

Joe turned Infiniti away. "Ignore him."

Death let out a booming laugh. His form blurred and stretched as it changed from Infiniti's mom to Joe's dad.

"Son, you've always been such a huge disappointment to me." Death crossed his arms and shook his head, sounding exactly like his dad, complete with the same mannerisms. "A huge disappointment."

Rage coursed through Joe's veins. Everything he had felt since the Cold Moon Ball mounted inside of him—heartache, pain, and fury—until everything boiled over and erupted inside of him.

"Back away," he ordered Infiniti.

His bones started cracking. His teeth elongated. His nails transformed into claws. He grunted as his muscles expanded, then contracted, as his clothes tore away and fur erupted over his skin. He fell over to the ground in wolf form.

Baring his fangs, Joe crouched low to the ground. He growled at Death, who had morphed back to his black-suited form.

"You gonna come at me, wolfy?" Death prodded. "You think you can take me?"

Joe snapped. He crouched low, and then pounced. He swiped at Death's face, then went for the jugular, not even knowing if Death had one, but doing whatever he could to shred the madman who wanted Infiniti.

Blasts of pain zapped Joe. He continued lashing out and biting, despite the agony coursing through his body, until a force slammed into him like an invisible freight train. He sailed through the air and thudded to the ground on his side.

Death marched over to him. He held his hand out, as if ready to choke the life out of him, when Infiniti lunged between them. She covered Joe with her arms, shielding his body.

"Stop! You can have me!" she yelled.

Death halted. He lowered his hand. He looked down on Infiniti as she protected Joe.

"What did you say?" he asked slowly, as if unsure of what he heard.

"Leave him alone and you can have me."

Joe whimpered. He didn't want Infiniti to give herself up for him, but he couldn't move. It felt as if every bone in his body had been pulverized.

Infiniti buried her face in his fur. She kissed his cheek and then stroked his head. "I'm so sorry," she whispered.

She climbed up to her feet. She straightened her spine and raised her chin. "Leave him alone and I'll go with you."

Death narrowed his eyes. He tilted his head. "You will trade your life for this wolf shifter?"

"Yes, I would. And I do. He loves me. And I love him. But you wouldn't know anything about that, would you? Death doesn't love anyone or anything!"

Death considered her words. He did know a thing or two about love. He turned away from the petite human, suddenly overwhelmed with thoughts of his own love. She was the most glorious and beautiful creature, created more than one hundred years ago, and lived in the Japanese underworld. Would she ever know that he loved her? Would she ever return the sentiment? Would she ever sacrifice herself for him?

Infiniti moved in front of Death. She narrowed her eyes while a look of recognition dawned on her face. "You do know. You do love someone."

Death scowled. He raised his hand to swipe at her with his power when she raised her arms.

"You need to tell her. Before it's too late. Before something happens to her and she's taken from you—the way you're going to take me from Joe."

Joe listened intently to Death and Infiniti, and when Infiniti compared herself to the person Death loved, he saw Death's expression shift. Was it doubt? A change of heart? Joe didn't know, but he lifted his head, pointed his muzzle to the sky, and let out a long, agonizing howl. The wail pierced through the cloudy day, drifting with the summer wind, letting every nearby creature know he was about to lose his one true love.

Joe's head fell down in defeat, his heart shattering for Infiniti, when a chorus of howls sounded in the distance. His pain had been heard, and if he and Infiniti had transported to the correct time and place, his pack would be on the move.

Infiniti's arms shook uncontrollably. "I'm just like her," she whispered. "And you're just like Joe."

Death moved closer to her. He glanced at Joe from the corner of his eye.

"Yes, I know something about love. I know the pain of not having it. The cruelty of it not being returned. I know every negative emotion associated with it." He stepped away from Infiniti. "But I've never experienced its joy. Or its pleasure. I don't know any of those things." Death clasped his hands behind his back. "I will let you have these things, human. And maybe one day I'll have the same returned to me. Consider it a quid pro quo. So, for now, you are off the top of my list." He brought his face close to Infiniti's with a swish. Infiniti saw the skeletal features beneath the thin layer of skin and shuddered. "But you are still on the list. And I'll be watching you."

With a gust of wind and a blast of light, Death vanished.

Infiniti lowered her arms. She sank to her knees. She huddled with Joe, holding him to her.

"Please be okay," she whispered. "Please."

Joe could feel the wetness from her tears on his fur. He nuzzled into her, relieved for her to be alive. But now he was broken, literally.

The pounding of animal paws and breaking of twigs rumbled in the distance, moving closer with steady rhythm. As the din grew louder, the earth started shaking.

"Please tell me that sound is your friends," Infiniti said.

A pack of wolves mixed with mountain lions burst onto the scene. The animals paced around Joe and Infiniti, circling them in a protective manner. Infiniti noticed two of the wolves had the same white fur as Joe but looked bigger and older. They stood closest to Joe. Infiniti figured they were his parents.

"It was Death," she said to them. "He did this, but now he's gone."

Suddenly, a tall elfish-looking man appeared out of thin air. He had long ears and a long flat nose. He eyed Joe with concern. "Move aside, young lady," he huffed.

Infiniti did as he said, backing away from Joe. The two white wolves joined her side. She watched as the man placed his hands on Joe. He moved them up and down his fur, holding them longer in some places and shorter in others. He worked methodically, probing and touching until Joe clamored to his paws.

"Joe," the man instructed, "escort this young maiden to the main road. The rest of you," he waved to the animals, "get back home at once."

The man vanished. The mountain lions trotted off, followed by the wolves, with the two white-furred ones lingering a little longer before they took off too. And Joe stayed. He pressed his body against Infiniti's leg and nudged her forward.

She kept her hand on his back. "You almost died, and then the supernatural dream team arrived," she said in an astonished voice. "And that elf guy healed you. And then he disappeared."

Joe huffed.

"Is that what your town is like? I mean, do elves walk around like it's no big deal and people transform into animals like it's nothing?"

He huffed again, wanting to explain everything, but figured it was best for him to still be in wolf form so she could process. They could talk later.

"I'm definitely not in Kansas anymore," she muttered.

They emerged onto a small dirt road. A Jeep was parked on the side. Joe's dad got out of the car and hurried over to them. He got down on his knees in front of Joe and hugged his neck.

"Son, thank God you're okay." He stayed like that for a while before standing up and hugging Infiniti. "And Infiniti, you made it, too. I'm so glad."

"Thank you," she said. "You must be Joe's dad."

"I am," he said. "You can call me Ivan."

He opened the car door and took out a stack of clothes. He placed them on the back bumper. "Infiniti, why don't you get in the car. I'll stay back here with Joe while he changes."

She sat in the back seat. After a few minutes, Joe climbed in next to her. She wrapped her arms around him. "Oh, Joe."

He hugged her back. "We made it," he exhaled. "We really and truly made it."

He wanted to say something about what she had said to Death about her feelings for him, but decided to wait. He wanted to hurry and get to the safety of Havenwood Falls before Death changed his mind about letting Infiniti live. But then he wondered if she still even wanted to go with him now that Death had backed down. He supposed if she wanted to go back to her place and time, the Court would help her.

"Now what?" Infiniti asked.

Joe moved closer to Infiniti. "Now we go to Havenwood Falls, if you still want to come with me."

Infiniti touched her fingers to her lips. She gazed up at Joe. Her expression told him she was thinking about what she should do. She sat quiet for a long time.

"Joe," she finally said. "I haven't felt right since the Cold Moon. But ever since I've been with you, I feel complete. Like with you I'm whole again. Myself again. And I'm not missing anything."

Joe's heart soared. "So you'll come with me?"

She smiled. "Yes."

"With that settled," Joe said, "let's go home."

Joe's dad opened the driver's side door. "Everyone ready?"

"Yeah," Joe said. "We're ready."

He clasped hands with Infiniti. They leaned against each other and sat in silence as they drove home, a deep understanding passing through them over everything they'd been through in such a short amount of time.

They rolled into town, the graying sky turning to night. Joe eyed the streets, realizing they weren't heading home.

"Dad, where are we going?"

"To City Hall. Addie wants to meet you both there."

When they got to the building, all the lights were turned off, and the parking lot was empty. Joe's dad parked at the far end of the lot, and another Jeep pulled up next to them. Addie got out of the other vehicle, and Joe, Infiniti, and Joe's dad exited theirs. Addie lowered her glasses. She studied Joe and then Infiniti.

"I'm impressed," Addie said with a wide smile. "I know rules were broken. We'll talk about all that later and do our big welcome orientation tomorrow, but for now I've got orders to shuttle the both of you to Dr. Underwood for a look over." She pointed at Joe. "Then you will go home." She pointed at Infiniti. "And you will go to my mom Lyra's house. But where are my manners?" Addie stuck her hand out to Infiniti. "You don't remember me yet, but I'm Addie. Addie Beaumont."

"That's right," Infiniti said. "Joe told me my memories from my time here will come back."

"Yep," Addie said. "Everything that happened when you were here will come back. Though I'm not sure when. Could be soon, could take a while since you're a time traveler and all that. It all depends. Now let's go. It's getting late."

After a quick visit with Dr. Underwood, Joe got the all-clear, while Infiniti was told to come back on a regular basis so she could be monitored for any residual side effects of time travel.

"What does that even mean?" Joe asked, as they stood outside waiting for Lyra Beaumont to pick up Infiniti, wondering if he should be worried.

"Apparently I've done so much time hopping, I need to be monitored for a complicated word Dr. Underwood told me that I forgot. He compared it to jet lag on steroids."

"Oh," Joe said. "That doesn't sound so bad."

"No, it doesn't." A hush fell down on them. "So I stayed at this lady's house the last time I was here?"

"Yes, you did. It's a great house with lots of room. And you'll love Ms. Beaumont. She's really cool."

"Oh," she said, suddenly looking unsure of everything.

"I can come over later tonight, or in the morning. Or both. Whatever you want," Joe offered, wanting her to feel comfortable but not wanting to overdo it.

"Tonight would be great. Thanks, Joe."

A car drove up, and Lyra Beaumont got out. She walked over to Joe and Infiniti wearing a huge smile.

"Joseph and Infiniti, reunited. It's so good to see." She hugged Joe and then Infiniti, but caught on right away that Infiniti still didn't remember anything. She stepped back. "My name is Lyra Beaumont, and I'll be your host, Infiniti. Are you ready to go?"

"Yeah, I guess." She turned to Joe. "See you later?"

"Yes, later. I'll be there."

Joe watched as Infiniti walked to the car, looking hesitant and a little scared. She got in the passenger side, and they started to drive off, when the car stopped. The door opened. Infiniti popped out. Recognition shone in her eyes as she hurried over to him.

"We got burgers and we went to the school. We watched movies together all night. You took me to the Cold Moon Ball, and I wore a purple dress. You were attacked trying to protect me." She slipped her arms around his waist. "And at the herbal shop, you kissed me. My first kiss. And you promised you'd come find me."

"And I did," Joe said, wanting desperately to kiss her in that moment. "I found you."

"Yes, you did. Now kiss me, Joseph Greg, or I might die."

He kissed her long and slow, thinking he never wanted to stop, thinking he never wanted to leave her, thinking he never wanted to be without her.

Thinking he could live like this forever.

EPILOGUE

*I*nfiniti peeled open her tired eyes and caught sight of the early summer sun filtering through her room. With a groan, she rolled her body away from the light and faced the wall. She'd only been in Havenwood Falls a few days, and each morning she had awoken exhausted with a racing pulse and a feeling of dread. She knew she'd been having crazy nightmarish dreams, but could never remember any of the details. Which was fine by her. She'd had enough chaos in her life to last her a good long while and didn't need any more. Even if it was in her sleep.

"Peace and happiness," she muttered to herself as she drew in a deep breath and stretched out her arms and legs. "And Joe."

She reached for the phone he had bought her and checked her messages. Sure enough, Joe had already texted.

Joe: Hey, beautiful. Text me when you're up

She smiled, her heart skipping a few beats as she thought of Joe. Eager to see him, she texted back.

Me: I'm up!

Joe: Can I come over? My mom made her special fritule pastries for you and Lyra

Infiniti had no idea what that was, but thought it sounded yummy. Plus, she'd be seeing Joe. She couldn't get enough of him.

Me: Yeah, come over
Joe: Ok, be there in a few

Flinging off her covers, she hurried to the bathroom. She splashed water on her face, ran her fingers through her long, wavy brown hair, then started brushing her teeth. She was in the middle of a gargle and spit when a knock sounded on the door.

"Hold on," she called out between the dribble, thinking there was no way that was Joe. He needed more time to get there, unless he had hauled ass, which was entirely possible.

She opened her bedroom door to find Lyra on the other side. Her host's short brown hair was tucked behind her ears and her usual pleasant smile was replaced with a worried expression.

"Infiniti, can you come to the living room? Addie is here and needs to speak to you."

"Addie?" Infiniti gulped.

Addie was Lyra's daughter. Infiniti didn't know Addie well, but the twenty-something woman had dropped by a few times since Infiniti had started staying there. She knew Addie worked for the mysterious Court of the Sun and the Moon. The only reason she was allowed to know this or anything about the Court was because of her own beyond-natural trips through time—and the fact that a wolf shifter was called to her.

"Uh, okay," Infiniti answered, suddenly nervous. "Let me change my clothes first."

"All right," Lyra said with a solemn nod.

Infiniti closed the door. She stood there for a while, wondering what the heck was going on, then quickly slipped out of her pajamas and into shorts and a T-shirt. A sinking feeling that she had done something wrong settled in her gut, even though she knew she hadn't done anything.

Dressed and ready for whatever Addie wanted, she entered the living room. Lyra and Addie were standing by the fireplace, talking in hushed voices. They fell silent when they spotted Infiniti.

"Um, good morning," Infiniti said with a half smile.

Addie's long brown hair was tied up in a loose bun. She eyed

120

Infiniti from over her dark-rimmed glasses. She was cool in a rocker chick kind of way with torn jeans and a healthy supply of tattoos, but also intimidating in a school principal kind of way. Infiniti wondered why she wanted to talk to her so early.

"Am I in trouble?" Infiniti asked with a nervous laugh. "Because with the way y'all are acting, it kind of feels like I am."

Before the mother-daughter duo could respond, the doorbell rang.

"Pretty sure that's Joe," Infiniti offered, relieved for him to be there because something was definitely up.

Addie eyed Lyra. "Guess he should hear this too."

"Yes," Lyra agreed. "It's good timing." She went to the door while Addie followed. Infiniti trailed behind, not wanting to miss anything.

"Um, good morning, Lyra," Joe said with a cocked brow when he saw the three of them at the door. He nodded toward Addie. "Good morning, Addie." He held up a tray wrapped in foil. "I've got some fritule from my mom. Enough for everyone."

Lyra took the tray. "Thank you, Joe. That's very kind of you and your mother. Why don't you come on inside? You're just in time for a special announcement from Addie."

Joe took Infiniti's hand and squeezed, tossing her a *what's going on* look. All she could do was shrug a little as they walked back to the living room and sat on the couch, because she was clueless.

Addie crossed her arms. She let a few seconds pass before she said, "We know it's you, Infiniti."

Tingles shot across Infiniti's skin while her mind scrambled for any clue to what Addie was talking about. "Huh?"

Lyra cut in. "But we also know you're not doing it on purpose."

Joe released Infiniti's hand and rose to his feet. "Hold on a second here. What are you talking about?"

Addie kept her focus on Infiniti. "Every night since Infiniti's arrival there have been space and time anomalies in the town."

Infiniti had been sitting, but stood up and joined Joe. Fear raced across her spine along with the realization that Addie was telling the truth. She had no idea what a space and time anomaly was, but she knew that whatever it was was connected to her because she'd been having crazy weird dreams since arriving and always woke up so drained.

Addie edged closer to Infiniti. "You know what I'm talking about, don't you?"

"Of course she doesn't," Joe asserted.

Infiniti took Joe's hand. She looked up at him. "I haven't been sleeping well since I got here, but I thought it was because of everything I'd been through." She turned her attention to Addie. "But I haven't been doing any space time whatever you said."

Addie's face softened. "You don't know that you have, but it's true. We've traced it to you."

Infiniti looked from Addie, to Lyra, to Joe, and then back to Addie. She was trying to process everything when Joe uttered, "Are you saying Infiniti has powers?"

Infiniti whipped her head in Joe's direction. Her mouth fell open. "Powers?"

"Yes," Addie answered. "That's exactly what we're saying."

"Probably from all of the time travel," Lyra added.

Addie nodded. "You need to learn about what you can do, as well as anything else that might have changed about you. Time travel is some freaky shit. And normally, we send young people who are awakening to their powers to night classes at the Sun and Moon Academy. But you're kind of old for that, and well, the timing just happens to work in your favor . . . anyway, the Court and I have come up with another idea." She narrowed her gaze on Infiniti and cocked her head. "If you can prove yourself."

Joe pulled Infiniti a little closer to him. An excited expression spread across his face.

"Addie, are you talking about SMA's College of Supernatural Guardians? Are you inviting Infiniti to test?"

"I sure am. The school has filled most of the spots for its inaugural class, but there's room for two more."

"*If* you can prove yourselves, that is," Lyra added.

Infiniti struggled to make sense of the information. "Wait a second. I'm not following."

Addie motioned to Joe so he could explain.

"It's a new college in town for supernaturals, but everyone who attends has to go through a series of trials. I was invited to test but turned it down because all I could do was focus on finding you. But now you're here, and you've got powers. So it appears we can both be tested now."

"Whoa," Infiniti whispered, hardly believing her ears. She had some sort of powers and could attend a college with Joe that had the words Supernatural Guardians in the name. She only had to pass a test or two first.

"Well, what do you say, Infiniti?" Addie asked. "It's either that or night classes at the Academy with the high schoolers. Your choice. But you have to decide quick, because the semester starts this month."

Excitement edged out Infiniti's nervousness as she thought of her favorite wizard movie where the students lived in a cool castle-like campus and had all kinds of magical adventures. She was totally down for something like that, especially if she could be with the guy she loved.

She smiled big at Joe, matching his emotions, and then faced Addie.

"I say sign me up."

We hope you enjoyed this story in the Havenwood Falls High series of novellas featuring a variety of supernatural creatures. If you loved this story, you can read more about Joe and Infiniti in *Sun & Moon Academy Book One: Fall Semester.*

ABOUT THE AUTHOR

Rose Garcia is the author of the critically acclaimed Final Life Series. The saga features gut-wrenching emotional turmoil and heart-stopping action with a diverse and dynamic cast. A lawyer turned writer, Rose has always been intrigued by science fiction and fantasy. More recently, she's been fascinated by a blend of science fiction and reality and the idea that some supernatural events are very real. Just ask her about the ghost she used to share a house with. Rose lives in Houston with her husband, two kids, and two dogs. Luckily, there are no ghosts in her current home. (That she knows of!) For information on Rose's releases and appearances, sign up for her newsletter at www.RoseGarciaBooks.com/newsletter. You can learn more about Rose at www.rosegarciabooks.com.

ACKNOWLEDGMENTS

WOW! My second installment in the Havenwood Falls High series has been born, and I have a ton of people to thank! First and foremost, I want to thank Kristie Cook, the amazing visionary, creator, and publisher of Havenwood Falls. I consider myself blessed that she invited me to bring my characters Infiniti and Fleet from the Final Life Series to her supernatural town. It's been a wild ride, and I look forward to cranking out many more stories with her phenomenal team!

To all the Havenwood Falls authors who helped me breathe life into my story: Kallie Ross who shared many of her characters with me including Joseph Greg and his family, Sheriff Ric and Kase of the Kasun pack, and Rose Howe; Justine Winter who let me set the deadly duo of reaper Shade StormIron and Death on Infiniti's heels; SF Benson who helped me SO much with my Death scenes; E.J. Fechenda who created Dr. Underwood; and Kristie Cook who created Lyra Beaumont. I have a super cool Court of the Sun and the Moon scene which includes Kristie Cook's Addie Beaumont and Saundra Beaumont; Morgan Wylie's Lilith Blackstone and Mathilde Augustine; Amy Hale's Lawrence Mills; Randi Cooley Wilson's Roman Bishop; E.J. Fechenda's Elsmed Fairchild, and T.V. Hahn's Barbie Stuart and Teeny Weeny Tahini. I loved writing this scene so much!

A huge thanks to Regina Wamba for my gorgeous cover and Liz Ferry for her eagle eye editing! And, of course, to my awesome publicist Amber Garcia.

And last, but not least, to my amazing beta readers and

critique partners who've been a part of my writing journey for many years: Heather Elliot, Jessica Ramirez, Olivia Moriarty, and Wade Moriarty. You guys ROCK!

But all the thanks really go to my amazing readers. Especially those in my FB reader group, Rose's Rebels. Thank you for your support, friendship, and encouragement! I hope you enjoyed *Finding Infiniti*!

UNICORN'S LAMENT

MEGAN LINSKI

HAVENWOOD FALLS HIGH

Unicorn's Lament

USA Today Bestselling Author

MEGAN LINSKI

~ A Havenwood Falls Young Adult Novella ~

BOOKS BY MEGAN LINSKI

The Fire Prophecy (Academy of Magical Creatures Book #1) – Co-written
with Alicia Rades

The Water Legacy (Academy of Magical Creatures Book #2) – Co-written
with Alicia Rades

The Earth Legend (Academy of Magical Creatures Book #3) – Co-written
with Alicia Rades

The Air Omen (Academy of Magical Creatures Book #4) – Co-written
with Alicia Rades

The Wolven Mark (University of Sorcery Book #1)

Kingdom From Ashes (The Kingdom Saga Book #1)

Fallen From Ashes (The Kingdom Saga Book #2)

Redemption From Ashes (The Kingdom Saga Book #3)

Prince of Fire (The Kingdom Saga Book #4)

Dawn From Embers (The Kingdom Saga Book #5)

Blessings From Ashes (A Kingdom Saga Novella)

Court of Vampires (The Shifter Prophecy Book #1)

Den of Wolves (The Shifter Prophecy Book #2)

War of Witches (The Shifter Prophecy Book #3)

Heir to Russia (The Shifter Prophecy Book #4)

Torrent (Angels & Demons Book #1)

Torture (Angels & Demons Book #2)

Truth (Angels & Demons Book #3)

Song of Smoke and Fire (Song of Dragonfire Book #1)

Change of Wind and Storms (Song of Dragonfire Book #2)

World of Gods and Men (Song of Dragonfire Book #3)

Rhodi's Light (The Rhodi Saga Book #1)

Rhodi Rising (The Rhodi Saga Book #2)

Rhodi's Lullaby (The Rhodi Saga Book #3)

Kiatana's Journey (Creatures of the Lands Book #1) – Co-written with Krisen Lison

Vera's Song (Creatures of the Lands Book #2) – Co-written with Krisen Lison

Wyntier's Rise (Creatures of the Lands Book #3) – Co-written with Krisen Lison

Vixen's Fate (Creatures of the Lands Book #4) – Co-written with Krisen Lison

Midnightstar (Creatures of the Lands Book #5) – Co-written with Krisen Lison

Angel's Rebellion (Creatures of the Lands Book #6) – Co-written with Krisen Lison

Breathless (Twisted Fairy Tales Shared Series Book #1)

Alora (Standalone)

These Starcrossed Lives of Ours (Standalone)

Sign of the Griffin (Standalone)

Eerie Tales (A Short Story Collection)

Webs & Roses (A Poetry Collection)

Anything But (Razberry Sweet Book #1)

Save Me (Razberry Sweet Book #2)

This novel is dedicated to all the unicorns out there—the people who society thinks are different, but really, they just shine brighter than all the others.

CHAPTER 1

The same dream haunted me every night.

I followed the silver unicorn through the gray, misty forest. I never got quite close enough to see many details, but I knew he was a stallion—he had huge muscles and stood at a height that would tower over me, if I dared to get near. His coat was shinier than the edge of a sharpened knife, and his rippling mane and tail went past his knees.

But the most incredible thing about him was the golden horn that stuck out of the middle of his forehead. It shimmered and sparkled, even in the cloudy day, and seemed to gleam when he looked toward me.

I chased the stallion through the woods. But though I ran as fast as I could, winding through trees and ducking branches, the unicorn was always faster. Just as I was about to reach out and pet his coat, he raced off into the trees and vanished.

Then I woke up.

I started upright in bed. My chest heaved as if I'd been running. I took a few deep breaths and tried to steady myself.

Just another dream, Thea. It's not real.

I hated that it wasn't real. Something about that unicorn made me feel empty inside without him.

But unicorns weren't real, and neither were dreams. Shaking off how vivid it felt, I stumbled out of bed and forced myself to take a cold shower, allowing the water to roll down my back, trying to wake myself up.

I couldn't. Even though I tried, the dream followed me around all day.

Havenwood Village was a nice apartment complex—certainly the best I'd ever lived in. I liked that I had my own bathroom. My mom had landed a good job at the Havenwood Falls Medical Center, and for the first time in a long while, we were doing fine.

First time since the fire, I guess.

I threw my white-blond hair up into a ponytail, slipping on a pair of jeans and a racerback top. I longed to grab the pink dress and sparkly heels in the corner of my closet and change into that instead, but I reminded myself that wasn't who I was anymore.

Ambrosia was already at the stove in the kitchen, making pancakes.

"How did you sleep, honey?" she asked as I sat at the table, placing a stack of pancakes in front of me. They were topped with raspberries, whipped cream, and sprinkles, just how I liked them.

"Fine, Ambrosia," I lied. My mother never wanted me to call her Mom, just always by her first name. It'd been like that since I was a little girl. It was a little weird to some people, but I was used to it.

She noticed the bags under my eyes and said, "You should be sleeping in. School will start pretty soon, and you won't be able to."

"I know." It was early August. My eighteenth birthday was thirty days away, at the end of the month. I'd be starting my senior year at Havenwood Falls High soon.

I hated starting a new school this close to graduation, but at the same time, Havenwood Falls High couldn't possibly be worse than Desmona Prep back in the Big Easy. That place had been hell on earth.

"Why don't you go to the lake later? There are plenty of people your age swimming, I'd bet. It's going to be such a nice day," Ambrosia suggested.

"I'm not one much for friends." I liked to keep to myself. I shoveled my pancakes into my mouth and enjoyed every bite of them. Yep. Solitude and food. Peace, quiet, and sweets were all a girl needed.

"You know," Ambrosia started, and she sat down on the other side of the table to eat her own pancakes, "I heard there's a riding stable nearby."

That piqued my interest. "Really?"

"Yep. Trains jumpers." She reached around to the drawers behind her, pulled open one of them, and handed me a brochure. I read it quickly.

Havenwood Stables. Looked like a fancy place, the kind where Olympians would train. I hadn't ridden a horse since I'd left Desmona Prep. I was dying to get back on one again. "How much do they charge?"

"What if I told you I already paid for a full semester's worth of lessons?" Ambrosia held her mug of coffee and smiled.

"No freaking way!" I shouted. "Ambrosia, you're the best!"

I got up and hugged her. It only took a few minutes for me to rush back into my room, change into a pair of breeches and knee-high boots, and grab my riding helmet.

"It's close enough you can walk," Ambrosia said. She got out a map of the town, took a red marker, and drew a path before she handed it to me.

I grabbed it and headed for the door. I was practically running to get there.

"Stick to the main road," Ambrosia warned me. She sounded serious about it. "Don't go into the woods. I mean it."

"Yes, Ambrosia." I hurried outside. It was still early morning, and a bit chilly out. I should've grabbed a jacket. I shivered, hoping the temperature would get back up to the forecasted seventy-five quick. The climate was way different here than it was in Louisiana. I was used to frying out there. Here I'd have to deal with snow, something I'd hardly seen before. I was a bit nauseated from the high altitude, though it was beginning to subside now that I was up and moving.

As I walked, I took in the sights of my new home. It was small, but Havenwood Falls was a nice place. Idyllic. Charming, even. But it was more than a little weird. The vibe that came off of it was . . . odd. It was nothing like New Orleans, which I missed, but not enough to want to go back.

I thought it wasn't a quiet town, either. I'd only been living here a few days, but just from walking around the area, I got the sense that every resident here had some kind of secret to hide.

I looked at the map Ambrosia had drawn. The stables were to the west, just outside of town. I could stick to the main road, as she said, and get there most likely in a half hour or so.

But it looked like there was a shortcut I could take—near the woods by the Mathews River. It seemed like rough terrain, but I bet it'd cut my walk time in half.

I was never very good at following the rules, so I left the sidewalk and veered into the trees, crossing over a creek by way of a small homemade bridge someone had built. I had a good sense of direction and could tell which way was west, so I kept walking that way, figuring I'd hit the horse stables sooner or later.

It didn't take me long to realize that I was lost. But I didn't mind it. I liked wandering. There's something nice about feeling like you are the only person in the world. I enjoyed my walk through the greenery, taking in the smells of fresh morning dew on the pine trees and listening to the birds chirping.

Then I heard something—the crack of a branch.

I whirled around. My eyes went wide when I saw what was standing above me.

On an embankment overhead stood a horse—but it wasn't a horse at all. It was the unicorn. Even more, it was *my* unicorn, and he was real. He stood proudly, his head held high and his ears pointing toward me. His silver coat shone in a halo of light the sun had formed around him, and his golden horn glistened, just like it did in my dream. His nostrils flared as he observed me, taking me in.

I took a step forward. But as soon as I moved, the unicorn took off and disappeared into the trees.

I stood there frozen for a few seconds, struggling to comprehend what had just happened. Yeah. Havenwood Falls was definitely different.

CHAPTER 2

I came out of the woods and ended up staring at a large commercial barn surrounded by paddocks. I could smell horses from here. The pastures were filled with all kinds of horses, of all breeds.

The barn was red in color and probably the biggest I'd ever seen. It was surprising that such a small town had such a huge training arena. I walked up the gravel road and looked to my right.

There was already a rider in the outdoor training arena, warming up. She rode a large Thoroughbred gelding and was sailing over jumps that had been set up in a pattern around the arena.

She was the most beautiful girl I'd ever seen. I had to stop in my tracks and watch her for a minute as she and her horse flew effortlessly over the jumps. Her hair was long and blond, darker than mine, and was in a ponytail under her helmet. Her skin was pale—looked fragile, even—and roses dotted her cheeks.

Her eyes . . . Something about her eyes was different. They were large and blue, and sparkled every time her horse took a leap of faith.

After she was done with the course, she stopped her horse for a moment and smiled at me. The expression made my stomach do flip-flops.

I was lame, so I more or less stood there frozen until the rider moved her horse on. I forced myself to head inside the barn, berating myself for how stupid I probably looked. Why couldn't I have waved or something? I probably looked like some zombie or freak.

My face was bright red. I could feel it. I headed into the barn and looked for someone who was probably in charge.

There were two people inside. One was a girl around my age. She had light brown hair and was mucking a stall. The other was a tall dude, middle-aged, with dark skin, short-cropped hair, and a look that instantly told me he was a hardass. He was muscular enough that he looked like he could lift a car no sweat.

I glanced again at the brunette. Her eyes shone just like the girl outside when she spotted me. Weird.

"Hi," I said. "My mother signed me up for riding lessons here. I'm looking for the person to talk to?"

The man turned my way. His expression seemed cold, distant. He barely moved as he raised an eyebrow and said, "And you are?"

"Uh . . ." What a rude way to start a conversation with someone. "The name on the list should be Aramanthe Amorea. Thea for short," I said.

His face changed when I said my name, but only slightly. A semblance of shock crossed over it before it quickly righted itself again, and he said, "We've been waiting for you. I'm the head instructor here at Havenwood Stables. You may call me Avalar."

"Oh." This guy had such a formal way of speaking. It was awkward. "Okay. So when should I come back for my first lesson?"

"You may start today," Avalar replied. "A group lesson will begin in about fifteen minutes. You're required to attend at least three before you move on to private lessons—to make sure you're serious."

He turned and waved his hand behind him as an indication

for me to follow. I certainly wouldn't get a warm welcome from him. He stopped next to the stall where the girl was.

"This is Ransom," Avalar said, gesturing to a gray Arabian gelding. "He'll be your mount for the time you are here."

"I prefer mares, actually," I said.

"Well, this should be a good challenge for you, then." Avalar said. His tone was harsh and rude.

I decided I hated the guy. Avalar was definitely a jerk. *He* was gonna be my jumping coach? Swell.

Avalar looked to the girl next to me. "Novah, can you help Thea tack up?"

"Sure thing!" Novah said brightly. Her smile was huge. She was the complete opposite of Avalar.

"Class will begin on time. Hurry along to make sure you're not left behind." That was all the goodbye he gave me before Avalar stalked off. I was left standing behind, wondering if it had been a good decision for Ambrosia to prepay for all of my lessons here.

"Don't worry about Avalar," Novah said, noticing my stricken expression. "He's a pain to get along with, but he'll lighten up once he gets used to you."

"I hope so," I mumbled under my breath. Something about the guy was just . . . off.

"Come on. I'll show you around." Novah led me to the tack room, where she helped me saddle up and put a bridle on Ransom. He was strong and high-spirited, which became apparent when I tried to put the bit in his mouth. He was going to be fun to ride, I bet.

"You been riding long?" Novah asked brightly. She led her horse out into the hallway, a fat quarter horse mare, to wait for me.

"Practically all my life," I responded. Ransom tried to headbutt me, and I had to push him away.

"Me too," Novah said. "Sera and I are both like that. It's so nice to meet new friends with the same interests as you."

Sera . . . "Was she the one practicing on the Thoroughbred earlier?"

"Yep." Novah said it like she was proud. "She's amazing, isn't she? I love watching her ride. She has a way with horses, but—" Novah giggled. "I think you and I can both say that we do, too."

This girl didn't even know me, but she acted like we were already best friends for life. Novah talked all the way out to the paddock, where Avalar was already instructing Sera. I didn't say much. I'd learned at Desmona Prep to keep my head down and stay in my lane.

Not that Novah needed any responses from me. She was the kind of girl who loved to talk.

When we got to the mounting block, I swung myself up onto Ransom and joined the lesson, taking a few warm-up trots and canters around the arena, watching Sera perform her jumps. Avalar noticed me immediately.

"Thea," he said. "I'd like to see what you can do. Take the course and try to copy Sera."

I took a look at the poles. They were set at a height that I'd jumped before, but never on a new horse and never after such a long span between rides. I'd hardly been on a horse all summer due to the move. It was clear that Avalar wasn't letting me off easy.

But I wasn't one to back down from a challenge. "Sure."

I urged Ransom into a canter, and set my sights on the first jump. Novah fell to the side, chatting with Sera, while Sera herself watched me with interest. I definitely felt the pressure.

I pictured myself sailing over the first jump. I steadied myself, and Ransom eagerly took it. I felt a thrill go through my body, entering through my stomach, as we crossed over it with ease. We took the next jump just as easily, and the next, too. My brain went numb with the thrill of it as we neared the end of the course. I was going to do a perfect practice round, on my first time!

Then my eyes glanced over to Sera, and I noticed her whispering to Novah. Was she saying something about me? I lost concentration, and the next jump came up too quick.

I misdirected Ransom. True to the Arabian he was, he slid to a stop before the jump and bucked, sending me flying off. I went hurtling through the air and crashed into the poles, destroying the jump completely.

"Thea!" I heard Novah call. "Are you okay?"

My head was spinning, but all my limbs were intact. Slowly, I got to my feet. "Yeah. Yeah, I'm okay."

Avalar expressed no sense of concern. "A fair attempt," he said. "Though clearly nothing special."

What was it with this guy? It's like he had something personal against me. I dusted off the dirt, grabbed Ransom's reins, and got back up on him, to show Avalar that I wasn't done.

Avalar was already reconstructing the jump. "Novah. You're up next."

Novah moved forward. I walked Ransom to the side of the arena with my head held down, not daring to look up at Sera. Great. I'd totally fallen on my ass in front of a really cute girl. She probably thought I was some amateur who'd never ridden a horse in my life.

A few minutes passed, and I smelled the scent of some sort of flowery perfume—an expensive one, like Versace or Coach. I didn't know anyone who wore perfume to the barn. I heard hoofbeats beside me, and looked up to see Sera beside me on her Thoroughbred.

"You shouldn't be embarrassed. I've fallen hundreds of times on these jumps," she said. "It's the first time I've seen a newcomer finish them so well."

Even her voice sounded beautiful—like musical wind chimes, or some celebrity singing your favorite song. My mouth went dry, and my mind went blank. *Say something!* my mind screamed, but I was too shy.

She seemed to notice that I wasn't going to say anything, and said, "I'm Sera. I've been here for a while. Did you just move to Havenwood Falls?"

I woke up then, and said, "Yeah, a few days ago. I'm still trying to get the hang of things around here."

"Novah and I will show you around later. This place is amazing. You'll see why." She winked at me, and butterflies danced inside my stomach.

We didn't get much time to talk after that, because Avalar started pushing us hard during the practice. We did lots of drills, and so many exercises that my muscles started to ache and I was sweating pretty badly. It no longer felt cool out. But I liked it. I could feel my skills getting better and better the longer the practice went on.

As much as I couldn't stand him, Avalar knew a lot about jumping and horses. He'd make sure I stayed focused and disciplined. He was the kind of coach that I needed to have if I wanted to make the Olympics someday.

Which sucked, because our personalities totally clashed.

"That's enough for today," Avalar said around noon. "We'll pick this up next session. You are dismissed."

I'd never had an instructor end a lesson like a military drill. Avalar ran a tight ship. The three of us walked to cool the horses off, then untacked them in the stables.

I listened to Novah and Sera chat about an album some singer had dropped while I brushed Ransom down. I'd grown to like Ransom during our lesson. He was headstrong, but fun to ride.

"You hungry, Thea?" Sera peeked her head around the stall door. "There's this amazing burger place in town that has the best shakes. It would be a great way to start off your tour of Havenwood Falls."

"Um . . ." I didn't know what to say. I hadn't been asked to hang with anyone in forever.

I decided to take a leap of faith. It wasn't a date, anyhow.

"Sure. I'll come." I gestured to my clothes. "Though I'm not exactly dressed for it." I was covered in dirt and horse slime from the ride.

"We can go to my house. It's not far. I'll lend you some

things." Sera flashed me another brilliant smile, and my heart skipped a beat.

There was the sound of boots, and I glanced up. A tall guy with brown hair and freckles was leaning against Novah's stall. He looked like he was a senior in high school, like me. I didn't pay much attention to him while I finished with Ransom. Boys were okay, but I wasn't into them.

Novah, though. She had guy crazy written all over her, and it showed. "Hey, Jas." She twirled a strand of hair around her finger. "How are you doing?"

He leaned against a stall door and gave her a smile that probably made her knees go weak. "Just fine, Novah Bell."

He reached out to tweak her nose, and she giggled.

"I was thinking you girls would like to come out to the lake," Jas said. "Big party going on there tonight."

"Not today, Jas," Sera said. "Today's a girls' day."

Her words seemed to carry a heavier meaning. His face became serious, and Jas said, "Right. Catch you girls later."

Jas walked away, and my eyes followed him as he left. What the heck. Did everything in this town seem to be one big teen movie?

Novah sighed. "That party sounds like fun. I bet Jas looks so hot in his swim trunks. I'm totally gonna miss out on that bod."

"Later, Novah." Sera's words seemed fierce. Then she looked at me, and her tone lightened again. "Come on. Let's get you changed. I'm starving."

Sera took me back to her car—a light blue turquoise truck that was probably older than most grandpas. It was vintage, and totally cool. She drove us a mile or so up the road to a big house up one of the mountains, one with a couple of fancy cars in the driveway.

I texted Ambrosia to tell her where I was, and the response I got from her was thrilled. She was happy I was making new friends already. I didn't have any, not for all the time I went to Desmona Prep.

I was impressed when we walked inside. Sera's house had

marble floors and chandeliers, with a staircase that wrapped upward in a spiral. I was wary about meeting parents, but I didn't see any.

Sera's room was bigger than my entire apartment. And it looked like the color turquoise blue had gone wild in here. It was everywhere, from the paint on the walls to the dresser to the fluffy throw pillows. Dozens of stuffed animals, most of them horses, were strewn on the bed and in piles beside girly magazines and makeup.

Sera's room looked like the sort you'd find in a teen movie, or in an interior decorating magazine. I was sort of jealous, before I thought a girl as pretty as her deserved it.

Sera instantly began rifling through her giant closet, which contained more blues. "Now, where is it . . ."

She finally pulled out a pink romper, one that was decorated with flowers, and jeweled sandals. "Here. Put these on."

"No, I—" I hadn't worn something that girly since . . . When was the last time I worn something girly, anyhow? I don't even think I'd worn anything with a flower on it in months.

"Please? You'll look amazing in it," Sera begged, her eyes large and pleading.

I couldn't really say no to her. I grabbed it, but hesitated. It didn't bother me to change in front of Novah, but Sera was a different story.

She seemed to notice my discomfort and turned around, busying herself by going to the bathroom. Novah kept going on and on about Jas while I changed.

"Do you think Jas will like this one, or this one?" Novah slipped on a pair of shorts and yanked off her shirt. She stood in her bra while she held up two different shirts, light green in color, asking for my opinion.

"No idea. I just met him," I said. I'd just met these girls, too, but it didn't look like it mattered. They'd adopted me, apparently.

"I'll go with this one. It makes my boobs look good," Novah said before she slipped it on.

When Sera returned, she was wearing a long blue sundress that amplified her curves. Sera let out a squeal when she saw me. "OMG! It looks amazing on you!"

"Does it?" I didn't know.

"Yes. You have such an amazing body," Sera said. She ran her hands up and down my arms, and I felt goosebumps rise there.

Novah and Sera weren't content to let us leave until they had done my makeup and curled my hair. When they finally nestled a jeweled headband between my curls, one that had a bow, I looked in the mirror and hardly recognized myself. I felt more like myself than I had in ages.

Sera spritzed me with some of her perfume and said, "There. You're perfect."

The compliment made me blush. We piled back in her truck, and Sera and Thea blasted the radio and sang along to country music. They had beautiful voices, I noticed, and harmonized in all the right parts. I sang along quietly under my breath, hoping they didn't realize I was off-key.

I noticed as we drove, Sera's clothes smelled like her, too. I really liked that.

When we got to the restaurant, some place called Burger Bar, amazing smells hit my nose. The three of us curled up together in one of the booths. I was worried about being the weird one, but I was happy when both Sera and Novah ordered veggie burgers and tater tots.

"We're both vegetarians," Novah explained when she saw my confused face. "Meat isn't really our thing. We don't like the taste."

"Me either," I admitted, shocked. Just how much did I have in common with these girls?

When I took the first bite of my veggie burger, I almost died. It was that heavenly. This place was the best. The other girls thought so too, because we didn't do much talking as we chowed down.

Some skater boy had sauntered up to our table. "Hey ladies," he said. "Who's the new girl in town?"

His navy-blue eyes were directly on me. Sera grimaced and said, "Thea, this is Dalton Underwood. Also known as our residential annoyance."

"So are you fitting in at Havenwood Falls?" The words seemed to have a double meaning.

"Dalton," Sera said in what seemed like a warning tone. "She doesn't know."

Didn't know? Didn't know what?

"Really? Seems like you two are hiding secrets." Dalton suppressed a laugh.

"Stick to your own kind, Dalton," Novah snapped.

Dalton grinned and added, "I get the point. I was just gonna get on out of here, anyhow. See you around, Thea."

He gave me a long stare—like he knew something about me that I didn't—before he left Burger Bar. I watched him cruise off on his skateboard from the window.

There was something . . . different about him. I wasn't sure what. I could just sense it. Like vibrations or something.

But that was weird. I pushed Dalton out of my mind and tried to focus back on my food.

"Ignore Dalton," Novah said. "He's an instigator. Likes to . . . tease us."

Like I knew what that meant. Were Sera and Novah hiding something? I wasn't sure. Maybe Dalton was just messing with me.

"You want to share my shake, Thea? I can't finish it," Sera started. She pushed it toward me and put another straw in.

I gulped, until I told myself it wasn't anything. I leaned forward and started drinking from the shake. As I did, Sera took a straw in her mouth and started drinking, too, so that our foreheads were nearly touching.

My mouth was so close to her lips. They looked so soft, wrapped around that straw. As I was drinking, I couldn't help but get sucked into her eyes again. Damn. This was a really good milkshake.

"Thea and Sera alert," Novah said, waving her hand and snapping us both out of it. "What are we doing after this?"

Sera pulled away from the milkshake and said, "I figured we could go to Callie's Consignments and look for new dresses."

"Finally," Novah said, exasperated. "I need a new wardrobe. I don't think the clothes I've been wearing have caught Jas's eye."

"You don't need to look nice to get a boy to like you. Just be yourself," I suggested.

Novah scoffed. "Believe me, honey, I've tried. But Jas doesn't have very much going on up there, and he doesn't even notice me unless I got these puppies out."

She grabbed her boobs. Sera fell on the table laughing, and I allowed myself to join in. These girls were kinda fun.

"That's not true." Sera wiped her eyes and looked at Novah. "Jas likes you, Novah. I know it."

"Well, at any rate, a new dress won't hurt," Novah insisted. She practically sprung up from the booth. "Come on, girls. I need to strengthen the artillery."

At the consignment shop, neither Sera nor Novah tried anything on unless it was blue, green, or so ridiculously feminine that its girliness punched you in the face. I mostly stayed on the sidelines and commented on their outfits as they tried on dress after dress.

Novah tried on some outfits that . . . uh . . . *endorsed* what she had to offer, while Sera remained pretty conservative. But whatever she tried on, I thought she looked great in everything. Even some weird old dress from the seventies that looked like drapery, had shoulder pads, and smelled like mothballs.

We weren't the only people taking up the dressing room. Some girl that looked like freaking Taylor Swift was ordering around her boyfriend as she tried on dress after dress, like she expected him to follow her instructions. I thought I overheard that her name was Celeste, and her boyfriend's name was Jonathan.

"Jonathan, can you please hold these?" Celeste put a ton of clothes into Jonathan's arms. I was surprised he didn't buckle under their weight. Celeste kept on piling on more clothes, until she went to the register and tried to talk the shop owner into giving her a deal. Jonathan didn't say much, just kept quiet and did as Celeste said. It was like he was trying to make himself invisible or something. For a moment, I thought he was, because I didn't see him anywhere, but I figured it was just a trick of the eyes. I felt the same weird vibrations coming off them as I did Dalton earlier.

"Thea, I think you should try this on." Sera had gone through the racks for the millionth time, and pulled out a pink dress, one that was floor length and made of satin, with a keyhole neckline. It had blue peeking out from underneath two swaths of pink fabric, decorative swirls adorning the dress.

It was daring, but I did like the outfit. It looked like a cosplay costume, or maybe a unique outfit someone had worn to prom. "Okay. I'll try it on."

In the changing room, my mind was going a million miles an hour. I really wanted to ask Sera if she liked girls, but I was too afraid.

I didn't want to get my heart broken and get turned down again, so I kept silent. I was probably fooling myself. Sera definitely had a boyfriend, and if she didn't, guys were probably lining up to take her on a date. She'd probably laugh in my face if I asked her out.

I was about ready to come out of the changing room and show the girls what I had on, but I heard whispering voices, one of which spoke my name. I shuffled around in the changing room to make it seem like I was still changing, when in reality, I was listening intently to the conversation going on outside my door.

"Thea just got here. She's not ready," Sera insisted.

"We can't keep it from her forever. We have less than a month before *she* shows up," Novah insisted. "Thea deserves to know the truth."

Sera hesitated before she said, "All right. Tonight it is."

It was hard to breathe. Who exactly was *she*, anyway? Had these girls been instructed to be my friends?

I felt offended. Of course they didn't really like me. Who'd want to be my friend, anyhow?

I stepped out of the changing room. Both girls gasped.

"Oh, Thea," Sera breathed. Her eyes ran up and down me. "It's gorgeous on you."

"You think?" I did a little twirl.

Novah nodded. "Yes. It's incredible."

I looked at the price tag. I didn't have much, but being a consignment dress, it wasn't expensive, plus it was on sale.

"Hey, Thea," Sera asked, and I looked up. "After the party at the lake, some of our friends are going to be camping out overnight. Novah and I are going. Would you like to come with, have a sleepover?"

This was my chance to get some answers about whatever they'd been talking about. "Sure. I'd love to."

"Great." Sera beamed. "Pick you up at eight."

I decided to buy the dress. Sera dropped me off at my apartment, promising to come back and pick me up tonight.

I tried to preoccupy myself until then by reading a book, but it was hard. I had a million questions. The unicorn in the woods. Avalar. Sera and Novah's strange behavior. It didn't add up.

Something weird was going on here. And I was going to find out what it was, tonight.

CHAPTER 3

*W*hen Sera came to pick me up at eight o'clock, Novah was already in the truck. It was obvious she and Sera were attached at the hip. I threw my sleeping bag and a change of clothes into the bed before I got in the cab.

I kept waiting for someone to break the ice by announcing some huge secret, but it never came. Sera and Novah kept talking about normal stuff. I waited anxiously, hoping they'd spill the beans about whatever they were hiding at any moment.

It didn't come before we arrived at the party, where a makeshift campsite had been set up by the lake. Novah and Sera got to setting up our tent, but Jas quickly stepped in.

"Let me help you with that, ladies." Jas got on with setting the tent up, but he wasn't very good at it. He kept falling on top of it and putting the poles in the wrong places. I sighed and took pity on him.

"Here, Jas." I took the stuff from him and had the tent set up within a couple of minutes. "It's seriously not that hard."

"My hero," Sera said, looking at me. I blushed again.

I looked around. It really wasn't a big party. About ten or so people, besides us. I went to grab a wine cooler, and I noticed at the table, all the food was vegetarian. No meat to be found.

Strange at a barbecue. Did Sera and Novah bring me to the Havenwood Falls Annual Vegan Picnic or something?

Parties weren't really my thing. It wasn't too long before I was bored. I had nobody to talk to, seeing as how Novah was too busy chatting with Jas to notice me, and Sera had just vanished shortly after we arrived. Where had she run off to?

I decided to try to find her. She wasn't at the party or the surrounding area, so I took a hiking trail around the lake to see if she was anywhere nearby.

No luck. I returned to the campsite feeling frustrated. By this time, it was past ten o'clock and dark. Novah was already inside our tent, putting on this gooey-looking face cream and wrapping her hair in curlers.

"I'd figure you'd be inside Jas's tent, trying to get your freak on," I teased.

"Oh, no." Novah blushed. "Jas hasn't even kissed me yet. Though I wish he would."

"Do you know where Sera is?" I peeked out of the tent one more time, just to be sure she wasn't there.

"No." Novah shook her head. "But she's fine. Trust me, she can take care of herself."

I didn't know what that meant. Was Sera some sort of tae kwon do master or something? Who knew.

I figured she'd come back when she was ready. I changed into my pajamas, then cuddled up into my sleeping bag, hoping that I'd wake up the moment Sera returned.

I woke up in the grass outside. I guessed it had to be past three a.m. by the lack of light in the woods. It felt like I'd slept for hours. I listened for the sounds of the campsite, and blearily looked around, but didn't see or hear any signs of it. I was in the middle of the woods.

I sleepwalked sometimes, but not often. Most of the time, it had been when I was little, and I always ended up in the grass. I was glad some freaking cougar hadn't found me or something. I went to stand up, to try to find the campsite again.

I yawned and walked to the river, to splash myself awake. But when I went to kneel down, I found that I couldn't. I extended my hand, only to see that my hand . . . had become a hoof.

Holy. Crap.

I startled awake when I saw my reflection in the water, for I didn't see a human, but a unicorn.

My coat. It was pink. A light pink, almost white. I had a dished nose and long ears. A sparkling white horn grew out of the center of my forehead, and a wavy mane and tail drifted in the wind behind me. A soft pinkness glowed around me, almost like . . . magic.

This was the craziest dream. But if this was a dream, it was a rad one, and I was going to enjoy every single moment of it.

I let out a whoop, but it came out as a whinny instead. I jumped over the river and galloped forward, extending my long legs.

This was a thrill. A gust of exhilaration flew through my body as I rushed forward, running as fast as I could under the light of the stars and moon. My mane and tail flew behind me, and the trees and grasses became a blur. I broke through the trees and entered into an open valley. I threw my head around happily, feeling more free than I ever had in my life. The feeling that was running through me was so strong and powerful it would've brought tears to my eyes, if I had the ability to cry. I just felt so . . . triumphant and powerful and strong.

I noticed that two unicorn mares came up beside me, one on each side. They were slower than I was and drifted behind me. They wanted to run with me. I nickered a welcome and charged forward.

"Thea, slow down! You're going to go over the border," a familiar voice in my head shouted.

That voice stopped me in my tracks. I skidded to a halt, panting and heaving. I'd been running for a while.

The other unicorns stopped beside me. I had the chance to get a good look at them. The first mare was green and had a horn that curled and spiraled instead of one that was straight. Her mane and tail hung like moss and vines from trees.

The second unicorn was gorgeous. Her coat was a turquoise blue, and she had a horn that seemed to be made of diamonds. Her mane and tail rippled like waves as she dared to step closer. I couldn't take my eyes off of her.

"What do you mean?" The question came out in my head, but it seemed like the other unicorns could hear me.

"We're within the ward. We're safe here, but not if you cross it, which you're about to do," another voice in my head responded. It also sounded familiar. It seemed like it was coming from the green mare.

"What's a ward?" It was like they were speaking Spanish. I had no idea what was going on.

"Think about your human self, Thea," the blue unicorn told me. *"Try it."*

I did. I thought about my old body, and quicker than I realized, I had changed back into a human. I was disappointed. My amazing experience as a unicorn was over that quickly.

Then, before I knew it, the two unicorn mares transformed in front of me. The green unicorn became Novah. The blue unicorn became Sera. All three of us were fully clothed, as if we hadn't been wearing horse hair and horns just a second ago.

I lost my mind. "What the hell!?"

I pinched myself in an attempt to wake up. But all I felt was pain, because this was real. I knew it was real. There was no denying it now.

"Thea, calm down." Sera held her hands out in front of her. "Everything's okay."

"You're a . . . I'm a . . ." I was at a loss for words.

"You transformed because you were in close proximity to us. Your magic could feel us nearby," Sera said. "Thea, you're like us."

"Like you?" I choked out. I could barely breathe. What was going on here?

Sera looked at Novah. "I think this is something we should talk about in private. Where others can't hear," she said. Novah nodded.

Sera headed back into the woods. "Come with us, Thea. We'll tell you everything."

CHAPTER 4

*A*pparently, whatever Sera had to say couldn't be said without a load of chocolate and junk food. We sat in a circle on Sera's bedroom floor, on a bunch of pillows and blankets, surrounded by chips, candy, and everything that was possibly bad for you at five a.m. Sera was playing soft music from a Bluetooth speaker, but it didn't help bring me back into reality. I couldn't stop imagining what it had felt like to gallop—actually *gallop*—through the fields near Havenwood Falls.

"I'm still waiting to wake up from this dream," I said. Novah had ripped into the Cheetos and chocolates and was eating both at once, completely unconcerned.

Sera, though, looked nervous. "You're not going to wake up. Magic is real. You experienced that today."

If she had told me that a few hours earlier, I would have thought she was crazy. But a few hours earlier, I didn't know I could grow hooves, either.

"Fine," I said. "I'm open-minded. I can believe in magic." I paused. "But I don't really understand. What am I? And what are you?"

Sera took a deep breath. "I know this might be hard to

understand, but you and I, we're different from other people. You're a unicorn shifter, Thea."

"And not just any unicorn shifter," Novah said. "You're a unicorn shifter *princess*."

"Yes," Sera started. "Like us."

I stared at them for a minute. Then I burst out laughing.

"Me? Royalty?" I wiped tears away from my eyes. My gut hurt, and I had trouble breathing. Being able to transform into a unicorn, I could believe. But a princess? No way.

"It's true," Sera said indignantly. "You're the third member of the Equestriad."

"The what?" I was seriously having a hard time comprehending this stuff. "Is this what Dalton was talking about at the Burger Bar?"

"Kind of. He knows what you are. He was picking on you. He's a fae," Sera said.

"A fae? Like a faerie?" My head was spinning.

"You need to start from the beginning," Novah said with a full mouth. Sera rolled her eyes and sighed.

"First, Havenwood Falls," Sera began. "It's not like any normal town. There are all kinds of shifters here. Wolves, kelpies, bears, dragons, the list goes on. And they're not the only supernatural beings. Vampires, witches, angels—they're all here, living amongst humans in secret."

I didn't want to believe it, but my gut told me it was true. This town was just too freaky for all this shit not to be real. "Okay. Go on."

Sera played with her hair. It was seriously distracting me from the conversation. "Havenwood Falls is run by the Court of the Sun and the Moon. They protect the supernatural races here and see that our secrets are protected. Most supernaturals know about each other in Havenwood Falls, but our herd is supposed to be a secret."

"Why?" I said, baffled. "If there's a whole bunch of magical freaky people running around, what makes us special?"

Novah and Sera glanced at each other before Novah said, "Unicorns don't come from Earth. They come from a different realm, an alternate dimension named Faerie."

"You guys are really stretching my abilities to believe here." I crossed my arms. "I have a hard time thinking this isn't just one big joke."

"Everything we say is true, Thea. I promise," Sera insisted. "Within Faerie was a country called Etheria. It was a land where the unicorns roamed. It was ruled by the Equestriad—the three reigning princesses."

There was a bit of silence, and I said, "Something tells me that Etheria isn't around anymore. Otherwise, the unicorns wouldn't be here."

Sera flinched, and she said, "Well, you'd be right. For thousands of years, our foremothers before us ruled Etheria in peace and harmony, centuries upon centuries of Equestriads, passing the crown on from mother to daughter. Our mothers were the last to rule, but Etheria was destroyed on your first birthday, Thea."

"By whom?" My mind was blank.

The girls hesitated. "Her given name was Malestraude, but by the time she rose to power, the unicorns were so afraid of her that she became known as Malevolent. She's your mother, Thea."

A coldness started spreading throughout my body, starting in my gut and spreading throughout my limbs. "No. No way. My mother is Ambrosia. She raised me."

"Ambrosia was your nursemaid. Just as Novah and I were raised by our nursemaids, who we just recently found out aren't our mothers as well. All of them are unicorns, too," Sera said. "They stole us away to Earth and kept us safe while Malevolent destroyed Etheria. If she had found us, she would've killed us all."

"Ambrosia would have told me about this," I insisted stubbornly. "She wouldn't keep this from me."

"She didn't have a choice. She was forbidden by Avalar," Novah said.

"What the hell has Avalar got to do with it?" I snarled.

"He's the temporary leader of the unicorn herd," Novah said. Then as an afterthought, she muttered meekly, "And your dad."

"*What*?!" Take back what I said about the princess thing. I would think I was marrying the next British monarch far easier than I'd ever believe the jerk who'd taught me jumping today was my dad. He was unfeeling, distant . . . nothing like a father should be.

"It's true," Sera said. "I know he's not the best role model—"

"If he's my dad, why didn't he raise me instead of Ambrosia?" I shot back.

Sera and Novah glanced at each other once again anxiously before Novah said, "He thought you'd be safer with her. That's why he split us all up, just in case Malevolent got out somehow and came looking for us, or him. He brought us all back to Havenwood Falls just before we turned eighteen. It was crucial we all survive."

I was furious. It felt like my father had abandoned me. And he kinda had. Did he not want me? Was I not a good enough unicorn princess, or whatever?

Even worse, did I remind him of my mother? Was I anything like her?

My hands were shaking, but I needed to hear more of the story, so I said, "Fine. Go on."

Sera waited a few moments to make sure I was really calm before she continued. "Malevolent was part of the Equestriad, and ruled Etheria with our mothers, Iristadi and Gwenavera. Iristadi was my mother. Her last dying breath was used to make a portal to get the three of us out," Sera said firmly.

I was still calming down from the whole Avalar-is-my-dad thing. "Why do they all have such fancy long names?"

"All unicorns do," Sera said. "My real name is Seravihne, spelled like S-E-R-A-V-I-H-N-E—pronounced *Sara-veen*." She drew the word out, so I could remember it.

"And mine is Novahrynne," Novah said. "Isn't yours something flowery?"

"Aramanthe," I whispered. I'd always wondered why Ambrosia had given me such a strange name, but I just considered it unique. Now I realized she hadn't named me at all. Malestraude— Malevolent—did.

"Malevolent wanted power. She wanted to rule Etheria for herself, and not share it with her friends," Sera continued. "When her friends refused, Malevolent sold the most precious part of herself, her horn, to acquire dark magic, and used that power to kill Iristadi and Gwenavera. She was going to kill all of us, too, to secure her place on the throne permanently. She wanted to be immortal."

"Why would Avalar go against Malevolent if he helped her . . . uh . . . make me?" I asked, turning red.

"I'm not sure." Sera looked down and grimaced. "The way Mom—I mean, Lucindiana—tells it, Avalar fell in love with Malestraude, and was crushed when his mate went to the dark side. He was a knight sworn to the good of Etheria. His country came first. He got the three of us out, then started locating unicorns who came to Earth, trying to get them all to Havenwood Falls. He's spent years looking, but the herd is still small. There aren't very many of us left."

"Which brings us to our next point," Novah added. "Unicorn horns are extremely valuable. They contain powerful magic. Other supernaturals will hunt us down for them, and there aren't enough of us to fight back."

"How many unicorns are left?" I asked.

"Less than fifty or so in Havenwood Falls. If even that," Sera said.

"Jas is one of us, too. His real name is Jaspirion," Novah said. She batted her eyelashes and sighed. "Isn't that such a perfect name for a unicorn stallion?"

Sera snapped her fingers. "Novah, focus."

Novah snapped out of it. "Oh, right. But the Court's offer for us to stay in Havenwood Falls isn't permanent. They know we have beef with Malevolent. If we don't kick Malevolent's butt, the Court will kick us out of Havenwood Falls, and we'll be left to fend for ourselves," Novah said. "The Court doesn't want any trouble, and the unicorns are bringing it here. If we don't stop Malevolent now, the herd will be destroyed forever. She wants to destroy us all, out of revenge for refusing to bow to her rule. There will be no more unicorns left on Earth . . . left anywhere."

I felt the blood drain from my face. "What do you mean? She's coming here?"

"Yes." Sera's expression was grim. "Iristadi and Gwenavera fought against her, but lost. Before they died, they used their magic to imprison Malevolent in a cage of magic, forcing her to remain in Etheria."

"But the spell will fade when the next Equestriad in line is supposed to take power," Novah said. "That's your birthday, Thea. Sera and I are already eighteen. Once you come of age, Malevolent is coming for our asses. And it ain't gonna be pretty."

I swallowed nervously. "So what do we do?"

"We only have one option. We have to learn how to use our magic, so we can beat Malevolent for good," Sera said. "Novah and I have already started training, but there's so much we need you to learn, Thea. And we don't have a lot of time."

No shit. My birthday was less than four weeks away. I'd been looking forward to it, but now I was seriously dreading it.

"Are you telling me my birthday is gonna turn into one big boss battle showdown with my evil mom?" I asked.

"That's a really positive way to look at it!" Novah said in a bubbly way. I glared at her.

"We're not gonna let you do this on your own, Thea." Sera reached out and put a hand on top of mine. "We're in this together. No matter what happens."

I looked at her warm hand on mine. Her touch made me feel better, even if it was only for a moment.

I had no choice but to believe them. I was a unicorn shifter princess, my dad was Avalar, and my mom was a raging, pissed-off evil queen who was on a rampage for revenge.

And if I didn't stop her, she was going to destroy the unicorns. Permanently.

CHAPTER 5

I fell asleep at Sera's house and didn't wake up again until ten that morning. Sera and Novah were still asleep on the floor—we'd all passed out on the blankets sometime after the girls had explained everything to me.

Sera looked so pretty, with her blond hair spread all around her on the pillow. She looked like Sleeping Beauty. I resisted the urge to stare at her—you know, because I wasn't a creeper—before I headed downstairs and called Ambrosia to pick me up.

As I waited, doubt and questions ran through my mind. Ambrosia knew what was best for me. She'd been the greatest mom ever, for years.

I knew what Sera said was true. Ambrosia wouldn't have hid this from me if Avalar hadn't forced her to keep quiet.

A woman appeared in the kitchen next to the entranceway, where I was waiting. She had curly black hair and high cheekbones.

"Hello," she greeted. "I'm Lucindiana. I raised Sera. You must be Thea."

"I am," I said. "It's nice to meet you."

She looked nothing like Sera. I wondered how much of an effort it took for Sera to keep believing over the years that this was her mother. But then again, Ambrosia didn't look anything like me, either, and I'd kept on believing the lie.

Lucindiana hesitated before she spoke. "We wanted to tell you girls," she said. "We just weren't sure of the proper time."

I didn't know what to say, so I nodded. Ambrosia pulled up, and I got in the passenger seat. It was hard for me to look at her. I didn't say much on the way home, and neither did she.

When we got home, I sat on the couch. There was a giant stuffed unicorn there—a ragged one that I'd received for my fifth birthday. I held onto it as Ambrosia sat across from me.

She handed me a plate of cookies she had made—sugar with multicolored M&M's. They were my favorite. She had made them for me after I got kicked out of Desmona Prep, as well as every time she had bad news to deliver. I dug into them, enjoying their taste. It seemed like they were the only thing left in my life that felt normal.

Ambrosia put a hand on the couch. "So now you know," she said. "We're unicorns."

My mouth was still stuffed with cookies, so I swallowed and said, "Why didn't you tell me?"

"It wasn't my place," Ambrosia said. "Avalar has authority over me."

I would never get used to this, this life of royals and class taking place in modern-day America. "Why do you care so much about what he thinks? Why do you do what he tells you to?"

"Because he risked his life to save all of us, years ago," Ambrosia responded. "My job was to keep you safe. That was the only responsibility I had."

My mouth went dry with a cookie still in it. "So you didn't care at all. You just raised me because it was your *duty*."

"No, sweetheart." Ambrosia sat next to me and put her arm around my shoulder. "I love you. I've loved you since the moment you came into this world. No matter what happens, I'll always consider you my daughter. In my heart, I'm your real mother." Her face turned menacing. "Especially compared to that vile . . .

woman." It seemed like the nicest word she could say about my birth mother.

"Should I be afraid of her? Malevolent?" I asked.

Ambrosia's eyes flashed. "Yes, Thea. You should be, because she's very powerful." Then she shook me by the shoulders. "But don't be too afraid. Because you're stronger than she ever will be, and you have the power to beat her."

"How do you know?" I asked.

"Because each new princess that is born is passed down the powers of all the queens that have come before her," Ambrosia responded. "You were born with more magic than she has. You can defeat her."

I looked down. "I'm not so sure."

"Don't give up." Ambrosia took me gently by the chin and lifted my gaze. She brushed back my hair. "You're a princess of Etheria. It is time for you to take the crown and lead the herd. And I know you, Thea. You won't allow anyone to steal your throne, no matter who it is."

She was right. I didn't allow people to mess with me or push me around. And if the unicorns needed me . . . well, I'd be there for them. "Thanks . . . Mom."

Ambrosia's eyes were watery. She leaned forward and gave me a hug. I hugged her back and forgave her. She'd loved me and supported me in every way throughout my entire life. She really did care. It wasn't her fault that all this had happened and that she couldn't tell me who I really was.

That was Avalar's doing. And I was going to make sure he heard about it. Whatever happened, I didn't think that I could ever think of him as my dad.

Ambrosia pulled away and wiped at her eyes. "Well, I suggest you get a nap and have some lunch. You'll be meeting with Avalar soon."

"I didn't know I had a jumping lesson today," I said, confused.

"You don't. You're going to be training with your magic," Ambrosia said.

~

Around one o'clock, Ambrosia drove me in the direction of Havenwood Stables. But instead of stopping there, she took a dirt road deep into the forest and stopped the car after we'd driven for about ten minutes or so.

"Here we are," Ambrosia said. She pointed to a dirt path by my side, and said, "Follow that path until you reach a clearing. Avalar will be waiting for you. I'll come pick you up around five."

"Aren't you coming with me?" I asked.

Ambrosia shook her head and said, "I think it's best if you and Avalar spend some time alone. You should bond with your father."

Bonding with Avalar sounded weird and kind of gross. I didn't want him to come near me. He was a stranger. I knew he was technically my dad, but he'd been rude to me from the moment we met. He'd known I was his daughter, too, and still treated me with disgust, which only added insult to injury. I didn't want anything to do with him.

But for Ambrosia's sake, I sucked it up and said, "Okay. See you later."

I got out of the car. I felt very lonely as Ambrosia drove away and I was left in the woods alone.

At least it was a beautiful day. I hiked along the forest path, enjoying the butterflies and the sounds of birds that echoed through the forest. It was really bright out, and the sun bathed everything in a shade of yellow. It was a nice change from the clouds that had coated the area recently.

When the path ended, I entered into a circular clearing, just like Ambrosia had said. In the middle of that clearing was the silver unicorn.

The stallion from my dreams, I thought. Seeing him took my breath away. He snorted as he saw me, nostrils flaring.

I dared to come close. The unicorn stood where he was. I reached out and laid my hand on his head, stroking the area below his horn.

The unicorn snorted and breathed heavily. His black eyes gleamed. Then he transformed, and my hand was suspended in the air.

It was Avalar. The magic was totally over. I dropped my hand, and Avalar stared at me with a disapproving stare.

"You're late," he began.

I wasn't about to acknowledge that. I was a princess, wasn't I? I could be as late as I wanted to. He didn't order me around.

"You're the unicorn in my dreams," I said, astounded.

"Yes," Avalar responded dully. "I've used my magic to check up on you and make sure you were safe for years."

"Can unicorns travel through dreams?" I asked.

"They can," Avalar said. "Although that isn't useful for what we're trying to accomplish, so I suggest we focus your training on magic that is actually helpful in defeating Malevolent."

My mouth dropped open before I quickly shut it. I wasn't feeling the fatherly love here.

"First things first," Avalar began. "The Court has drawn us a ward around Havenwood Stables, where the unicorns may transform and stretch out their shifter sides. It circles around us by a mile or so. You are not to go outside the ward in your unicorn form. Ever. It is the only thing keeping you safe."

That's what Sera and Novah were talking about when they mentioned the border last night. "Will I fight Malevolent here?" I asked.

"We will attempt to lure her here to this clearing, so yes," Avalar responded. "I expect you to be able to defeat her."

"You aren't making me feel any less pressured to succeed," I stated.

"Good," he replied. "That will decrease the chances you will fail."

I really wanted to say something back, but nothing came to mind. He kinda had a point. If I didn't succeed, the unicorns were doomed, and probably Havenwood Falls with them. There was no room for error.

"To start your lesson, transform into a unicorn. Just imagine yourself taking shape," Avalar said. "Now that you know you can, it should be easy for you, like breathing."

I doubted that I could do it that easily. Yet when I thought about my unicorn form, I changed, and my body elongated and morphed to become the pink unicorn again.

Joy rushed through me. I was amazed I could still do it. I wanted to run around and kick my legs into the air, then rush off into a gallop again, but Avalar's harsh gaze made me stay put.

Avalar changed too, back into the silver stallion. For some reason, I felt like I could relate to him more when he was a unicorn rather than a human.

Avalar pointed his horn at the ground. He focused on a certain spot, and a flash of purple light came out of his horn. I jumped back, frightened by the noise it made. The purple light landed in the grass, forming a circle with strange runes I'd never seen before.

"Magic traps," Avalar said as he lifted his head. *"If you can lure Malevolent into one, you can hold her within it for a time. She'll be unable to move while you do your work."*

Avalar made it sound like a job, and not like I was trying to kill somebody. *"How am I supposed to off her? Stab her with my horn?"* I asked sarcastically.

"A princess doesn't speak in such vile terms," Avalar stated. *"And no. That is not how things will be done."*

Avalar was the type of guy who cared about stupid things, like what fork to use at dinner and what color the napkins were. He was so overly proper about everything.

"'Kay. So I ain't gonna do that," I said, speaking in the worst manner possible. *"What now?"*

His nose flared. I was annoying him. *"We'll begin with the magic traps for now. Focus your attention on me. Imagine binding me to the place I stand, and put all your intent into doing so. With that intent, the magic will rise up out of your horn and force me to stand in place."*

"Sounds easy enough." But it wasn't. I tried to make the magic

trap and failed. I managed to make a few purple flashes come out of my horn, but it was nothing spectacular. When I'd finally managed to make a circle on the ground around Avalar, it faded before I had the chance to really look at it. I made several more circles, but they were all gone in moments.

"Your magic is barely holding me," Avalar complained. *"You must perform the spell with force. With feeling! What you're doing now will barely contain Malevolent's hooves for a millisecond."*

"It's my first day," I replied, discouraged. *"I don't know what I'm doing. I just found out about all this!"*

"I understand time is short, but it is also of the essence," Avalar said. *"If you don't learn this magic proficiently by the time Malevolent arrives, we are most certainly done for."*

I'd had enough. I shifted back into a human and crossed my arms. Avalar changed back, and I said bluntly, "Just give it to me straight. What exactly do I have to do in order to end this thing?"

Avalar sighed. "To defeat Malevolent, you must be able to conjure the Unicorn's Lament. It is the most powerful spell known to unicornkind, and can only be performed by the Equestriad. With the spell, you, Sera, and Novah will combine your magic into one in order to take away Malevolent's magic and destroy her for good."

He then shook his head. "But Malevolent is fast, and she's deceptive. If you don't capture her in one of these magic traps and hold her in place long enough for you and your fellow princesses to perform the spell, she'll overpower all of you. You'll have to use other types of magic to wear her down before she's even weak enough to be conquered by the Lament. We will train every day, until you are ready."

This was sounding more and more impossible every minute. "If this is all so important, why didn't you bring me here to learn this stuff years ago?" I shot back at him.

"It wasn't safe. Malevolent's minions are everywhere. I had no choice," Avalar responded.

"No choice but to send me away?" I ask. "I can't believe that."

"You don't understand my motives. You're just a child," Avalar said.

"I'm not going to be a child for much longer, so tell me what to do," I said through gritted teeth.

"I cannot tell you! Only you can decide for yourself whether you are capable," Avalar said.

I curled my hands into fists. The thing was, I didn't know if I was capable of this. But I was trying my hardest, and I was fighting for a cause, and a people, that I hardly knew anything about. I was seventeen freaking years old!

"Maybe if you hadn't abandoned me as a kid, I'd be better at magic," I spat. I didn't mean to say it that way, but the words just came out.

"I didn't mean to abandon you, Thea. I can imagine why it looks that way," Avalar said.

"Looks that way? It is that way!" I shouted.

"My people—*our people*, I may remind you—come first before any personal duty to family. I have to do what's best for the herd!" Avalar roared.

"What about what's best for me? I'm your daughter!" I yelled.

I didn't wait to hear a response. I whirled around and stomped out of there before Avalar could give another condescending answer. Screw waiting for Ambrosia. I'd walk home.

I hated it, though tears burned in my eyes. I forced them to go away, though. I didn't care that I had a dad who had walked out on me, even if it was for a noble reason. I'd never needed him anyway.

I'd been just fine on my own. And if I needed to, I'd defeat Malevolent on my own.

I just didn't know how I could.

CHAPTER 6

The next day, I walked down the block to go to the gas station, because I had a craving for Cheetos. I saw Novah and Sera at the drink station, giggling and making heaven knows what.

Novah was wearing a turquoise crop top with blinged-out shorts. Sera had on a tight white shirt and a blue skirt that was big and poofy. Sera wore heels, while Novah had on high-tops. They looked like anime characters.

"What are you guys doing?" I asked, looking at the mess they had made on the counter.

"Making unicorn slurpees!" Novah said in a high-pitched, thrilled voice.

"Unicorn slurpees?" I asked, confused.

"They're the best," Novah said. "Trust me."

Novah and Sera mixed cherry and blue raspberry slushies together before they crushed up a bunch of multicolor candies, sour and sweet, pouring them into the mixture before ripping open a bag of cotton candy and placing it on top. They paid for the drinks and candy before handing one to me.

I had a bag of Cheetos in my hand, but Sera grabbed it from me and paid for it. "Here," she said. "For you."

I tried not to blush, and took a sip of the slurpee. It was packed with sugar, sour, and probably awful for you. But I loved it.

We left the gas station. Sera started by saying, "So I hope your first training session with Avalar went better than we've heard."

I shook my head, still sucking on the slurpee. I lowered my voice and looked around to make sure no one overheard us. "Nope. It was awful. I officially suck at being a unicorn."

"You don't suck," Sera said. We made our way down the street. I followed the girls, not really sure where we were going.

"I totally do." I frowned. "I couldn't even make a magic trap."

"I couldn't make a magic trap either my first day," Novah piped up. "You'll get it. Once you learn unicorn magic, it's easy to do. Unicorns are natural spellcasters."

I wasn't so sure. The girls knocked on the door of a little bungalow house and waited.

"Why are we here?" I asked, looking around.

"Every shifter is required by the Court to get a tattoo, for security purposes," Sera said. "Addie does them. She's a witch, and you're next. Ambrosia got hers yesterday."

"What!" I yelped. I was totally afraid of needles.

"We got ours." Novah showed me her tattoo, one of a horseshoe with an exploding star in the middle.

"Where'd you get yours?" I asked Sera nervously.

Sera wiggled her eyebrows. Then she pulled down the top of her skirt ever so slightly, to show a unicorn head in rainbow colors tattooed on her ass.

"Sera!" I hissed, then giggled obnoxiously. "You didn't!"

"I totally did." She grinned as she pulled up her skirt. "Where do you want yours?"

I wasn't sure. I didn't even know what to get. "Has this been paid for?"

"Avalar took care of it," Sera said. She dragged me toward the house. "Come on!"

I wondered what Avalar had as his tattoo. Probably a frowny face, or the word NO written in big red letters.

A woman opened the door. She was young, with tattoos, piercings, and ripped up jeans. She intimidated me a little.

"Hi, Addie." Sera beamed, and her smile made my heart skip. "We've brought her."

"Thea, right?" Addie asked, and I nodded. She gestured for me to come inside. "Let's get you started."

I decided on a tattoo of a galloping unicorn in color on my shoulder. It was smaller than the size of my hand. The needles didn't hurt as much as I thought they would, but I still held Novah's and Sera's hands like I was giving birth while getting it.

"I love your tattoos," I told Addie as she finished up my own ink.

Addie smiled. "Thanks. A lot of them are for decoration, and not necessarily magical purposes."

"So why do I need this tattoo, anyway?" I asked.

"Your tattoo is a part of the Registry for supernatural creatures in town," Addie explained. "The ink has magic within it. The tattoos connect with the protective wards around Havenwood Falls. Kylo Ren, get down."

Addie pushed her tuxedo cat off the table next to us and got to work cleaning my new tattoo. As a witch, Addie had four familiars, all named after Star Wars characters. I liked pets, and Addie had so many; besides Kylo Ren, she also had Chewie, a wolf, Skywalker, a raven, and Princess Leia, a miniature dragon. I thought that the dragon was the most amazing.

I kinda hated Star Wars, but I didn't tell Addie that, because I thought it would offend her, and it wouldn't be smart to piss off a witch. I was a novice unicorn, and I was pretty sure in a fight, she'd win.

When we waved goodbye to Addie, I felt more confident. For some reason, just getting a tattoo made me feel like a part of this town—not just someone who was supposed to save it.

The three of us walked back to the gas station and got into

Sera's car, and she drove us out of town. She parked near the stables. We sat in the truck bed and shared the Cheetos as I complained about Avalar.

"I just don't think I'm cut out for this, guys." I leaned against the truck and looked up at the clear blue sky. "I'm supposed to be this awesome unicorn princess that's full of power, but I can't even cast a simple spell. Plus, lately, I can't stop eating."

"Same, girl. It's stress," Novah said. A Cheeto popped out of her mouth, and I laughed.

Sera stood up in the truck bed. "The protective wards around the stables aren't far from here. Let's practice. I bet you aren't as terrible as you think."

"Girl, you're in heels and a skirt. You can't hike through the woods," Novah said skeptically.

Sera shrugged. She pulled off her heels and tossed them before jumping down into the mud, not caring if her feet got dirty. "No time like the present."

My stomach wiggled. Sera was so adventurous. I really liked that about her.

"Ugh . . . fine." Novah stood up, too, and I had no choice but to follow. We walked until we hit the boundary line for the ward, then we transformed. I followed Sera and Novah through the forest as a unicorn until we reached the same clearing I'd been practicing in with Avalar yesterday.

Sera turned toward me. *"Okay, Thea, show us what you've got."*

I tried. I attempted to make a magic trap, but all that came out of my horn was purple smoke.

"This is pointless." I stomped my hoof in frustration. I'd never get it.

"Don't give up. Try a different way," Sera offered.

"Yes. Imagine fixating a person to one spot, like glue," Novah said.

I tried again. I pointed my horn at Novah and imagined that she was stuck in a giant, sticky vat of glue. A purple shot flew out of my horn and made a circle on the ground with the strange runes again.

"*Hey! I can't move!*" Novah squealed. Sera laughed, and the sound was like jingling bells.

"*I did it!*" I cheered.

Sera danced on her hooves, like she was clapping. "*Well done! Do it again!*"

Sera and Novah were way easier to practice with than Avalar. I picked up the magic trap within ten minutes with them teaching me and had mastered it within twenty.

"*Show me more!*" I demanded. Now that Avalar wasn't around, the pressure was off, and I was actually getting excited about magic.

"*Try this. It's an offensive maneuver. Imagine focusing all your magic as a weapon, like shooting a water gun.*" Sera bowed her head, and a blue light shot out of her horn this time. It surrounded me and felt like a dozen feathers tickling against my sides.

"*Hey! That tickles!*" I laughed. Sera withdrew her horn, and the tickling went away.

"*It wouldn't tickle if I didn't want it to. It'd really hurt if I wished it,*" Sera said. "*Unicorn magic is all about your intention. If you can think it, you can do it. Watch.*"

She pointed her horn at a tree, and another blue blast came out of it. It hit the tree, and what was left behind was a large, sizzling black spot in the trunk that was still burning.

"*Woah,*" I said. I tried to copy her, and although the blast was smaller, I was still able to copy the spell. I left a tiny black burn spot in the trunk of the tree, right above Sera's.

I turned my head toward Novah instead and imagined her surrounded by bubbles. As I thought of the image in my head, bubbles began sprouting out of my horn. They surrounded Novah, hundreds of them, and she snickered as she popped them with her horn.

"*You're getting it,*" Sera encouraged, and I felt myself swell with pride. I was feeling much more confident.

"Is there any more?" I asked eagerly.

"That's all we know," Novah said. *"Avalar didn't teach us much. He wanted to wait for you."*

"Has he taught you the Unicorn's Lament?" I asked them.

Sera shook her head. *"Avalar was waiting to practice it until the three of us were together."*

That was a disappointment. I was hoping the girls could teach me, instead of Avalar. They made it fun.

"We should go back. Avalar warned us not to stretch our magic too far," Sera said.

We headed back, changing at the ward boundary. On the way back to her truck, I said, "You really seem to respect Avalar."

"He's the leader of the Etherian herd," Sera said. "At least he is for now, until the three of us take over. He's sacrificed a lot to make sure the unicorns don't go extinct."

"He's not easy to get along with," I pointed out.

"He just wants us to succeed. He has to push us. He doesn't have a choice," Sera said.

When we got back to Sera's truck, Novah was patting her face down, trying to wipe the sweat that was on her forehead with her shirt.

"Ugh. I *so* need a facial," Novah complained. She acted like she was wilting.

"Agreed. We're having a spa day, tonight," Sera said. "It's the only way to get rid of all this stress."

"Mani-pedis and veggie pizza!" Novah sang out.

"And makeovers, too," Sera said, and she looked at me. "I got a new makeup kit I've been dying to try out, Thea. I'd love to make you feel more relaxed."

"Oh, um, sure," I said. I got tongue-tied, and the words came out kind of slurred, but if Sera noticed, she didn't say anything. She just smiled at me.

Was it just me, or did her words seem to imply something more? She held my gaze, and I felt myself getting hot all over.

"I totally need this," Novah groaned, and the spell was broken as Sera tore her gaze away. "I need to vent about guys."

"You always need help with guys," Sera said.

Novah flipped her off before she added, "By the way, are we watching our show tonight?"

"The one with the ponies? Absolutely," Sera said, and Novah squealed. I was pretty sure the show they were talking about was a cartoon made for a much younger audience, but I didn't care . . . because I secretly loved it, too.

Sera and Novah acted so girly. They were always feminine, all the time. I don't think I ever saw them wear jeans. It reminded me of how I used to be, before the fire. I missed that.

But at the same time, I didn't think I could ever return to being that person—the girl I used to be. She was dead. She'd died in the flames.

Still, mani-pedis and veggie pizza sounded amazing right now. Especially since it was at Sera's house.

"I'm in," I said.

Sera wrapped her arm around my waist. "I didn't know you had a choice," she said playfully, and she shook me.

My heart stumbled as I felt her tight hold around my hips. When she touched me, it felt . . . amazing. A warmth started in my chest and spread throughout my entire body. What she'd said had more weight than she could ever know.

Nope. My feelings had been spoken for, and there was no turning back now, not even if I wanted to. I already knew I could try to make myself like someone else, and it wouldn't work. I'd only known Sera for two days, yet that was all it took. I didn't believe in love at first sight before I got to Havenwood Falls, but I did now.

When it came to Sera, there was no choice involved whatsoever.

CHAPTER 7

Two weeks passed so quickly in Havenwood Falls I didn't realize my birthday was only a few days away until I looked at the calendar.

I started school at Havenwood Falls High on August 21, along with Sera and Novah. I thought it was a normal high school, until I found that it was packed with supernaturals mixed in among the unknowing humans. The classes were pretty normal. Sera told me there was a Sun and Moon Academy for supernaturals in the town that was kept completely under wraps from the non-magical community. They offered magical classes, which I was interested in taking, but Sera told me that the three of us weren't allowed to attend until after we defeated Malevolent, as Avalar wanted all of our attention focused on the task at hand.

I wasn't surprised. Avalar ruined everything.

My favorite class was Art, which was taught by Mr. Weaver. He was a fairly young teacher who seemed enthusiastic and excited about starting a new semester. I instantly liked him, even when my painting didn't turn out quite right. He said it looked beautiful even though I was certain it looked like shit. I think it needed more glitter. At the same time, I was a unicorn, so *everything* could always use more glitter. Weaver gave me an A anyway.

At the same time, there seemed something spooky about him, but I couldn't quite put my finger on what. I wondered if he was supernatural, too, but didn't have the balls to ask.

While at lunch, I spotted a beautiful girl with a body like a supermodel. It took one look at her gold-flecked eyes to see that she was a supernatural.

I was surprised when Sera and Novah made a beeline for her and sat at her table. I didn't know what else to do, so I followed their lead.

"Thea, I'd like you to meet Miranda Saunders," Sera said as we sat down. "Havenwood Falls High's resident sassy and fearless chick." Sera leaned in and whispered under her breath, "She's a vampire."

Miranda flashed me a smile. I thought I saw a glimpse of fangs, but I could have been imagining things. "Well, hello there, Thea. The girls have told me so much about you."

"You guys have been talking about me?" I asked Sera, raising an eyebrow.

"Only like, a bit," Novah confessed. I rolled my eyes.

Miranda dropped her voice to a whisper and leaned in. "Don't worry about me, little unicorn. I don't bite." She laughed. "Much. I'm a bit of a *unicorn*, too. One of a kind."

She winked at me, and I didn't quite get what she meant. But whatever. It seemed like the more secrets you uncovered in this town, the more you had to discover.

"Miranda's great," Sera said. "You want to know the latest fashion, you go to her."

"Yeah, when she's not drooling over Kai Reynolds," Novah teased. Miranda reached across the table and smacked Novah on the shoulder.

I noticed a designer purse sitting on the table in front of Miranda that I was dying to have. The girl had a great sense of style. I wanted to raid her closet *so* badly.

"Fan of labels?" Miranda asked me, wiggling her eyebrows.

"Yes," I confessed. "Though I don't really have the extra cash to spend." I blushed.

"We'll go shopping sometime," Miranda said. "I know how to get some great deals."

I relaxed. For a vampire, Miranda was actually pretty nice. Havenwood Falls High was a lot more welcoming than most of the other schools I'd been to. Especially the last one. I had a feeling I'd fit right in here.

Despite us having to go to school, Avalar trained us every day. Thankfully, he'd moved on to group sessions, training all of us at once as opposed to working with me one-on-one. I was better with the girls around, but I still couldn't seem to conquer my powers unless Avalar wasn't there and either Sera or Novah were teaching me. I felt too pressured to succeed when Avalar was watching me, and I couldn't take the disappointed look in his eyes every time I failed to perform a spell. Clearly, I wasn't the daughter he'd been hoping for.

We didn't get a lot of time to ride horses, which made me kinda grumpy. The few rides we got were scattered here and there around our training, and Avalar limited our time with the horses because he wanted us to focus on beating Malevolent.

I personally thought riding would help me de-stress about the whole thing and make my magic better, but I didn't speak up, mostly because I was too afraid to. Voicing my opinion had been beaten out of me at Desmona Prep, and it was a habit I found hard to break.

Still, it was nice the few chances we did get to ride. Like on the Saturday before my birthday, which was August 31.

"Can you believe we're going to be facing Malevolent a week from today?" Novah asked. Her usual cheery tone was there, but it was tainted with a bit of fear. She, Sera, and I had snuck the horses out of the stables and were riding them in the farthest pasture from the barn, where hopefully Avalar wouldn't see. Novah and I were watching Sera fly over the jumps while we waited for our turns.

"It doesn't feel real," I responded. I kept my eyes on Sera as she sailed over the jumps. As long as I kept my eyes on her, I was calm.

"It doesn't." Novah shook her head. "Are you nervous?"

I nodded. "I'm not really afraid of Malevolent, though."

And I wasn't. She was scary to think about, in a way, but I wasn't terrified of her. I didn't know if that was because I was foolish, or because I didn't know what I was truly up against.

"Really?" Novah was surprised. "Then what are you afraid of?"

I didn't hesitate to answer. "Of failing. I want to prove myself. I want to show these people that I can lead them."

Avalar had introduced me to the rest of the herd, and he hadn't been lying when he said it was small. Most of them had been at that barbecue Sera had taken us to. So many unicorns came up and thanked me personally for saving them, and defeating Malevolent, though I hadn't yet done anything but train.

I didn't want to let them down. If they died by Malevolent's horn, their deaths were on my hands.

"You aren't going to fail. None of us are," Novah said.

"How can you be so sure?"

"I am." Novah looked at me. "I know we can do this, as long as it's together."

I didn't answer. I was too busy watching Sera effortlessly finish the course.

Novah reached across and nudged me. "Someone's got a crush on Sera."

My cheeks and ears immediately burned. "What! No, I don't!"

"You do," Novah teased. "Why don't you ask her out already? It's getting old watching you pine over her."

"She probably doesn't even like girls," I mumbled.

"She likes you," Novah said. "She told me so."

I wanted to do backflips on my horse. "You're not making it up?"

"Why would I make something like that up?" Novah asked.

Sera came back from finishing the course. Novah urged her

horse forward to take his turn, and Sera stood her Thoroughbred beside my Arabian. My hands were shaking. Why not ask now?

"Hey, Sera?" I asked.

"Yes?" She looked at me, and I almost lost my courage. Ransom sensed my nervousness and danced underneath me. I had to pull on the reins to get him to stand still.

"After this, do you want to . . . go out tonight?" I asked.

"Like on a date?" Sera batted her eyelashes.

I forced myself to pick my jaw off the ground. "Um, yeah. I mean, no. Unless you want it to be, that is." *I screwed that up.*

She gave me a smile and said, "It's a date. Pick me up at seven."

Novah came back from her course. I urged my horse forward, and we flew over all the jumps. I felt so confident and elated. It was like I was flying. I was going on a date with Sera tonight!

But by the time I got back to my house later to take a nap, I was freaking out. I didn't know what to do. I'd had crushes on girls, but I'd never asked one out before on an official date. My nap ended up being nonexistent as I tossed and turned, wondering if Sera liked me too.

Ambrosia was so excited when she came home from work and I told her about the date. She spent the entire evening helping me get ready. By the time she was done with me, my hair was curled and I was wearing a brand-new dress, decorated with multicolor florals, along with heels and a pearl necklace.

I swallowed as I saw my reflection in the mirror. I hadn't dressed like this in a really long time. Maybe things could be different now, in Havenwood Falls.

Before Ambrosia took me to Sera's house, she dropped me off at Fairy Tale Florists. I couldn't decide what kind of flowers Sera would like best, so I just went with a bouquet made of irises and forget-me-nots, because they matched the color of her pelt.

When Sera answered the door, my heart skipped a beat. She looked amazing. Her hair was in a high ponytail with a bunch of curls, and she had on a lacy blue dress with exposed shoulders and a tea-length skirt.

She squealed when she saw the flowers. "Oh my gosh! They're amazing, Thea."

She leaned over and kissed me on the cheek as she took the flowers from me. My entire body glowed. She walked inside her kitchen and put the flowers in a vase before she joined me on the porch.

Ambrosia waved goodbye. "Have fun, you two!"

She drove away, and I turned to Sera.

"You'll probably have to drive," I said, a bit embarrassed. "Seeing as how I don't have a car."

Sera jingled her keys at me. "Fine by me. I like taking the wheel in relationships."

Despite the bad pun, I couldn't stop my insides from flip-flopping. Sera implied that we could be something more.

We hopped in her truck, and Sera started up the engine. "So, where are we off to?" she asked, looking at me.

"Um . . ." I was the one who asked, so I should've come up with a plan on where to take her. I was really bad at this.

Noticing my blank expression, Sera laughed and said, "That's okay. I really wanted Chinese, if that's cool with you?"

Sera could want to eat dirt, and it'd be cool with me. "That actually sounds really good," I said. "Let's go."

She parked at Miller's Plaza, and we walked into Sakura Buffet. When we went inside, it was pretty full, as it was a Saturday night. We managed to get a small booth at the back, but instead of sitting on the other side like she was supposed to, she sat next to me. Sera pressed herself up against my body in the booth, and I went lightheaded. I could barely talk as the waiter handed us the menus.

I decided on the deluxe stir-fried vegetables, and Sera ordered veggie lo mein.

When the waiter was gone, I turned to Sera with an apologetic smile. "Sorry. I'm not an expert on this dating thing. I've never taken another girl out on a date before."

"That's okay." Sera reached under the table and interwove her fingers with mine, clasping our hands tightly together. "I've never been on a date with another girl, either."

Her skin was soft and warm—nothing like holding a guy's hand. I looked at her manicured fingernails on top of my hand and thought that I'd never been happier in my entire life.

We held hands the entire time until our food showed up. We didn't really say much, but Sera rested her head on my shoulder and leaned into me even more than she already was. I knew we were cuddling in view of the entire restaurant, but I didn't care what people thought. I bet we looked really cute together.

Only when food was on the table did Sera loosen her grip from mine. After dinner, she took me to this crazy bookstore called Into the Mystic New Age Books and Gifts. She talked about crystals and yoga, and showed me all these books about magic and reaching your inner potential. She was really into this psychic stuff. She told me she took yoga classes at NamaStays Inn, and wanted to know if I'd like to come to her next class . . . after Malevolent was defeated.

I obviously said yes immediately. Watching Sera do yoga sounded like heaven. If I didn't have a good enough motive to survive before, I did now.

When we were done at the bookstore, after Sera had practically bought the place out, she noticed I was carrying a small bag, too.

"What's that you got?" she asked curiously when we hopped back in her truck.

I hesitated. It was supposed to be a surprise, but she had already seen.

"It's for you." I took it out of the bag. It was a crystal pendant on a necklace, blue and pink in color. The colors mingled together and made a beautiful pattern within the crystal. "It reminded me of us."

I looped it around her neck and fastened it. We were so close in her truck our faces were almost touching, and there wasn't a lot of space to move around.

Sera lifted her face so that her lips were only centimeters away from mine.

"Do you believe in fairy tales?" she whispered. Then she leaned forward and kissed me.

I didn't expect the kiss, so I was surprised. I sat there in shock for a moment, trying to process that my dreams were coming true, before I realized that I should probably kiss her back. I closed my eyes and placed my hands on her lap as I kissed her, feeling fireworks explode in my chest.

Kissing a girl was a lot different from kissing a guy. Sera was soft, she smelled good, and she was gentle. She went slow. Her lips felt like velvet against mine as she moved them. Her mouth is smaller, and she didn't bite or suck on my lip like guys did, or be aggressive. Instead, she acted like my mouth was something to treat with the most tender care. She was in no rush to go further, but instead drew out the kiss like it was the best kiss she'd ever had in her life. Her hands lifted to part back the curls from my face, and I felt like I was in heaven. I didn't have to tell her how far to go, or to stop, because it was like she was naturally attentive to my needs and just knew.

It was kind of cheesy, but as I kissed Sera, I felt . . . sparkly. Just sparkles, everywhere. I felt like my body was going to start projecting rainbows. It was a very unicorn way of putting things.

When Sera pulled away, she looked shy. It was a weird look on her. She wasn't a shy person. She was always brave.

"I've never kissed a girl before, either," Sera confessed.

"Me neither."

I blinked at her, and she put her hands on the wheel. "Come on. I want to show you something."

Sera drove until we stopped at Town Square Park. She held my hand again and pulled me along to a large wooden gazebo at the southeast corner of the park. When we stepped inside the gazebo, Sera began playing a song on her phone. She took my hands in hers, and we started slow-dancing to the tune that was playing low in the background.

"What is this place?" I asked.

"It's my favorite place in all of Havenwood Falls," Sera said. She spun me around before she drew me in, even closer this time. "I thought that when I found someone I liked, I'd bring them here, and we could dance."

"I didn't know you liked me." I looked downward. "I thought you would laugh at me when I asked you out," I confessed.

Sera stared at me and said, "If you thought I would laugh when you asked me on a date, you don't know me very well."

"I didn't back then," I said. I wrapped my arms tighter around her waist. "I know you now."

I kissed her this time. The way we held each other when we kissed again was like nothing I'd ever experienced. It was like being embraced by a cloud, and I could tell Sera would never hurt me. She was so sensitive to my needs it almost made me emotional.

When Sera pulled away, she said, "I changed my mind. You're the best part of Havenwood Falls."

I smiled and continued swaying us to the music. I didn't know how to respond to that. Probably because it made me too choked up.

"How did you end up in Havenwood Falls?" Sera said. "Obviously Avalar summoned you here, but where did you grow up?"

The happy moment faded, and the cloud of joy lifted. I cleared my throat and frowned.

"It all began two years ago," I said. "Ambrosia had this great job, and we lived in this huge house in New Orleans. Life was so perfect."

Tears were starting to dot my eyelashes. I really didn't want to cry in front of Sera. "Then our house caught fire one day. The gas line wasn't hooked up to the stove correctly, or something stupid like that. Ambrosia and I got out okay, but we lost everything, and the hospital she worked for had massive budget cuts and she ended up losing her job. We had to live off the insurance money. I had to quit riding lessons, and Ambrosia couldn't find work. We were so poor."

"That's so terrible." Sera reached out and brushed away a tear that fell down my cheek that I didn't even know was there.

"After the fire, I was angry. I'd always had daddy issues." I shook my head. "Ambrosia told me my dad had left when I was a baby. I didn't understand why he would just run off on me and Ambrosia like that. And after the fire, after we lost everything, I couldn't handle it. I ended up getting in trouble, and the judge sentenced me to a year at Desmona Prep. It was a school for troubled kids outside New Orleans. It had a great riding program, but that was the only good thing about it. I got picked on a lot there."

"That's horrible." Sera seemed shocked.

"It was pretty bad." I had trouble meeting her eyes. "I was a girly girl growing up. Pink was my favorite color. I loved dresses and doing my hair and makeup. Bows, pearls—they were my favorite. I liked ponies and watching rom-coms and reading love stories."

My voice was getting wobbly. "But at Desmona Prep, anything feminine was considered a weakness. They made boys and girls wear the same uniforms and didn't separate anything based on gender. At first, I thought it was a good thing, because it helped make us all feel equal, but at the same time, I felt like they pushed masculinity over femininity. Romance novels were banned. They were considered a lower class of literature. They didn't allow dances or parties. No one was allowed to dress up or accessorize, even on the weekends when we could wear our normal clothes. Everyone was forced to wear T-shirts and jeans. If you acted like a girl in any way, you were a target."

I looked down. "I had the girliness beat out of me by bullies. And criticized out of me by teachers. So I kind of learned that being a woman was considered weak."

"Being feminine isn't a weakness," Sera argued. "It's actually harder to be soft and kind than it is to be harsh and tough, especially in this world."

"I know that now. You taught me." I leaned upward and kissed her forehead. "And I am really tired of pretending to be something I'm not."

"I'm so sorry that happened to you," Sera said. I could tell she truly meant it.

I shrugged. "It was what happened. I'm past it now."

Sera's expression was doubtful when I said that. "I grew up in Louisiana too. I had a pretty great life. I was always popular."

"I can imagine that." I pictured Sera, lounging on Florida beaches with tons of popular preps around. She was so nice and sweet, so extroverted and so pretty, that I bet people flocked to her. She'd never been an outcast like me.

"I never really went through anything tragic," Sera said. "I came to Havenwood Falls last year, along with Novah. We didn't know we were unicorns until we shifted together the first time we met at the stables. It was a pretty big shock. We were just as surprised as you were, at the beginning."

I nodded. "It's hard to know you've been lied to all your life."

"Right. But honestly, it was more of a relief than anything. There was a part of me I felt like had been hiding my entire life. Then it came out once I became a unicorn."

"Me too," I confessed. "Even though this is all crazy new to me, knowing about this world actually makes me feel better. I always knew in my heart there was something more. I just couldn't put my finger on what."

Sera frowned. "I just wish I could've met my parents. Novah feels the same way. We have names, but don't know anything else about them. Neither one of us have asked much, because we don't want to upset our adoptive moms. You're lucky that your parents are still alive, Thea. Even if your mother is totally evil."

"Avalar isn't exactly an outstanding father," I mumbled.

"No. But at least he's alive," she whispered.

"Your friends probably made up for his absence." Now that I

had Avalar in my life, I was quickly learning fathers weren't all they were cracked up to be.

She shrugged. "I had a lot of friends growing up . . . a lot of boyfriends, too . . . but it always felt like something was . . . missing." She brushed my cheek lightly with her hand, and cupped the side of my face. "I didn't know what was missing was you."

My heart melted. I brought her in close for a really tight hug —you know, the kind that crushes you to another person and makes you feel like you're one.

"Thea," Sera started, and her lips moved against my ear as she whispered. "Ever since I found the Equestriad, I feel whole. Being a unicorn is what I've been meant to do my entire life. I won't be able to stand it if Malevolent takes that away from me."

I nestled my face in her ponytail, and made myself a promise. I was going to defeat Malevolent. For Sera's sake as much as mine.

CHAPTER 8

I'd learned in the past month there was nothing unicorns loved more than sugar— and there was a coffee shop in town that apparently made the best drink ever, according to Sera and Novah. Even better, it was named after us—though I didn't really buy that from the girls.

Coffee Haven was owned by a gorgeous woman named Willow with a petite build and amazing turquoise eyes. It took a lot for me to rip my gaze away from her. Like, seriously, if I was a few years older, I'd be all over that. If I didn't know I already liked girls, Willow would've made me realize.

Sera and Novah forced me to order a drink called Unicorn Farts. I thought the name was kind of dumb (and a bit gross). Like, really, you don't want to see my farts, because they're disgusting. But at the first sip, I fell in love. This seriously was going to be my new favorite thing.

Willow smiled at me as I sipped. "Good?"

"Very." I was downing it in seconds. "I'd love another."

Willow laughed. "Coming right up." She paused, and then added, "Don't worry. I know you're nervous, but whatever it's about, I'm sure it'll all work out. It usually does."

She gave me a smile before continuing to make my drink. I

was standing there speechless with my mouth hanging open. What did she just say?

"Willow is an empath." Sera leaned over, whispering to me. "She can read emotions."

Did everyone in this town have crazy magical powers? It was kinda hard to get used to. I figured I'd meet an alien on the street next. Sera and Novah placed the same order before we started the walk down the street to Jas's house, who was having an end-of-summer pool party.

There were only five days left until Malevolent would arrive, and all of us were starting to freak out. We'd mastered as many spells as we could, but Avalar still hadn't taught us the Unicorn's Lament—which he promised he was going to do this week.

"Hey, lovebirds," Jas said as we arrived, giving a pointed look at me and Sera. There were already a ton of unicorn shifters in the pool, and he was at the grill, cooking veggie dogs.

I blushed, but Sera said back playfully, "You're just pissed you can't get between this, Jas." She gestured between me and her.

"Right you are," Jas said, and he gave us a wink. "Though I think the chances are slim in that department."

Sera giggled, and I said nothing. We weren't officially girlfriends yet, but that was because I'd been too nervous to ask Sera, and it had become pretty clear she wanted me to ask her out first. We'd kissed a few more times, but since Novah was usually with us, we kept the PDA to a minimum.

Novah took her opportunity to slink up to Jas's side and wrap an arm around his waist. "How you doing today, Jas?"

"Oh, just fine, darlin'." Jas bent down and kissed Novah's forehead. She gave a girly squeal, and hopped up and down. Sera made a gagging sound, and I rolled my eyes.

"Like you two are any better," Novah shot at us. I snickered.

I stayed at the pool party until night fell, and Sera wanted to go. We left Novah with Jas. She was sitting on his lap in a lawn recliner and obviously didn't even notice we were leaving.

Sera had been in a good mood at the party, but when we left she seemed kinda . . . upset.

"What's wrong?" I asked her as we walked toward her truck. "You look troubled."

Sera paused for a moment, before she said, "Avalar didn't want me to tell you this, but the Court warned him that if we can't deal with Malevolent, they'll go outside the town wards to defeat her themselves. If she hurts or kills anyone, or exposes the supes to humans, the Court will end up kicking all the unicorns out of Havenwood Falls. He told me because he thought I could handle it." Sera sighed. "The thing is, I don't think I can."

"Why didn't he say anything to me?"

"He didn't want to make you feel more pressured than you already are," Sera explained. "He knows he's been pushing you harder than Novah and me."

Avalar cared about my well-being? That was a first.

"We're going to win," I told Sera. "I know we are."

"I hope so." Sera stopped at the ward line for the unicorns. "You wanna go for a run?"

I longed to stretch my unicorn legs. "Sure."

We entered into the woods, and once we were in the cover of the trees, Sera and I changed. We ran freely through the forest like unicorns were meant to do, and I enjoyed the feel of the sunset shining down on my back, and the flash of Sera's hooves as she ran in front of me.

But it wasn't enough. In the past month, Sera, Novah, and I had galloped all around this ward, and I'd already seen everything in the area. I wanted more. I wanted to explore.

At nightfall, I stopped at the edge of a known border, and shifted back. Sera changed beside me, and I said, "What is it with the dumb boundary, anyhow? Why can't we cross it?"

"Thea, it's not safe," Sera repeated. "The Court set up the ward so we can change, but Avalar's magic isn't able to extend out that far. He set up protective boundaries that nobody but unicorns can cross within the ward. If we go outside of that, we're unprotected."

I rolled my eyes. "If it's a vampire, we can just stab it with our horns or something."

"It doesn't work like that in Havenwood Falls. Thea, you're too curious," Sera said nervously.

I gave a mischievous grin. "I just like a bit of excitement. Catch me if you can!"

"Thea!"

I had already changed back and was galloping through the woods over the boundary line before Sera had even shifted, giving me a good head start.

I heard Sera's hooves behind me and laughed. This was so much fun. I liked the thrill of the chase. *"You've gotta be faster than that, slowpoke!"* I laughed.

"Thea, this isn't funny!" Sera's voice was panicked. What was she so worried about?

Then the area grew darker. It was like the light of the moon went away, and the stars vanished. I could barely see. My breathing became ragged, and my heartbeat was so loud, I could hear it in my ears. I slowed to a halt, and Sera came up beside me.

"What's going on?" Even in my head, I sounded out of breath.

Sera didn't answer. *"We have to get back to the boundary line."* There was an edge of fear to her voice.

I heard growls. Barks. And howls. Out of the shadows stepped wolves, a whole pack of them, all black in color, with red eyes that glowed in the darkness.

I was freaking out. *"I thought the pack wasn't allowed around the stables?"* I asked, frightened.

"They're not Havenwood Falls shifters! They're Malevolent's minions!" Sera shouted. *"She's getting more powerful! It won't be long before she can break out of her cage! Run, Thea, run!"*

I turned on my hind legs and bolted back in the direction of the boundary line, but it was dark, and I had lost my way. Sera was right behind me. The wolves chased us through the bushes, and got closer and closer. I could feel their hot breaths on my hooves.

I was faster than Sera, and at the moment, all I wanted was to get the wolves away from her. I galloped as hard as I could, breaking away from her and leading the wolves in a different direction.

"*Thea, don't!*" Sera's cry was lost to the wind as I led the wolves away from her. I jumped over fallen logs and rocks in my way, galloping through a river, but nothing stopped or slowed down the wolves, and I was getting tired. They started approaching me from all sides, surrounding me.

I aimed a kick at one of the wolves. It hit true, but instead of dealing a powerful blow to the wolf's body, all it did was go right through.

It hit me. The wolves were made of magic. Malevolent's dark magic. I couldn't touch them, but they could hurt me.

One of the wolves jumped and sank his teeth into my flank. I gave a cry of pain, and two more wolves latched onto my ankles. I went down, and the whole pack of them jumped onto my body, sinking their teeth into my flesh and tearing with all their strength.

Blood gushed out of the wounds, and I realized that I couldn't get up. The wolves were too heavy, and there were too many of them. I tried to fight back, but my hooves and horn went through smoke.

I felt weak as my blood pooled around me. I was dying. There was no way out of this.

"*Thea, no!*" There was a blinding, flashing light, one I realized came from Sera's horn. The great light seemed to burn the wolves on impact, and they howled with pain. They ran away from me as Sera came galloping near.

"*Sera,*" I thought, just before I passed out. I saw a white, healing light glow from Sera's horn, and felt my broken flesh knit together as the world vanished around me.

CHAPTER 9

*W*hen I woke up, I was lying on my couch at home, a group of figures around me. As the room became clearer, I recognized faces. The Equestriad. Ambrosia. And Avalar.

Who looked pretty pissed.

"What were you thinking?" he demanded.

Sera had tear stains on her face, and her nose was pink.

"What happened?" I asked blearily.

"Sera healed you and brought you back home. You could've been killed," Avalar said through clenched teeth.

A rush of anger went through me. "I know that would've been a tragedy, seeing as how you still need me to do your dirty work," I spat.

"Thea, that's enough," Ambrosia snapped. She rarely got angry, but she was furious now. "You made a reckless, childish decision. You put yourself and Sera in terrible danger."

I fell silent. I knew when to shut up.

"Do you realize what you nearly jeopardized?" Avalar bellowed. "Years of preparation were almost ruined!"

"I get it," I said sourly. "You could at least be happy that I'm still alive."

Avalar looked surprised. "I . . . I am glad," he stated. "I'm relieved to see that you're unharmed. But that's no excuse for your behavior."

"I'm sorry," I said, though it was more to Sera than to him. Watching her cry felt worse than the wolves' teeth in me had.

Avalar straightened up. "Rest. I expect the three of you to arrive in the clearing at dawn. Tomorrow, we work on the Unicorn's Lament."

Avalar stomped out. He slammed the door, which seemed out of character for him. I'd never seen him truly lose his temper before.

Ambrosia's harsh glare vanished when he was out of her sight. "I'm very upset with you," she said, stroking my hair back. "But I'm so grateful you're alive. Those wolves could've torn you apart."

Sera ran out, covering her face and heading into my room. Novah looked at me and thumbed her hand in the direction she'd gone. "You'd better go handle that."

A pit of guilt settled in my stomach. I slowly got off the couch, but I found I didn't feel sore, dizzy, or disoriented. Sera's healing magic had made me as good as new.

Horrid terror wrapped itself around me as I remembered what had happened. Those wolves weren't even the worst of it. They were Malevolent's minions. Those were her lackeys. She had to be a million times more powerful. How could we stand up to that?

I entered my bedroom. Sera was sitting on my bed, clutching a pillow and crying into it.

I sat beside her. I wanted to touch her, but I figured I should keep my hands to myself right now. "Sera, I'm so sorry," I started. "I should've listened to you. We had no business going over the boundary line."

"It was stupid," Sera snapped.

"I agree that what I did was stupid," I said. "It never should've happened."

Sera's lip quivered. "You don't understand. You could've been killed. If I hadn't been able to heal you—"

She got off the bed. She crossed her arms and whipped around, turning her back to me.

"Hey." I got up. I turned her back around to face me, though it was hard to do, because tears were streaming down her face. "I really am sorry, Sera. I am so, so sorry." I was crying now, too, because I couldn't watch Sera bawl for long without it giving me some sort of waterworks.

"I was watching them rip you apart and hoping I could get to you in time." Sera's voice was muddled with tears. "Do you know how awful that is?"

I tried to picture myself in Sera's position and couldn't, because the thought of her being devoured by wolves was too hard to handle. "I can't even imagine. But thank you for saving me."

Sera continued to cry into my shoulder while I rubbed her back. I felt like a jerk, because it was me who'd made her feel this way.

I wasn't afraid of Malevolent before. But after dealing with those wolves, I was scared out of my mind.

On Tuesday morning at dawn, I suppressed a yawn, knowing I had to be at my best today. Even before the school day began, the three of us were working on channeling the Unicorn's Lament, but I really wasn't feeling it. If Avalar wanted me to do this spell right, the least he could do was let me sleep.

"The Unicorn's Lament is a test of your powers. It is all the strength of your magic combined with your fellow princesses'. Done correctly, the spell will form a rainbow appearance," Avalar said.

"How do we cast it?" I asked. Avalar barely looked at me. He was still mad, obviously.

"The Unicorn's Lament is forged by combining the three values that are most important to the unicorns—friendship, beauty, and love," Avalar continued. "Each of you must embody and produce the truest form of this magic, and combine them together in order to stop Malevolent and break the dark magic that protects and controls her."

I raised an eyebrow at that. Did Avalar truly think that Malevolent didn't have a choice when it came to her use of dark magic? After all these years, did he really think he still stood a chance at getting back together with my mother?

"Stand in a triangle," Avalar said. He motioned for us to change, and we did. He positioned us at three points across from each other, then put a hay bale in the middle—a target that stood as Malevolent.

"Think of the truest form of your value to you, and use it to channel your magic," Avalar said. "Sera, you'll be given the value of beauty. Novah, friendship. And Thea, your value will be love."

I immediately focused. I tried to think of what love meant to me, and what I would consider the truest embodiment of it. My mind went blank, and I couldn't think of anything. I tried to think of Sera and of Ambrosia, and though I knew that I loved them and that they loved me, I didn't know why. I realized I didn't truly understand love, or beauty, or friendship.

On our first try, we merely managed to get multicolored sparks to fly from our horns. On the second, flashes of color popped out, but they were nothing like the beautiful rainbow I'd imagined. We struggled to combine our magic, and the rainbow that was supposed to result just ended up looking like a pastel-colored sludge all over the hay bale.

"This isn't working," Avalar said. "Let us try something else."

We switched roles, changing up the values each of us had to embody to see if we could perform the spell easier. A few times, the magic exploded on us and caused injuries. Avalar had to heal us with his horn.

"Again," Avalar demanded. "Get it right this time, girls."

I felt frustrated. Avalar didn't even know what he was doing. He'd never performed the spell himself. He could be teaching us totally wrong.

We broke for school, but as soon as class was over, we were back here practicing. By the end of the day, my knees were shaking with tiredness. Avalar noticed and said, "That's enough. We'll pick it up again tomorrow."

Sera and Novah sighed with relief. But I didn't feel relieved at all. We were so close to my birthday, and so close to Malevolent arriving, and we were totally unprepared.

~

Avalar worked with us all week, from sunrise to sunset, and only took time off so we could go to school. We could almost, but not quite, pull off the Unicorn's Lament by Friday night. We'd gotten far enough that we could make the rainbows come out of our horns, but they wouldn't combine. None of us could perform our part of the spell properly on our own. Not even Sera.

Avalar was on the point of looking hopeless. "Stop," he said, after the hundredth time we'd tried and failed. "You'll exhaust your magic. It's too late now."

The three of us stood in the clearing, exhausted. Our heads hung so low our horns almost touched the ground.

"You have to be able to perform the Unicorn's Lament by tomorrow," Avalar said firmly, as if we didn't already know the obvious.

"What if we can't?" I objected.

"You must," Avalar insisted. "There's no other way."

He turned his back on us. "Get some sleep. You'll need to be ready when Malevolent comes."

The three of us looked at each other warily. I felt as prepared as a puppy going to a dragon fight.

"We should be together tonight," Sera voiced. "Let's have a sleepover, my house."

"We won't sleep if we're all together," I pointed out.

"We can try," Sera said, before she added, "I have a feeling sleep isn't going to happen for us, anyway. And I don't want to be alone."

The look on Novah's face, and probably mine too, said the same.

We headed to Sera's house. Lucindiana made us dinner—pasta primavera, which was my favorite—but we barely ate. None of us were really hungry. When Novah refused to have any ice cream or cake after, I knew something was seriously wrong with us.

Ambrosia and Esmeralda, Novah's nursemaid, had come over, too, to spend the night. It seemed the Etherian unicorns wanted to be as close together as possible.

Eventually, darkness approached. We left the house and headed into the woods, beyond the protective wards around the town and the stables, in order to fight Malevolent.

When we got into the woods, I saw a bunch of unicorns standing in a protective circle. All of them were stallions. Jas was among them, though he hadn't changed yet. All above us, dark clouds had gathered above the mountains. A storm was brewing.

"Jas!" Novah said. She threw her arms around him, and he hugged her tightly.

"Jas, what are you doing here?" I asked as we approached.

"I'm part of the Unicorn Guard," he said. "I'm a knight sworn to protect the monarchy, like Avalar. All of us will gladly lay down our lives to protect the three princesses."

"No one is sacrificing themselves tonight," I said. I looked at Sera, and she nodded.

"I'll make sure you guys are protected," Jas said. "Don't worry about me. I can last the night."

Jas leaned down and gave Novah a kiss on the lips. Novah stood completely still, and Jas brushed his hand through her hair as he pulled away.

"Princess," he said, and nodded his head.

Novah looked stunned, like she was floating on clouds. She gave a girlish sigh. "Okay, Jas kissed me. I'm ready to die now."

"No one's going to die," I told her sharply. "There's a bunch of us and one of Malevolent. We can still win, even if she has her minions."

"But we can't perform the Unicorn's Lament," Sera objected. She seemed depressed and hopeless. It wasn't like her, and I hated it.

"We can't yet, but maybe we should give it one more try," I suggested. "We might get it this time."

Sera's look of despair became one of determination. "Right. Let's do this."

By this time, it was around eleven o'clock. We tried again and again, but the spell wouldn't work. I could hardly make bubbles pop out of my horn at this rate. We all shifted back, looking desperate.

"This is useless!" Novah said. "We're never going to get it!"

"Don't give up!" I encouraged them, but even I was downtrodden. I didn't know if we could pull it off, either.

"I think I'm getting closer to figuring this out. We need to use the best parts of ourselves to beat her," Sera said firmly. "There's no other way."

"How are we supposed to do that?" Novah wailed. Sera didn't have an answer for her, and I didn't, either.

The dark clouds had only grown bigger and more foreboding. They covered the sky and blacked out any light from the moon or stars. Thunder rolled above my head, and I looked up at the exact time lightning rippled across the sky, making the clouds appear in fragmented cracks. The sound from the thunder was so loud, it made me jump. I could feel it vibrating in my bones.

Rain began pouring from the sky, and within seconds, that rain had turned to heavy hail. I put my arms up to shield myself from it. A storm was whipping up, the most powerful I'd ever seen.

"Girls!" Ambrosia called. "Get ready!"

The three of us huddled together. The knights shook their manes and steadied themselves against the hail that was pouring down.

I had a bad feeling I knew what was going on and where the storm had come from. I checked my watch. It was only an hour past midnight. My eyes met Sera's. She'd had the same thought. She wore the same horrified expression I did.

This couldn't be right. We had expected to have a little bit of time before she arrived. We were completely unprepared!

Yet Malevolent had wasted no time. She'd already broken out of her prison by the time the clock struck twelve.

And she was already here.

CHAPTER 10

*S*era, Novah, and I gathered together. We watched as hundreds of wolves streamed into the open area. The knights turned to face them, lights glowing from their horns. They began battling the wolves viciously. The hail increased, and we watched in horror as the wolves began to bring down some of the knights, in search of us.

"We have to find Malevolent," Sera said. She turned to look at us. "You girls with me?"

We weren't ready. But I knew we'd never be ready. The moment had come, and it was do or die.

"We're with you," I replied. "Now until the end."

"Let's go." Novah changed, and we did the same. Our maids—Ambrosia, Lucindiana, and Esmeralda—followed us.

Ambrosia was a beautiful unicorn. She was pure white, from her horn to her hooves. Lucindiana was lavender, and Esmeralda was orange. We raced through the battle, dodging the fighting that was going on all around us. The knights kept Malevolent's minions off us so we could search for the evil queen.

Thing was, I wasn't entirely sure I wanted to find her.

I saw a flash of silver in my peripheral vision. Avalar had

arrived. He galloped up beside me, and I noticed with horror part of his pelt was covered with blood—his blood.

"We need to get to the clearing!" Avalar shouted. *"Follow me!"*

Avalar turned and headed into the forest. Multiple minions went to follow us but knights blocked the way, chasing the wolves back with the light from their horns. Jas successfully burned three wolves that were hot on Novah's tail before he brought up his head to watch us race by.

"Jaspirion!" Avalar cried. *"We need you!"*

Jas left his post and took up the rear. The minute we entered the deeper forest, the world got even darker. The trees shielded us from the hail, but it was still difficult to know where we were going. We made light gleam from our horns so we could see.

Avalar slowed down to a walk. He was being cautious now. The rest of us allowed him to take the lead.

The sounds of battle and the howls of the wolves died out behind us.

But once we reached the clearing, there was someone already waiting for us.

Malevolent. She stood before us in her unicorn form, a devious gleam in her eye.

Her pelt was midnight blue, and she had a curled mane and tail that fell nearly to her hooves. A long cloak of starlight upon velvet hung from her shoulders, clasped in place by a gold brooch on her chest. Her horn was gone. She'd sold it to obtain dark magic, I remembered. In its place was a long, black icicle, curved like a knife and glinting like glass.

As we approached, Malevolent changed. She became a woman with long black hair, wearing a cobalt-blue velvet gown. A crown of black icicles glittered on top of her head, and her nails were long, painted, and sharp. Her skin was as pale as mine, and her eyes were brown and cold. She looked every part the evil queen from the darkest fairy tale I could imagine.

She was gorgeous. And the worst part of it was, I could see myself in her. We had the same facial features, same body structure. I'd taken little from Avalar. Besides my light hair, I was basically a younger copy of her.

As we approached, Malevolent opened her arms. "Aramanthe," she said. She gave a wide smile, revealing perfect teeth. "I've waited seventeen years to meet you again, my daughter."

Avalar changed back, and we all took it as a sign to do the same. Avalar stepped forward, planting himself in front of me.

"Surrender, Malestraude," he said. "You are outnumbered. Let us end this quietly."

My heart beat fast. Maybe we wouldn't have to fight. Maybe we could talk things out.

"Oh, I have no intention of talking. I did enough talking to myself, for nearly two decades while confined in a cage you helped put me in, Avalar," Malevolent said coolly. "You said you loved me. That clearly was a lie."

"I did love you. I don't love what you've become." Avalar stood his ground, but his expression seemed conflicted.

"I have no more business with you, Avalar," Malevolent said, and she waved her hand like she was disgusted. "My concern is with Aramanthe."

Malevolent extended a hand to me. "Come, my daughter. Take your rightful place by your mother's side. Together, we could rule the unicorns and Havenwood Falls. Our joined power would be unstoppable."

I shook my head and backed away to stand by Ambrosia. "I have a mother, and she isn't you."

Malevolent threw back her head and laughed. "The nursemaid? I have more power in my hooves than she has in her horn. Do you think she can protect you from me?"

"I will until my last breath," Ambrosia vowed. "Come close to her, and I'll spear you with my horn."

Malevolent chuckled, like this was a game and all of us were her pawns. "This is an embarrassing display. I've had enough of these jests."

Malevolent moved faster than any of us could think. In the

blink of an eye, she transformed into a unicorn and sent a black bolt of magic shooting from her horn. It was directed at me, but since Avalar was standing in front of me, it hit him in the chest. He went down, making wheezing sounds with his chest.

"Avalar!" I cried. I rushed forward, putting my hands on his back. He was still struggling to breathe.

"It was a mistake to bring you here," Avalar gasped. His eyes seemed panicked and afraid.

"No." I shook my head. "No, it wasn't a mistake."

"Abandon the unicorns," Avalar breathed. "Run away, Thea. I just want to make sure you're safe."

"What a disgusting display of affection," Malevolent said. *"It's wholly boresome."*

She sent another black bolt at Avalar, but I pulled him out of the way and to the ground before it could hit him. Malevolent started firing, this time shooting bolts that looked like lightning from her horn. Sera and Novah dove out of the way, and our nursemaids sprang into action.

Ambrosia, Lucindiana, and Esmeralda charged at Malevolent from three different directions. Lucindiana sent a stream of vines from her horn, intending to wrap Malevolent within them, but Malevolent stepped aside and the vines wrapped around a tree instead. Malevolent aimed a lightning bolt at her, and it hit her target. Once Lucindiana was struck by the bolt, she froze in place. Marble began crawling across her pelt, and she was captured in an expression of fear and shock, her form completely made of stone.

All of us were frozen in shock as we looked at the statue of Lucindiana, frozen in place. Sera's screaming could be heard in the background.

While we were all distracted, Malevolent took her chance. She shot a beam at Esmeralda, and like Lucindiana, she became a statue.

"Esmeralda!" Novah screamed. She ran to her nursemaid and threw her arms around the statue, crying. Jas dragged Novah away from Esmeralda just before another one of Malevolent's bolts hit her.

Then my worst nightmare happened. Ambrosia reached Malevolent, and the two mares rose up on their hind legs, batting their hooves at each other as they dueled. Malevolent's right hoof hit Ambrosia in the face, knocking her down. Ambrosia attempted to get back up, but Malevolent shocked her, and quick as a flash, the only mother I knew turned to stone.

"Ambrosia!" I screamed. I rushed to her and put my hands against her marble form, but she didn't move. She was captured in a prison of marble.

With the loss of Ambrosia, I went numb. If I didn't know what to do before, I was completely helpless now. I couldn't feel anything.

"You're going to pay for this!" Jas screamed. He lost his temper and transformed. Jas left Novah's side and galloped at Malevolent full speed with his horn down.

The moment he neared her, Malevolent spun around and kicked out with her back hooves. The blow caught Jas in the side of the head and sent him flying backward. He transformed mid-fall and slammed against a tree. He slumped against it, bleeding from a cut on the side of his head.

"Jas!" Novah went to his side, kneeling next to him and shaking him in an attempt to wake him up. But although he was still breathing, he was totally out of it.

She'd reduced us to four in a matter of seconds, and she hadn't even broken a sweat. It'd all happened so fast.

Malevolent changed back. The smile on her face was bigger than before. "Well, daughter, have you changed your mind?" she asked.

I backed away from her again. "I'll never join you!" I swore.

And I meant it. It didn't matter what she promised me. She'd turned Ambrosia to stone and hurt my dad. She could go to hell.

Malevolent's welcoming, generous smile instantly turned into a snarl of hatred. "Then perish!"

She shifted, and sent a lightning bolt at me. Everything from there happened in slow motion.

Avalar was no more than a few steps away. He was still recovering his breath, and noticed the spell Malevolent had cast in my direction.

"No! You won't take my daughter!" Avalar roared.

He changed into a unicorn and charged in front of Malevolent's blast. He reared up on his hind legs just as the spell hit him. Like Ambrosia, the spell spread until his form had become a statue and he was left frozen in place, an expression of rage and anguish on his face as his mane rippled behind him.

Avalar had sacrificed himself for me. The reality hit me like a landslide.

Sera, Novah, and I glanced at each other with panicked faces. We were alone. Malevolent had changed everyone to stone. Jas lay unconscious against a tree. We were on our own.

Malevolent went to attack me again, and I changed on instinct. I leapt out of the way just as she blasted a large hole in the tree behind me.

Sera and Novah changed, too. The three of us darted around the clearing and avoided Malevolent's blasts from her horn. We couldn't get close enough to hurt her with our horns or hooves. She sent spells so fast that it was difficult to think of any of our own.

One of the bolts was headed straight for me again. I managed to conjure up a magic shield just in time to stop the bolt from hitting me. Novah and Sera copied me, and Malevolent's spells bounced off and ricocheted everywhere. Defending ourselves was the best we could do in this situation.

This was impossible. We were overrun. We couldn't handle this. Malevolent was going to win.

Sera's words broke into my head. *"We need to use the best parts of ourselves to beat her."*

But the best parts of me weren't strong or brave or wise. The best parts of me were girly and playful and colorful. What use were those kinds of things in a fight to the death?

I figured we were dead anyway, and I might as well try something different. While she was distracted with chasing Novah and Sera, I used my horn to summon the biggest jet of bubbles I possibly could and sent them streaming at Malevolent full blast.

Malevolent wasn't expecting them. The blast of bubbles hit her in the face. Surprised by the onslaught, she stopped casting spells and backed away. She shook her head violently, her eyes full of bubble goo and temporarily blinded.

"Girls, that's the key!" I shouted to them. *"Think of something silly! Something happy!"*

Sera's and Novah's expressions were bewildered, but they did as I said. Sera sent fluffy blue hearts puffing out of her horn that surrounded Malevolent like a fog. When the hearts popped, they released a blue gas that filled Malevolent's mouth. She coughed and snorted, struggling to breathe.

Novah pointed at the ground, and green teddy bears popped up out of the dirt. Malevolent stepped on them, and they squeaked as she did, throwing her senses off further. She stumbled around and tripped, trying and failing to gain back her surroundings.

"This is childish! Stop this behavior at once, and fight me!" Malevolent demanded, still gasping for breath.

She sent more lightning bolts, but they were scattered and missed their target. She couldn't predict which spells we were going to cast next, as they were nonsensical. Their purpose was to throw her off her game, and it was working.

Novah sent a sticky pink substance out of her horn at Malevolent's hooves. It turned out to be gum. Malevolent tried to pull her hooves out of it, but even as she was able to free one hoof, another became stuck in the goo.

While Malevolent was held by the gum, Sera cast the magic trap. Malevolent stopped immediately within the circle, and struggled to break free.

She could've if she gathered her bearings. But I kept Malevolent disoriented with the bubbles while Sera grew the power of the magic trap and Novah kept tossing teddy bears that hit her in the face. Novah was laughing as she did so. Malevolent looked furious.

"When I break this spell, the three of you are going to be begging for mercy," Malevolent snarled. Her mouth and eyes were the only part of her that she could move now. The magic trap had her bound.

"Girls! The Unicorn's Lament!" I cried. *"Do it now!"*

The three of us galloped to our places to form the triangle. We only had a few moments before Malevolent would be able to break out of the magic trap. We had to move quickly.

There was no doubt we could do it. We had to. I closed my eyes and thought about how Avalar had sacrificed himself for me, and all that he had done to keep me safe, even if he couldn't be there while I was growing up—even if he wanted to. I understood what love was in that moment and had never felt more powerful in all my life.

"For love!" I cried.

"For beauty!" Sera added.

"For friendship!" the three of us said at once. We sent colors shooting from the tips of our horns, and in the air, the three spells combined to make a rainbow that vibrated with intensity and power. As the rainbow claimed her, Malevolent began to scream in fury. Her form waved and dipped within the colors as she tried to escape and failed.

"You might be powerful, but you're no match for the Equestriad!" I yelled triumphantly. *"You're finished!"*

Malevolent gave one last scream of rage before the rainbow overtook her, and she exploded into an array of colorful sparkles. They coated the area and gleamed throughout the clearing, trailing through the air to the ground like falling stars.

The three of us looked at each other in amazement. We had done it. Malevolent was defeated.

Once Malevolent was gone, the unicorns that had become statues turned back to normal. Ambrosia, Lucindiana, Esmeralda, and Avalar broke free from the marble, emerging from the stone in their human forms.

"Ambrosia!" I screamed. I threw myself into her arms and hugged her tightly. Beside me, Sera and Novah did the same with their nursemaids.

"Thea, I'm so proud of you." Ambrosia put her face in my hair, and I felt her tears soaking into my head. "You're truly the princess everyone knew you would be."

"Thanks, Mom." I pulled away from her and wiped the tears from her eyes.

I turned. Avalar had come out of his statue, and he was staring at me.

"Well done, Thea," he said gruffly. "I always knew you had it in you."

I looked at him. Then I ran forward and embraced him as tightly as I could, trying to thank him for what he had done. There weren't any words I could say that would indicate how much gratitude I felt in that moment.

Avalar stiffened with the touch, like he didn't know how to react, before he relaxed and wrapped his arms around me.

"You don't know how long I've waited to hold you in my arms," he said. "Since the moment I gave you away."

"You don't know how long I've waited to have a dad," I whispered back.

Avalar pulled away and tweaked my chin. "What do you say we go for a gallop later?" he asked. "Just some father-daughter time."

"That sounds amazing." Images of me and Avalar galloping through the forest together, as silver and pink unicorns, burst into my mind. It was more than I had ever hoped for or dreamed of growing up.

There was a groan behind us. Jas was waking up. Novah was at his side, helping him sit up and looking concerned.

Jas blinked his eyes wearily, looking around the scene of crushed marble, gum, and teddy bears. He shook his head once or twice, then slurred, "Hey. Who am I?"

~

We had lost a few knights in the fight, but the unicorns had emerged victorious. Avalar had organized a party at Creekwood Country Club that night, to celebrate my birthday and the fact that Malevolent was finally defeated. The unicorns could live on in peace.

I wore a big dress, the pinkest and the prettiest I owned, along with high heels and a big, glittering tiara. Sera and Novah wore gowns in their respective colors, tiaras on their heads, too. Everywhere we went, unicorns bowed to us and said, "Princesses." It was surreal.

The food at the country club was so good. Avalar had rented out a large empty space with a dance floor, and a DJ played all of the Equestriad's favorite songs. Sera, Novah, and I danced all night with the rest of the unicorns, who, I learned, did love something more than sugar—and that was getting down with their bad selves.

I was surprised Avalar had thrown the party together so quickly, until I learned that he'd been planning it all month as a surprise for me. He assumed that we could defeat Malevolent. He hadn't even had a doubt, as he'd already paid for the food and the deposit for the ballroom.

He'd believed in me all along. He just wanted to push me to succeed.

While Sera, Novah, and I were dancing, a familiar face appeared. Jas was there, wearing a suit with his head bandaged in thick white wrappings.

"Hey, girls," he said. "Happy birthday, Thea."

"Jas! So nice of you to come," Sera said politely.

"Are you sure you should be here?" Novah asked, looking worriedly at the wrappings around his head.

"It's just a small concussion," Jas said. "I'll be fine. The doctors wanted me to rest, but I never miss a party."

Jas took Novah in his arms and spun her around a few times. Novah giggled, lighting up as he twirled her around.

"It's so sweet that you guys get to be princesses," Jas said offhandedly. "At least for a day."

The three of us looked at each other with wary expressions. "Yes," I said. "Of course."

"I'm starving, by the way," Jas said. "I'm gonna grab a plate. Coming, Novah?"

She shook her head. "I'll be there in a minute."

"All right. Don't keep me waiting." He gave her a wink, then whirled around on his heel and went to the buffet line.

Novah seemed crushed. Sera put her hand on Novah's shoulder.

"He'll come back to you, Novah," Sera said gently. "Give him time."

Novah gave a watery smile. "I hope so."

Jas had amnesia from Malevolent's strike to his head. He'd forgotten that he was a unicorn, about Malevolent . . . everything. He thought that this was just a normal birthday party.

Avalar said it was best to let Jas remember everything on his own, and allow him to think he was a regular human for a while. There was no telling how he'd react if we told him the truth about everything, or if he'd believe us.

He'd also forgotten he'd kissed Novah. Which was devastating to her.

"It's okay. I've got my girls," Novah said, and she threw her arms over Sera's shoulder and mine. "The Equestriad's all we need, as long as we're together." Then she frowned. "So long as you two lovers don't treat me like a third wheel."

"We would never do that to you," Sera said.

"Yeah," I agreed. "Besides, we're going to make great aunts, once Jas's memory comes back and you two start making all kinds of cute unicorn babies."

"Shut up!" Novah laughed, and slapped me on the arm.

A slow song came on. Novah left the floor, presumably to look for Jas. I reached out and grabbed Sera, taking her into my arms. Couples flooded onto the dance floor.

We swayed slowly to the music, all the other unicorn couples twirling around us. Avalar looked on proudly from the sidelines, Ambrosia next to him.

"Do you believe in fairy tales?" Sera asked sweetly. She straightened the crown on my head, and spun me around before bringing me close once again.

"Yes," I replied. "I'm living in one."

As the song went on, Sera laid her head on my chest. Just before it ended, I whispered in her ear, "Sera?"

"Hm?" She lifted her head and looked at me.

I wasn't afraid to ask now. "Do you want to be my girlfriend?"

Sera smiled at me. She leaned over and gave me a deep kiss, taking my hands in hers. "Thea, I think that would be the most magical thing of all."

∾

ABOUT THE AUTHOR

Megan Linski is a *USA Today* bestselling author and a disabled writer from Michigan. She writes books for teens and young adults in the fantasy and romance genres. She enjoys ice skating, horse riding, and traveling the world. In her spare time, she advocates for mental health awareness and suicide prevention, and also battles Common Variable Immune Deficiency Disorder, a rare primary immune condition.

You can find her at www.meganlinski.com.

ACKNOWLEDGMENTS

Thank you to all the Havenwood Falls authors who allowed me to use your characters in my story— Kristie Cook for Addie, Liz Ferry for Celeste and Jonathan, E.J. Fechenda for Willow and Dalton, and Amy Hale for Miranda. It was quite the magical experience!

PAPER BIRD

AMY RICHIE

HAVENWOOD FALLS HIGH

Paper Bird

AMY RICHIE

~ A Havenwood Falls Young Adult Novella ~

BOOKS BY AMY RICHIE

To my kids, you're stronger than you think.

PROLOGUE

EIGHTEEN YEARS AGO

The air was crisp with an October chill. Up ahead, he could make out the bar where Elias had asked to meet him. He still wasn't sure what this meeting was all about, but when his old friend had called, Ralph couldn't resist his desire to meet him again after so many years apart.

Elias had fallen off the grid completely, almost like he was gone from Earth, but Ralph knew better than that. Elias was one of the few angels left here that he could trust.

Inside the bar, an old country song blared from the jukebox. In one corner, a couple was so twisted up in each other, it was hard to tell where one stopped and the other began. His heart clenched a little for his Beth. If she were here, they would be in a similar position.

He quickly shook his head to dispel such thoughts. He was here to meet Elias, and then he would go home and . . . He grinned as his thoughts ran away from him again.

"Ralph," a familiar voice boomed out. A dark-haired man waved from a stool at the bar; Ralph hurried to join him.

"Elias." He smiled wide. "It's been a long time, my friend."

"Indeed it has." Elias beamed back at him. "Sit. I'll buy you a drink."

Ralph sipped on his drink while he listened to Elias talk about the town he had come from.

"Sounds pretty . . . ideal," he commented when Elias took a breath. Being an angel himself, Ralph knew what a town that offered that kind of protection must mean to Elias.

"It is," he agreed, "but that isn't why I asked you to meet me."

"Then?"

"I've been hearing some . . . rumors about you."

Ralph stiffened slightly. "What kind of rumors?"

"Word is that you've become attached to a human."

His eyes narrowed as he took a forced drink. "I don't see how that is any of your concern."

Elias's hand tightened around his drink. "I'm only looking out for you, friend. There are some who won't take kindly to your . . . transgressions."

"What exactly are you trying to say?"

"I'm telling you to end this before it's too late."

Ralph stood up from his stool. "Are you threatening me?"

"Not at all," he said calmly. "Just trying to help."

"Did Daniel send you to talk to me?" He ran a hand over his face. He was a fool to think he could trust Elias. "What I do isn't any of your business, and you can tell Daniel that too."

"I'm not here for him."

"Whatever."

"If you run into trouble, come to this town of safe haven. They might be able to help you there."

"I don't need anyone's help."

Ralph was fuming as he slid off his stool and stormed out of the bar. So Elias was doing favors for Daniel now? Who did they think they were to tell him what to do? He didn't take orders from anyone. His feet slapped against the pavement as he made his way toward the only person who offered him any comfort these days: Her.

CHAPTER 1

PRESENT DAY - AVA

I sucked in a deep breath and held it in my aching chest. Pushing my senses out, I could just make out the argument going on in front of me—on the big porch attached to an equally large farm house.

"Did you get my letter?" Uncle Ted asked the man who hadn't stopped scowling since we pulled up.

"Mail's slow here," he grunted in reply.

"If I had your phone number . . ."

"No phone."

"Ava is in the car." He jerked his thumb back to me.

From my distance I couldn't be sure, but I thought I saw the man's eyes bug out. "Why?"

"If you would have read my letter . . ." He scowled, letting his words trail off in a grumble.

"Why is she here?"

"There's been more trouble."

"What kind of trouble?"

"The girl can't stay out of jail."

I sank lower into the seat. There was no reason for me to hear this part, no matter how exceptional my hearing was. Uncle Ted and his lovely wife Jane didn't want someone like me around their perfect children. I was a bad influence.

Or so I had been told.

"Hey." Uncle Ted was suddenly back at the car, yanking open my door. "You can come out now."

"I thought you said we were coming to see my dad."

"What?" Distracted, he pressed on the trunk button that was hidden in the glove compartment. "We are," he grunted, still close to my face. "That's him up there."

I peered through the glass at the man glowering at us. He couldn't have been more than a few years older than me. Why was Uncle Ted lying?

"Come on out now," he ordered curtly, moving around to the back of the car to take out my suitcases.

Reluctantly, I pushed the door open farther and stepped out onto the unfamiliar grass. So this was where they were banishing me to? For one stolen shirt?

I really hated being a bad influence.

Uncle Ted had already dug all my things from the trunk and had most of it tucked in his arms and in his hands by the time I reached him—clearly he was in a hurry and I wasn't moving fast enough.

"I got these," he panted when I offered to help. I had little choice but to follow him back up to the house.

"Ralph." Uncle Ted reached out to the man who was obviously not old enough to be my father. "This is Ava."

Ralph's mouth fell open and stayed that way.

Now that I was closer, it was clear that something was different about Ralph, something I couldn't put my finger on. Even if Uncle Ted and Jane wanted to get rid of me, it wasn't right to just dump me off with a stranger in a town I had never heard of. We had a hard time finding the place; that should have been a sign.

"Who are you really?" I asked Ralph.

"He's your father," Uncle Ted sputtered. "I know this is—"

"He's not my dad," I cut him off. "He's too young."

"Well . . ." Uncle Ted rubbed his hand across his top lip.

"How did you find me?" Ralph asked, suddenly finding his voice again. "You shouldn't be here."

"We did get lost," Uncle Ted admitted, still not acting like himself. It must have been the stress of abandoning me when he promised his sister that he would take care of her only daughter. "There was a man—Brad, I think he said his name was—he pointed us in the right direction."

"We followed a bus," I piped in, taking pity on Uncle Ted and his stutters. I had never seen him so flustered.

Ralph's eyes strayed to me, as if he'd just remembered I was standing there. "Brad." He snorted. "Figures."

"So"—Uncle Ted cleared his throat—"anyways . . ."

"She can't stay here," Ralph suddenly snapped. "I don't want her."

Uncle Ted had the decency to shoot me a look of pity. "She . . . needs somewhere to go."

"She can go back with you."

"We don't . . ." He cleared his throat again. "She can't stay with us."

I was glad he hadn't said out loud that he didn't want me either. I mean, it was pretty obvious, but at least he didn't say it out loud.

"I'm . . ." Uncle Ted took a deep breath. "I'm sorry how this all worked out. If your mom . . ."

Was he really going to say he wouldn't dump me off here if she didn't die? If I hadn't killed her?

"Whatever." I shrugged. "Hope you and Jane . . . you know . . . do your thing." Despite how it was ending, I had lived with Uncle Ted for the last seventeen years. If nothing else, he was comfortable, and until he married Jane, he was even kind of nice.

"Yeah."

There were no tears or hugs or heartfelt goodbyes. He gave one last shrug, then slouched off the porch and practically ran back to his waiting car. If he got his way, I would never see Uncle Ted again. Feeling sad would have been appropriate, I realized. Too bad I couldn't bring myself to it.

"Hey," Ralph screamed, running off the porch after him. "I said you can't leave her here."

Uncle Ted was already pulling out of the driveway, though—without me. He didn't turn around.

"Ted!" Ralph stood alone in his front yard, screaming after the retreating car. All that was missing were the chickens and the beer-stained T-shirt, and this would be an episode on a reality TV show. "Come back here!"

Could today get any worse?

"He left," Ralph panted, stopping in front of me. "He just left."

"I noticed."

"You can't stay here."

My eyes slid closed and then opened again slowly. "I'll be eighteen soon."

"In seven months," he thundered.

It came as a bit of a shock that he knew my birthday. "Did you even know my dad?"

"Umm." He pinched the bridge of his nose. "I guess so."

"And my mom?"

At this, his hands dropped back down to his sides. "What did you do to get kicked out?"

"Stole a shirt." I shrugged, glancing down at the offending top. It wasn't even worth all the trouble I had gotten into, ten bucks at the most. Why didn't I just pay for it? "Is there a room in there I can use?"

His lips pursed tightly, but when he spoke again, his voice was soft. "Just until we get this figured out. A night . . . maybe two."

CHAPTER 2

I glanced around the handkerchief-sized room with mounting concern. I could just make out the bed under piles of boxes and what looked like car parts. Boxes were also stacked along the walls and blocked the closet.

This was the room he was giving me? The house was huge. There had to be an empty bedroom in here somewhere. I wasn't even going to be able to sit down, let alone use the bed and closet.

"You can, uh . . ." Ralph ran one hand through his already messy hair. "Clear this out if you want."

"I thought you said I can't stay," I mumbled without looking back at him.

"You're here right now," he gruffly pointed out.

"True." I crossed my arms over my chest. "Where can I put all this stuff?"

"Anywhere really. There's a few rooms upstairs with boxes in them, shed out back. Where ever you want."

"Ok."

"This is the only bedroom downstairs," he explained in halting tones, "and there's no bathroom on the second floor."

"I don't need an explanation." It was still too weird to turn around and actually look at him.

"Don't worry . . . Ava," he stumbled over my name. "I'll talk to Ted. He's a decent guy—for a human."

"A human, huh?" I didn't smile at his weak attempt at humor.

"He'll take you back."

Even if Ralph could convince Uncle Ted to take me back, I didn't want to go. He had already thrown me to the curb like a bag of trash. Why would I go back? Ralph knew my dad and although he didn't want me, if it was a choice between here and back with Uncle Ted's family . . .

"I'm staying here," I informed him flatly, turning just enough so I could see him in my peripheral vision.

His face paled further. "Why would you want to stay here?"

"Just until I'm eighteen."

"That's . . ."

"It's better than some of the places I've stayed." I raised my chin defiantly.

"But you were with your uncle since you were born."

Again with him knowing things about my life.

"Not always." I wasn't going to relive those memories with him, though. I just needed a room for a few months. I could figure things out and get a place of my own after I turned eighteen. I didn't have to burden anyone then.

"Why do you want to stay here?" he asked again.

"You're not much older than me. It'll be like having a roommate." That was a good enough reason.

"I'm older than I look." He raised his chin slightly. "They have good water here in town."

So far I hadn't seen much of the town. An old black man, the back of a bus, mountains that rose up from the ground all around us, and then the farm. No fountain of youth so far. "How old are you?"

"Older than you."

"Okay." I let my eyes widen in his direction. "How did you know my dad?"

"He's . . . my brother."

Another uncle.

"Do you know where he is?" Not that I was going to live with him, even if I did know where he was or what he looked like or anything about him really. I didn't even know his name. I always assumed Uncle Ted didn't know him either, but evidently he had some contact with his family.

"I need to run into town," he announced suddenly. "You stay here."

I had already planned on it.

"You can just"—he waved his hands at the room—"clear this out and . . . wait."

"Good idea." I scowled.

"Or don't." He moved his shoulders nervously. "I don't know how long I'll be." With that, he turned and darted away from me. He was so weird.

Sighing deep enough to move my shoulders, I slipped my jacket off and hung it on the door knob. Pulling a hair tie from my wrist, I quickly twisted all my honey-colored hair up into a messy bun.

Cleaning the room would be hard work, but maybe that was exactly what I needed. A distraction from all the things going on around me. That's how things usually happened—I never felt like I had control over anything.

Except for . . .

I shook my head quickly. The room wasn't going to clean itself.

Rolling my shoulders back and forth to get the stiffness out, I sank onto the soft bed. It had been a long afternoon and Ralph was still gone. Even if he found Uncle Ted and made him come back to get me, Uncle Ted couldn't take me home—Jane would never allow it.

The more I uncovered, the more surprises the room gave me. It turned out I now had a desk, dresser, and a nice mirror. As a bonus, the closet was empty except for a few boxes on the top shelf. And it was a big closet, partially making up for the tiny room.

This would do for now.

"Hey."

I looked up; Ralph was standing in the doorway, his face suspiciously calm.

"You're back?" I asked stupidly. He lived here. Of course he would eventually come back.

"I decided that you could stay."

He must have talked to Uncle Ted. I cringed away from the thoughts of what had been said to make him look like that and change his mind so completely. I didn't want to know. "I was going to anyways."

"Room looks good."

"Thanks."

"Where did you put everything?"

"I took most of it upstairs to that first room. It was already pretty full but . . ." I let my words fall away. He had said I could put the stuff anywhere; there was no need to ramble on.

"I . . . talked to . . . the Court."

"Who?"

"You don't have to register for now," he forged ahead despite my confusion. "I told them you weren't staying and you haven't come into your . . . you know . . ."

"No." My face twisted. "I don't actually know what you're talking about."

"Doesn't matter." He scowled back. "You're fine for now."

Fine for now? Court? Register? And come into my what? Was I supposed to understand any of that? "I . . . don't know . . ."

"Just forget it." He turned away from me.

"Do you have any food?"

"What?" He spun back, surprised by my sudden change of direction.

"This room was a lot of work. I'm hungry."

His eyes widened briefly, then narrowed back out. "Maybe." He shrugged. "I don't shop a lot."

"Homeless people can't really be too picky," I said softly, moving past him to get to the kitchen. No matter which way I tried to look at things, I was pretty much homeless now, clinging onto the only straw I had left.

I almost felt bad for Ralph, but I was determined not to be a burden on him. Starting with making my own food.

There wasn't much to choose from. He obviously didn't cook much. I found some bread that didn't have mold on it and some lunch meat that still smelled okay; a sandwich was within my wheelhouse of culinary skills. My stomach rumbled at the thought, reminding me that I hadn't eaten much of anything since the night before. A sandwich was perfect.

Ralph watched me while I worked. I tried not to be uncomfortable; this was his house after all. He had only given me one room—a room that I had to work for—so I didn't feel guilty about taking ownership of it.

"I'm staying here for senior year," I declared, not looking at him. "Then I'll leave."

Ralph nodded. "You won't have to stay that long."

"I'm still going to." I searched the empty fridge and found a lone bottle of ketchup in the door. Good enough, I inwardly shrugged. It appeared that good enough was going to become my mantra for a while.

Not forever.

"You won't always be underage," Caleb sighed, twisting one of my stray hairs around his finger. "Soon enough, he won't be able to tell you what to do anymore. You can come stay with me." He smiled softly, showing off all his perfect teeth.

"It feels like forever, though." I pouted, sinking into his velvety voice.

"Not forever."

"Don't worry." Ralph sighed loudly, effectively bringing me

back to the present and his understocked kitchen. "I'll talk to your uncle."

"You are my uncle," I reminded him.

His teeth worked his bottom lip.

"He'll take you back," he went on relentlessly. His eyes went in and out of focus as he worked out how exactly he was going to get rid of me.

I hated to burst his bubble; nothing would work, though.

"I'm not going back there." I scowled. "I don't care if Uncle Ted agrees to it or not; I'm staying. I just did all that work." I half-heartedly gestured back to the room he had lent me. "Don't worry, I won't cause any trouble here." It was hard to stay out of trouble, but I needed to. At least until I turned eighteen, but it would be better to be able to graduate.

One step at a time.

Without waiting for him to sputter any more excuses at me, I made my way back to the small room with the comfortable bed. It wasn't exactly my room, but it had all my stuff in it, and that would have to be good enough for now.

CHAPTER 3

a bird of some sort called loudly right outside my bedroom window, making my eyes shoot open. I bolted upright in bed, my heart pounding in my chest.

"What the hell was that?" I whispered to no one.

Inching my body forward, I peeked through the slit in the curtains, searching out the monstrous creature. It wasn't even fully daylight yet. A quick scan showed that I was in no immediate danger. I rubbed sleepily at my gritty eyes and let out a small groan.

Sleep was out of the question, since I hadn't actually seen anything out there. That meant it could be anywhere—plotting its attack on me. No, it would be no use to lie back down until I knew for sure that I wouldn't be killed by Big Bird.

I slid the rest of the way off the bed and shuffled out to the kitchen. My mouth dropped open at the sight that waited there.

"Morning," Ralph awkwardly greeted. "I made you some food."

"I see that."

The circular table was full of various plates of breakfast foods and even some that weren't breakfast. Sausage, eggs, toast, pancakes, pizza, jello, a bowl of butter, what looked like an entire chicken . . .

"I couldn't remember what humans liked to eat when they first wake up." He swallowed hard.

"How did you do all this?"

"I got up early."

"It's early now," I pointed out. "Did you go to bed at all?"

"I just sleep when I'm tired." His shoulders jerked upwards. "Are you going to eat?"

I slid into an empty seat at the table. There was no point in being rude, I told my still racing heart. Besides, the food really did smell delicious—better than the sandwich I had eaten the night before.

"You look scared," he noted, as I began piling sausage and toast onto my plate.

"It's not because of the food," I blurted out, suddenly remembering the killer bird.

"Then?"

"It's nothing." I had already resolved not to bother him. As long as I stayed inside where it was safe, I would be fine. It's not like birds could open doors.

"You want to go to school?"

"Today?" I poured syrup on my sausage links, mouth already watering.

"Probably tomorrow," he clarified. "In general though, you want to go?"

"Not really." I had never been very good at school.

"I thought you said . . ."

"Yeah," I sighed. "I guess I need to finish it up after all the time I've put in already."

"You haven't even started yet." His eyebrows furrowed together in the middle of his normally smooth forehead.

"I've been going since I was six." I stabbed one of the links and took half of it in one bite.

"I'll sign you up. I'm not sure how long you'll be here, so you might as well go. I think the year just started at Havenwood Falls High. I hear it's a decent school."

It was the middle of October, but good enough.

"How will I get there?" As far as I had been able to tell, Ralph didn't live anywhere close to a school, so walking was out. If there was no school bus . . . "Will I have to fly there?"

"What?" His eyes widened. "Of course you can't fly."

"I know," I said dryly. "I was kidding."

Shaking his head, he began piling his own plate with pizza and jello. "You can drive. It's not too far. Eight minutes and thirty-six seconds if you drive the speed limit the entire time. Take into account traffic"—he shrugged lightly—"I would say no more than ten minutes anyways."

He stared at me until I snapped my mouth back closed again. "You timed it?"

"Last night." He nodded. "I thought you would need to know so you can plan accordingly."

"That's, um . . ." Weird. "I don't have a car." My face scrunched up at his obvious oversight.

"I bought one for you."

My mouth seemed to be on a hinge. Realizing it was hanging open again, I snapped it shut and watched as he chewed calmly. "Are you serious?"

"About which part?"

"The part about buying me a car."

"It's just a used one." His forehead creased. "It's not a big deal. I got it from Josh over at the garage."

It was a very big deal.

"Do you have a license? I probably should have asked first."

"Yeah."

"Good." He nodded. "That's all settled then."

"Yeah." I took another bite, chewing slowly.

I did have my license—that was true enough. The rectangular plastic card was tucked away in an ugly wallet I had gotten for Christmas one year. But I knew I didn't deserve that thing. In fact,

I didn't actually know how to drive very well. I had only done it three or four times.

When I turned sixteen, I was determined to prove my worth to whoever was looking. Even though I didn't have anybody willing to teach me, I didn't let that stop me. At the actual test, I freaked out and refused to even turn the car on.

It was easy to convince the instructor that I had driven perfectly—the best he had ever seen. I didn't know why people believed the things I told them, but it came in handy sometimes.

Now I'd have to drive myself to school every morning? Oh well, I could do it. It was better than asking Ralph to drive me. Time to be a big girl.

"Fine." I took a bite of buttered toast. "I'll drive myself to school."

"If you need me to take you the first day . . ." He trailed off, not quite offering.

It didn't matter, though. "I don't need you."

"Good," he grunted in reply. "It's better to . . . you know . . . rely on yourself. Makes life easier."

"So I've been told." My mom died the day I was born, and my dad left a few minutes after she took her last breath. I was pretty good at relying on myself.

"I'll go into town again today," he announced. "I can get you enrolled and stuff."

"Should I go with?"

"No," he answered quickly.

Whatever. I didn't really want to go anywhere with him anyway. It would have been nice to get a look at the school and to know where it was, but I would just do that in the morning.

"Thanks for breakfast," I said, getting up from the table. "And . . . for the car." He didn't acknowledge my gratitude, which was fine. Grabbing up my half-eaten toast, I made my way back to my room.

Now that the sun had risen properly, I scanned the place

beside my window for the bird that had woken me up. Everything was quiet, though—way too quiet to be natural.

Shuddering, I hurried over to the closet and flung the door open. I randomly pulled out a pair of jeans and a pale pink V-necked tee shirt. It had been a weird morning, and the sun was barely even up yet.

CHAPTER 4

"*O*kay," I whispered to my reflection. "First days aren't that bad." Having gotten myself kicked out of several schools, I had had my fair share of first days. They sucked.

Taking a breath, I scanned a critical eye over my appearance. My heart-shaped face was too puffy; my lips and cheeks looked swollen, but they weren't. That was just how I looked. I was slender enough not to be made fun of at school, but I wasn't what anyone would call skinny or athletic. Curvy—that's what Caleb said. My honey-colored hair hung most of the way down my back, cascading in gentle waves. It was my favorite part of myself, even if it did sometimes border on frizzy instead of wavy.

"Good enough." I sighed deeply.

Ralph wasn't anywhere to be found when I came into the kitchen. My stomach was too full of nerves to eat, but I did manage to chug down a glass of orange juice from the recently restocked fridge. As much as he didn't want me here, it was good of Ralph to make an effort.

After one glance at the big clock above the door, I knew I needed to hurry if I didn't want to be late on my very first day. Considering it wasn't everyone else's first day, everyone was bound to notice me.

Despite his warnings, the car that Ralph had bought for me wasn't bad. A cute silver thing with no rust or dents. Four wheels, a windshield, and four doors. Seemed perfect to me.

I gripped the steering wheel tight enough to make my knuckles turn white. Driving was definitely not my favorite thing to do, but I needed to rely on myself more. I wasn't willing to burden Ralph when I could do this myself.

How hard could it be?

Having lived in the nearby town of Montrose, I was used to the sight of the mountains that blotted out the skyline and seemed to bring in the crisp air of fall earlier than other places, but Havenwood Falls was different. The mountains were on all sides of me as I drove, boxing me in. I expected to feel suffocated by the sight of them but was pleasantly surprised by the comfort they gave me.

The three-story building of the school came into view not long after I got into town. Relieved, I pulled into a parking spot and killed the engine. Was this my life now?

Still jittery from the drive, I made my way up to the large front doors, then to the office, where they would have my schedule and books ready for me.

Puffing out my cheeks, I pushed open the heavy glass door that led to the school office. A woman looked up when I entered, smiling pleasantly.

"You must be Ava Tate?"

"Yeah." I bit lightly on my bottom lip, willing myself not to say anything she might consider rude. Although I usually didn't mean to be, people always thought I was being disrespectful. That's the word Uncle Ted used.

Get through senior year; that's what I needed to focus on. If I got good enough grades here, I'd be able to get into Harper, a trade school back home. I knew better than to hope college was

AMY RICHIE

possible, but Harper offered all sorts of career choices. I could do hair, or tend flowers, or . . .

"Here's your schedule," the woman called out, bringing me out of my silent musings. "And your books." She patted a stack of textbooks, still smiling kindly.

"Umm . . . thanks," I told her, smoothing my top lip out before it got out of hand.

"Welcome to Havenwood Falls High, Ava. I'm sure you'll enjoy your time here."

Eager to get away from the talking brochure, I left the office, all my books in tow and my schedule clutched tightly in one fist.

It wasn't hard to find the row of lockers. Following the numbers, I was able to find mine and deposit my books inside. Heart hammering, I checked the schedule to see which class I had first. History with Ms. Bast. How in the hell was I supposed to find it?

"Hey there," a gorgeous girl called out, a few lockers away. Her blond hair was swept dramatically off her face. "New here?"

"That obvious?" I chuckled nervously, then immediately wished I could suck the sound back in.

"I'm Miranda Saunders." She grinned.

"Ava Tate," I replied back in the socially acceptable manner.

"You need help finding your class?"

Nodding eagerly, I held the paper out to her. "History."

"Follow me." She spun on one heel away from me. "I think you'll like this school," she called over her shoulder.

"Thanks," I mumbled, keeping my eyes on the back of her shoes.

As soon as I entered Ms. Bast's class, I knew I wasn't going to like this school. At least twenty pairs of eyes swung around to take in my loose-fitting jeans and frizzy hair.

"Ava Tate?" Ms. Bast's eyebrows disappeared into her hairline. She was gorgeous, by far the prettiest teacher I had ever had. Her tight green skirt was short enough to show off her long copper legs. "Do you have family in Havenwood Falls?"

Why was that any of her business?

"An uncle," I grunted, swallowing past the dryness in my throat.

"Also a Tate?" she continued to probe.

"I didn't ask him."

There were a few scattered giggles from the room. Ms. Bast's eyes narrowed. "You may take an empty seat at the back."

All around the full classroom, eyes kept straying back to me. It was a small school; their curiosity was understandable. No one smiled. What did I care though? It wasn't like I needed or wanted to have a sleepover with any of them.

Ralph probably wouldn't let me even if I did.

The only other person sitting in the back row with me was a dark-haired boy. He stared at me with his deep coffee-colored eyes. He didn't turn away when I caught him staring. It was going to be a long forty-five minutes.

"Don't forget to study tonight, boys and girls," Ms. Bast called from the front of the class when the clock had finally clicked down. The dark-haired boy had looked at me more than he looked at his book. "European geography test tomorrow. The map is on page 43."

She directed the last part at me. Would I be expected to take the test too? How was I supposed to know anything about Europe? I had never been outside of the United States, and I never planned to be.

CHAPTER 5

*P*ursing my lips, I tapped my pencil against an open map I was supposed to be learning for the Europe test. I had never been good at tests, and I had a feeling this one wasn't going to be any better. I had to prove myself to Ralph, though.

The rest of the school day had passed in the same fashion it had begun—a whirlwind of awkward staring and nervous smiles. I didn't return any of the smiles.

Ralph wasn't home when I got back, so I made myself another sandwich and retired to my room, where I planned to stay until I knew Europe. Even if I didn't understand why it was so important for me to learn it. I wasn't going to be going on any trips to Paris or anything. I didn't like to fly.

By the time Ralph came home, my resolve was starting to waver.

"Oh my god," I half growled at the offending maps. "I can't look at this anymore."

Outside, the sun was starting to set, creating streaks of purple and orange in the vast sky. A sudden longing to see the mountains washed over me. I could use some air, I decided on a whim. I had all night to study.

"Where are you going?" Ralph asked, when I passed the table to get to the front door.

"Outside." Wasn't that obvious?

"I'm making food for you."

"I had a sandwich earlier." We didn't need to be making habits here. I was only staying the year.

As soon as I stepped out on the porch, the hair on my arms stood up and goose bumps broke out all over my skin. The air was starting to chill, and small patches of snow were piled everywhere. I was used to the cold, though.

Something else was causing it. There was no one out there with me, and yet . . .

I squinted, scanning the semidarkness around the house. Dark, impregnable shadows lined the forest in the distance. It was probably fine, I told myself weakly.

"Why did you come out here, anyway?" Ralph asked, joining me on the porch. "I thought you were studying."

"I'm done," I lied easily.

Although obviously not convinced, he let it drop. His gaze followed my own line of sight. "What are you looking for?"

"I'm not sure," I breathed. "It felt like someone was watching me."

"Really?" He sniffed the air deeply. "Are you sure?"

"No." I straightened up, suddenly realizing how paranoid I sounded. "It was probably just the wind. Or that killer bird from yesterday morning."

"I already told you that was a rooster." He scowled, not taking his eyes from the tree line.

"I'm going back to Europe," I told him with a roll of my eyes.

"Europe?" He twisted wildly to look back at me. "Is that what he told you?"

He? "You mean Ms. Bast?"

"What did he tell you?" he sneered. "Was it some cheesy pickup line? And did you fall for him?"

"You're a really weird guy."

251

"What?" He blinked several times.

"Ms. Bast didn't tell me that," I informed him, my nose scrunched. "I figured it out by myself."

"I don't . . . understand what you're saying."

Was this my real life?

"I'll see you later," I scoffed, stomping back inside the house.

CHAPTER 6

I chewed relentlessly at the skin on my bottom lip. I really hated taking tests; it hardly seemed fair to make me take one on my second day. How was I supposed to learn all those places overnight? I didn't even know how to pronounce half of them.

And if I failed . . .

My chest clenched at the thought, my hand falling back down to my side. There was only one thing I could do, I decided. Ms. Bast was alone at her desk—it was now or never.

No one needed to know.

"Hi." I waved stupidly at the woman sitting behind the desk. "Can I talk to you for a second?"

"Sure." She smiled kindly.

"I was just wondering if you remembered that you already had me take this test yesterday." If I just pushed a little with my mind, she would think I was telling the truth. Then I could give myself an A . . . maybe a B.

Her head jerked back slightly at my words. "Why would I do that?"

No one had ever asked that before. Why wasn't she just

agreeing with me? "Because I'm new," I stammered. "So you wanted to see what I already knew."

Ms. Bast's eyes narrowed—also something I didn't expect. "Take your seat, Ava," she ordered dryly. "Class will begin soon."

What?

"Did you really think that would work, new girl?" An amused voice chuckled behind me.

"What?" I whirled around to find the boy I had noticed the day before—the one with the deep brown eyes.

"I saw you trying to get out of today's test." He jutted his chin in the direction of Ms. Bast, who had gone back to ignoring us.

"Mind your own business." I clicked my tongue against the roof of my mouth. Fully irritated with my failed attempt, I slouched back to my seat.

"I can help, if you want," the boy offered, holding his hands wide. He had followed me to my desk.

"How can you help?" It was too late now. The bell would ring in a few minutes. "You want to be study buddies?" I widened my eyes sarcastically.

"I hate studying," he snorted. "I was thinking of something more guaranteed."

"Like what?"

"Like a list of the answers." He pulled out a narrow sheet of paper that was numbered to twenty-five. I couldn't read what it said after the numbers, but I didn't need to.

"This seems a little . . ." My tongue felt swollen. How did that happen? It was normal-sized a few moments ago.

"Brilliant?" He flashed a wide grin.

"Obvious is what I was going for," I corrected with a pronounced frown, "and risky."

"Maybe." He shrugged. "But if you don't know the answers . . ." He waved the paper in front of me. "It's up to you."

Ms. Bast had gotten up from her desk.

"Fine," I hissed. "How much?"

"No money." He held my gaze briefly.

"Then?" I prompted impatiently.

"You'll owe me a favor."

"I'll owe you a favor?" I snorted. "What is this, the eighteenth century?"

"Agreed?"

"Whatever." I shrugged, snatching the answer sheet out of his hands. "But I'm not giving you my virginity or anything."

"You're a virgin?" His eyes traveled slowly down to my feet and back up again, making my face flame hot. "That's . . . unexpected."

"What the hell is that supposed to mean?"

"Tuck that into your sleeve," he ordered as the bell shrilled, ignoring my embarrassment. He turned away from me toward his own desk. Before he went far, he turned back to me. "If you ever want to do a study session without the studying, I'm here for you, Ava." His eyelid dropped into a ridiculous wink.

"You are—"

"Toby," he cut me off with another small wink. "Good luck on your test."

"Find your seats," Ms. Bast called above the din of conversation. Without preamble, she handed the test sheets out and sat back at her desk. Whatever she was reading must have been more interesting than maps of Europe.

A few seats over, Toby nodded encouragingly. He was probably right. I would fail if I didn't cheat. Especially since my mind thing didn't work; I wasn't sure exactly how that thing worked, so it was impossible to know if I could fix it. Maybe I was just a normal girl now.

Kind of normal.

Fingers tapping furiously against the desk in front of me, I slipped the small paper out enough to see the tiny writing. Okay, this wasn't so bad, I thought, relaxing slightly. If I just got through this one, I'd be sure to study harder next time.

"Ava Tate?"

My head snapped up at the sound of my name. My heart almost stuttered to a complete stop when I looked up to see Ms. Bast glaring down at me. Why wasn't she still at her desk?

"Yeah?" I croaked.

"I'd like to see you out in the hall," she declared angrily.

~

The longer I sat in the hard plastic chair, the hotter my ears became. Why wasn't the principal talking? I had been sent to see plenty of principals, having been kicked out of several schools, and they all loved to fire up their throats and yell down to me. But this one so far had just told me to sit and wait. Maybe this was like when the police took me in —he must be waiting to question me until my parents got there.

He'd be waiting a while.

The door opened behind me, making my spine stiffen— especially when I heard Ralph's familiar angry voice. He wasn't my parent. Why would they call him?

"What's going on here?" he grumbled, sinking into the chair next to me.

"Mr. Tate?" The principal sifted through the papers on his desk, his eyes narrowed. "I thought we called Ava's father . . ." His voice trailed off awkwardly.

"I'm close enough." Ralph scowled. "What did she do?"

"It's not really a big deal," I told him nervously. This was all I needed, to be in trouble before a full week even passed. Now he would see exactly why Uncle Ted didn't want me. Where would I go if he decided he didn't want me either?

"We take cheating very seriously," Mr. Friske boomed out from behind his desk.

"Mr. Friske." Ralph smiled silkily. I had never seen him so charming. "Ava is new here."

Mr. Friske made a small grunting noise, but his stony expression softened.

"I realize that." He sighed. "I understand that she just came to live with you recently?"

"Very recently," he cooed.

My mouth fell open. Who was this guy?

"We've taken that into consideration and decided to suspend Ava, rather than expel her."

"For how long?" Ralph asked before I could find my voice.

"Two weeks."

"Suspended?" I sputtered.

"For two weeks," Mr. Friske repeated, holding up two steady fingers.

"For cheating on one stupid test?" Ridiculous. I shouldn't have even been taking a test on my second day; this was all Ms. Bast's fault.

"This is your second day at our school."

"I know." It was like he could read my mind.

"I think it's important to set a precedent here." He didn't crack even the tiniest of smiles.

"Am I supposed to know what that means?"

"We'll see you in two weeks, Miss Tate. At which time you will retake that test without cheating."

"Thank you." Ralph smiled just enough so he didn't look happy but he didn't look mad either.

I had no such luck hiding how I felt. Going by the look Ralph shot me, my thoughts were displayed clearly on my face. It was so annoying, just like Mr. Friske.

"Let's go home, Ava." Ralph sprang up from his seat, pulling me along with him—all the way through the school and back out to the parking lot.

"I'm sorry you had to come down here," I murmured, trying not to look at him.

"I'm going," he declared curtly. "I assume you're okay to drive home?"

"Of course," I squeaked.

He stared at me, unblinking, for several long moments. "Why is your heart beating so fast?"

"Wh—" As usual, Ralph caught me off guard with his words. "Can you hear it?" I pressed my hand against my chest, willing my heart to slow down. "How?"

"Hmm." He shook himself out of whatever he had been thinking and whirled away from me. "I'll see you at home."

What the hell? He was so weird.

"Whatever," I grumbled, moving toward my car. It was pretty decent of him not to flip out on me over the whole cheating thing.

My shoulders slumped at the fresh memory of trouble. Uncle Ted was right about me; I couldn't stay out of trouble. I just wasn't a good person.

"You're not going to cry, are you?" Toby called out. His tall frame was leaning casually against my car.

"Shouldn't you be in class?" I scrunched my face angrily.

"They won't miss me." He shrugged, unconcerned.

This was all his fault. "Go away."

His face fell dramatically, comically.

"That's not very nice." He jutted his bottom lip out.

"I'm not a nice person." I reached for my door handle, but Toby moved himself to be more in my way.

"I thought we were going to be friends." He grinned. "Didn't you offer me your virginity and everything?"

"You got me in trouble," I accused, trying to elbow my way past his infuriating smirk.

"You're the one who got caught."

He was right, of course, but I wasn't about to admit that. It was easier to be mad at him. "I should have never listened to you."

"I was just trying to help." He chuckled. "Passing that test seemed important to you." His head tilted to one side, obviously making fun of me.

"Move."

"Ava," he purred, flashing his straight teeth. "Don't be mad at me."

"Move," I repeated. I wasn't giving in to him. Did he think I was born last night?

"You're going to break my heart." He clutched his chest.

"Find someone else to bother." I pushed at his shoulder, attempting to make him move, since he wasn't doing it himself.

"Ava."

"I've known plenty of guys like you," I growled. "I'm just trying to get through my senior year, so stay away from me."

"That's where you're wrong."

"About?"

"You've *never* known a guy like me."

The wind changed suddenly, bringing something different to his expression. Something sinister. It happened so fast, I wasn't sure what I saw exactly.

The hair on my arms stood straight up, a ringing started in my ears, and my chest clenched. My body was telling me, very clearly, that I was in danger.

Without knowing why, I found myself calculating how long it would take me to run back inside the school. Would Toby be faster?

"Ava?"

Blinking rapidly, I shook off the strange feeling. Dangerous, really? Geesh, what was wrong with me? "I have to go home," I said thickly. "Don't follow me."

"Follow you home?" He chuckled, his eyes shining. "Why would I follow you home?"

I slid into the front seat of my car and pulled the door closed. "I'm not sure why I said that," I told him through the open window. "I'm just . . . upset about getting suspended."

"So . . . you do want me to follow you?"

"No!"

"Mixed signals"—he held his hands up between us—"that's all I'm saying."

I pushed my lips out in an exaggerated pout. It was still hard to believe that I got two whole weeks for one little test. Hopefully the school wasn't always going to be this strict. "See you in two weeks."

Moving suddenly, Toby leaned far into my window.

"I seriously doubt that," he growled. Then he was gone, leaving me gasping for air.

"What the hell?"

CHAPTER 7

*G*roaning loudly, I let my head fall backward until it hit the soft cushion of the desk chair. Ralph had dug out the comfortable chair for my studying pleasure, or so he said.

It was more for torture though. Studying was by far the worst pastime. I would rather have gone outside and dug for worms than study that map of Europe.

"Ugh." I pinched the bridge of my nose in an attempt to chase away the headache that was trying to eat my brain.

I grabbed my useless phone from the corner of the desk and glanced at the time. I must have been studying the maps for hours . . . like nine or ten hours at least.

"Forty-five minutes?" I sputtered. No way was the clock working. It must have stopped working when the signal went out.

Ralph had warned me that my phone wouldn't work this far out of town, and even in town it was spotty. The mountains made it that way. But I insisted on keeping it charged just in case.

Even though I didn't have any friends that would text me. Or call me, or miss me. Or even notice I was gone.

Rubbing furiously at my eyes, I forced my attention back to something that mattered.

Suddenly a welcome distraction came from the kitchen in the

form of Ralph banging around. Grinning, I slammed the book shut and bounded from the room.

"Hey," I greeted him, careful not to show my happiness. "What are you doing?"

"I should ask you the same thing," he called over his shoulder. He was haphazardly piling groceries into the fridge. "You need to prepare for the retake. Mr. Friske said—"

"I know," I cut him off. "I got the same email." Apparently suspension wasn't enough of a punishment. I had to retake the test when I went back. "But I still have a while. I've been studying all morning."

"You have?" He frowned, putting several boxes on the counter.

"Well, I mean . . . most of it." I hadn't been awake for long, but he didn't need to know everything.

"Mmm." He nodded, unconcerned as always. Really, Uncle Ted should have dumped me off here a long time ago.

"You went shopping?" I sniffed hopefully. Maybe he had picked up a few of those bagels from town.

"I'm leaving town," he announced.

"What?"

"And I wanted to be sure you had food."

"What do you mean you're leaving town? Is it because I got in trouble?"

"No." His eyebrows furrowed in the middle of his forehead. "I'll only be gone a few days."

"Where are you going?"

"It's . . ." He cleared his throat lightly. "I don't pry into your life," he pointed out. "And this is something . . . something I don't want you to pry into."

Fair enough. "Are you coming back?"

"Yes."

"In a few days." He had already said he would be gone a few days. There was no reason to panic.

"You can't come with me."

"Yeah"—I shrugged—"I get it."

"I mean"—he sighed and ran a hand through his hair—"you aren't registered, so you can't leave town."

"Umm . . ."

"Just . . . stay close to home." His tongue ran over his bottom lip.

"Where else would I go?" I whispered. No reason to be scared. He's coming back.

"Here's some money." He laid a stack of bills on the counter next to the boxes. "Just in case."

In case he didn't come back?

"I don't think I'll need it. I'm not going anywhere," I reminded him.

Ralph crossed the room and pulled open the front door. Just before leaving, he turned back to me. "I'll be back in a few days."

"Promise?"

He smiled wide. "I promise."

Good enough.

CHAPTER 8

My eyes wouldn't close. No matter what I told myself, it wouldn't work. It was too bad my special powers didn't work on me.

Outside my window, a tree danced wildly in the wind, creating shadows across my ceiling. It was the middle of the night—I really should have been sleeping. I had never felt this alone, though.

I lived most of my life with Uncle Ted, where there was always commotion of some sort. He and Jane had four small children; noise was inevitable. When things got hard there, I stayed with Caleb from time to time. He didn't have a house, and the streets never slept.

Blowing air out loudly through my puffed-up cheeks, I rolled to my side and forced my eyes to close.

"Ava!"

My recently closed eyes popped back open. Was that my name I heard? It was hard to hear anything over the thudding of my own heart. Why was I so jumpy? I was clear out in the middle of nowhere. Who was going to be out there? No one was around—not even the police could come here quickly if I called. It would take them a while . . .

I sat up in my bed. Pushing my senses out, I listened as hard as

I could. I had exceptional hearing. No one I knew could hear like I could.

"Ava!"

"Oh," I hissed, letting my held breath back out. Someone was calling me; someone who knew my name; someone who knew I lived here. I couldn't just lie here and pretend I didn't hear them. Heart still pounding, I threw my blanket aside and hurried to the kitchen.

I opened the door just enough to let myself slip outside to the front porch. Even if it wasn't smart, I needed to know who was calling me. Maybe someone was in trouble out there. Maybe it was Ralph.

Squirming uncomfortably at the thought, I scanned the yard where the light from the house touched. I wasn't surprised that no one was there. It wouldn't be that easy. I hugged my arms over my chest.

The late night air was cold, even for fall. In my haste to get outside, I hadn't bothered to grab a jacket or hoodie. All I had on was a flimsy tank top and short shorts.

Goose bumps rose on my bare skin, but I couldn't be sure if that was from the cold or . . . something else.

"Don't let your imagination get crazy," I whispered firmly.

Deciding I needed the sweater, I turned back toward the house. But I stopped before I'd taken a step.

"Ava!"

"Who's out there?" I turned back to the voice. "What do you want?"

It was too dark to see much of anything past my own bubble of light, but I knew where the voice was coming from. I knew it before I ever came outside. So many children's stories centered on the evil things that lurked in the woods, ready to eat us. Every irrational fear I had ever had told me not to go one step off the safety of the porch. And yet . . .

There was someone out in the trees calling to me.

I opened my eyes as far as they would go, searching for any

sign of a person or even light. I would settle for light. There were only shadows and even darker shadows. It was stupid enough to be out here at all. Was I really that crazy, to be considering going out farther?

No way.

"I'm going back inside," I told the disembodied voice in a shaky whisper. "I'm not going out there."

Very suddenly, from one breath to the next, everything became crystal clear to me. There was nothing out here to be afraid of. My whole body relaxed, feeling lighter than it had in such a long time. What was I thinking to be afraid?

A friend was out there—a really good friend. They didn't need my help. They just wanted . . . to play. Grinning widely, I skipped down the few steps and out onto the grass.

"I'm here," I called out, spinning in fast circles. "I'm sorry I was afraid before, but I'm ready now. Please don't hide from me."

A light flared to life from the center of the tree line. It was a light so beautiful that it almost hurt to look at it. Shocked, I ducked my head into my shoulder. "I know you," I whispered. "I remember."

There was only one thing that mattered now—I had to get to that light before it hid again. I had made it scared by yelling from the porch when it had reached out to me. But I would fix that.

No matter what.

Taking a quick breath, I starting running toward the tree line. A low-level panic had started in my stomach, urging me blindly forward. My foot caught on something jutting out from the grass, and I sprawled forward.

"Ouch," I hissed to the darkness. Bright spots of blood oozed up on both my knees. I didn't have time to be injured. He wouldn't wait for long.

Raising up to my hurt knees, I searched out the light. It was almost gone, I realized with a fresh rush of urgency. I could just make out the faint glow now. I had to hurry.

Pushing myself back up to two feet and mostly solid ground, I took off again in the direction of the light. It was a good thing Ralph wasn't there, I realized as I ran. He would never have let me go running off into the woods in the middle of the night.

Just inside the woods, I paused against the first tree I came to. Which way did I go now?

"Ava."

"I'm here." I looked around wildly, searching for the voice that had called me out into the night. He had to be here somewhere.

"Ava."

"I don't understand what you want me to do!" As I turned in a complete circle, my foot snagged on a clump of grass, and I lost my balance.

Laying there on the cold ground, I sucked in a deep breath and watched the stars burning in the sky above me. This all seemed so strangely familiar.

"You need to get up now."

Of course I did. Why was I lying on the ground anyway? It was cold. I rose up on steady legs, waiting for my next instructions.

"Do you see the tall tree to your left?"

I nodded. I had fallen right next to it.

"Climb to the top of that tree."

"I can't climb a tree."

"You can."

He was right again, obviously. As soon as I started climbing, I realized how easy it was. My feet found the right knobs and branches, like I had been climbing trees my whole life.

The higher I got, the more excited I felt. This, whatever it was, was the right thing to do. I wasn't even cold anymore.

Once I got to the highest branch I could get to, I twisted around so I could swing myself onto it. "There," I grinned triumphantly. "I made it."

It was higher than I expected. The wind blew stronger up here than it did on the ground; I had to grab tight to the tree to stop myself from falling. "What do I do now? I'm going to fall!"

"Jump."

"What?"

"Jump."

"No, I can't jump from up here." I peeked down and instantly regretted it. My stomach rolled at the sight of the ground so far beneath me. "I'm scared."

"Jump!"

I leaned forward as far as I was able to, then . . . I let go.

It was amazing. The wind ruffled my hair and pushed it away from my face so I could see everything that was going on around me. Everything . . .

In an instant, the fog that had held me captive lifted, and I realized that I had just jumped from the top of a tree. I was going to die. Everyone would just assume I had killed myself. I didn't even have enough breath in my lungs to scream.

Just when I was sure I would crash face first into the ground, the wind seemed to catch me and hold me in its embrace. Instead of falling to my death—I was flying. Or, at least, floating. To my complete shock, I landed softly back on the earth on two legs.

Then immediately crumpled to my knees.

My breath rasped in and out of my ragged lungs. Somehow, despite everything they had been through, my lungs and heart still seemed to be working.

I leaned forward until my forehead made contact with the hard ground. I felt like I was going to throw up, but I didn't think I could move, so I just sat there with my knees against my chest. Maybe they would be able to prevent me from falling apart completely.

What the hell had happened to me? Was I going crazy?

"Ava?"

I peeked up enough to see a real person walking toward me. At least I hoped he was real and I wasn't hallucinating again. I recognized him.

"Toby?" I squeaked out of trembling lips.

"Are you all right?" He dropped down beside me.

"No." I shook my head, my forehead swishing along the grass.

"Let me see," he ordered gently. "Are you hurt?"

"I don't understand what's happening," I choked, not moving.

"I just want to see if you're hurt."

"I think I'm going crazy." Saying it out loud was so much worse than thinking it.

"What happened here?" He gently poked my bloody knees.

When had I moved? "I . . . fell." Shuddering, I glanced back up the tall tree that loomed over both of us. "I fell out of this tree."

Toby's brow puckered. "I don't think you did."

"I jumped," I sobbed, letting my head fall back down. He caught me before I went all the way down.

"But . . . you didn't hurt your knees when you jumped."

"Who cares about my knees," I wailed, the sound coming out muffled. "I'm crazy. Like . . . for real crazy. I jumped out of a tree because someone told me to." And now I was blurting it out to him.

"I think I would question the sanity of whoever told you to jump."

At this, my head snapped up. "How can you make jokes at a time like this? Didn't you hear what I said?"

"I heard." He went back to examining my knees. "Do they hurt?"

"I . . . no, they don't."

"I'll help you get back home," he cooed. "You're not really dressed in enough clothes to be hanging out here in the woods."

Sobbing more, I flung my arms around his neck. "You don't understand," I explained thickly. "You don't understand what I'm telling you." I wasn't entirely sure I understood.

He must have thought I had a bad dream or something. Obediently, I got up from the ground and let Toby lead the way back to the empty farmhouse. He let me cling onto him until we got inside.

"Do you think you'll be okay now?" he asked, looking down at me in the chair he had set me in.

"You're not going to leave, are you?" Cold panic shot through my veins.

"I . . . was thinking about it. Yeah."

I clutched wildly for his hand. "Please stay here tonight," I begged.

His head jerked back at my odd request. We weren't exactly friends. The last time I had seen him, I had yelled at him to leave me alone. I didn't blame him for being surprised. I didn't know why he had been out by our farm tonight, but I still wanted him to stay.

"I don't think that's a good idea," he said slowly, prying his hand away from my fingers.

"Ralph is gone," I cried, refusing to let go. "I can't stay here alone. What if . . ." My eyes darted back and forth. Saying anything else about hearing voices would scare him away for sure. "What if I have another bad dream?"

"You had a dream?" His eyes narrowed as he watched me freak out.

"I . . . don't know what it was," I admitted. "It's not like any dream I've ever had before. But . . ." It must have been a dream. Why else did people hear voices in the middle of the night—voices that wanted them to die?

"You don't look so good."

Even though I knew I shouldn't cling on to an almost stranger who gave a bad vibe, I couldn't stop myself from holding on to his arm so he couldn't leave me.

"To be fair," I croaked, "I did just fall out of a tree." Or jump, I silently corrected.

"You really want me to stay?" His dark eyes searched my face. "I thought you wanted me to leave you alone."

"I don't want to be alone tonight. I don't know Ralph's number." Not that I could call him even if I did know it.

"I doubt he has a phone," he chuckled weakly.

"You know him?"

Toby pursed his lips out. "I'll stay here tonight," he declared suddenly. "If you're sure you want me to."

"I do." I nodded quickly. I didn't want to be alone, and Toby was here already. It wasn't like I knew anyone else in town.

"Okay." He tried to straighten back up, but I was holding him too tightly. "You can let me go. I promise I won't leave."

My tongue darted out to glide over my lips. "I'll make a bed up on the floor."

"Are you going to let go of me first?"

"I don't know."

"You're safe," he soothed. "I promise you're safe."

He was making an awful lot of promises to me, but what good were his words? I didn't trust him at all.

"We can go together." I jumped up from my seat. "My room is this way."

Not giving him much choice, I pulled him into my room. Only after the door was shut behind us did I let go of him. If he tried to bolt, the room was small enough that I could get to him before he got the door open. I set to work quickly making up a blanket bed on the floor next to my real bed. It was too small to share, and I wanted to sleep next to Toby.

If I heard the voice again, he wouldn't let me follow it. Probably. I really hoped so, anyway. But what did I know about Toby? Not even his last name.

I hurried to swallow my panic before I got crazy. He was better than no one; that was the one thing I was sure of.

"We can both sleep here." I scurried under the top blanket and patted the place next to me.

"Are you sure Ralph won't be back tonight?"

"He said he'll be a few days."

"Where did he go?" Toby eased himself under the blanket beside me, still fully clothed.

Maybe it would be better if he took some of his clothes off, I thought frantically.

"Don't you want to be more comfortable?" I asked in place of an answer. Willing my voice back to normal, I tried again. "You could at least take your shoes off."

"I'm comfortable," he grunted, rolling onto his back—not looking comfortable at all. "You try to sleep."

In a childish gesture, I linked my pinky with his and held it tight. "Just . . . you know . . . in case," I panted.

"In case of what?" I saw his eyebrow shoot upwards to join the lines on his forehead.

"In case you decide to leave."

"You think this is going to stop me if I really wanted to go?" He tugged lightly on our entwined fingers.

I knew he was right, of course. Sniffing lightly, I scooted closer to him. I still wasn't sure what had happened to me out there. It wasn't a dream, though. It was real. But if it was real . . .

"Hey." Toby moved so he was halfway on his side, looking down at me. "Are you crying?"

"No," I lied.

"Hey," he said again, nudging me with his shoulder. "You don't have to be afraid."

"I'm not," I choked.

"He wasn't going to hurt you," Toby's voice dropped to a whisper in the night.

Without meaning to, I copied his volume. "How do you know?"

"He only meant to show you the truth."

"He wanted me to die."

"Never." In a surprisingly gentle movement, he reached across our joined hands with his free one and wiped away a tear that had escaped my eyes. "Try to sleep. I won't leave."

CHAPTER 9

$\mathcal{M}$y forehead furrowed dramatically before my eyes were fully opened.

"Oh my," I groaned, rubbing away the lines on my head and by my eyes.

I had had the weirdest dream ever. A strange voice in the woods, climbing a tree, then jumping from the tree. And Toby had been there too. In fact . . .

"Morning," a deep voice greeted me huskily.

My eyes popped open. "What are you doing here?"

A grin splashed across his face. "You wouldn't let me leave." He winked. "You were all over me last night."

"I was not."

"You made us this nice little love nest." He patted the blanket we both seemed to be laying on.

"Why are we on the floor?" Scrambling backward, I untangled myself from the blanket and plopped heavily on the bed. "Did you stay the night here?"

Toby leaned back against the pillow, his smile growing with every awkward second that passed.

"Don't worry," he taunted, "you still have your virginity."

My mouth fell open. All I had on were my shorts and tank top

273

I slept in. Definitely not something I wanted Toby to be seeing me in—let alone sleeping next to him in. What in the world had happened last night? "But why are you here?"

"I told you." He propped himself up with one hand. "You wanted me to stay."

"I mean"—I breathed deeply, hoping he couldn't see how hot my face became—"how do you even know where I live? How did you get out here?" I didn't call him. We weren't friends. Why was here?

His grin slipped. "I came out here to talk to you."

"About what?" My eyes darted to the closet. If I got up now, it would just bring more attention to the fact that I had very little on. It was probably better to wait until he left. If I didn't get up at all . . .

"It doesn't matter right now." He jumped up from the floor and moved to the door. "Get dressed. I'll make breakfast."

"No," I said quickly, holding up one hand. "You don't need to make breakfast. I'm good."

"I'm hungry." He shrugged. "I was stuck out here all night, watching you sleep."

Heat spread through my cheeks. "Watching me sleep?"

That wasn't creepy or anything.

"You're so cute when you sleep." He chuckled. "Until you started snoring." He shuddered dramatically. "I feel sorry for your future husband, having to sleep next to that every night."

My eyes popped open. "Are you serious right now?"

Forgetting my embarrassment, I sprang to my feet and hurried across the room to help him out of my room.

Toby's eyes dropped to my knees. "Do your knees still hurt?"

"Just get out," I hissed. I knew exactly what he was trying to imply, and I also knew it wasn't true. Nothing had happened . . . at least nothing like that.

"I was just asking."

"Now. I need to get dressed." Laughing loudly, he finally left so

I could slam the door after him. "Holy . . ." I leaned my entire body against the cool wood of the door.

How could he be here? Last night was a dream—I couldn't even remember most of it. There was a voice calling my name, and I followed it. Like an idiot. Where did Toby come into it?

"Hurry up." He pounded on the door, startling me upright.

"I thought you left."

"Nope. I'm waiting for breakfast."

With one more sigh, I hurried across the room and grabbed the first clean clothes I could find. It only took a few minutes to change and pull my hair back into a loose ponytail. Normally I would have changed in the bathroom so I could clean up, but I needed to be dressed before I went out there, since Toby didn't appear to be leaving.

Toby chewed loudly, I noted as I watched him shoveling spoonsful of cereal into his mouth. I had never been much of a cook, and he wasn't picky, so a box of sugary cereal and a gallon of milk was good enough for breakfast.

At least for him. I didn't eat.

"Aren't you hungry?" he grunted around a full mouth. "This stuff's not bad. Ralph knows how to pick cereal."

"How do you know I didn't pick it?"

He shrugged.

Toby seemed to know entirely too much about me and Ralph, considering he was just a boy at school who had convinced me to cheat.

"I'm not hungry." I sniffed. He needed to hurry up and go. I really wanted a hot shower and some time to think.

"What do you remember from last night?"

"Hmm?" I sat up straighter. "I know nothing happened between us," I snapped. "So don't even try spreading rumors at school."

"You were in the woods when I found you," he reminded me. "Do you remember what happened to you out there?"

"I was in a tree." I swallowed hard. "At the very top."

"How did you get up there? Do you remember that part?"

I couldn't tell if he was making fun of me or not. "I climbed up."

"To the top?"

"In my dream," I hurried to clarify. "I climbed up and then I fell out."

"You didn't fall," he argued.

"I jumped." I cleared my throat. "But I wasn't trying to kill myself, so you don't need to tell Ralph or anything."

"You flew." He took another bite, as if he hadn't said something ridiculous.

"I can't . . . fly." Even if I could in my dream, Toby wouldn't have seen that part.

That's all it was. A dream. Toby found me at the end of that dream, when I was laying on the ground and confused. If I really did ask him to stay, I was grateful he did. But I didn't want this to get around. Crazy and a slut—all in one night.

I'd had worse nights, I inwardly shrugged.

"You weren't dreaming"—Toby caught my gaze and held it— "and I think you know that."

"I . . ." I swallowed again. He was right that it felt real, but then again—it couldn't be real. Maybe I was still asleep, actually. "I don't know anything right now." I really wished Ralph were home.

"Well I do know. It wasn't a dream."

My eyes narrowed. "How do you know?"

How in the world could he be so sure? He hadn't been inside my head. He didn't hear that voice.

"You heard a real voice."

"No, I didn't." I closed my eyes. The world seemed to be going in and out of focus, changing from the things I knew into the things that couldn't be true.

"Ava."

My eyes snapped back open.

"I was the voice, so I know it wasn't a dream." He finally put his spoon down and leaned across the table, his eyes boring into mine.

"There's no way . . ." But maybe I had already known. I saw a flash of it at the school, didn't I? "Why would you want to kill me?"

He sat back in his chair again, huffing a deep breath out through his pursed lips. "I already told you," he grumbled, "I wasn't trying to kill you."

My eyebrows lowered on my forehead. "You called me from my bed to go out to the woods and climb a tree. Then you made me jump out of the tree."

He glanced up, his expression dark. "I guess so."

"But not to kill me?" Yeah, right. If he really did do all that, why did he stay the night?

"It's getting awfully boring having to keep telling you the same thing over and over again." He tapped the table with several long fingers.

"This all . . ." I ran my tongue across my bottom lip, trying to think of a good word to describe what this was. Weird seemed too tame.

His stormy expression suddenly changed. "You can't go and tell Ralph that I tried to kill you," he hissed with a strong hint of desperation.

"He's not here." Obviously.

"When he comes back," he clarified quickly. "You can't tell him that when he comes back."

"I'm not going to tell him about any of this." He already didn't want me to stay with him and then he got called to the school because of me. I wasn't adding any crazy to the table as far as Ralph went. "He wouldn't believe me anyway."

"You're probably right." He shrugged, going back to his cereal. His eyes kept flickering to my face.

"What did happen last night, though?" I carefully avoided eye contact.

"We've already—"

"No," I cut him off. "I mean, how did you do all that? And how did I . . . not get hurt when I jumped?"

"Are you sure that you're ready to know?" He shifted his gaze back to my face, making me squirm uncomfortably.

"Of course I'm ready," I tried to say bravely through my clenched teeth.

"It's because you're a Nephilim."

Was that supposed to be some grand reveal? I had no idea what that meant. Was that someone who walked in their sleep? Now that I thought about it, I might have heard of that before. "A what?"

"You have a human mother . . ."

Obviously.

"And your father is an angel."

"How do you know my father? I don't even know my father. And he can't be that great . . . he left me with Uncle Ted." An angel? That was going a bit far and it had nothing to do with hearing voices.

"I mean," he said forcefully, widening his eyes at me, "he's an actual angel. Wings and everything."

"That's . . . stupid. There's no such thing."

"Well . . ." He shrugged. "He's fallen, so the wing thing is iffy."

"I . . . you're not making any sense."

"Your dad is an angel that fell to the earth. Your mom is human. That makes you Nephilim," he explained slowly, in choppy sentences.

Half human, half angel? I had never heard of a person like that. But maybe that explained things. People believed me when I told them things—things that were very clearly not true.

"You tried to use your compulsion with Ms. Bast," Toby echoed my thoughts. "To pass your test."

I knew what he meant without the prompting. "It didn't work."

"The school is warded against that sort of thing."

My eyes widened. "Is everyone at the school Nephilim? Are you?"

"No and no."

"But you said . . ."

"I said you couldn't use any sort of magic or powers at school."

Magic? Just what kind of school did I go to now? Did Ralph know? Ralph. "But wait." I held up my hand. "Ralph and my dad are brothers."

"That was a lie."

"Then tell me the truth," I demanded, my breath making my voice raspy.

"You already know the truth, Ava," he said softly, so softly that I barely heard the words. If I hadn't been staring at him so hard, I might have missed them. "Ralph is your father."

"He's an angel?" Because he seemed so normal. And way too young to be my dad. "Uncle Ted," I recalled out loud, "he said Ralph was my dad. But . . . how did he not know he was too young? It's not possible."

"Ralph can be whoever the other person needs him to be. It's part of our charm."

"Why does he look young like that for me?"

"Doesn't work on you."

It was all too much. "You're an angel like Ralph?" He nodded. "What do you look like, then?"

"I don't use any sort of glamour." He grinned. "I like being young."

No one could like high school that much.

"Anyway." Still grinning, Toby pushed his chair away from the table and stood up. "I have to be going."

His words shook me out of my stray thoughts and exploding questions. "You're leaving?"

He grinned wickedly down at me. "I know you're infatuated

with me now, but I can't move in here." There were too many things rolling around in my head for me to be annoyed. He must have seen the panic clearly on my face, though. "I'll be back soon," he assured me with a roll of his eyes. "Take a shower, try to relax."

"Relax," I sputtered. "How am I supposed to relax?"

"Read a book or something." With one final wink, he was gone.

Left alone at the table, I sucked in a quick breath and tried to hold it in my broken lungs. It was no use.

"What just happened?" I gasped. Toby couldn't just tell me stuff like that and then leave me alone to deal with it. It wasn't right.

How could this be real? I had never heard of Nephilim. And angels? Weren't they women in white dresses that you put on the top of Christmas trees? Was I going to believe that Ralph was an angel?

But I couldn't deny that I was something. I had always known there was something different about me.

Uncle Ted knew it too.

He avoided touching me at all costs; I used to think it was because I killed his sister. She died giving birth to me. Of course I was to blame. Now I wondered if that was the reason he didn't like me. He must have known I was different, and he was afraid of me.

Afraid.

Tears gathered in the corners of my eyes, making them sting. Ralph shouldn't have left me there with him all those years ago. He should have realized that a human would never be okay with raising someone . . . like me.

I had never given my absent father much thought. He was always someone from a fairy tale—not tangible. I was more right than I could have imagined.

"Okay." I shook my head to dispel the negative thoughts. They never did me any good. "No point sitting here crying," I told myself firmly. Tears wouldn't change anything.

I needed to stay busy until Toby came back . . . or Ralph. He had a lot to answer for once I saw him again. Hopefully he didn't ghost me again.

Sniffing lightly, I rose up from the table and closed the cereal box that Toby had been eating from. It was some fruity crap that Ralph bought for me. He must not have realized I wasn't a little kid anymore. Although age didn't seem to hamper Toby any.

I stowed the box back in the cupboard and gathered the dirty bowl filled with used milk. With a nod of my head, I ran water over the dishes, happy to have something to do.

CHAPTER 10

*O*utside my bedroom window, the sky had gone from purple to dark blue to black while I sat at my desk and pretended to study maps. The curtains were pulled back so I could see if any cars happened to pull into the driveway. The aspen trees formed a nice little cocoon around the house, effectively cutting me off from the rest of the world. It was like Havenwood Falls was an entire other planet.

It had been a long afternoon, long and boring all on my own.

A knock sounded on the front door, taking the rest of my attention away from the map. I had been waiting for Toby to come back all day. He had promised he would come back.

Hopefully that was him.

As if I were a jack-in-the-box, I sprang up from my seat and hurried out to the kitchen.

"I'm coming," I yelled, just in case. *Don't leave, Toby.*

It wasn't my dark-haired prince though. It was Ralph. Rolling his eyes, he gave me a sheepish shrug.

"Can't find my house key," he explained by way of an apology.

"Dad!" My gasp came out before I could stop it, surprising us both.

Ralph's eyes narrowed before he slipped past me into the kitchen. "Dad?" he grunted.

"I just . . . I'm surprised . . . I didn't expect you to be here yet," I stuttered, embarrassed by the accidental affection.

Ralph set his bag heavily on the kitchen table and crossed over to the sink.

"I don't mind if you call me Dad," he said with his back to me.

"What?"

"You know," he turned back around, his eyes darting everywhere but at me, "if you want to call me Dad, I'm okay with that."

"Ummm . . ." *Dad* didn't feel right. I had never called anyone Dad before, and I wasn't entirely sure I could start now.

Without waiting for an answer, he turned back to the cupboards and began pulling out boxes of food. "It's not a big deal either way." Although he tried to sound nonchalant, I had to wonder if he was hurt by my hesitation.

If Toby was right, though, Ralph was an angel—a full-blown angel. How old was he? I already knew he wasn't as young as he looked. Why did he care what I called him? After my mother died and left me alone on the earth, Ralph hadn't come for me.

"Were you bored out of your mind here?" he asked suddenly, bringing my attention back to his small kitchen.

"Not really." Maybe he wouldn't notice the airiness in my reply or the way my heart pounded at the thought of the past day. "It's all right here."

"Oh yeah?" His hands paused on the loaf of bread he was reaching for. "Any return of the killer chicken?"

"Very funny." I rolled my eyes. "How did your trip go? Did you . . . get whatever you needed done?" I still had no idea where he went, and he still wasn't giving me any clues.

"Undetermined."

"Am I supposed to know what that means?"

"Do you want some food?" he offered. He was really good at avoiding my questions. It was so annoying.

"It's late."

"People still eat when it's late," he grunted. "Don't they?"

Would it be weird to ask him if he was an angel? Would he tell me the truth? What about Toby—did he know Toby?

"Some . . ." I swallowed hard over my awkwardness. "I'm sure that some people do. Not everyone is the same."

Ralph's eyes bored into mine, making my pulse speed up again. "What kind of person are you, Ava?"

"A tired one," I muttered, shifting my eyes away. "I'm going to bed."

"Okay."

"I'm glad you're home." The words tumbled over each other in an effort to get out of my mouth.

"Yeah."

I turned away and crossed to my still-open door.

"Ava."

"Yeah?"

"You want to go get a coffee with me tomorrow at Coffee Haven? It's a nice little place in town."

"Sure." I shrugged slightly. "I'd like that."

The line at Coffee Haven was already almost to the door by the time Ralph and I walked in. A few eyes flickered our way, but most people were more interested in their own coffee orders to give us much notice.

"It's cute in here," I whispered happily to my quiet coffee date. "Very . . . small-town vibe."

"It has good coffee," Ralph commented in his usual gruff way. "Some of it's a little frilly."

Ralph was probably a black coffee kind of man, I decided, crossing my arms over my chest. Behind the counter, a girl who must have been part Japanese was smiling wide at a guy stuttering over his order. The girl was really pretty. I didn't blame the guy for being distracted. As I watched, she twisted her finger in her long hair and laughed out loud.

"What kind of coffee do you drink?" Ralph asked awkwardly, with enough eye contact to give the illusion that he actually cared.

"I'll probably just get some hot chocolate." I had never liked the taste of coffee. I could never resist a good coffee shop though.

"I heard the blueberry scones are quite good," he offered.

"Scones?"

His eyes widened. "That's what I heard," he repeated.

"What will it be?" the girl behind the counter asked when it was our turn to order.

"Hot chocolate and a blueberry scone." What the hell, I mentally shrugged. I noticed the small name tag pinned to her shirt read *Harlow* as she spun away from us and prepared our order.

Despite his advice, Ralph skipped the scone and only got a small black coffee.

"Here's a seat." He gestured at an empty table, where we both sat. The hot chocolate was delicious and perfectly coated the back of my throat.

"You were right about this place," I whispered, leaning across the tabletop. "It's perfect."

"I'm glad you approve."

Actually, the whole town of Havenwood Falls was nice. Even if it did look like an entire pumpkin patch had thrown up in the middle of town square. "Halloween is no joke around here, huh?"

Ralph chuckled at the sight of witch decals on a window. "Comes with the territory, I guess."

I knew the people in Havenwood Falls weren't exactly normal, but I didn't really know much about them. Being trapped out there with Ralph on his stupid farm didn't exactly do any favors for my social life.

For the first time in recent memory, I missed going to school. At least there, I had an opportunity to talk to people my own age. And if I was being honest . . . I wanted to see Toby again. I hadn't been able to talk to him since he told me I has half angel.

Why didn't he come back like he promised?

Behind me, the door opened to let in a gust of chilly morning air. The hair on my arms stood straight up, but it didn't have much to do with the cold.

Already knowing who had walked in, I whirled around and saw Toby standing just inside the door. Our gazes locked for several long hours—or maybe it was just a few seconds. Either way, excitement coursed through my veins. I could hardly sit still in my chair. Every nerve inside of me stretched tight, waiting to snap. I wasn't going to be able to sit there; soon I was going to embarrass both of us and throw myself at him.

"What the hell is he doing here?" Ralph grumbled. I had practically forgotten he was there with me.

"Who?" Tearing my eyes away from Toby, I looked to see who Ralph was looking at. He was staring right at the door. "Do you know Toby?"

His gaze moved swiftly to me again. "How do you know him?"

"He goes to my school."

Ralph nodded slowly.

"And he stopped by while you were gone."

His face fell almost comically. "At our house?"

Despite his outrage, my ears burned at his pronoun choice. Our house? "Yeah. He wanted to help me . . . study." I had never been a very good liar when it really counted. "I'll just go talk to him real fast."

"No way." He slammed his hand on the table between us, making me jump.

"What do you mean, no?" It wasn't like we were going to start going at it here in Coffee Haven. In fact, we hadn't kissed yet at all.

"You're not talking to him."

"I'm just going to—"

"Hey," Toby's familiar tone said from above us. I didn't even realize he had moved away from the door, and now here he was right next to our table. "Nice to see you again, Ava."

"We're leaving," Ralph growled, popping up from the table. "Let's go," he ordered me, without taking his eyes away from Toby.

"I'm not finished with my scone."

"Take it with us."

Mouth opening and closing like a fish, I helplessly followed Ralph from the shop. Toby didn't move from his place.

CHAPTER 11

"*Y*ou're not allowed to see him," Ralph thundered, his words vibrating against the walls in our cozy little kitchen. "He should have never been here in the first place." His nostrils flared as he glared wildly around the room. "What did he do to you?"

"Nothing." I wasn't about to tell him about the whole tree-jumping thing.

"Never"—he put his finger out toward my face—"ever talk to him again."

"You can't tell me who I'm allowed to talk to."

"Yeah, I kind of can."

"Why?"

"In case you've forgotten"—he rounded the table to put himself closer to me—"I'm your father."

Oh, he wasn't actually going to pull the dad card on me, was he? "Why do you not want me to talk to Toby?"

"He's toxic."

"Uhh . . . could you be a little more specific?" I raised both eyebrows in his direction.

"I said no."

What a dick thing to say.

"You are ridiculous," I huffed. More irritated than I could handle, I turned on my heel and disappeared inside my room, slamming the door behind me.

If this was what having parents was like, I was better off without them.

"Ava," Ralph yelled, pounding on the door. "Come back out here; we weren't done talking."

We were done talking all right; maybe I would never talk to him again. Did he think after seventeen years, he could just waltz back into my life and tell me who I was allowed to talk to? Did he think I was seven years old?

"Don't act like a child," he continued to bellow through the wood. "There are things you don't know about him."

Of course there were things I didn't know about him. We had just met and he told me I was half angel and that he and Ralph were angels—there was a lot I didn't know. But that didn't mean I didn't want to know.

"Come out so we can talk."

I took a deep breath and blew it out forcefully. Hiding in my room was immature—he was right about that. And maybe he would be able to answer some of my questions. Even if he didn't, there were a few things I had to say to him.

Flinging the door open, I stomped past him back out into the kitchen. "What do you want to talk about?" I snapped.

"You know what you are." It wasn't a question, but I still nodded. "And you know what I am."

Uncomfortable, I crossed my arms over my chest. "Toby said you're an angel."

Hopefully he wouldn't hear the fear as it gulped down my throat, or the way my heart galloped away inside of me.

"He's right," Ralph nodded.

So, he was finally going to open up and tell me the truth—but did that change anything? Not really. I still wasn't human. I was still living with my nonhuman father in a town full of people who had something to hide.

Most importantly, it didn't change the way I felt about Toby.

"Do you know why Toby was kicked out?"

"Kicked out of . . . Heaven, you mean?" My eyebrows puckered at the implications his words stirred up. "It never really came up."

"Angels aren't kicked out for just anything, you know," he huffed, his eyes wide with anger. "It has to be something serious."

"Okay." I let my arms fall back to my sides. "Should I sit down for this story?"

"This isn't a story, Ava," he growled. "This is serious."

"You've already said it was serious." I held up one hand to stop him from saying useless things. "What happened? What did he do?"

"Violent crimes against humanity." He said it like a declaration, like the information should have shocked me, but truthfully, I didn't know what that meant to an angel.

"I'm not sure what . . ."

"Toby isn't a nice man," Ralph continued to explain. "His idea of a good time is to torture humans."

"How?"

"Set their things on fire, confuse them on the roads, make them think they're crazy—fun things like that."

"He's not like that now." I shook my head back and forth.

"You have no idea what he's like now."

That day at the school, out in the parking lot, I had felt a vibe from Toby—an evil vibe. And then that night when he called me from my bed. Toby made me climb a tree to the very top and then made me jump out of it. How many times had he done something like that to other people?

Enough times to be kicked down to Earth.

"I don't care." I raised my chin. "Nothing you say is going to make me stay away from Toby."

"You're grounded."

"What?"

"That means you can't leave this house."

"I know what it means. You can't ground me."

"Yes, I can," he panted. "You're not leaving this house again without me. Not until your suspension is over."

"That's . . . insane."

"Grounded," he said again, pointing one long finger at me. "Don't even think of going out to meet Toby. Not now, not ever."

The trees surrounding Ralph's farmhouse were thick, making it look dark even in the middle of the day. Since it was October, it was cold in the woods—really cold.

Shivering, I pulled my thin sweater closer to my body. It didn't seem this cold when I left Ralph's house not more than ten minutes ago. He had left to make a run to town, leaving me with the most freedom I had been allowed for days.

I was out the door before his car was completely gone from the driveway.

Toby had played a starring role in my dream that morning. He told me to wait for Ralph to leave and then to come meet him. Even though he gave good directions in the dream, it was proving more difficult to fight my way through the trees than I expected.

"As soon as you clear the woods, you'll reach Devil's Peak. I'll be waiting for you there."

Apparently, Devil's Peak was a great big rock where teenagers went to make out years ago, until a flood nearly wiped it out. Now the ground was uneven and dangerous, so it wasn't seeing any more action.

Just when I was sure I was going to be lost in the woods forever, the foliage opened up to a flat piece of land. Not more than twenty feet away was a lone rock jutting from the ground, and on top of that stone was a familiar dark-haired boy, grinning at me so wide that his eyes crinkled.

"Toby," I breathed. "Finally."

"Well lookee there"—he whistled low through his teeth—"if it isn't my own little paper bird."

"Paper bird?" I hurried to cross the distance that separated us.

"Half bad-ass angel and half fragile human."

"Tsk—not all humans are fragile," I said, tilting my face up toward him. It was like we had known each other for years instead of mere days.

"I've missed you," he admitted, his voice dipping low.

"I've been on house arrest."

"What did you do?"

Ralph wasn't mad because of something I did; he was mad because of Toby. He was mad because of all the evil things Toby had done to get himself into trouble.

And because I insisted on defending him.

"Ralph told me about you," I blurted, trying and failing to pull my eyes away from his perfect face.

"That I'm an angel?" He wiggled both eyebrows.

"He told me"—my tongue slid nervously across my bottom lip —"why you were kicked out."

Toby's grin froze, then faltered. "Did he, now?"

"Yeah, and he told me I'm not allowed to talk to you. He said you're dangerous." Maybe not in so many words, but the implication was obvious.

"I don't . . ." He cleared his throat uncomfortably. "I haven't always liked humans."

"Oh."

"I found some needed to be . . . taught a lesson."

I tried to imagine the avenging angel that Toby painted.

"What did you do to them?" I whispered.

"Only what they deserved. Eye for an eye, you know?" I watched his teeth work against the loose skin on his lip. "Humans can be vile creatures."

I took a deep breath, then moved to wrap my arms around his waist. "Lucky for us," I said as loud as my voice would go, "I'm not human."

"I've learned a lot since those days." He wrapped his arms around my shoulders to hold me close to his body. "I don't mind most humans now."

"Most?" I squeaked.

"There are some who annoy the shit out of me." His deep laughter vibrated against the side of my face.

"Despite my father's best efforts, I like you." Keeping my face buried in his chest, I waited for my heart to settle down before looking up at him.

The look on his face didn't do my nerves any favors.

"I like you too." His voice had turned husky, somehow sexier than any other sound I had ever heard in my life.

"What if Ralph doesn't let me see you?"

"What is he going to do, tie a blindfold around your eyes?"

"Sounds kinky." I tried to raise one eyebrow, but I might have failed.

"Mmmm."

His lips turned up into a small grin just before they moved close enough to press against mine. Tiny lights exploded behind my eyes. It was like I had waited my whole life for this moment with Toby at Devil's Peak.

CHAPTER 12

I couldn't seem to let my eyes relax enough to even blink as I watched the brunette across the table from me pulling stuff from her oversized bag. Things that I didn't recognize. Things she needed to give me a tattoo. An actual tattoo.

Tempers had been heated with Ralph and me on the home front after my forbidden outing with Toby. For weeks, the two of us barely spoke at all. Going back to school had come as a blessing—both to get me away from Ralph and so I could see Toby again. I was worried for a while that Ralph and I would spend the rest of my senior year in silence, but then one day, he made breakfast.

Right at this very table, we ate bacon and let our disagreement dissolve on its own. Although we didn't talk about Toby anymore, we did talk about other things. It was strange to me, discovering how much I had in common with a father I never knew until a few months ago.

And now this.

I came home from school, and Addie was in our kitchen, waiting to give me a tattoo that she said I needed in order to stay in town.

"You ready?" She wiggled her eyebrows at me.

"Will it hurt?" I glanced from Ralph to Addie and then back again.

"It's nothing to worry about." She laughed, a soft tinkling sound that filled up the nervous air between us. "It's just going to be a small white bird; the same one Ralph has. He thought it would be special if you two got the same design. Is that all right with you?"

"You have one too?" I looked again to Ralph.

Nodding, he pulled back his sleeve to show off a small white bird etched into the skin on the inside of his upper arm.

"It didn't hurt at all," he assured me.

Ralph and I would have matching tattoos. In an odd way, I felt like it would connect us somehow. Maybe it would help bridge the time we had lost.

"Yeah, it's all right with me," I murmured, still staring at Ralph's arm.

"You know, Ava, this isn't a normal tattoo," Addie said, bringing my attention back to her and the task at hand.

"Because it's white?"

"Because it's magic," she corrected with a shake of her long hair. "With this," she tapped my bare arm where the tattoo would go, "you'll be able to leave town without losing your memory. It protects you; it makes you one of us."

One of us. "That sounds . . . good," I finished lamely. The emotion that suddenly gathered in my throat didn't let me say all that I was feeling.

"Here we go." She shook her hands out and set to work on the mark that would make me part of the town.

Excitement coursed through me, replacing the nervousness. As much as I liked to piss Uncle Ted off, I had never imagined myself getting a tattoo. Grinning wide, I let my eyes slide closed as Addie worked.

It was over quickly and with way less crying than I thought would happen. Running my fingers over the slightly raised skin, I was surprised at the tears that gathered in my eyes.

"Did it hurt?" Addie wrinkled her nose and ran her thumb over her artwork.

"No." I swallowed hard and tried again. "No, it didn't hurt."

"You know, I didn't even know Ralph had a kid."

"I'm sure he never expected me to show up on his doorstep."

Addie smiled as she packed up her supplies. "It's cute how proud of you he is."

Proud? Addie was wrong about that. We were getting closer but not on that level. I couldn't even call him Dad yet. But maybe this small white bird was the next step we needed.

"Okay, kids, I'm out." Addie waved from the doorway with two fingers.

"I'll walk you out," Ralph hurried to offer.

"I'm fine." She waved him away. "I can find my own way out. See you around, Ava." She winked, then disappeared into the falling snow.

"She's nice," I declared, still fingering my new art. "I like her."

"Nice tat." He came closer to inspect it.

"Thanks."

"Now it's official."

"What is?" I looked up at him.

"You're staying here."

"I was staying here even before this." I chuckled. Still, there was something warm about hearing it from him. He brought Addie here. Did that mean he actually wanted me to stay now?

CHAPTER 13

"Who did you have to pay to get study hall?" Toby demanded, kissing the tip of my nose.

"Everyone is in study hall," I scoffed, choosing to ignore his insinuation.

"Some people have tutoring this hour," he needlessly pointed out.

"I don't need it." I pursed my lips and tilted my head playfully. In fact, I did need it, but study hall with him was so much more amusing.

"It's fine." He kissed my pursed lips. "I'll tutor you later."

"I'm sure we'll study into the wee hours of the morning."

"Who talks like that?" His top lip snarled upwards. "You've been around Ralph too much. You're going to need an intervention soon."

"Whatever."

"Seriously though, I'll make sure you get an A in history." One eyebrow arched high on his forehead. "At least a C."

"Let's talk about something more fun," I pouted.

Toby caught my bottom lip between his teeth, sending shivers down my spine.

"What do you want to talk about?" he asked, letting go of my flesh.

"You already know."

"Not the Cold Moon Ball?"

"Why won't you go with me?"

"I haven't been to that thing in years."

"That's because you didn't know me."

"How about"—he ran one finger along my jawline, stopping to add a little pressure against my lips—"if I promise to think about it."

I knew he was trying to distract me with that magic touch of his, but thinking about it was better than the flat no I had gotten so far. "Deal."

Even if he didn't go to that dance with me, I was happier here with Toby than I had ever been in my life. Not that I had much to compare it to. Back in Montrose, I had thought I loved Caleb, but now I knew the difference—I barely even liked Caleb.

"Christmas is like three weeks away." Toby scowled.

"I know." It was hard to believe I had been in Havenwood Falls that long already. I opened my notebook to the first page, pen poised and ready to jot down a few notes. "Are you going to finally tell me what you want?"

"I already have all I want." He gently kissed my forehead.

"Very sweet, but I was being serious."

"Me too."

Christmas had never been a joyful experience when I lived with Uncle Ted and Jane. They bought me gifts, because they had to, but it was always awkward with them. I knew they didn't want to.

Now was my chance to make this Christmas better. I had Ralph and Toby. They didn't like each other, but they both liked me.

"What are we going to do for Christmas?" I asked Toby, trying to keep the childish glow out of my eyes.

"Probably the usual." He shrugged. "A make-out session in the backseat of my car followed by an awkward drop-off in front of your house."

"Toby. I'm being serious."

"Ralph isn't going to open his arms to me and invite me over for Christmas dinner."

"He might." Ralph was being seriously decent about my insistence on dating Toby. "He waved at you last night."

"He was swatting the snow out of his face."

My nose scrunched up. "I told you that wasn't true."

"If you say so."

"If I only had one Christmas wish," I held a finger up between us, "it would be for all three of us to be together for Christmas." They were the two people I cared for the most in the world. Of course I wanted to be with them.

Toby's low chuckle quickly turned to a full-blown laugh. "That is never going to happen, Ava."

"It could if you tried."

The feud between my dad and Toby went back too far for either of them to remember. Besides, it was never a personal issue with one another—Ralph just didn't like how Toby treated humans. And Toby wasn't like that anymore.

"How about we talk about something better?" He threw my own words back at me.

"What should we talk about?" I growled.

"On second thought, why do we need to talk at all?"

"The teacher will be back any second," I hissed, wanting him to kiss me anyway.

"And?"

Toby pressed his lips lightly to mine, applying pressure just as my heart was starting to speed up. My lips parted with a contented sigh, allowing his tongue to touch mine briefly. Much to my disappointment, he stopped the kiss before it could get too deep.

"I have an idea—one that you'll like."

"What's your idea?" It had better be good if he stopped kissing me just to say it.

"Let's go Christmas shopping."

"Shopping?" That was his great idea?

"In Montrose."

The furrow on my forehead smoothed out. Shopping in Montrose—that changed things. "Really?"

"Why not? You can leave town now."

"Ralph said I can't, though."

"'Cause he worries too much," Toby scoffed. "What can happen? I'll be right with you."

That was true. I hadn't been back to Montrose since I left it; I would love to go visit with Toby. Even if we did do some shopping while we were there.

"I'm in." I grinned widely.

CHAPTER 14

I inhaled a long breath of frigid air and held it in until my lungs felt like they were going to burst. Standing on the porch, too nervous to go inside, I chewed mercilessly on the inside of my cheek. How was I going to get permission to go to Montrose with Toby?

Oh well, I decided, *I can't just stand outside forever.*

"Hey, Ralph," I greeted in what I hoped sounded like a naturally high voice.

"Hello," he replied, staring at me from the side of his eyes.

Shit. He didn't buy my false bravado at all.

"What are you doing?" I sniffed the kitchen experimentally.

"Cooking." He held up his hot pads proudly. "Are you hungry?"

"Why do you always think I want to eat?" I scoffed.

"So . . . is that a no?"

Without answering, I crossed to my room so I could have more time to make my breathing normal. Pinching the bridge of my nose, I debated just giving up on the shopping trip with Toby. Maybe I should just stay and eat whatever Ralph was cooking. His food was usually good. It was Saturday, after all—a day Ralph and I usually spent together.

"Ava?" Ralph's voice called from the kitchen. "What are you doing in there?"

"Nothing." I frowned as I marched back out to him. "I was grabbing something in my room."

"How were the chickens?"

"Fine." Still terrifying, despite his best efforts.

"Hmm." He turned back to his work space. "Are you eating?"

"I can't." I pressed my lips together hard enough to make them hurt. "I already have plans, actually."

"What plans?"

"Christmas shopping."

He didn't say anything.

"In Montrose."

Still silent.

"With Toby."

He spun around, his lips pulled back into a smile that was anything but amused. "Is that supposed to be some kind of joke?"

"Depends. Are either of us laughing?"

"You're not going anywhere with Toby."

"We already have plans. It's not like we'll be out late."

"No."

"You can't just say no."

"I just did."

"Why can't you give him a chance?"

"Why would I?" He scowled, the lines on his forehead furrowing deep.

"You don't even know him."

"I'm sure I don't know him the way you do." I would have blushed at his words if they weren't so accusing. "You know how I feel about . . . him."

"He's changed," I told him—again. It didn't seem like he was going to believe me this time either.

"Do you think I want my daughter to be hanging out with scum like that? A murderer?"

"Stop calling him that."

"Ava."

"Ralph." This conversation was getting on my nerves. We'd had it too many times in the past few months.

"Regardless of your . . . company," he sneered, "you need to stay in Havenwood Falls, where it's safe."

"Safe from what?" Or whom? I didn't really understand why Ralph had come to this town to begin with. Who was he hiding from?

"You don't need to know all that. That's my business."

Ralph was hiding out here, and although he wouldn't tell me why, it couldn't be for something good. "You're my father. It's my business too."

"Fine." He crossed his arms over his chest and glared at me, a small vein throbbing in his temple. "I came here to escape the radar of other angels—fallen ones."

"Why don't you like other angels?" My eyes narrowed as I waited.

"They don't like me," he barked.

"Why not?"

"Don't worry about it."

"Tell me."

His eyes darted wildly from side to side. "I'm not . . ."

"Ralph, why are the angels hunting you down? Enough that you had to hide here?"

Just when I thought he wasn't going to answer, he blurted, "It's because of you."

As if his words physically touched me, I stumbled backwards. "What are you talking about?"

"Because you were born. These angels asked me to destroy you at birth, but I didn't do it."

"Is that why you left me behind?" I was the reason his angel pals were after him. I was the reason he had to hide here.

"I left you with your human uncle so you would be safe."

"How is that safe? I could have come here with you."

"I only came to live here about five years ago. It was best to cut ties."

"I . . . I need some air," I gasped, moving toward the door.

"Don't go far," he warned, as I slipped out onto the front porch.

Ralph blamed me for the things that had happened to me? But that wasn't fair. I didn't ask to be born. One thing was for sure: I needed some retail therapy with Toby. Screw what Ralph said.

CHAPTER 15

*T*he pavement under my feet was slippery from all the snow that had fallen that week and was still falling even as I walked through it. I didn't know where I was walking to, but I knew I didn't want to stay in that kitchen with Ralph anymore.

I sniffed back my tears before they could fall and freeze on my face.

Behind me, a car pulled up and slowed down.

"What are you doing out here alone?" Toby called from the window he had rolled down. "It's cold out here."

"I just . . . wanted to walk." I shrugged helplessly.

"What's wrong?" His eyes were instantly alert, his eyebrows lowering down on his forehead. "Have you been crying?"

"I'm not." My voice broke and gave me away.

"Get in the car, Ava."

There was no reason not to listen to him. We had plans to go shopping anyway. Being careful not to start wailing, I opened the car door and slid into the passenger side. "I take it you're driving?"

"You still want to go to Montrose?"

"Of course."

His sigh was audible. "All right."

Besides his tapping on the steering wheel, we made the entire drive to Montrose in silence. He didn't even turn the radio on.

I knew from Addie that I could go past the town's wards without losing my memory, thanks to my bird tattoo that she had given me. Today was the first test of her words.

The only way I was going to get through this ill-planned shopping trip was if I didn't think about Ralph at all. His words rang in my ears, so it was going to be hard to not think of them. But I was willing to try.

For Toby, if nothing else. He was only taking me shopping to appease me.

"Phew." The air that I blew out made a whistling sound as it passed through my teeth. "I almost forgot how much more traffic there is out here."

"Yeah," Toby chuckled. "We get kind of spoiled in Havenwood Falls with no traffic at all." He expertly maneuvered into a parking spot in front of a small store I had never seen before.

"I've never been here," I commented as I joined Toby on the sidewalk. "What is it?"

"Secondhand store." He shrugged. "I used to come here a lot . . . a while ago."

"How long ago?" There was something elusive about his answer that immediately piqued my curiosity.

"When the new owner first took over. I think he was just over eighteen, inherited it from his grandparents."

The bell over the door jingled when we entered the musty shop, catching the attention of the old man behind the counter. He had to be in his eighties, at least. Looked like the grandparents still worked here too.

"Hey, Archie," Toby greeted warmly. The old man nodded but didn't greet Toby by name.

"Wonder if the grandson is here," I whispered, "so you can say hi."

"You mean the new owner?" Toby grinned.

"Umm . . ."

"That's him."

"You said he was eighteen."

"When he took over."

My face drained as I understood what he meant. "You knew this guy when he was eighteen?"

"Yep." My mouth fell open.

"They have kitchen stuff over here," he pointed out. "You should be able to find something here for Ralph."

All in all, the trip to Montrose hadn't been all that I hoped it would be. Toby was on edge the entire time, hovering over me as if I were about to be attacked any minute. We didn't go anywhere besides the old secondhand shop. Although I managed to find an apron for Ralph that said *Kiss me, I'm an Angel,* I didn't feel successful. All I wanted to do was get home.

"You sure you don't want to stop for food? We could go to Napoli's and grab a pizza."

"I'm not hungry."

"Tell me what happened today."

"Ralph and I got in a fight."

"Because you wanted to hang out with me," he guessed correctly.

"Do you know anything about fallen angels?"

"A little," he snorted, "considering I am one."

"There are . . . bad ones . . ." Did I sound like a baby? Because it felt childish to ask like that.

"They would say that we're the bad ones." He took a deep breath that made his nostrils flare. "Ralph would say that there is good and bad in all of us."

"What would you say?"

"I would say that it depends on which side of the line you're on." He glanced at me. "There is one of them that's after your dad. He goes by the name of . . ."

Toby's words were cut off by a car horn honking behind us. A car that hadn't been there just seconds ago. Its appearance caused a deep pucker to form on Toby's brow.

"Who's that?"

"How would I know? Just somebody cruising these back roads." On either side of us were fields that turned into mountains. We weren't far from Havenwood Falls; a few miles and we'd be within the wards.

Everything next happened very quickly. The car slammed into the back of our car and then pulled up beside us. I just had time to register that the driver was wearing a black mask before he rammed into our side, knocking us off into a ditch.

CHAPTER 16

"*Ava.*" Goose bumps rose up on my arms and the back of my neck.

"Did you hear that?" I raised my head to search around the outside of the car for its source.

"Hear what?" Toby asked, still scowling at the back of the car that had run us off the side of the road, then peeled away.

"Someone just called my name."

"No one called for you. It's your imagination."

"This has happened before," I continued stubbornly. "I definitely heard it."

"*Ava.*"

"Stay here." His grip tightened on my shoulder. "Don't move."

"You did hear it?" I whispered excitedly. It was nice to know that I wasn't going crazy.

"I don't think they're here to play." He pressed his finger against his lips. "At least, not any game we want to play."

What kind of talk was that? Was he trying to scare me on purpose?

"Let's just go," I suggested, pushing my panic down. "Can you take me home? Will the car still work?"

AMY RICHIE

"Yeah," he said slowly, not moving. "I'm going to look at the damage. Stay here," he ordered again.

"I'm not staying here," I hissed, getting out with him to round the front of the car. Several long scratches ran along the shiny black paint, but Toby wasn't even looking at the car. "What is it?"

"Well, isn't this a pretty picture?" a familiar voice taunted from nearby.

My eyes raced until they found the lone figure staring at us. How was it possible? Why was he here?

"Caleb," Toby called out to him before I could find my voice.

"Indeed it is," Caleb purred. "It's nice to see you again, Ava."

Toby moved quickly, deliberately putting himself in front of me. "Don't say her name," he growled. "Don't even look at her."

"Relax." Caleb rolled his eyes. "Me and Ava go way back."

"What did I just say?" In his anger, sparks of light flew from Toby's fingertips. "Don't say her name."

It wasn't really a big deal. I silently rolled my eyes. Caleb was never my boyfriend. Sure, I was a bit obsessed with him—who wasn't? But those feelings were never reciprocated. Toby was overreacting. *Don't say my name?* What did he think would happen if Caleb called out my name? Would I turn into a frog—or was I mixing up my scary creatures?

"I thought I was going to find just one little birdie out here." Caleb grinned—a large toothy thing that sent chills up my back. "But look what I found instead."

"What do you want?"

"You know what I want. Don't ask useless questions." His eyes shot briefly to me and then back to Toby again.

"How do you guys know each other?" I asked from behind my human—or not human—shield. "Caleb, are you . . .?" I let my question trail away, not sure if I should reveal that Toby was an angel and I was half angel. It didn't matter. Neither one of them were paying attention to me.

"What did you do, attach yourself to her?" Toby asked him.

310

"You found her with her human uncle and you . . . befriended her?"

"A favor for a friend." He smiled in his lopsided way, the kind of smile that made my heart do funny things.

"A friend?" Toby repeated his words back to him. "What friend?"

"You wouldn't know him."

"Try me."

"Where's Ralph?"

"No idea."

"He wouldn't leave his bastard unprotected."

"He didn't." It was impossible not to hear the unspoken threat that emitted from Toby.

Unprotected bastard? Was Caleb talking about me?

Toby clicked his tongue against the roof of his mouth. "Actually, I changed my mind. I don't know anyone named Ralph."

He crossed his arms over his tight chest and glared at Caleb.

It was hard not to be impressed. Hopefully the two didn't decide to fight. They were both too perfect for violence.

"You really know how to irritate me, don't you, bird?" Caleb hissed.

Was bird supposed to be some kind of insult? It didn't sound all that menacing. It was probably best not to say that out loud, though, just in case Caleb decided to show me just how big and bad he could be.

Too sudden to be natural, dark clouds gathered over our heads. A streak of lightning ripped the sky open, followed immediately by a clap of thunder that had me cowering behind Toby. Maybe he had heard my silent musings.

"You don't want to make me angry," Caleb roared, raising his hands just as more lightning flashed.

"Holy shit." I took a small step forward, closing the space between me and Toby. "Is he making the storm?"

Toby turned just enough so I could see the side of his face. "I won't let him hurt you," he vowed. "Don't worry."

It was too late for that. I was full-out scared.

"You need to leave," Toby told Caleb, in a tone that made the hairs on my arm stick up. "This isn't a fight that you're ready to have."

"Is that supposed to scare me?" He cocked one eyebrow high on his forehead. "A lot has changed since the two of us last met."

So they really did know each other.

Huh, I thought stupidly. *What a small world.*

"You heard me, snake."

Caleb's laughter started low, but soon his shoulders were shaking with it. "Snake," he roared with twisted humor. "I haven't heard that one in a while. Do you know what snakes like to eat?" he asked, suddenly sober again.

How could I have missed that he was a complete lunatic? All that time spent drooling over him and here he was—stark raving mad.

"Baby birds." He let the *s* ring out in a low hiss.

"Leave while I'm still letting you walk."

"I'm not going anywhere without the half-breed."

"That's never going to happen," Toby responded lazily, as if he didn't just call me a half-breed.

That meant Caleb knew what I was, before I ever knew. Was that why he wanted to be friends in the first place, if you could consider us friends? What did that mean? The implications made my head spin.

"Why do you want me to go with you?" I squeaked out. "We were barely even friends."

"I can assure you," he snapped, "I'm not after a friendly visit."

"I mean, we talked sometimes." I shrugged, trying to make sense of what was happening. Things like this didn't belong in real life.

"I would never be friends with someone like you," he sneered.

It was strange; I had never heard any words that physically felt like a slap. Until now. "Someone like me? What am I like?"

"You are an abomination, a disgusting thing that shouldn't exist." His top lip curled up, revealing two rows of sharp teeth.

"What is wrong with you?" I sputtered. "This is like, next-level evil."

"Oh please." Even from the distance we were apart, I could see his eyes roll up. "Why would I care what you think?"

"We hung out," I reminded him. He was always nice to me. How could someone lie so easily?

"I only kept you close to me for one reason." He held up one thin finger. How was it possible that even that finger was attractive?

"What . . . what reason is that?" It didn't matter, when it came down to it. He wasn't my friend or even someone I should have been talking to—clearly.

"Ralph."

"He won't come here. He doesn't even know where I am."

"Ralph!" Caleb flung his head back and screamed at the sky like a crazy person. "I have your offspring."

That was sort of an exaggeration. Just because he was looking at me didn't mean he had me. He was still at least ten feet away. I could turn around and run if I wanted to. Who was he kidding?

"If you don't show your face, I'll kill her."

That's a bit much, I inwardly scoffed. What did he think, we were in some old Western movie?

"I won't let you hurt her," Toby warned him.

"Oh, please," Caleb sneered, "you can't stop me. You gave up your powers."

"Not all of them." Fire shot from his fingers—fire that was easily blocked with a lazy swish of Caleb's hand.

"Any other tricks?" he taunted my would-be protector.

A light flared to life, a flash of light that momentarily turned the whole world around us to white. In front of me, Toby let out a string of profanity.

"What is that?" I had to yell to make him hear me.

"Just stay back," he ordered instead of answering me. *Typical*.

"I heard you were looking for me," Ralph bellowed from the middle of the field. He was just suddenly there between us and Caleb—he appeared from nothing. From his back, two enormous white wings had sprouted. My mouth fell open and wouldn't close. He was so beautiful. No wonder my mother fell for him. She didn't stand a chance.

Caleb's eyes lit up hungrily. "So nice of you to join us."

"Are you serving a new master, snake?" Ralph demanded.

"Never," Caleb hissed back.

"What are you doing here, trying to threaten my daughter?" Something shifted in my chest at his words.

"I've come for you, of course. You're a pretty hot commodity right now, worth a lot—alive or dead."

"No," I cried out, terrified of Ralph getting hurt because of me. Desperate to reach him, I clawed at Toby's arm holding me back.

"Stay back," Toby grunted. "He's got this."

"But Caleb . . ."

"Is no match for your old man," Toby finished for me. "It's best for you to stay out of the way in case things get ugly." As far as I was concerned, things were already ugly.

"You're a disgrace to your kind," Caleb jeered. "You don't deserve to walk the earth."

"Get some new material," Toby threw in loudly.

"Don't egg him on," I hissed through clenched teeth. Toby spared me one eye roll before turning his attention back on the two men in front of us.

"I'm here to make sure you get what you deserve," Caleb continued, his attention solely on Ralph and his impressive wing span.

"You think you're big enough to get that done, do you?" Ralph's head tilted dramatically to one side. "You should run along and find your daddy. Tell him you weren't big enough for the job. I'm sure he won't blame you." He shrugged. "Probably."

"I was big enough to find your offspring, wasn't I?"

Ralph's lips tightened.

"No one else could find her, but I did." His eyes were definitely giving off the crazy vibe. "I knew she was the way to you. You couldn't stop yourself from finding her." He laughed loudly. "I knew."

"You will leave Ava alone," Ralph ordered quietly. His kind of crazy was way scarier.

"Actually, I'll be finishing her off after I'm done with you." Caleb smiled widely. "I know an old friend of yours that will be very happy to see you again. You might remember him. Daniel."

A low sort of hum radiated off the name and swept across the field.

"We both know that isn't going to happen."

"You think you'll be able to get through both of us?" Toby asked boldly. Ralph's eyes flickered briefly to the pair of us. Evidently, we'd be talking about my choice of company later—after the crazy . . . whatever he was . . . was taken care of. I flinched at the thought of that conversation.

"I know I can."

"Enough!" Flames shot from Ralph's fingers and hit Caleb right in his chest. They weren't like the small flames Toby had produced earlier. Ralph's fire was blue and burned so hot that it seemed to singe the air it touched.

Caleb stumbled backward several steps, clutching the place over his heart that was still burning.

I slapped my hand over my mouth to stop my screams. Ralph was going to kill him. I mean, Caleb deserved to get his ass kicked for sure—but to be killed?

"Toby," Ralph thundered, "take Ava home."

What? "No way. I'm not leaving here until you come too."

I needed to make sure neither one of them got hurt.

"This has nothing to do with you," Caleb butted in.

"I'm the bastard offspring," I gasped. "It has everything to do with me."

"Does the worm have any say in matters once the fish is caught?" Caleb taunted.

Was he calling me a worm? The insults were kind of hard to keep up with.

"Come on." Toby took my hand and pulled me back toward the car.

"No." I dug my heels into the ground. "I'm not leaving."

"Don't make me throw you over my shoulder and force you away."

"You wouldn't do that."

"To keep you safe"—his wide eyes bored into me—"I would do just about anything."

"Is Ralph going to kill him?"

"No." Toby pulled more forcefully against my futile resistance. "He'll . . . convince him he's wrong and then alter his memory."

Before I had enough time to abandon Ralph and leave with Toby, the sky opened up and a cloud of fire descended down to join us in the field.

"What is that?" I breathed.

"Daniel."

"Oh my . . ."

I peeked around the bulk of Toby's car, where I had been exiled when Daniel arrived for the fight. The four men were glaring at each other so hard that I could practically hear it from my hiding spot. Daniel and Ralph both had their wings showing.

Despite my fear, I couldn't help but be impressed.

I felt split in half. Part of me wanted to rush into the fight to help Ralph and Toby; the other part of me, the part that was still human, was too afraid to leave the safety of the car. What if one of them got hurt?

"You have pretty good seats here," Caleb purred, crouching down beside me.

My whole body stiffened at his voice. "What are you doing?"

"I've been waiting for you for a while now."

"How sweet," I murmured from my dry lips.

"I feel like the big boys are going to be a while. How about you and I go somewhere safe?"

"You go ahead by yourself," I choked out. "I'll let them know that you left."

"Nice try." His false smile disappeared. "You're coming with me, half-breed."

"No, I'm not." Hoping to catch him off guard, I jumped up and darted around the car.

He was just as fast. His arm circled tight around my waist and clutched me back to him.

"How about we borrow your boyfriend's car?" he panted. Without listening to my protests, he flung me into the passenger seat and crawled in over me to get to the driver's side. "I'm sure he won't miss it." He grinned without amusement.

"Where are we going?"

"It's a surprise," he laughed, roaring the car back to life.

The sky was almost dark by the time Caleb pulled up next to a large building in Montrose. There were no windows on the side that I could see, just a large slab of gray concrete.

"Honey, we're home," he taunted.

"Where are we?"

"Montrose."

"I know that much." I rolled my eyes. I was scared, for sure, but a part of me still held on to a hope that Caleb wouldn't really hurt me.

That misplaced hope faded when he pulled a needle from a small case that I hadn't even noticed before.

"I don't want you spewing filth in there." He jutted his chin toward the mystery building. "You don't mind taking a little nap, do you, bird?"

"I won't say anything in there," I cried, panic setting in.

"Truer words have never been spoken." With one last dark grin, he leaned across the car seat and jabbed the needle into my arm.

"What did you . . ." My words slurred away, darkness pulling me under.

CHAPTER 17

$\mathcal{M}$y head was throbbing wickedly before my eyes fully opened.

"Oh," I groaned, forcing my eyelids the rest of the way open.

The thought of him brought me more fully awake. I didn't recognize the room I was in, and it was too dimly lit to make out much of anything that was in it with me.

I was handcuffed to a small wooden chair. The shadows across the room from me might have been people—maybe. If Caleb was over there watching me, he would have known already I was awake.

No. I was alone.

Yanking hard on the cuffs, I knew right away I wasn't going to able to break free. I had enough experience with them to know how screwed I was.

A door high above me creaked open, flooding my eyes with bright light. Caleb stood there, glaring down a staircase at me.

"Finally awake?" he sneered.

"Let me out of here," I yelled, even if I knew the demand was useless.

"Where would the fun be for me then?" he asked, coming

down the steps. "We're just getting started. What are we going to do with you?"

"You could let me go," I suggested. "I won't tell your boyfriend."

His hand arced back and slammed heavily against my face. As much trouble as I got myself into, I had never been in a real fight. The pain was surprising.

"You're not going anywhere. You and I are going to stay here and see if Ralph comes for you."

I experimentally rotated my jaw.

"If he got away from Daniel, he's going to come after you."

With one last kick at my shin, he went back up the stairs and left me alone again.

The room was so dark, I couldn't tell if my eyes were open or closed. The air whooshed loudly in and out of my lungs. In my entire life, I had never been so utterly alone. Even with my extra sensitive hearing, there were no sounds to pick up.

I swallowed hard, willing myself to stay calm.

Ralph and Toby.

I grasped tightly to my life boats. They were my family now. The only thing that mattered to me. Before I went to live with Ralph in Havenwood Falls, I was a mess. No one wanted me, and I didn't belong anywhere. Now I had a place to belong. I had a family.

Tears slid down my face, more tears than I had cried in a very long time. If Daniel killed Ralph, I would never get the chance to call him Dad. He would never know how much I cared for him . . . how much I loved him.

I had finally found someone that I loved, who might even love me back, and now he was being taken away from me. And here I was, trapped in some basement room by Caleb.

Helpless.

Why was I always so helpless with the things that happened to me?

The first time I talked to Toby was in the back of the history classroom, the day I decided to cheat on that test. He was trying to take my virginity. My chuckle turned into a sob.

Two months in and my V card was still intact. I should have let Toby take it when I had the chance.

Then again, it was kind of hard to sneak time alone with Toby when we had Ralph glaring over our shoulders. Even if he kind of accepted my feelings for my newfound boyfriend, that didn't mean he liked it.

Oh, I really needed to see if those two were okay.

And I was really, really tired of being the victim of my life. How dare Caleb kidnap me, drug me, and lock me down here like some animal? The only reason he was able to do these things to me was because I was letting him. I allowed myself to be weak.

Not anymore.

I took a deep breath through my nose and let it out slowly through my mouth. Concentrating only on the cool metal of the handcuffs, I willed them with all I mentally had in me to break in half.

I never expected it to work, but suddenly my hands were free from their restraints.

"Holy shit," I whispered, jumping up from the chair.

I wasn't sure how I had done it, but I was free, and I wasn't going to waste that by being all shocked like an idiot. In the next few seconds, I darted up the steps to the door where Caleb had disappeared. It was locked, of course. It didn't take much more than a small nudge with my mind to unlock it.

The door led to a very short hall with only one door at the end of it. There were no people there. Caleb never expected me to break out of that basement. I hurried over to the only exit and tried the handle. It was unlocked.

Just like that, I was back outside.

It was dark out, the air cold enough to make my eyes burn. I had no time to worry about that. I had no idea where Caleb was or when he was coming back.

I took off running without any idea where I was going. This wasn't a part of town I was familiar with, but I knew there were many different alleys all around us.

I didn't stop running until I was several streets over. Panting hard enough to make my chest hurt, I leaned against the dirty wall of the alley and wiped away the last remnants of tears on my face.

I was away from Caleb—now what? I didn't know how to find Toby or Ralph. I could probably find my way back home, but they wouldn't have gone there without me.

I closed my eyes and focused on Toby. *"Where are you?"* I whispered into the nothingness.

Suddenly, there he was, inside my head. I saw him walking along a street I recognized here in Montrose. I saw him as clearly as if I were there with him.

"Toby," I said out loud. In my head, he stopped and looked all around him.

He heard me.

"Toby," I cried out, excited by this new connection. "Meet me at the shop we went to earlier. The one Archie works at."

His lips moved, then the connection was gone. I would just have to hope he had heard. I flung myself off the wall and began running again.

CHAPTER 18

$\mathcal{J}$t took me longer than I expected to find the shop. I had to first find a street that I recognized and then backtrack to find the shop. Luckily for both of us, I had a good memory and an excellent sense of direction.

Toby was already there when I stumbled to a stop in front of the locked doors.

"Ava." I saw his lips move, but I couldn't hear the words over the sound of my own breath echoing inside my ears.

My arms snaked around his neck at the same time his reached for me. "You came," I sobbed. "You really did hear me."

"You disappeared," his muffled voiced accused angrily.

"It was Caleb. He brought me here."

Toby's lips were everywhere all at once. He kissed my forehead, my eyelids, my cheeks, my lips. It made it hard to talk, but I didn't exactly mind at the moment.

"I was so scared," he murmured. "Scared that you were . . ."

"I'm alive. He didn't even hurt me." I was just bait. For . . .

"He's lucky he didn't," Toby growled.

Ralph wasn't with Toby. Why did only one of them get away? Surely, they didn't kill him, right? "Where's my dad?"

"Daniel took him."

Took him; didn't kill him. My shoulders sagged with the weight of my relief. "Where did he take him?"

"I know where they took him, but . . ."

"But what?" I gripped his arm tightly, willing him to tell me what he knew.

"You don't have to do that," he chuckled, poking my forehead with one finger. "I was just going to say that it will be dangerous."

"I don't care about that."

"I figured you would say that."

"Toby."

"I don't suppose there's any way I could convince you to go back home and wait for us there?"

"That is not going to happen. We have to go save my dad."

"Yeah, I guess we do."

"Where is he?"

Toby's sigh echoed through the air between us. "Being the bad guy is easier than being the hero."

"No one said anything about heroes." I rolled my eyes at his dramatic choice of words. "We just need to get my dad."

"Let's go, then."

"Do you remember the plan?" Toby hissed, his eyebrows furrowed to their usual height.

"Yes." We had only been talking about it the entire way to . . . wherever this was. This part of town wasn't a place I came to on purpose, but I had been here before.

I recognized the yellow door on the side of the brick building across the street from where we were hiding. Caleb had brought me here once. The details were fuzzy, but I definitely remembered that door. Whatever went on in that building probably wasn't good.

Goose bumps rose up on my arms as the chill in the air dropped several degrees.

"You're sure we can't fight?" Powers that I never knew I had were waking up in me. Maybe Toby and I together would be enough.

"I'm sure," he cut off my budding hopes. "I told you, there are too many of them."

How did he know? Daniel took Ralph; Toby came to look for me. It's not like he had X-ray vision and could see through the walls. Maybe.

"You're going invisible," he firmly reminded me, "and then going to get him."

Toby could go invisible, but he could still be detected by the other angels. Since I was part human, they wouldn't be able to see me. I knew the plan, and it made sense on the way here. Thinking about walking up to that door now was starting to shake my resolve though, in a big way.

My lips shook as I nodded my agreement. If this was the way to save my dad, I was willing to do whatever it took. Even if that meant going into a den of snakes. "I'm ready to go in there. If I don't come back . . ."

"Stop talking like that," he snapped, running a hand roughly down his face. "You're going to be fine."

"I was just kidding." Sort of.

Not really kidding, but when he looked at me like that . . . and just before I was going into that room where Daniel was.

Toby suddenly moved his hands to cup my face. "I love you, Ava." He kissed the shock off of my lips. "I'll see you soon."

"Yep."

I didn't give myself time to overthink things. Just like Toby had taught me on the way here, I gathered heat along my spine and down my legs and let it shimmer inside my chest.

"Good," I heard Toby mutter. "Hurry up. In and out."

Even if he couldn't see me, he had to have heard me gulping in air like a dying fish. This was it—go time. I turned away from Toby and half ran, half stumbled to the yellow door. Thankfully, it was unlocked. It wasn't even shut all the way.

Ralph was easy to spot amongst the stacked boxes and layers of dust inside the room. Careful to be as quiet as possible, I moved across the room and stood next to him. The biggest problem wasn't the chains that held him to the wall or the blood seeping from his leg and side—it was the two men standing in the small space with him.

Caleb and Daniel.

At the moment, they were completely focused on a paper taped to the wall. They didn't even turn around when I pushed the partially opened door further so I could come inside.

"Dad," I reached out to him with my mind, not even sure if it would work.

His head moved ever so slightly in my direction. My heart leapt.

"I don't know how to get past these guys." Toby and I made the plan for me to get in here and get to Ralph, but we didn't talk about how I would get back out.

From outside, there was a loud crash that finally made the two men tear their attention away from the paper.

"What was that?" Daniel boomed.

"I'll go look," Caleb quickly offered.

As soon as the door opened all the way, a huge ball of fire made him stumble backwards. "What the hell?"

Both men ran outside to investigate.

This was our chance.

"Don't worry, Dad," I whispered out loud. "It's me. I've come to get you out of here."

"It's dangerous," he hissed. "Hurry up and get out of here before they come back."

"I'm trying."

"Leave me," he snarled.

"Not going to happen." Using the same power inside of me that had freed me from the handcuffs, I made quick work of the chains around my dad. "Can you stand up?"

"I can see you."

My eyes locked with his. Strange how much of myself I could suddenly see inside of him. "You're not going to get all mushy on me, are you?"

"I just meant that you're not invisible anymore."

"Toby said that if I lost my concentration, it would interfere."

"Toby?"

"Let's just get out of here." We could talk about Toby later.

Ralph limped, but was still able to walk back outside with me. Thank goodness, too, because I wouldn't have been able to carry him. We didn't stop to wonder why Caleb and Daniel weren't out there waiting for us. They must have gone after whatever made that flash.

Which had to have been Toby.

"Toby isn't out here," I stated the obvious.

Ralph tried to help me look, but had to give up when his body fell limp. I managed to catch him before he hit the ground, but it was pretty obvious that we needed to get somewhere safe.

There was only one place I could think of.

"Come on, Dad," I grunted under his weight. "Let's get you home."

"How?"

"We can go see if the shuttle is around to take us back to town."

"And Toby?"

His name sent a spasm of pain through my chest, but I couldn't do anything about him until I made sure Ralph was safe. Hopefully Toby had gotten away and would be back in Havenwood Falls waiting for us.

"Let's go home. We'll worry about him later."

Ralph didn't nod. It seemed like even that was too much.

CHAPTER 19

"You're up early," Ralph said quietly, coming to join me on the large front porch. The sun was just starting to peek out over the mountaintops.

"I haven't been to bed yet." My voice came out as a croak after sitting in silence all night.

"Any sign of him?"

"Nope."

I had waited up all night for Toby to show up, and he still wasn't there. I had even tried to find him inside my head like I did in Montrose, but that didn't work either.

"Do you think he got away from them?" Even though I didn't want to hear the answer, I asked anyway. "What if he's dead? I shouldn't have left him last night."

"You did what you had to do." Ralph sat down beside me. "Toby knows that. He's fine. He will come back to Havenwood Falls, but he can't do that if he's being followed. Have patience."

"He risked his life to save us."

"I know that."

His change in tone caught me by surprise. I looked over to him. "I love him, Dad. I really do."

"I know that too." He nodded slowly. "I'm sorry that I put you in danger."

"You didn't put me in danger. I'm the one that left the safety of this town."

"Those guys were only after you because of me." He turned to look out at the trees. "I didn't even know Caleb was around you. I've been watching, making sure you were safe, and I missed it. I hate that he . . ."

"Don't do that," I hurried to cut him off. "It's not your fault that the bad guys are out there."

We fell into silence, both of us uneasy with the mushy stuff. The sun broke free of the trees completely before he spoke again.

"I like when you call me Dad," he blurted out, then hurried inside to bang around in the kitchen.

My lips tried to curve up into a smile, but thoughts of Toby out there somewhere sobered me up again. Where was he? Was he hurt? If he didn't come back soon, I was going after him, no matter how much Ralph tried to stop me.

My eyes popped open at the first sign of light outside my window. Today was the day—Christmas. This was the deadline I had given Ralph for Toby's return. He promised that if Toby wasn't back by Christmas, we would go looking for him.

It had been a long few weeks.

"Dad," I yelled as soon as my head cleared my door frame. "Are you up?" I sniffed the wide array of food that filled the table. "Don't forget what today is."

"It's Christmas," a voice answered. It wasn't Ralph's voice, though.

"Oh my god!" My hands flew up to cover my mouth. Toby was there—just standing there by the door as if he hadn't been missing. "What are you doing here?"

"Ralph invited me." He shrugged, his eyes dancing.

"He did? When?"

"Back in Montrose, in that field. He said if we made it out alive, I was invited to Christmas dinner."

Tears gathered in the corners of my eyes. "We were coming to get you."

"No need." He held his arms wide. "I know my way home."

Running across the kitchen, I flung myself into his still-open arms and buried my face into his chest. "Where the hell have you been?"

Somehow he understood me. "I took a detour, just to be sure there were no nasties following me."

"I've been worried," I sobbed.

"I know." He laughed gently and pulled my face upward to look at him. "I don't know why you're so obsessed with me," he said softly.

"It's because you're cute." I sniffed.

He moved ever so slowly until finally, at long last, his lips pressed against mine.

Behind us, Ralph cleared his throat loudly.

"Is this Christmas dinner still happening or what?" He banged a large bowl down hard enough to make me jump away from Toby.

"Nice apron," Toby chuckled.

"Nice to see you too," he grumbled dryly. "Glad you didn't die."

Swiping the tears from my face, I scurried around the table to give Ralph a one-armed hug. "It smells great, Dad."

"Mmm." He scowled down at me.

But I knew he was happy.

And so was I. It had taken a while to get here, but I finally had a place I could call home. I might have to eventually deal with Daniel and Caleb, but for now, it was Christmas dinner with my family.

We hope you enjoyed this story in the Havenwood Falls High series of novellas featuring a variety of supernatural creatures. The series is a collaborative effort by multiple authors.

ABOUT THE AUTHOR

Amy Richie has lived in a small town her entire life. She lives with her three kids and their bird, Perry. She began writing in high school but never took it seriously until a few years ago. She enjoys writing because it takes her out of her everyday life and gives life to the people in her head. "When I was little I wanted to be a mermaid, then when I was in high school I wanted to be a vampire; now as an adult I'm a writer, which is better because now I get to be both."

You can visit her on her website: authoramyrichie.com

ACKNOWLEDGMENTS

Being an author can be a lonely road, so the people who are in your corner are exceptionally important. Thank you to all my family, my friends who are like family, my work friends, my book friends, the authors who continue to amaze me, and all the fans who show their support. Even a simple "how's your book coming along?" helps in a big way.

AN EXCERPT

Predestined (A Havenwood Falls High Novella) by Valia Lind

From *USA Today* bestselling author Valia Lind—She goes on a hunt for answers, only to discover what she never realized she wanted until now.

Niccola knows two things: her mother has disappeared and she needs to find her long-lost father.

By some providence, Niccola ends up in Colorado, with nothing but a backpack. When she arrives at the small town of Havenwood Falls in the Rocky Mountains, she quickly realizes that her family's history is much more complicated than she ever knew. She's no stranger to keeping secrets, but even she's not prepared for what she finds.

While Niccola tries to unravel her past, she meets a gorgeous deputy-in-training who could be her future. She's spent her whole life protecting her secret, because being a half witch, half shifter is not something that goes over well with her coven. Yet, Warren sees past the labels and straight into her heart. She doesn't believe in destiny, but maybe she needs to rethink that.

Together, they must do whatever it takes to find the truth and save her mother. Time is running out, and Niccola must find it in herself to trust the town and its people, or lose it all forever.

PREDESTINED

BY VALIA LIND

Find your father.

For the hundredth time, I stare at the piece of paper with my mother's handwriting and the three simple words that shatter every notion I've ever had. I thought my mother hated him. I've hated him my whole life. Now I have to find him?

My mother's magic is all over the paper, but I can't tell if it's meant to help me or just residual from whatever happened here. We were supposed to go to dinner together. I ran out to pick up mail from our PO box and came back to my whole life ruined.

Looking up, I glance around the disarray that is our living room. The apartment is small, but we've lived here long enough to collect all kinds of keepsakes. Which are now thrown all over the area.

The panic I felt when I first walked through the open door hasn't really subsided. But Mom has taught me how to control it— and my magic—enough that I can keep a clear mind.

Whatever happened here, she's in trouble, and I have no choice but to follow the clues she left. Which is why I don't call the police or the coven. Instead, I walk over to her room, picking up a few discarded items, then I settle myself in front of our coffee table. After I flip it over back on its feet.

Next I light a candle, then I place my phone facing up in front of me. It's the closest thing I have to a black mirror, and I need it to scry. I pull my necklace over my head, the small quartz crystal dangling on the bottom. It's all I've got.

Holding the crystal in my hand, I close my eyes and set an intention. When I open my eyes, I place a tip of my finger against the phone, and ask for my mother's location. My body buzzes with magic, heating the crystal I'm holding. Leaning in, I look closely, studying the fuzzy image appearing on the surface of the phone.

But it's gone before I can make out too much of it.

"Come on," I whisper under my breath, as I try to force myself to stay calm and focused. The crystal heats up again, a town's name coming into focus before it's gone again.

"Denver?" I mumble, incredibly confused and a bit frustrated. This isn't giving me much information. When I try the third time, I end up with nothing but some mountains in the distance.

"This is useless!" I snap, sending some of my unchecked magic at the candle and throwing it against the opposite wall. Thankfully, the flame goes out, or I would be in so much trouble.

But that brings me to the problem at hand. I can't be in trouble, because my mother is not here to declare I'm in trouble. My chest grows heavy, and I try to keep my breathing centered.

"Think, Nic. You got this," I say out loud, just to hear a voice. Reaching for my phone, I open a browser and type in Denver, followed by mountains.

"Denver, Colorado? What the heck is in Colorado?" As far as I know, my mother has never been to Colorado. Or anywhere near it. I spent my whole life between California and Nevada. But if there is one thing she has taught me, it's to trust my magic. So that's what I'm going to do.

I walk over to my room, pulling out my backpack and stuffing three changes of clothes into it. After grabbing a toothbrush and paste, I search for my favorite lotion but can't find it anywhere. My body moves on autopilot, reaching for what I need, but my mind is completely on my mother.

What did she get herself into?

She's been acting weird for weeks now, but she wouldn't exactly share what was going on. Maybe I should've pushed harder and tried to figure it out. But I'm only seventeen. It's not like she was going to trust me with a huge problem, no matter how close we are. She's still my mother, and she will do anything to protect me. Of that, I have no doubt.

But she's gone now. And it's my turn to do the protecting.

Determination fuels my every move as I do another sweep of the apartment. Satisfied that I have everything I'll need for the trip, I swing the backpack over my shoulder and walk out of my room.

One last long look at the mess of our apartment, and I'm out the door. It's no time to be sentimental, or to let the feelings creep in. If I break down, there's no going back. I have enough problems as it is. Like figuring out how I'm going to survive a plane ride, since I hate flying.

It doesn't take me long to land in Colorado, but it's way longer than I'm comfortable with. Surprisingly, I got a flight out in just a few hours. Even though I tried, I couldn't sleep on the plane. My body is in constant hyperawareness; every person I meet is a possible threat.

With my backpack slung over my shoulder, I step outside the airport doors, trying to think of my next move. My eyes are instantly drawn to a pair of vans parked at the curb. They're nothing special, standard-issue passenger vans, except for the gorgeous images wrapped all around the body of the vehicle. Before I realize what I'm doing, I've taken a few steps toward the vans.

I freeze in my tracks, confused by this sudden pull toward the vans and the town painted on the doors. It's not like I'm sentimental about outdoorsy places, or unknown towns in a state

I've never been in, so the only explanation must be magic. My mom taught me to trust my instincts, and my instincts are telling me to get in the van.

"Looking for something?" The deep raspy voice reaches me before the man walks around the front of the van. Dressed in a flannel shirt, jeans, and a leather coat that is much warmer than my own, he looks like what I would imagine my grandfather would look like. If I had one.

"A ride?" I don't sound sure of myself, so I clear my throat and try again. "A ride please. To . . ." I wave my hand toward the van's décor, and the man smiles.

"It would be my pleasure."

For someone who doesn't trust people, I find myself completely okay getting in the van with this stranger. I'm not the only one. A few people get in after me. I can tell they're human right away, dressed to go skiing, so I move to the back, keeping my eyes on them and the driver.

My hand reaches into my pocket to make sure my mom's note is still in there. I find instant comfort the moment I touch it. It's like a part of her is with me. For just a second, I let myself feel. The worry, anger, and emotions all rush in at once, and I have to keep myself from audibly gasping. Tears well up in my eyes, but I'm done feeling sorry for my situation, so I push them back. Along with the feelings. The only thing that's left is determination.

Maybe I should be more scared. Maybe I should be a crying mess on the floor. But my mom raised me to take care of myself, and a part of me thinks she's been preparing me for this exact moment. I may only be seventeen, but I'm no weakling. I will do whatever it takes to find my mother. Even if that means finding the man who abandoned us before I was even born.

I blink my eyes a few times, completely lost in my thoughts, when

I see a sign flash by as we drive. I'm so out of it, the six-hour drive just flew by.

Welcome to Havenwood Falls.

Can't say I've ever heard of the town, but then again, I don't know everything there is to know about Colorado. The people in front of me are chatting away, but all I can do is stare at the passing trees. I don't even know what I'm doing here. Once I get to town, I'll need to do another spell to try to get myself out of this mess.

A few miles down the road, the town opens up below us. It looks like something out of a movie. I think that even more once we pull up at the inn. Everyone piles out, so I have no choice but to follow. The crisp late autumn air and the altitude hit me at once, and I pull my jacket tighter around me. I'll probably need to invest in something warmer if I'm to stay any length of time.

"I hope you find what you are looking for," the old man says as I reach to give him cash for the ride. "This one is on me." He smiles warmly, and for some reason, I think he knows more than he's saying. But before I have a chance to ask, he's talking to someone else, and I'm on my own once again.

I study the building in front of me, Whisper Falls Inn. The name is a bit strange, considering. Shouldn't that say Havenwood Falls Inn? Shrugging, I study the three story Victorian-style manor. It's gorgeous. Like something out of a gothic novel. A Christmas garland, red bows, and lights adorn the exterior. From where I'm standing, I can see a large tree in the front window. If I had my camera with me, I'd probably walk around the property and take some pictures. But that's not why I'm here.

Instead of going inside, I turn my back to the door. Right in front of me is what I can only call the town square. It's like this town stepped right off the front of a postcard. I shake my head as I start walking. The decorations are everywhere. Even the lampposts are sporting garlands and bows. My eyes are drawn to the large gazebo off to the side, with its lights and Christmas decor. When I look closer, I notice a few sun symbols and decorations, which makes me think someone here celebrates Yule. Snow blankets the area around me, completing that magical small-town look.

School must be out for break, because even though it's early afternoon, there are kids and teenagers everywhere. Thankfully, that means I don't stand out. As I walk, I can't help but feel like I belong here. I'm not what my coven calls a reader witch, so I'm not as in tune with emotions, but I do have a few reader talents.

With my own magic, I can decipher humans from supes pretty easily, and I can tell this town is full of both. But I don't know how many of them are friendlies. I have to tread carefully. Glancing up, I see that I'm on Main Street. This seems like a perfect place to start, so I decide to head away from the inn.

The town square is surrounded by businesses on every side, each decorated for the holidays. From what I can see, there's everything from a music store to a pawn shop to a coffee shop. My stomach growls the moment my eyes land on Coffee Haven, and I realize it's been a while since I've had anything to eat.

When I step inside the cafe, the smell of coffee is instantly welcoming. But there's also an undercurrent of something otherworldly here. My eyes scan the area, landing on a few strategically placed crystals, pine cones, and candles. I smile to myself. Someone here definitely loves Yule. I bet norms eat this atmosphere up. But I'd be lying if I said I didn't enjoy it myself. It's nice to know there is someone like me here. Even though I'm not about to broadcast it.

"Hi. What can I get you?" The woman behind the counter is a few years older than me, with silvery hair and the most beautiful bluish eyes I've ever seen. Her voice is soft, and she seems friendly enough. I can absolutely see her as the one who placed all the crystals around the place.

"Hi. Could I get a caramel coffee and one of those blueberry scones, please?" I glance down at her name tag: Willow. She gives me a smile before ringing up my order, and I hand over the cash. The exchange makes me a bit apprehensive, since I have a very limited supply of money at the moment. Getting that flight to

346

Denver took more of my savings than I would've liked. With that worry, all the others rush in. The only reason I would be drawn to this town had to be because somehow it would help. But I have no idea where to start, and the panic starts to set in.

Willow's demeanor changes just enough that I know she must've seen something in my eyes. Even though her customer-friendly smile hasn't left her face, she's studying me carefully. With a quick thanks, I grab my order and move to one of the tables. But I can still feel her eyes on me. Clearly, I need to be even more careful about keeping my demeanor neutral. Maybe they just don't trust outsiders. If there's a magical community here, I can understand that all too well.

It takes me five minutes to eat my snack, and then I'm up and out. A part of me wants to march back in there and demand answers. But I doubt Willow knows about my father or what happened to my mom. She might have her own reasons to be suspicious. I shake my head again, trying to keep the panic at bay. I need to shut it all down. I can't afford emotions right now.

When I leave the cafe, I just walk, looking for some kind of a clue as to why I was led here. I probably should've seen if there was a room at the inn before I decided to explore, but it's too late now.

When I stop in front of the old red three-story building, all thoughts of cold and homelessness are forgotten. There's something curious about the building, and when I look over at the sign, I read it out loud.

"Havenwood Falls High."

Of course a small town would have one of these movie-esque high schools, and something inside of me twinges at the idea of attending one. But this isn't why I'm here, and once the fascination subsides, the frustration sets in.

After taking a deep breath, I pull out my necklace and Mom's note, closing my eyes in concentration. My magic sparks as I try to see past what's here. I don't even know why I'm doing this, except that it seems like a locator spell would be a good idea. But after a few tries, there's nothing.

"Now what?" I ask out loud, wishing my mother were here to help.

"Now I think you should answer some questions."

I spin around at the voice, coming face to face with a gorgeous dark-haired guy. He seems to be a few years older, and definitely a few inches taller, than me. His dark blue eyes are narrowed as he studies me in turn. He's wearing jeans and a dark-colored shirt with no jacket.

"Excuse me?" I finally seem to find my voice. "Did you need something?"

Maybe I'm being a little rude, but the way he's watching me is making me uncomfortable. I've never had to use my battle magic as of yet, but my mom has taught me, just in case. There's something about him that's putting me on edge.

"As I stated previously, you need to answer some questions."

Purchase *Predestined* where books are sold.

www.ingramcontent.com/pod-product-compliance
Lightning Source LLC
Chambersburg PA
CBHW020930260626
47169CB00006B/1648